The Turn-coat

Also by Jack Lynn
THE PROFESSOR

The Turn-coat

JACK LYNN

DELACORTE PRESS / NEW YORK

Library of Congress Cataloging in Publication Data

Lynn, Jack, 1927-
  The turncoat.

  I. Title.
PZ4.L98936Tu   [PS3562.Y444]   813'.5'4   75-31896
ISBN 0-440-09133-0

FOR LINZI.

March 16, 1975
Mougins, France

Although this book is fiction, parts have been written in the historical setting of the Korean conflict. The reader will find certain errors of fact. Times and places of specific circumstances in actual military operations, names and missions have been distorted purposely to suit the story. The fictitious figure of Gerald Howard Hawthorne has been contrived from a study of numerous case histories to motivate the central situation and is *not* a portrait of a real person.

Jack Lynn

AUGUST 17, 1961
WASHINGTON, D.C.

1

IT WAS MIDMORNING of a bright and clear August day in the nation's capital. The marble surfaces glistened in the sunlight as the tourist brigades inspected and photographed the imposing complex of public buildings, grounds and monuments.

On the inside, the Washington pace was unusually hectic.

The Department of State had been bustling with priority activity and late-night strategy sessions since the government had severed diplomatic and consular relations with Cuba on January 3.

An additional staff workload could be attributed to the fact that Patrice Lumumba, the ousted premier of the Republic of the Congo, had been murdered in the secessionist province of Katanga on January 17.

Color television sets, in certain privileged Department offices, had offered the conscientious workers some diversion on April 12, when Major Yuri Gagarin of the Soviet Union was launched into orbit from Siberia in a spacecraft called *Vostok 1*.

However, the organization was thrown back into chaos on April 17, when the abortive invasion of Cuba was crushed by Fidel Castro.

The most recent blow was felt by the Department on August 12, when East Germany closed the border and created the Berlin Wall.

It had been a hard year for the American State Department.

In a modest office on the second floor, Neil Porter studied a brief communication from Hong Kong, China. He shook his head, looked up at the oil painting of the President of the United States and smiled.

Christ, sir, he thought. The shit will soon hit the fan.

Mr. Porter was a pencil-thin, thirty-five-year-old Deputy Secretary of State. He was well dressed, well educated and part of the fresh, new Washington scene. The hustling deputy personified the flash and brash approach to government which had become the trademark of a young Administration.

He made an automatic move for the secretarial button but then decided against it. Instead, he picked up the communiqué and hurried out of the room.

"I'll be with Mr. Taylor," he mumbled as he walked quickly past his secretary in the outer office.

The woman, a stern, dark-haired State Department veteran, buzzed ahead in order to alert the secretary to Elton Taylor, the Deputy Secretary of State for Foreign.

Porter moved briskly down the corridors of the old government building, nodding to several associates, but mainly he had his mind on the message from China. The importance of the dispatch was clear and he increased his pace, ignoring the familiar morning traffic in the halls of State.

"He's available," grunted Taylor's secretary as Porter walked past without the slightest display of recognition.

Elton Taylor was a balding, thickset man with a warm smile and a cheerful manner. He was liked by all members of the staff, including the Secretary. In fact, the President had called him Elton on several occasions and this, of course, added to his personal popularity on the job, and at the same time guaranteed steady invitations to exclusive Washington social events.

However, it was a known fact in most of the inside circles that Elton Taylor had reached his political peak and was now

operating on the final rung of a rather laborious governmental climb.

The man was aware of his limitations, still enthusiastic
about most of the work in the Department, and was very
happy to be considered an outsider in the political rat race
for glory.

He looked up as Porter moved quickly into the room.
"Good morning," he said.

His smile faded as he watched the young man take a seat
in a leather lounge chair facing the desk.

After a moment, the senior official asked quietly, "What's
the problem, Neil?"

Porter leaned forward and lowered his voice. "Our friend
is out."

Taylor stared at him curiously before speaking. "What
friend?" he asked. "Out of where?"

"Red China," Porter replied quickly.

Taylor remained puzzled. "Neil, I don't have time for games
this morning," he said, a shade uneasily. "We're in the middle
of the Hammarskjöld mission. Can you get to the point?"

"I'll get to the point, Elton." Porter hesitated. "The Turncoat is out," he whispered.

Taylor's face creased into an immediate frown as the words
registered. There was silence in the room.

Porter stood and walked to the window. He looked out on
Constitution Avenue and thought to himself: Be cautious. Do
not become involved. This is a very hot potato and it happened before your time. Pass it on to your immediate supervisor and then bail out.

"Where is he now?" asked Taylor.

"Hong Kong," answered Porter, continuing to study the
sights of Washington.

"Why in hell did they let him out?" He seemed incredulous.

"I don't know," Porter replied. He walked back to the
desk and took a seat.

"Is he on his way back?" asked Taylor.

"No. The man is broke and stranded. The Red Cross is
taking care of him in Hong Kong."

Elton Taylor took a deep breath as Porter handed him the official communication from China.

The younger man felt a touch of sympathy as he watched Taylor fumble with the paper. The senior official was long on experience and short on guts and theory, thought Porter. From observation, he knew that most of Taylor's work with the Department was produced from rote rather than reason. There was a lack of sophistication, very little initiative and absolutely no individuality and never a true understanding of the job. Just a damn nice guy going smack down the middle until the final whistle.

"What are you going to do, Elton?" Porter asked with sincere concern.

"I'll take it to the Secretary right away," he replied.

The Secretary admired forthrightness and swift decisions because these were the methods he used in managing his department.

He was aware of the advantages of delegation and took pride in his selection of supervisors. But he also had an intense personal interest in everything that went on within his own department. He expected and demanded instant understanding and prompt action.

Roger D'Allesandro was used to the responsibility of control and management. Several of America's most powerful corporations had been, at one time or another, carved, molded, and under the direct supervision of this handsome, fifty-five-year-old dynamo from Illinois.

He was feared, respected and admired by his associates and he had the complete trust and personal friendship of the President of the United States.

He stretched his lanky frame full-length on the plush office sofa, removed his glasses and rubbed his eyes. He was still feeling the strain of the unexpected early-morning conference with the President and the Secretary General of the United Nations.

Hammarskjöld was a brilliant man, he thought, but a little thick and sure as hell stubborn as a mule when he wanted things his own way. D'Allesandro was certain that the diplomat would have a difficult mission trying to set up a cease-fire between the UN and Katanga forces in the Congo.

He sighed, closed his eyes and began to doze.

The short nap was interrupted by Robert Adler, his administrative assistant.

"Mr. Secretary."

D'Allesandro opened his eyes.

"Sorry to disturb you, Mr. Secretary," Adler continued. "I think we have a priority. Mr. Elton Taylor would like to see you immediately, sir." He paused. "If it can be arranged."

"Taylor?"

"We can do it, if you see him now," ventured Adler.

"What the hell does he want?"

"Mr. Taylor said it was sensitive and quite important. Elton Taylor is certainly not the pushy type. I think the man truly has something important on his mind."

D'Allesandro looked up. "All right, Bob. When can I see him?"

Adler checked the pad.

"You have to be on the lawn with the President at twelve-fifteen."

"For what?"

"Captain Virgil Grissom and Commander Alan Shepard." D'Allesandro nodded.

"The afternoon is jammed, Mr. Secretary." Adler glanced at his watch. "You could see him in about ten minutes and give him a half hour."

"Very well," said the Secretary. "Set it up."

Exactly twenty minutes later, the United States Secretary of State, Roger D'Allesandro, had been informed of the situation.

"Dammit!" he blurted. "This is tragic."

Robert Adler, seated on the sofa, seemed unperturbed, but Elton Taylor, who was across the desk from the Secretary of State, turned white. He nodded several times, unable to speak.

A secretary walked briskly into the office and deposited a thick file on the oval desk.

"This is all I could find for the moment," she said, positioning the material for D'Allesandro. "Do you need me, sir?"

"No," he snapped, interested in the file. "And make certain that we're not disturbed."

The young woman nodded, moved to the door and hesitated. "You're expected on the lawn, Mr. Secretary."

"Make apologies," mumbled D'Allesandro as he studied the material. "I'll explain to the President later."

She left the office and the State Department's top official adjusted his glasses and began to scan the official documents on his desk.

Elton Taylor caught a quick glimpse of several Chinese inscriptions on the front of the folder. There was also a serial number, a special reference designation and a State Department classification: "*Secret Sensitive.*"

There was complete silence in the office as the Secretary of State examined the official documents.

In a few moments, he looked up and removed his glasses.

"What does the man want, Elton?" he asked, trying to keep his voice even.

"I don't know exactly, Mr. Secretary," answered Taylor. "I imagine he wants his passage home. He has no money."

D'Allesandro stood and walked to the window. "Can we prevent him from coming back to this country?" he asked with his back to Taylor and Adler.

"I don't think so, sir," answered Taylor, now completely under control. "The man is an American citizen and entitled to return home."

"After eight years with the Communists in Red China?" growled D'Allesandro.

"His citizenship was never revoked, Mr. Secretary," said Taylor, feeling that he was within his rights to be emphatic.

The Secretary walked back to the desk and leaned on it heavily. He looked at both men. "One thing is certain. If this man comes home we'll have to buy some silence."

D'Allesandro sat and drummed his fingers on the desk top

as Adler left the sofa and took a chair close to Taylor, facing the Secretary. Experience had taught him when to observe a D'Allesandro silence and exactly when to break through.

"What about the press, Mr. Secretary?" He broke through.

D'Allesandro thought for a moment and then glanced at Taylor. "What do you think, Elton?"

"He was hot in 1953," said the Deputy as he shifted in his chair. "I don't think the boys will play him up too much now."

"Bob?" The Secretary looked at Adler.

"Feature stuff. I don't think they'll probe."

The Secretary of State leaned back in his chair and fingered the border of the brown folder in front of him. "I want to talk to Ed Atken," he said.

Edward Atken was the Chairman of the Senate Foreign Relations Committee and a close personal friend. The Secretary knew that the senior senator from his home state of Illinois would be very interested in the news from Hong Kong.

D'Allesandro checked several pages in the folder and then looked intently at both men before speaking.

"I want this Hong Kong affair kept down to a minimum. We do not need departmental group therapy."

The meeting was brought to an immediate halt the moment the intercom sounded. A secretary informed D'Allesandro that the senior senator from Illinois was on his way over, without an appointment.

D'Allesandro smiled. "The old bastard must have received the word already."

Adler and Taylor smiled and stood, as the Secretary of State rose.

"Thank you, gentlemen," he said warmly. The meeting was over.

Senator Atken stormed into the office without being announced. The tall, seventy-one-year-old senior senator from Illinois stopped in front of the oval desk and looked down at Roger D'Allesandro.

"Why in hell didn't this wretched boy expire in Tsinan, China?" he blasted.

The Secretary grinned. "Sit down, Mr. Chairman, before you do yourself an injury."

Senator Atken took a seat, pushed the hair out of his eyes and leaned across the desk, pointing his finger.

"Roger, this is serious."

"I know."

"Damn serious."

"I know."

The Senator took out a small cigar and stuffed it into his mouth.

"You'd better find a way to keep this boy over there," he said dryly.

"Impossible, Senator."

"Then shut him up when he gets here."

D'Allesandro lit the old man's cigar and commented calmly, "Now, Ed, you know as well as I do that we cannot do any such thing. All we can do is pray that nothing much comes of the situation."

"And the President?" he asked, puffing his cigar.

"We'll include him in our prayers," said D'Allesandro with a shrug.

Senator Atken leaned back and studied the Secretary for a moment. "You know something, Roger. I don't believe you fully realize the potential danger here."

"I think I do."

"If you did, you wouldn't treat this affair so lightly," the Senator countered.

The two men looked directly into each other's eyes.

"I seriously suggest that you do something drastic," said Atken coldly.

D'Allesandro was annoyed. "I'm running the State Department, not the KGB."

"Let this mess bubble and you might be in a lot of hot water," said Atken.

The Secretary of State checked his watch and then opened the file once again. He located a particular page and then looked up at the Senator.

"Do you remember the names of the two lawyers who were involved in 1953?" the Secretary queried.

Atken grimaced. "Frank Barlow and Thomas Whiting," he answered.

"Where are they now?"

"I don't know. Somewhere deep underground, I hope."

"These two men could mean real trouble," the Secretary said thoughtfully.

"The whole damn thing could mean real trouble," Atken said caustically as he stood and began to pace the length of the office. "What's your immediate plan, Roger?"

"I have no plan. We'll just keep our hands off the gentleman, in every way."

"You won't pay his passage out of Hong Kong?" the Senator asked.

"Absolutely not," D'Allesandro responded.

Senator Edward Atken crossed to a bookcase and glanced at some of the historical titles. For a moment, he too remembered the period at the close of the Korean war.

"What about standard interrogation and possible surveillance when he returns?" he finally asked without turning from the bookcase.

"No interrogation and no surveillance," said D'Allesandro. "He doesn't exist."

Senator Atken left the bookcase and crossed to the chair facing the Secretary of State. His face creased in a malicious grin. "Well, maybe God will give the Democratic Party one more miracle. Perhaps this strange boy will go home and quietly melt into the hills of Michigan."

"I hope so," said D'Allesandro softly.

"You'd better pray so," asserted Atken. He leaned forward and touched the folder on the desk.

"If this thing opens up . . . ," he paused, "our able and distinguished vice president will not be on the ticket in 1964."

The elderly politician stood and squared his shoulders. "In fact, my dear friend, there might not be a ticket in 1964 unless our charming and handsome president can cover up the smells."

AUGUST 21, 1961
NEW YORK CITY

2 ROBERT CALHOUN SPANGLER leaned back in .is chair, propped his boots on the edge of the ornate desk and prepared himself for another session with his people.

He took a quick, professional look at the small piece of yellow teletype paper in his hand and smiled. In ten minutes, the program staff of Amalgamated Broadcasting Television would file into the executive office on Park Avenue and then sit poised with pads and pencils. He knew that the group anticipated these unscheduled afternoon briefings and realized that any meeting in his office could possibly produce another unorthodox Spangler program assignment. Another penetrating documentary, an award-winning drama, a music-special with a fresh, inventive approach.

Publicity pictures, plaques, framed certificates and various awards were displayed prominently around the walls of the office.

Spangler pressed the button for his secretary.

"I'm ready. Let them in as soon as they arrive." He snapped off without waiting for her reply.

The executive had come up the hard way in the American radio and television business and he was now beginning to reap the rewards.

After spending many lean years as a mediocre announcer and newscaster on local radio outlets around the country, he had discovered the secrets of clawing his way over certain key colleagues. After this awakening, he had moved rapidly into television program production and management.

Now Spangler was operating close to the top, in New York City, as the Vice President in Charge of Programming for America's largest and most successful chain of broadcasting stations. Amalgamated's outlets were spotted strategically in lucrative markets across the United States, including New York, Los Angeles and Washington, D.C. Robert Calhoun Spangler was the hot-shot executive responsible for all program activity in the group.

He looked at the paper in his hand once again, thought for a moment and then pressed the secretarial button.

"Fran, get Wineburg up here from Legal. I want him to hear this briefing."

Again he snapped off without waiting for a reply. He placed the yellow piece of paper on the desk, adjusted his tie and jacket, yawned, stretched and waited for the arrival of his troops.

Arnold Dorfman, Amalgamated's news director, made his brisk entrance, followed by Tim Henderson, the publicity director. Fred Schroeder, one of Amalgamated's talented young staff television directors, entered a few seconds later.

Frances Patterson took a seat on the sofa and they were now set and ready for the Spangler treatment. The program executive surveyed the group carefully, then leaned forward and squinted at his secretary.

"Where the hell is Wineburg?" he demanded.

"He'll be up in a minute," she answered quickly. "The chairman is on the phone from California."

Spangler ignored the reply and held up the yellow piece of paper.

"Do you people know what this is?"

"A news item," said Dorfman.

Spangler tapped the yellow paper in front of him. "This is not a news item. To me, Mr. Dorfman, it's a two-hour special for the group and possibly for major syndication." Spangler paused and studied the reporter. He allowed the situation to register with the staff before speaking again.

"Perhaps another Emmy or Peabody Award for Amalgamated Broadcasting Television," he added.

Dorfman was becoming irritated and restless. He was a well-trained member of the Spangler program squad and knew exactly when to pose tough and when to run.

"What in the hell is this all about, Bob?" he barked.

Spangler smiled and picked up the yellow teletype copy again. "I'll read the item, Arnie."

There was a tap on the office door and Morris Wineburg moved in quickly, mumbling "Sorry." He pushed himself into a seat next to Fran Patterson on the sofa and Spangler waited until the lawyer was comfortable.

Then he began to read the news copy aloud.

"Turncoat stranded in Hong Kong without funds." He looked up and his eyes roamed from one member of the staff to the other. He checked for reaction, found very little at the moment and went back to his copy.

"Gerald Howard Hawthorne, the Korean veteran who refused repatriation and defected to Red China in 1953, has been refused free passage back to the United States by State Department officials."

Once again, Spangler glanced up and surveyed his audience. The staff seemed mildly interested and perhaps a little curious but certainly not overwhelmed by the impact of the news item.

Spangler had counted on this reaction. He continued to read.

"After spending eight years in Tsinan, China, Hawthorne secured his release from the Communists in order to return to his home in Waverly, Michigan. He is now being cared for by the American Red Cross."

He placed the news item back on the desk, folded his arms and waited for response.

"Thinking of a straight documentary, Bob?" Tim Henderson, the publicity director, opened the session.

"I'm not thinking of a documentary at all," answered Spangler. "I want a two-hour, in-depth interview with the Turncoat."

"Impossible," mumbled Dorfman.

Spangler's eyes darted to the news director. He stood and walked slowly to the front of his desk and sat on the edge, facing him.

"Tell me why, Arnie."

"Complications," answered Dorfman without looking up

from his pad. "Governmental complications, for example. And besides, the networks are probably in touch with the State Department now, setting up some action with Hawthorne in Hong Kong."

"You give me a pain in the ass, Dorfman," snapped Spangler.

The news director looked up and their eyes met for a moment. He turned away and Spangler continued icily. "I don't give a damn about complications. We have an able staff here, capable of doing the impossible, and I sure as hell don't worry about networks." He paused and then added, "Ever heard of flexibility, Dorfman?"

"Many times, Mr. Spangler."

The program chief walked back and sat behind his desk. He picked up the teletype copy and waved it. "I want Gerald Howard Hawthorne. And I'll get him."

There was silence once again in the room until Henderson cleared his throat loudly and asked, "Bob, what have you got when you've got him?"

Spangler took his time and lit a cigarette. He looked down at the paper and stroked his chin thoughtfully with thumb and forefinger. He spoke slowly and with great intensity.

"You've got a filthy, yellow, traitorous little son-of-a-bitch. That's what you've got."

The staff watched and listened with curious interest as Spangler continued, speaking almost to himself.

"I spent nearly four years in the Marine Corps. Iwo, Okinawa, Ie Shima. I saw guys with their guts blown out and their balls shot off. They were United States Marines, not gooks. This yellow shit-bird would have crawled under Surabachi Yama."

He rose to his feet without looking at the staff and walked slowly to the window.

"He cooperated with the Reds, defected, lived with them, even married one of them. Then the bastard gets tired of it after eight years and wants to come home." He shook his head slowly in exaggerated disgust. "Home. To the United States of America."

He continued to stare out of the window as the staff watched him very closely.

"Bob," said Tim Henderson with understanding, "if it aggravates you so much, why play with it?"

Spangler regained his composure, turned to the publicity director and smiled. "I have just expressed my personal feelings about the gentleman in question," he answered pleasantly. Then added, "Now, as the Vice President in Charge of Programming for Amalgamated Broadcasting, I say that Gerald Howard Hawthorne will make an exciting subject for an important interview. Make some notes," he barked good-naturedly. "Get started."

In Hong Kong, another meeting was in progress. Paul L. Tramler, a special representative of the American State Department, was having a difficult time explaining his country's position.

The small, sparsely furnished room in the American Red Cross building was hot and uncomfortable. There was a strong, nauseating smell of dried fish in the air and the noise from the crowded Hong Kong streets made normal conversation almost impossible.

Tramler's jacket was draped over the back of a wicker chair and the sleeves of his white shirt were rolled up. The slowly rotating fan on the ceiling seemed to increase the heat and add to the general noise and discomfort.

He was stout and middle-aged. His ginger hair was thin on the top. The official mopped his brow with a handkerchief as he thumbed through various documents on the table.

Mainly, Tramler was disturbed by the strange, almost pathetic-looking figure sitting across from him. The man could have been a Chinese rice laborer. His complexion had the coloring and tone of a chronic invalid's. The thick black hair was cut short and unprofessionally. He was dressed in the simple garments of a Chinese peasant.

Tramler knew that the man was about thirty years old and yet the penetrating eyes might have belonged to an elderly man. Not once did they leave the official's face as he perspired and rifled mechanically through his papers.

There was a strange quality of Oriental calm about the man and yet Tramler knew that this was an American, Gerald Howard Hawthorne, and that he was negotiating his way home after spending eight years in Communist China.

Tramler had felt from the beginning that the entire assignment was a humiliation. The official had seen better days in the service of the American government and he considered the Hong Kong trip to be a subtle but deliberate punishment for certain errors in judgment which had occurred during his two-year tour of duty in Japan.

He was concerned about the manner in which the job had been handed to him. Ordinarily, instructions were received from Mr. Elton Taylor. He had been briefed on the Hong Kong trip by Neil Porter.

Porter had told him that the meeting had been arranged by Mr. Jarvis Sinclair of the International Red Cross after Hawthorne had received an official statement from the American Embassy in Hong Kong, stating that free passage to the United States and to Waverly, Michigan, could not be granted by the government.

After obtaining his release from the Chinese Communists, Hawthorne was destitute, and in order to avoid any embarrassment or confusion later, Tramler was flown from Washington in an attempt to clarify the government's position as quickly as possible.

Sinclair, a dour Red Cross veteran, sat next to Hawthorne and acted as his personal representative. Both men watched carefully as the State Department official located a particular document in his briefcase.

"Here is a copy of the official ruling in this matter. You may keep it." He handed the paper to the Red Cross official and added, "As you must know, Mr. Sinclair, I am not here to alter this decision in any way. I can only answer your questions and try to clarify the government's position as well as I can."

Sinclair quickly scanned the document and then put it down on the table. "Same damn thing we were told by the Embassy," he said dryly.

"That's right," said Tramler.

Sinclair slid the document over to Hawthorne, who ignored it as he continued to stare suspiciously at Tramler.

The official was now becoming even more uncomfortable. He mopped his brow and neck once again and wished that the session would wind up quickly so that he could retire to the Alamo for a very tall Scotch on the rocks.

"Let me be very clear about one thing," said Tramler politely. "The United States government is in no way preventing Mr. Hawthorne from returning to his country."

He glanced quickly at Hawthorne and then back to Sinclair. He continued, avoiding Hawthorne's eyes. "Although he was dishonorably discharged from the United States Army by the Secretary of Defense on December 12, 1953, his citizenship was never revoked. Mr. Hawthorne is free to go back to his home in Michigan but he must do so under his own power. Are we clear about this?"

"Very clear," Sinclair answered promptly without trying to conceal his irritation. "But the man is without funds," he continued. "My agency has gone as far as it can at the moment. We expected some help from the government."

Paul Tramler began to place his papers back into the briefcase and at the same time he tried to decide which of the two men he disliked the more.

"I understand," he said without looking up, "but there is very little that I can do."

Trying to keep the contempt out of his voice, Sinclair asked, "What about his back pay, while he was serving time as a prisoner of war?"

The State Department representative was beginning to lose his patience and he was aware that a loss of temper usually followed. These particular character faults had contributed to his breakdown in Japan.

He hesitated briefly, in order to exercise practiced control. "All back pay and allowances were forfeited at the time of his dishonorable discharge."

Tramler glanced at Hawthorne and then leaned toward the Red Cross official in a clumsy attempt to be relaxed and informal. "Let's be frank about this thing, Sinclair." His tone

was now confidential. "Mr. Hawthorne has received a dishonorable discharge from the Armed Forces. He is a known
and well-publicized defector to Red China."

He lowered his voice even further. It was now almost a
whisper. "The man also has a record of collaboration in the
prisoner-of-war camps."

Tramler paused, straightened up, and mopped his forehead.

"The American government cannot be a party to any of his
actions now that he wants to come home from Red China.
However, we are not restricting him in any way."

He turned back to the former prisoner of war and forced
a smile. "As the saying goes, Mr. Hawthorne, you are on
your own." He snapped his briefcase shut.

"I did not defect," said Hawthorne. "They told me that I
could go and I went."

His voice was cold but without bitterness and it took
Tramler and Sinclair by surprise. It was a monotone without
inflection or resonance. His face was a mask and the expression did not change. But the eyes disturbed Tramler once
again and the official had a difficult time answering.

"You are now out of my area, Mr. Hawthorne," he stated
quietly. "I'm only authorized to discuss your passage home."

Hawthorne lowered his eyes. He appeared to be studying
the Embassy paper on the table in front of him.

Tramler watched him for a moment and realized, with
relief, that the meeting was over. He decided that a few
sympathetic words were in order. After all, regardless of the
circumstances, he was in Hong Kong as a representative of
the United States of America.

"Do you have any funds at home?" he asked placatingly.

Hawthorne did not look up. Instead, Sinclair answered. "He
owns a house in Waverly, Michigan. His father passed away
while he was in China and the place was left to him."

"What about his mother?" Tramler asked without a trace
of sincere interest.

"She died before he went into the Army."

The official stood and tried his best to deliver a warm, closing message. "When you went to Red China in 1953, there

was a great furor in the country. You were the first and it shocked the American people. No one could understand how an American boy could choose Red China over his own country."

He picked up his jacket and continued. "That was a long time ago and things have changed. I don't think you'll have any trouble."

Sinclair stood. "That's it?" he asked coldly.

"That's it," answered Tramler.

The Red Cross official frowned and nodded toward Hawthorne, who was still sitting at the table with his head bowed.

"This man spent eight years in Communist China. Are you telling me that Washington doesn't want to talk to him?" he asked with more than a touch of bitterness.

"I didn't say that, Mr. Sinclair," Tramler answered sharply. "My instructions do not call for any interrogation of this man in reference to his experiences in prisoner-of-war camps, Red China or anywhere else. I am here to verify the Embassy directive only and to clarify the situation as well as I can."

Sinclair shook his head and did not answer as Tramler continued.

"I was sent from Washington because the government has a great deal of sensitivity and understanding in matters of this kind. A piece of paper from an Embassy can be very cold in a case like this."

"And your words are warm, Mr. Tramler?" Sinclair asked.

Tramler gripped the door handle. His voice was now harsh and grating.

"Hawthorne is not the only man on earth who is paying for a serious mistake, Sinclair. I know. I've paid for some of my own."

Hawthorne looked up slowly and this time his expression had changed. The skin on his face seemed to have tightened and there was bitterness and anger in his eyes.

He stood and glared at Tramler. Then he nodded to Sinclair and walked quietly out of the room.

Robert C. Spangler's New York program meeting was rolling in top gear.

He read from a neat stack of typewritten papers on his desk, pausing frequently for staff questions or comments.

"Hawthorne enlisted in the United States Army on September 17, 1950. He was nineteen years old. His hometown is Waverly, Michigan, a small, quiet suburb outside of Detroit."

Fred Schroeder tried his best to keep up with the pace of Spangler's delivery but he was fighting a losing battle. "I should have brought my secretary," the director muttered.

Tim Henderson picked up the comment. "Bob, it would be a lot easier if Fran could type up your notes and give us each a copy."

"No," snapped Spangler. "I want to give it to you myself and I want to watch it sink in."

Henderson shrugged and smiled. Spangler added, "This is a program meeting, Tim, and these are important research notes, not one of your damn press handouts."

He stood and began his familiar pacing.

"After basic training, Hawthorne was assigned to a combat unit and sent to Fort Upton, North Carolina. On December 10, 1950, he was shipped to Korea."

"How was his record as a recruit?" queried Schroeder.

"Nondescript. But he was pretty good with a rifle," answered Spangler. "Research will have more on this phase later."

He walked slowly to his favorite spot near the window, stared down at Park Avenue.

Still facing the window, Spangler continued, "After spending three weeks in Korea, he picked up a Silver Star for rescuing a Private First Class Robert Bean while their patrol was under heavy enemy fire."

"That I didn't know," interrupted Dorfman as he continued to write in his pad.

Spangler twisted abruptly from the window and walked to Dorfman. "You didn't know what, Arnie?"

Dorfman looked up and was surprised by the tone and the strange expression on Spangler's face. "That the bastard had a Silver Star," he said a little nervously.

"What do you know about Silver Stars, Arnie?"

Dorfman studied his boss for a moment. "Only what I see in war movies," Dorfman replied.

"I know all about Silver Stars, Arnie," Spangler asserted bitterly, "and I'd love to talk to this gook lover about the way he won his."

Spangler took a deep breath and continued. His voice seemed to be softer. It was obvious that he was trying to exercise more emotional control.

"Regardless, the man won a Silver Star in Korea, and this fact must be considered in the research and in the preparation of the program itself." He scanned the staff and added, "This product will be valid from start to finish. I will insist on it."

He walked quickly back to his desk and took a seat. "Now, let's get down to the guts of this damn thing," he said, checking his notes. "On January 29, 1951, Hawthorne and his platoon were involved in an engagement near Usan, North Korea. The enemy stormed the position, Hawthorne froze, threw his rifle to the ground and quit. He was captured by the Chinese Reds and taken to Prison Camp Six near Pyuktong."

"A Silver Star and then he throws his rifle away," commented Dorfman, shaking his head. "Why?"

"I have my own feelings about that," answered Spangler as he tapped the yellow piece of teletype paper on his desk. "But your question, Arnie, is part of the reason for this program. We'll ask Hawthorne."

"Camp Six, near Pyuktong, was one of the roughest. Isn't that correct?" asked Schroeder.

"For most prisoners," said Spangler without embellishment.

"I remember reading that Hawthorne had cracked up at Usan," said Henderson. "Mainly, because he had killed several American soldiers by mistake a few weeks earlier."

"I don't have much on that incident," said Spangler promptly. "I'm waiting for research." He paused and glanced at his notes once again. Then, almost as an afterthought, he said, "I don't know if he cracked up at Usan but he did kill five American soldiers during a particular engagement.

"Hawthorne was in the Red prisoner-of-war camp from January 29, 1951, until August 20, 1953. He was a known progressive and collaborator during this period. It has been confirmed by several witnesses who were in the camp at the time, that Hawthorne was directly responsible for the starvation and deaths of many American prisoners of war."

He paused, surveyed his subordinates for a moment and then returned to the briefing.

"This man lived in comfort with the Reds, worked for them in the camp, eventually read and spoke their language, signed propaganda documents and finally refused repatriation. He defected to Red China and arrived in Tsinan on August 22, 1953."

Abruptly Henderson cut in. "I don't think it's fair to say that he defected."

All eyes turned quickly to the publicity director.

"Just what the hell would you call it then, Henderson?"

"There was a repatriation agreement," he challenged. "Hawthorne had a choice. Stay or come home. He chose to remain in Red China. This shocked the American public at the time but he did not defect."

Spangler was determined not to be provoked. Instead, he stared at Henderson for a moment and then turned back to the rest of the group.

"We won't dig into the fine print at this first meeting," he said quietly. "We'll have a complete and detailed briefing when all the research is in."

Dorfman, who was becoming increasingly interested in the project, cut through the obvious tension in the room. "So, he went to Tsinan. Was he dishonorably discharged right away?"

"A few months later," answered Spangler without consulting his notes. "American public pressure was building and the Secretary of Defense was swamped with thousands of petitions from various veterans' organizations and loyal, patriotic citizens. On December 12, 1953, the Secretary announced that Gerald Howard Hawthorne had been dishonorably discharged from the United States Army. The Secretary personally assumed the responsibility for this edict."

The group, with the exception of the news director, made notes.

"Wasn't he married to a Chinese girl?" Schroeder asked as he continued to write.

"Yes," answered Spangler. "A Chinese Communist. He met her in Tsinan."

"Why didn't he bring her out?" Henderson queried.

"She died in November, 1959."

The office was quiet for a few moments as the staff checked their information.

Spangler watched them all very carefully and decided that there was enough interest and enthusiasm to guarantee complete cooperation.

"Fantastic," mumbled Dorfman. "Eight years in Red China. How in the hell did he live? He must be Chinese by now."

"He damn well looks it," Henderson contributed. "I saw a picture of him sitting in the Red Cross building in Hong Kong."

Spangler sat back, watched and listened. He knew that healthy side conversation at this stage of any briefing was a good indication that the project had the feel of a winner.

Spangler turned to Morris Wineburg. "Well?" The executive smiled.

"Interesting," said Wineburg. "But as usual, you talk as if you have a deal. Have you?"

"No."

"Then isn't this meeting a bit premature?"

"I called this meeting, Morris, in order to get a reaction from my staff. Now, I'll get Hawthorne."

"How?" asked the lawyer suspiciously.

The chatter around the room stopped abruptly. This was the fascinating part, the magic of Robert Calhoun Spangler, winner of four Peabody Awards, twelve Emmy Awards, and the proud owner of scrapbooks loaded with industry scoops and national program upheavals. The impossible made easy before your very eyes.

"We'll buy the bastard," Spangler announced.

He stood, moved to the front of the desk and leaned, facing the members of his staff. "He's stranded in Hong Kong and the government won't touch him with a ten-foot pole. I'll pay his passage here to New York and we'll tape a two-hour, in-depth interview."

He nodded to Morris Wineburg. "You'll set up a syndication contract and we'll give him five percent of the sales after recoupment of costs. Then I'll ship his ass on to Waverly, Michigan."

Several members of the group exchanged glances and Wineburg placed his notes in his jacket pocket.

"The networks might be doing the same," the lawyer suggested. "And they can offer him more money and straight national exposure."

Spangler smiled. "Hawthorne is a public news item at the moment, Morris. The networks will not buy news. It's against their religion."

"There's always a first time," countered Wineburg.

"Correct, counselor." Spangler put his hands into his pockets. "That's why I'm doing it for the first time. I intend to buy Hawthorne and I can assure you that I will protect my investment."

"May I ask how?" Wineburg was now concerned about Amalgamated and Mr. Frederic G. Bateman, the Chairman of the Board, who was involved in many delicate corporate transactions. And, in addition, the Federal Communications Commission was breathing down the organization's neck. The chairman was not in a position to tolerate any nonsense from the television program department.

"Trust me," said Spangler, smiling broadly. "I'll explain it all at another meeting."

"Who does the interview, Bob?" asked Henderson.

"Arthur Fremantle," said Spangler. "I'll fly him in from the Coast when we're set here. I want this job staged in New York and I want it done perfectly, under my direct supervision." He added firmly, "Not one goddamn word released about any of this, Tim, until I say move. Understood?"

Henderson nodded as he continued to scribble in his pad.

"Straight interview and nothing else?" asked Schroeder.

"I don't know yet, Fred," answered Spangler, now loving

every minute of the session. "Maybe a brief discussion front and back, if we can get top people. We'll see."

Spangler glanced at the news director.

"Dorfman," the program chief said quietly, "you look like a man with something on his mind. Why don't you sound off? You might feel better."

"I know for a fact, Mr. Spangler, that the networks are in touch with the State Department in Washington right now. In a few days they should have clearance for an interview in Hong Kong with Hawthorne. I think we're late."

Spangler's tone was elaborately casual. "I don't want an interview in Hong Kong, Dorfman. I want a *program* in New York."

He pushed himself away from the desk and walked slowly to the news director's chair.

Spangler was now in complete control. "I know that the networks are in touch with the State Department and I don't give a damn because I know that the State Department doesn't give a damn about Gerald Howard Hawthorne. So, I intend to bypass Washington and save plenty of time. And, I intend to do that with my secret weapon. A telephone. A telephone, ladies and gentlemen," he snickered. "A simple telephone. Tonight I will place a person-to-person call to Mr. Gerald Howard Hawthorne at the American Red Cross building in Hong Kong. The networks will be playing with the State Department while I purchase the Turncoat."

"What makes you think he'll sell, Bob?" Henderson asked politely. "He sure as hell must be a strange and unpredictable character."

"The package I'm offering this man will not be turned down," answered Spangler. It was a declaration.

"Five percent of nothing?" Wineburg disputed. "By the time you pull your costs out of syndication, he'll have nothing."

"Not money, Morris," said Spangler. "Trust, friendship, protection from exploiters, an opportunity to put his case before the American people professionally, honestly, openly, without restrictions. And, the right to edit the tape. A chance to come home and a chance to look good."

Robert Calhoun Spangler took a long drag of his cigarette, returned to his chair, sat down and blew a perfect smoke ring toward the ceiling.

"I have a feeling about this gook. It isn't money. The man is afraid. He wants to start fresh in this country and he needs help." He paused and looked directly at Arnold Dorfman. "I'm going to give it to him."

AUGUST 27, 1961
HONG KONG

3 THE AMERICAN PRESS was treating the Hawthorne release from Red China with mild curiosity rather than sincere journalistic interest. Reports were being filed by various news agencies but mainly in reference to the man's financial dilemma in Hong Kong and the fact that the American government had refused to pay his passage back to the United States.

Radio and television networks were represented but the coverage was limited to dull visuals and bland commentary, without a word from Gerald Howard Hawthorne. The Turncoat had ceased to be headline news.

It was a drastic change from the bombardment and saturation in August 1953. The press had represented a shocked and humiliated nation and Hawthorne had been the evil eye of the storm.

The Chairman of the Permanent Subcommittee on Investigations for the United States Senate had truly set the stage.

Senator Joseph McCarthy had launched one hundred fifty-seven inquiries, notably into the "Voice of America" and the Army Signal Corps installation at Fort Monmouth, New Jersey.

Later it was discovered that his search had failed to unearth any cases of actual subversive activity or disloyalty, and to put it mildly, the manner in which he conducted his investigations brought him into open conflict with the United States Army.

But in the midst of the fear and suspicion created by McCarthy in 1953, reports on the morally weak and unpatriotic conduct of the American prisoners of war in Korea were slowly filtering back to an aroused and confused nation and Gerald Hawthorne was becoming the scapegoat for the American conscience.

The press had played the situation from every possible angle. Radio and television had followed with analysis, commentary, discussion and documentary. The American Legion, Veterans of Foreign Wars and other organizations had screamed protests and placed the blame on the "new" Army and a lack of discipline and training. Others felt that the young soldiers had been brainwashed, drugged or hypnotized.

The label "Turncoat" was created by an inventive journalist and Hawthorne became a symbol, a slogan, a warning and a target. He had been the first, and as far as the American people were concerned, he personified all the others. This particular veteran had carried the insult and humiliation all the way by rejecting his own country in order to live in Communist China.

Parents, widows and the children of the dead in Korea had cursed his name. Returning heroes had vowed to shoot him on sight. Even the guilty, as they came home to face charges and punishment, spat at the name of Hawthorne.

The small, quiet town of Waverly, Michigan, had also been caught up in the public disgust over his defection. From the steps of the Town Hall, the mayor had proclaimed that the proud and patriotic town of Waverly would have to live with the shame of Gerald Hawthorne.

Now the Turncoat was out of Red China and there was a strong possibility that he would soon return to Michigan.

Journalists were treating the event cautiously as though Hawthorne were an ugly thought which had been hidden away for years and forgotten. He was a feature article, representing a distasteful period in American history, and most of the competent reporters were trying not to stir it up again.

Still, many were interested in the prison camp phase of his story and every writer was genuinely curious about the man's life with the Communists in Tsinan, China. But they all discovered very quickly that the Hong Kong assignment was nothing more than a frustrating experience.

A few pictures were taken in the American Red Cross building but Gerald Howard Hawthorne was silent.

His room was a small storage area located in the basement of the cramped Red Cross building in the center of town. He was fortunate to have found the space. It had been furnished with an Army cot, a chair, a dilapidated card table and a small reading lamp. Hawthorne had seen much worse in his time and he was appreciative.

He relaxed on the cot, closed his eyes and tried to get used to an American cigarette. Sinclair had given him a carton of Pall Malls in exchange for a framed poem, poorly written in Chinese by an unknown Communist in Tsinan.

Home was now a reality.

The glib program executive from the American television company in New York had presented a complicated proposition on the telephone. There had been a poor connection, and in addition, Hawthorne knew that the man had not taken the time to explain the details properly.

Yet he had accepted the basic terms of the agreement and funds were on the way from Amalgamated Broadcasting Television.

Representatives from numerous publications had presented vague, confusing propositions to Jarvis Sinclair in exchange for exclusivity but Hawthorne was not interested. Spangler was the only person to promise immediate passage out of Hong Kong. Nothing else was important.

Hawthorne sat up and stubbed the cigarette in a metal ashtray near the cot. He stood and walked to the small window. There were two iron bars and the opening was covered with chicken wire. He had to look up in order to see out and this was very familiar.

He wanted to go home.

The house on Elm Drive was now the most vital thing in his life. In fact, it was the only thing in his life. He would close and bolt the front door and wait for the strength to face another set of staggering challenges.

He returned to the cot and sat with his back propped against the cool basement wall.

There was a polite knock on the door of the small room. "Gerald?" It was Sinclair's voice.

"Yes."

"Can I talk to you for a minute?" he asked quietly.

With an effort, Hawthorne pushed himself off the cot and stood for a moment. He glanced at his watch and realized that it was only five-fifteen in the afternoon. He took a deep breath, lit a cigarette and then opened the door.

Sinclair walked in, holding an official-looking document. The Red Cross representative took a seat in a chair near the bed and looked up at Hawthorne.

"I think you've got the coolest spot in the building," he said, noticing that Hawthorne did not look well at all. Sinclair continued, "A Morris Wineburg just arrived in Hong Kong. This man is your ticket home, Gerald."

Hawthorne moved slowly to the cot and sat on the edge facing Jarvis Sinclair.

"Amalgamated is a solid firm and this man Spangler is certainly a professional," Sinclair was saying. "You fell into responsible hands."

There was silence as Hawthorne sprawled on the bed, smoked and stared up at several prominent cracks in the basement ceiling. The Red Cross official took out his own pack of cigarettes and lit up. Then in a soft and careful tone, he said, "You look lousy, Gerald. Would you like a drink?"

Hawthorne turned and looked at the official as if seeing him for the first time. He squinted, thought for a moment and then said politely, "No, thank you."

He turned back to his study of the ceiling and was only dimly aware that the man was present.

Soon he would be forced to honor his bargain with the American television producer and disclose the personal details of his life in exchange for a ticket home.

Hawthorne pledged that Robert Spangler was going to receive a worthwhile sketch but no one on earth would ever be allowed to view the completed portrait.

The Red Cross official opened the dossier on the card table.

"Routine stuff," he said as he glanced through the contents. "It proves to the boss back in the States that you received our goods and services and that I did not cheat the organization."

He smiled as he handed the papers and a pen to Hawthorne. "Everything is detailed and itemized. I suggest you read it before signing."

Hawthorne scribbled his name quickly, without a look or a pause, and handed the documents back.

"You should be on your way sometime tomorrow," said Sinclair, and then he added with great sincerity, "I can imagine the strain."

"I'll make out," Hawthorne whispered.

There was a brief silence. Sinclair arranged the papers on the table.

"I suppose you speak and read Chinese fluently?" he asked.

"Yes."

"Did you learn it in China?"

Hawthorne looked at the Red Cross official and decided that he would satisfy the man's curiosity, up to a point.

"The guards in the prison camp taught me a little." He paused and then spoke very softly. "My wife taught me a lot."

"Did you go to any formal school in China?" the representative asked.

"Cheloo University."

Sinclair shook his head in disbelief. "Amazing. It must have been very difficult. Did you finish high school in America before the Army, Gerald?"

"No."

Hawthorne leaned his head back and felt the dampness of the basement wall.

"They were junior classes." He thought of the pleasures at Cheloo. "Studies in Chinese history, culture and language. Designed for the young."

"Quite an accomplishment."

"I had many friends," Hawthorne said pensively.

"Did you meet your wife in Tsinan?" Sinclair asked, prepared for silence or an outburst.

"Yes," Hawthorne answered. "Her father was a doctor in my prison camp."

The Red Cross representative paused and thought about the statement for a moment before continuing.

"How long were you married?"

"Five years."

"I was married for sixteen years," he said softly. "My wife died four years ago and I still cannot adjust. I loved her very much."

Hawthorne was silent as the official moved into a very delicate and private area.

"How did your wife die, Gerald?"

"Cancer," he answered quickly.

"My wife was killed in an automobile accident outside of Pittsburgh," said Sinclair. Then he was aware of Hawthorne's expression.

"I'm sorry," he mumbled.

Hawthorne pulled himself off the cot and walked to the small window. He stood with his back to the Red Cross official.

Sinclair rose to his feet, collected the dossier from the table and started slowly for the door.

He paused for a moment before leaving. "I'll stop by for you when Wineburg arrives," he said, realizing that the words were being wasted on the frail, brooding figure near the window. Hawthorne's head was bowed and he seemed to be deeply absorbed.

Sinclair left the room and closed the door quietly.

SEPTEMBER 10, 1950
WAVERLY, MICHIGAN

4 THE TOWN WAS SMALL, picturesque and orderly. It was located exactly thirty-four miles from Detroit and this was an ideal situation for the fifteen thousand inhabitants, who seemed very friendly to an outsider. They were close enough for big-city action and far enough away to enjoy the clean, fresh air and suburban quiet.

Waverly in 1950 was an active and productive community and there was very little poverty. There were broad streets, magnificent lawns and trees. The houses in the better sections of the town were large and quite impressive.

The Hawthorne residence was not situated in the most exclusive section of Waverly, Michigan, but the neighborhood was clean and quiet and the street was lined with stately elm trees.

The house was a large wooden structure with a comfortable porch and ample grounds. It was old and in need of paint and repairs, but it appeared homey and unpretentious.

Hawthorne was born here, in his mother's room, on the second floor.

As far as he was concerned, she was the most beautiful woman on earth. Her face was exquisitely boned and delicately formed. Her long black hair was always clean and fresh and shining. It fell to her shoulders and he remembered the colorful ribbons she used to wear.

Her eyes were deep blue and they were large and arched with very dark brows. They would sparkle when she smiled and sometimes tear when she laughed. His mother was small but her body was curved and slender and graceful.

He loved her very much, and when she died in an automobile accident, he was deprived of all warmth, understanding and love and left to the violent rages of a drunken father.

Hawthorne was a sensitive-looking boy with a pale, thin face, dark eyes, dark hair and a very slight body.

Timidity and shyness, in his early childhood, had slowly developed into pessimism and at nineteen, despair and futility. His time was spent alone without laughter or interests of any kind.

His father was a plumber, a big man with a scar just to one side of his mouth, where five years before three men had attacked him with a bottle. Howard Hawthorne was forty-two years old on this date in 1950.

He had a thick neck and a brick-red face. His eyes were large and deep-set, and at times they were cold and barbaric. His full head of black hair was seldom combed and his eyebrows were dark and bushy.

The plumber was a chronic drinker. He used to proudly admit to his few close drinking companions that he had "started at birth. My old man gave me a shot of booze instead of a slap on the ass."

During sober intervals he seemed to love his wife and feel some compassion for the boy. After drinking, however, he became brutal and capable of instant violence.

Each night, while his mother was alive, Gerald would cringe in bed, smother his face in the pillows and try to block out the terrifying screams and drunken commotion.

Sometimes the boy would cower in a corner on the floor and cry uncontrollably until he fell asleep.

"Take a good look at him, Marion," he remembered his father shouting. "A goddamn emaciated little queer. Your son is a goddamn queer! Your fault. YOUR FAULT!"

And the man would strike her and she would scream and Gerald would shrink away from the sounds and the meaning of his father's words. He would draw his knees up and force himself deeper into the corner. Many times he had managed to press his forehead into the wall until the pain blurred all reality. Once he had felt blood.

Usually, the next morning, when his father went to work, if he was able to, his mother would console him and he would try to comfort her.

THE TURNCOAT | 33

One day on the sofa in the living room she had cried bitterly and he had stroked her hair. She took his hand gently and Gerald looked deeply into her eyes. He kissed her tenderly on the cheek and felt a slim arm around his shoulders. Her eyes had a strange, slightly confused expression, but they were very soft and radiant.

For the first time, and the last, the boy leaned forward and kissed her gently on the mouth.

Her lips were moist and full. They parted as Gerald felt the warmth of her response.

His father had been mistaken. Gerald Howard Hawthorne, at the age of sixteen, had made tender, passionate love to a very beautiful woman. His mother.

She was crushed to death three weeks later as she returned from work in Detroit. The station wagon was completely demolished in a violent head-on collision with a heavy truck belonging to a local construction firm. The driver was also killed instantly.

Marion Hawthorne had worked as a beauty operator in a small shop on Fulton Street and her weekly earnings were mainly responsible for the adequate, middle-class existence of the family in Waverly since her husband had been dismissed from both local firms which had previously employed him. He now worked from his home as a "free-lance plumbing technician."

The man leaned heavier on alcohol after the death of his wife. He worked less, cursed more and drove his basically unstable son to the point of madness.

On the night of the accident, in a drunken rage, he had locked and bolted Marion's bedroom door. The room had remained unopened since the news of her death.

Gerald was happy about the arrangement. He felt that everything genuine and beautiful was now contained in one isolated chamber of the house and that the spirit of his beloved mother would rest in peace.

Soon after the tragedy, local whores had taken over his father's world. One afternoon, because of a holiday schedule, Gerald had returned from school earlier than usual to find the front door locked from the inside and all the shades drawn. He rang the bell several times but there was no reply.

Finally, he saw his father's face peering through the curtained glass of the living room window. Gerald considered getting away from the porch when he saw his father's expression, but it was too late. The door opened slowly.

His father was completely nude. He reached out for Gerald and swayed drunkenly.

"Come on in, Gerry boy," he slobbered, "the water's fine."

Young Hawthorne started to pull away but the strong hand gripped him and yanked him into the hallway.

The plumber leaned back against the wall, wiped the saliva from his mouth and roared with laughter. "Caught your old man in the act, eh, Gerry?"

He punched the boy playfully on the arm.

Seventeen-year-old Gerald kept his eyes riveted straight ahead, realizing that he felt like vomiting.

"I'm gonna show you what a real man is like, kid," his father mumbled. "Get your skinny ass in the other room."

He was shoved roughly through the heavy red portieres.

A woman was on the floor of the living room. A repugnant prostitute with her naked legs spread wide. She was an unshapely mess with large, flabby breasts and a coarse, hard face.

Her features softened into a smile as Howard Hawthorne pushed his son closer.

"This is my kid Gerald," said the plumber, standing over her. He put his muscular arm around the boy's shoulders.

"He's a little strange. I've got to learn him a few things."

The whore looked up at Gerald and rubbed her crotch seductively. "I'll learn him for you, Howie," she said.

Howard Hawthorne convulsed with laughter. "Ain't she somethin'."

He wiggled his naked toe between her legs.

"Ever seen one of these up close, Gerry?"

The boy closed his eyes and turned away in disgust.

His father's brawny arm clamped around his neck and he

was twisted back violently to face the repulsive flesh sprawling on the floor of the living room.

"*I asked you a question, boy!*" The red face was close and the voice bellowed. "*Answer me!*"

Gerald Hawthorne froze, paralyzed in mind and body.

A strong, beefy hand gripped the hair at the back of his head and pulled until the pain was unbearable, and he was forced to the floor on both knees.

His head was pressed forward until it was between the legs of the prostitute. He heard the sound of obscene laughter as she maneuvered her hips and stretched wider.

"Taste it, you little freak," his father muttered drunkenly, shoving the boy down to the large, curly patch of black pubic hair.

The hand pressed harder on the back of his head and the smell of the woman's damp organ nauseated him. He tried not to breathe.

"*Taste it!*" his father screamed. "*Grow up!* you goddamn little queer!"

The whore spread wide and then shrieked with laughter as Gerald's mouth was shoved down to her opening. He twisted and struggled desperately but soon tasted the sour juices of the woman and felt the flabby pulp of her body against his tightly clenched lips.

"Hey," she cackled, "you're not as good as your daddy, Junior."

Finally, his head was pulled back and his father yanked him to his feet and gave him a mock salute.

"Congratulations, my boy," he spluttered, pretending to pin a medal on his chest. "You have tasted a woman and I'm proud of you."

The whore applauded enthusiastically.

"Now, Gerald," his father continued, "sit down, and watch a real man knock off a piece." He patted the boy paternally on the cheek. "You might learn something."

Gerald felt ill. He could taste the vaginal juices on his lips and he wanted to wash and scrub away the sight and the stink of the woman.

"Please," he begged. "I feel sick."

Howard Hawthorne raised a huge fist and moved it threateningly in front of the boy's face. "Watch," he said with cold, drunken menace. "Or I'll break your fucking neck."

The plumber shoved and Gerald fell backwards to the floor.

He forced himself to watch as his father teased and then mounted the squirming monstrosity. The action was too grotesque to register with any reality, and he sat dazed as the two figures rolled and slobbered and moaned.

Gerald saw his father fumble between his legs and then thrust. The whore groaned and he knew that the performance would soon be over.

The scene was no longer horrific. In fact, he was beginning to see the comic aspects of it. He suddenly saw that the plumber had a mat of thick black hair covering his broad behind. He watched it bob and weave over the woman.

Gerald watched his father quiver and then push deeper into the whore. The woman wrapped her legs around his wide back and eased his head down on her breasts.

For a brief moment, the boy caught her eye and she grinned. He turned away quickly.

Howard Hawthorne pulled out and away from the woman and stood swaying in front of his son.

"Well, boy," he asked in a whiskey-thick voice, "did you learn anything today?"

Gerald Hawthorne did not flinch or tremble.

"Yes, sir," he said firmly without lowering his eyes. "I did learn."

The plumber tried to smile but his contorted features refused to respond. Instead, tears began to roll down his cheeks as he moved closer. He wrapped his arms around Gerald's neck.

"Good," he mumbled. "Very good." Then he released his hold and slapped the boy good-naturedly on the shoulder.

"We ought to spend more time together, Gerry. Get to know each other."

Young Gerald Hawthorne was basically intelligent, alert and receptive but he lacked confidence and drive. His sullen manner and unsociability stamped him as a "character" and his fellow students at Waverly High School tended to exclude him from their activities.

Mrs. Beatrice Powell was the only member of the school staff, and indeed, the only person in the community, with an ounce of interest in the strange, brooding young man from Elm Drive.

The boy resented the attention and did his best to discourage any attempt to break through his protective wall.

Mrs. Powell was a forty-six-year-old widow with thinning blond hair and severe, hawk-like features, although she had a youthful figure with firm breasts and well-shaped legs.

She was considered to be a very able teacher, a good citizen, a loyal churchgoer. When she received an official note from the school administrator, informing her, as the homeroom teacher, that Gerald Hawthorne was terminating his classes at the school, she was sincerely disturbed.

"You will regret this move, Gerald." She had detained him after class. "A seventeen-year-old boy without a formal education will face a mighty crooked and uphill path."

He sat back quietly and watched as she paced back and forth in front of the blackboard.

He could no longer concentrate on schoolwork. His father had been nursing a blind and steady four-month drunk and the violent rages were becoming even more frequent. It was now impossible for him to find employment. His father had settled in Waverly nineteen years ago after selling his share of a lucrative family plumbing business in Toronto, Canada. Marion Dunhill had been born in the town and had met Hawthorne at a Christmas charity dance.

According to the pictures in the family album, young Howard Hawthorne was tall and good-looking with a roguish smile and manner. He also had money at the time and Gerald was certain that the man was able to hold his whiskey much better during the early years of courtship and marriage.

As the years went by and the whiskey flowed freely, he had squandered a substantial investment in a local plumbing establishment and grew increasingly unable to hold any sort of job. Arguments, violence and numerous separations had destroyed all his wife's love and respect. Cheap booze and whores took care of the Unemployment Compensation, which his father was still collecting illegally.

"It's your father, isn't it, Gerald?" Mrs. Powell asked.

The boy stood and picked up his books without answering.

"I know," the teacher continued. She took hold of his arm gently but he pulled away. "If you want me to do something about him, I can, you know."

He stared coldly at Beatrice Powell. She did not change her expression or the calm and deliberate tone of her voice.

"Let me help you, Gerald."

Mrs. Powell moved a cautious step closer.

"Gerald," she practically whispered. "Change your mind. Don't leave."

The boy looked up at a spot on the ceiling and bit his lip. He was certainly not in a proper frame of mind to endure another meaningless lecture, but for some reason this woman had become his very last connection with normalcy. It was difficult for him to step away.

"I'll go to Peter Barstow at Welfare," she was saying, "or even to Senator Brewster. Something can be done." She paused to catch her breath. "Please let me try."

Hawthorne shook his head and started for the door.

"I could report him to the authorities, you know," she blurted.

The strident pitch of the woman's voice stopped him for a moment.

He turned and stared at her curiously.

"Your father," she said without waiting for his question.

Gerald hesitated for a moment and studied her face.

"Forget it, Mrs. Powell," he said quietly. "Goodbye."

Gerald Hawthorne had moved from a bad dream into a nightmare.

It was difficult, nearly impossible, for him to muster enough courage for employment interviews. Many times he would set an appointment, arrive on time and then walk repeatedly around the block, trembling and perspiring, until it was too late to go inside.

Once, while being interrogated by the manager of Pittman's Shoe Store, his mind had gone blank and he had forgotten his home address and his date of birth.

On another occasion, while applying for an apprentice position at the Thompson Plumbing Corporation, he had lost the use of his voice completely. The assistant manager had asked Gerald about his father, and the boy had been unable to reply. In fact, it had taken him two days to regain his speech.

Finally, Mrs. Powell had arranged a trial position as a general helper in Moran's Texaco Service Station on Cable Road, just outside of town. The hours were long and unpredictable but it was an excellent opportunity for Gerald Hawthorne.

In less than two weeks he had managed to disrupt the general routine of the service station by creating a tense and morbid atmosphere which Mr. Moran considered to be detrimental to morale and productivity.

Hawthorne was released with a lecture and one week's pay.

He accepted the dismissal with a feeling of relief and began to spend most of his time locked away in his room on Elm Drive.

He wasted hours toying with fantasy and dwelling on memories of his mother. Her framed photograph, taken only a few months before her death, was situated prominently on the bureau top and it was the nerve center of the small room. All of his love and attention were focused on the delicate figure, posing so regally on the porch swing.

He had taken the picture himself.

The thought of her eased his fears and depression and the sight of her turned every other woman on earth into a replica of the slobbering whore he had watched rocking under his father.

On several occasions, he had heard his father's raucous laughter and the screams of drunken prostitutes but he had not seen the man for nearly a month.

Gerald knew that his father would soon run out of whiskey and that they would both need food. For the moment, the boy was relieved and happy that his father did not seem to be aware of his presence in the house.

One night Gerald had awakened abruptly, screaming wildly at the top of his lungs. Cold perspiration had soaked his hair and pajamas.

He realized that someone was pounding on his bedroom door.

His father entered, hesitated for a moment and then moved to the bed.

"What the hell is the matter with you, Gerry?" he asked softly and with obvious concern.

The sober sincerity of the man's voice forced the boy to look up.

He had to squint and struggle for focus. His father's face was chalk-white and the skin was drawn tightly over sunken cheekbones. Blood-red eyes were circled in sickly black and the boy noticed a tremble in the man's hands.

"I heard you scream," his father said.

Gerald reached under the pillow, removed a handkerchief and wiped the cold sweat from his forehead.

"I'm okay," he muttered.

Howard Hawthorne adjusted a worn black silk bathrobe, which was much too short.

"I guess we're in the same boat," he said thoughtfully.

Gerald pulled the covers up and did not answer. His father sat wearily on the edge of the bed and glanced at the photograph on the bureau. "God rest her soul," he said.

The boy said nothing.

"I have a proposition for you, Gerald," his father said. "We can't get work, and we both sure as hell need it badly."

He stood and began to move around the room. "Suppose I kick the booze?" He turned and looked at the boy intently. "And I mean kick it, as of now."

He walked toward the bureau and stood looking at the photograph for a moment. "We throw in together. What you don't know about plumbing, I'll teach you fast." He moved back to the bed and sat. "Hell, I know of two jobs already, out by Hammond's Stables. Old Bert Fry will give them to us in a minute, if he sees that I'm straight on the line."

Gerald watched him suspiciously and without a noticeable change of expression. His father turned and looked directly into the boy's eyes.

"I've got to do something fast, Gerry," he said softly. And then he walked to the door and added, "Or I'm gonna die."

He left the room without glancing back.

Gerald spent the rest of the night thinking about his father's desperate proposal. He rationalized that the booze, the whores, the violence and the cruelty would not equal the sheer terror of leaving the house in order to make his own way in the community.

The thought was appalling but Gerald decided to take the risk and go to work with his father.

It was a complete disaster from the very beginning.

Howard Hawthorne had tried. In fact, he had stayed away from the bottle for nearly two weeks but the experience had shattered his nerves. The venom, which had been stored and pickled for so long in his bitter, alcoholic body, was suddenly released and Gerald was forced to think of immediate escape.

Humiliation piled on humiliation as the boy struggled to get through each day. Howard Hawthorne's violent and derogatory outbursts smashed any small amount of confidence which his son might have had.

His actions became more frenzied and belligerent as the weeks passed. On a particular job, in a home located several miles from Waverly, he beat Gerald severely for forgetting to pack a wrench when the tools were boxed in the morning. He never called a doctor; instead, the boy remained in bed for five days.

Gerald thought seriously of escape but a solid wall seemed to block every possible path. His mind was not prepared for challenges or competition.

One month later, however, he was forced into an unexpected showdown with reality.

Beatrice Powell had miraculously arranged a contract with

the Waverly School Board, procuring Howard Hawthorne and his son some of the plumbing assignments which were ordinarily given exclusively to the Thompson Company each year.

The first assignment, a simple job in the Roosevelt Junior High School auditorium, was to have been a test of their competence. Several important Board members were poised for inspection and evaluation.

Early in the morning, before reporting to the school, Gerald was sent by his father to Anderson's Hardware for the specialized tools needed to complete the auditorium job properly. It had been the first time that his father had ever trusted him with any kind of responsibility and the boy knew the importance of this first assignment.

The air was clean and fresh and he walked home briskly, feeling a slight touch of confidence and optimism for the first time in years.

The house was unusually quiet when he returned. He checked his watch and wondered if his father had left early in order to conduct a preliminary inspection before beginning the actual work. It was eleven o'clock and they were due in the auditorium at twelve noon.

He called his father several times and then put the package down and searched the downstairs rooms for a note. There was nothing to indicate that the man had left the house.

Reluctantly he opened the door of his father's room upstairs. The man was nude and swaying crazily over the crumpled, fully-dressed figure of a young woman on the bed. Gerald immediately recognized the crippled daughter of some neighbors who lived several houses down on Elm Drive. The girl was mentally retarded and could not have been more than fifteen years old. She seemed to be unconscious.

His father, holding an empty whiskey bottle, turned slowly when he heard the door open. He did not seem to be surprised or alarmed by his son's interruption.

"I didn't touch her," the plumber said quietly. He tossed the bottle into a corner of the room. "The damn dummy was asleep on the bed when I came out of the shower." He staggered toward Gerald, who stood motionless in the doorway. "Everybody knows the poor, sick bastard roams the neighborhood." He stopped in front of his son. "I'll call her daddy as soon as I get dressed."

He poked his finger against Gerald's chest and whispered, "Now go downstairs and get me another bottle of hootch."

The boy studied his father carefully but did not move. "You deaf?" the plumber asked impatiently. "I said, go get me some hootch." Young Hawthorne did not lower his eyes. His father stepped closer, swayed and nearly fell to the floor. He raised his fist and moved it slowly in front of Gerald's face.

"Don't play games with me," he said with cold menace. The fist paused and clenched tighter. "Get it, you goddamn little queer."

The deep-set eyes were mocking him once again. Every word out of that cruel mouth was vulgar. For the first time, disgust turned to deep hatred and Gerald Hawthorne vowed that he would die on the spot rather than obey any order from this sick and worthless human being who called himself his father.

"Go to hell," Gerald said bitterly. He turned and walked away.

The plumber was stunned and unable to react immediately. Instead, he leaned on the door frame and watched incredulously as the boy began to descend the stairs.

"Gerald."

He continued to walk without turning back.

"*Gerald!*"

He hesitated for a moment and heard his father shuffle from the doorway to the railing, overlooking the stairs.

"GET YOUR ASS UP HERE, GERRY!" the man bellowed, leaning far over.

The boy turned slowly and looked up.

Howard Hawthorne's eyes were wild and blazing, maniacal, and veins protruded from his neck.

This time, however, the boy felt that the threat was wasted.

Suddenly Gerald's deep-rooted hatred turned to sadness and then to pity.

"Go to hell," the boy repeated quietly. He left the house on Elm Drive.

AUGUST 29, 1961
WASHINGTON, D.C.

5

THE GENTLEMAN, WEARING a conservative gray suit and carrying a thin black briefcase, smiled, nodded and then walked quickly past the desk of Mrs. Andrea Colt, appointments secretary to the Vice President of the United States.

She checked her watch and realized that the visitor had been inside only two minutes thirty seconds. Strange, she thought. It was certainly one of the shortest meetings on record, unless of course he had delivered or received a dispatch of some kind.

The Vice President had personally scheduled the brief meeting without consulting the appointments log and this was rather strange. Security clearance had not been handled in the normal manner and no one had mentioned the man's name.

She thought she remembered seeing him years before, at a fund-raising dinner at the Waldorf-Astoria in New York. If it was the same person, then he was a multimillionaire with giant holdings in Latin America, a major contributor to Party election campaigns and a close personal friend of several high-ranking government officials, including the President and his wife.

If it was the same person, and now she was beginning to doubt it, she recalled seeing his name on several classified documents, part of a Securities and Exchange Commission dossier, marked for investigation. The name she remembered was Rhinebow or Rainbow or something similar.

An hour later, the internal house phone buzzed and she lifted the receiver. The voice on the other end was deep and clipped.

"Mrs. Colt, this is Hector Rambeau. I know that the Vice President is on the telephone at the moment. Please inform him that Mr. Whiting and Mr. Barlow will be in his office tomorrow at 3:30 PM. And tell him that someone will be in touch with the television fellow very quickly." There was a pause. "And, Mrs. Colt. There is no need to list the 3:30. Just arrange it. I'm sure the Vice President will explain. Thank you."

Andrea Colt did not make a note of the Whiting and Barlow meeting. She thought for a moment and then sat back and smiled. Her curiosity had been satisfied.

Studio B, in the Amalgamated Television operation in New York, was small, compact and used mainly for one- and two-camera situations, ordinarily interview or commentary for news inserts. On this particular night, however, the limbo work area was serving as battlefield headquarters for the programming commander-in-chief, Mr. Robert C. Spangler.

He sat with his arms resting on the back of a folding chair. His actions typified an important military briefing prior to action.

"They get in at two-thirty in the morning," Spangler instructed. "So let's go over the operation in detail.

"Arnie Dorfman is in charge of the airport phase of this project." The news director nodded and Spangler continued. "This is the touchy part, so listen carefully." He glanced at four burly, uniformed security guards. "You boys step in with Arnie and Tim Henderson the minute you see his face at the arrival gate. Surround the bastard and start moving fast. You know the layout at Idlewild, so hustle him quickly and stay away from the action in the VIP lounge. Media will be set up there with mikes and cameras."

"That could be trouble," said Dorfman.

"No trouble," Spangler replied quickly. "We bought him.

We own him. Let them take a few shots as you move but Hawthorne doesn't stop or open his mouth. Understood?"

They understood and Spangler continued. "The cars will be standing by. Shove him in, bundle him up and head for the Carlton Hotel. I'll be waiting in the security suite."

"What about us, Mr. Spangler?" asked the largest of the four hefty guards.

The program chief stood and walked closer to their chairs.

"Fellows," he said very seriously, "you were hired because I received special recommendations from certain people around town. I can't tell you how to run your business, but let me say this. Arthur Fremantle can't get in from California until tomorrow evening.

"I want this man bottled up in the room," the executive continued. "You boys will eat, sleep and crap with him. If he gives you trouble . . ." Spangler paused. "Well, handle it any way you can."

He studied the four guards carefully for a moment and then asked, "Do you men know his background?"

"Yes, Mr. Spangler, we sure do," answered a hard-looking, pock-marked member of the group.

The program chief started a slow walk back to his chair. "You were at Okinawa with the Sixth, weren't you, Travis?"

"Yes, sir," the guard answered proudly.

Spangler took a seat and then winked at the security men. "Then I don't think I'll have any trouble," he said with a grin.

Dorfman felt a slight turning of his stomach as he surveyed the guard detachment. He wondered about those special recommendations from certain people around town. The longshoremen's union, he thought, or the Mafia, or perhaps the Nazi Party.

"The minute Fremantle arrives from the Coast, we move out of the Carlton and into the studios," said the leader.

"When can I release?" asked Henderson, the publicity chief.

"Go in stages, Tim," answered Spangler. "Release the first shot as soon as the tape rolls with Hawthorne.

"When we complete the interview with Hawthorne," he continued, "we rush him on a plane for Waverly, or China, or hell. Then we go to work."

"What about the press after he records and takes off?" asked Fred Schroeder, the director.

"We have an exclusive contract with this character for one year, commencing with the date of the interview," answered Spangler.

"What the hell does he know or care about contracts and exclusivity?" countered Dorfman.

"Arnie," said Spangler calmly, "we have to gamble."

"Why doesn't Fremantle shoot him as soon as the interview is over?" kidded Dorfman.

The staff laughed.

"Not so funny," said Spangler with a broad smile. "Knowing my boy Fremantle, he might do just that anyway."

"Knowing your boy Fremantle," said Dorfman, "Hawthorne might shoot *him*."

The staff laughed again. Spangler joined in and then nodded to the security guards. "I understand that the guy is queer. You fellows might have to shoot him at the Carlton."

"Or love him at the Carlton," said Travis.

Spangler had to sit back and wait for the laughter to subside.

A young messenger entered the studio, leaned close to Frances Patterson and whispered. She nodded, looked puzzled and made a note.

"What is it, Fran?" asked Spangler, noticing her expression.

"There is someone in reception without an appointment," she said.

"So?"

"His name is Pantell."

"So?"

"From Washington."

"The station?"

"I don't think so."

"So throw him out."

"He mentioned Gerald Howard Hawthorne and said that it was urgent."

Spangler also looked puzzled. "Tell him to wait. We have to finish this meeting."

* * *

Morris Wineburg placed the magazine back into the rack and made himself comfortable in his first-class accommodations as the huge jet streaked toward home.

Christ, what a lopsided world, he thought. Primitive, restless natives in Katanga forcing an urgent visit from the Secretary General of the United Nations, and at the other end of the scale, the most sophisticated destruction on earth about to be ignited by the Soviet Union. Nuclear blasts of twenty-five and over fifty megatons would soon rock the universe, while the Congolese committed barefoot murder. And, in addition, the return of the defector, Gerald Howard Hawthorne. He wondered about the man's controversial war record, his life in Red China and the motivation for making so many unorthodox moves. And he doubted that anyone on earth would ever be told the truth.

Amalgamated's legal counsel yawned and thought of the forthcoming slaughter, which he had helped to arrange for the television broadcasting arena.

Gerald Hawthorne had roamed the streets of Waverly for hours after cursing his father.

He had walked to the foot of Elm Drive and then up to Poplar, his favorite, a much smaller street where you were never exposed.

When the street widened at the intersection of Poplar and Main, he turned left and walked past the Pizza Palace and the Tivoli Theatre.

The boy kicked an empty cardboard milk container into the gutter and cursed as he neared Anderson's Hardware. He lowered his head and moved quickly to the other side of the busy thoroughfare.

He stopped abruptly next to Woolworth's.

A new display in the front window of an abandoned storefront had attracted his attention. A black headline on a red, white and blue poster announced that America was in need of men who loved their country. This was part of a massive, nationwide recruitment drive.

Ordinarily, Hawthorne would have moved on quickly without giving the advertisement a thought or a second glance. This time, however, he stayed and looked carefully, ignoring several roughnecks who were jeering at the recruitment officers seated at a desk in the store window.

"Up your ass, Major, with a big, fat bazooka," one young roughneck screamed from his strategic position against the fender of a parked car. The others in the group were convulsed with laughter.

This action would ordinarily have caused Hawthorne to continue on his way. But on this particular afternoon, he was interested in the United States Army.

Two impressively uniformed recruiting sergeants were seated behind a metal desk in the large storefront window. They were surrounded by colorful posters, banners and catchy promotional slogans.

Hawthorne found himself trying to square his shoulders as he watched the men sort papers on the desk. Carefully he considered the exciting possibility that the United States Army might provide an escape route from Waverly, Michigan.

He moved closer to the window and inspected the soldiers. A man in a military uniform was always respected, he decided. He thought of travel to faraway places, small islands and big cities, where the faces, languages and customs were all new and exciting.

The pay was adequate and steady, he reasoned. And the Army offered a routine to follow each day, difficult perhaps, exacting, but practical and predictable. Not like his father's crazy behavior.

Suddenly he realized that one of the recruiting sergeants was motioning for him to come inside.

The boy looked at his watch nervously, pretended to be late and, with an awkward bit of pantomime, he gestured that he would return in two hours.

The soldiers laughed and Hawthorne moved away from the department store window.

After a few steps, he found himself face to face with the roughnecks, who had been waiting patiently for him to make his move. Ordinarily, he would have walked the other way in

order to avoid a scene in public. But now, after his unexpected contact with the military, he straightened up, and with
eyes-front marched briskly past the hooligans.

He had finally discovered an immediate escape route but he
had ignored several important factors.

North Korea had blasted into South Korea, over the 38th
parallel, on June 25, 1950. The troops had moved quickly
southwards, taking Seoul, the capital, while the Republic of
Korea was making a vain attempt to halt the enemy.

Douglas MacArthur was appointed commander of the
United Nations forces and the ROK Army was placed under
his control. Troops and officers of the United States were
flown in but an effective defense was not made until they
had poured in more supplies and men at Pusan and set up
along the Naktong River.

Troops of other nations arrived and finally an impact was
made on September 15, 1950, when the United States made
a substantial landing of Marine and Navy forces at Inchon.

On September 17, 1950, Gerald Howard Hawthorne, age
nineteen, enlisted in the United States Army.

AUGUST 30, 1961
NEW YORK CITY

6 "LADIES AND GENTLEMEN, fasten your seatbelts,
please. We will be landing at Idlewild Airport,
New York City, in just a few moments. Thank
you."

"Here they come," shouted an excited, demonstrative soldier with a broad Texas drawl as an elderly couple moved
wearily through the arrival gates at Idlewild. They were the
first of the TWA Flight 575 passengers from Hong Kong.

Others were also waiting.

Arnold Dorfman had to admit that the entire Hawthorne

affair was interesting and quite exciting. Spangler had managed to set up the assignment like a Hitchcock thriller, using
intrigue, suspense, tight security and even Gestapo tactics.

He glanced at his four companions. The muscular guards
were wearing civilian clothing.

"They should be out soon," said Travis, who was obviously the spokesman for the group. "We'll make a wedge and
move fast, Mr. Dorfman."

The executive producer nodded.

"If we lose you," said Gallagher, another guard, "we'll
meet at the cars."

Dorfman nodded again as he kept his eyes riveted on the
passengers, who were now moving more quickly through the
arrival gates.

Then he surveyed the immediate area of the sprawling airport and spotted a few reporters, photographers and com-
mentators, but the majority of the press representatives
seemed to have ignored the arrival, or were standing by in
the lounge, waiting for the subject to be brought to them.
He wondered what the hell was keeping Tim Henderson,
who had gone off earlier to reconnoiter.

The director focused his attention on the gate and thought
for a moment about Robert Calhoun Spangler. There was no
doubt that he was competent and effective as a program
executive. The Hawthorne piece, for example, regardless of the
dramatic preliminaries, could possibly become a valid and
important contribution to television journalism.

Yet he shuddered to think just how far Spangler might go
in order to protect his investment in Gerald Howard Hawthorne.

Tim Henderson arrived, out of breath and slightly disheveled, after maneuvering his small frame in and out of
every known press hangout in the airport.

"Spangler was right," he said, breathing heavily. "They
have mikes and cameras and they *are* waiting for Hawthorne."

"Too goddamn bad," muttered Dorfman with his eyes on
the gates.

"They won't smell him," added Travis.

"There's Wineburg!" said Henderson.

All eyes shifted immediately to the attorney. He paused at the gate and then waved.

For a moment, the entire Amalgamated squad stood frozen as they caught a glimpse of the short, thin man who was standing next to the lawyer.

Hawthorne's suit had been crumpled out of shape and his shirt was soiled and open at the collar. He was carrying a large cloth bag, embroidered with colorful Oriental dragons.

He stood blinking into the glare of the airport lights, trying to absorb the scene.

"Let's go!" blasted Travis, and the security guards moved out on the double.

Dorfman and Henderson watched the operation without making an attempt to follow. In a moment, the four men had surrounded Hawthorne, and he was lost in a muscular wedge which began a swift drive through the airport, past a group of furious reporters and photographers.

Travis and Blanco, with a bewildered Hawthorne sandwiched between, piled into car number one, while the other two security guards, with Dorfman and Henderson, climbed into the second.

"Take off like a fucking streak," said Travis with a triumphant smile.

The driver pulled away fast and the second car followed as Gallagher waved politely to several disgruntled members of the press who were assembled near the airport exit.

"Don't rub it in," ordered Dorfman. "It's bad enough as it is."

The Carlton Hotel security suite had been used on various occasions by presidents, kings, millionaires, pop singers and Mafia leaders. Total protection and complete privacy were offered along with luxurious furnishings, gourmet cuisine and impeccable service.

It was the only suite on the fifteenth floor and it was accessible without formal authorization. It was also very

expensive but Spangler had smartly finagled his yearly programming budget to work in the Carlton tab.

"They should be here in a minute, Bob," said Fred Schroeder, the assigned director, who was aware of Spangler's agitation.

Spangler ignored the remark, walked to a bar and poured
himself a small drink. He downed it and then faced Schroeder, who was relaxing on the sofa next to the secretary.

"Fred," said Spangler, "I want you to meet this guy and
then leave right away. I don't want too many people hanging
around this joint."

"Right," the director answered.

Spangler poured another drink and moved to a comfortable chair near a window.

"We'll all take off together and let the character get some
rest," he added.

"Will you be at home, Mr. Spangler?" asked Fran Patterson.

"No, I'll be with my friend on Beekman Place," he
answered. "Do you have her number?"

"Yes, sir."

"Give it to Travis and make sure he doesn't call me there
unless the bastard jumps out of a window or something."

"Yes, sir."

"Your four apes won't help his nervous system," Schroeder
remarked.

"Can't be helped. I'm not taking any chances with this
character," said Spangler.

"I don't blame you, Bob," Schroeder responded. "When does
Fremantle get in?"

"Tomorrow night, very late."

"Tape the following morning?"

"No," answered Spangler. "Afternoon." He paused for a
moment and then said thoughtfully, "I need a lot of time
with Arthur before he gets into this boy. The situation is
delicate and the results have to be perfect."

"To your good health, Gerald." Spangler raised his glass
and the others did the same. Hawthorne and the airport

detachment had arrived ten minutes earlier. "And to your good luck," he added.

They drank and watched Hawthorne as he nearly drained the large whiskey in one continuous gulp. His chair had been positioned strategically near the center of the spacious living room.

For at least a half hour, the group in the living room had forced light chatter and stale jokes but it was apparent that the mask-like features of the Turncoat would never respond. And there was no possible way to avoid his cold, searching eyes.

"We'll be leaving in a few minutes, Gerald," said Spangler. "Remember, this is your place. Order what you want and make yourself comfortable."

"Yeah, just sound off," Travis interjected. "We'll be at your service."

Hawthorne suddenly turned and took a long look at the guard. His eyes moved to Blanco, Todd and Gallagher.

"Who are these men?" he asked.

"Security officers," answered Spangler, avoiding the term guards.

"The Army?" Hawthorne asked sharply.

"No."

"The police?"

"No," Spangler answered patiently, "from a private concern."

"Why do you need them?" he demanded.

"To make certain that no one disturbs you." Spangler paused, realizing that his point was not well made. "Gerald, these men are trained and qualified. They've been hired to keep things in order until we complete our business and get you home safely to Michigan. Understand?"

Hawthorne finally turned away from the guards but Spangler knew that he would have to spend some time later on the telephone briefing Travis and the others.

"When does this man Fremantle get here?" Hawthorne asked coldly.

"Tomorrow night."

"When can I go home?"

"The next day," Spangler replied. "After we tape the interview."

For the first time, Hawthorne leaned back in the chair and relaxed just a little. Spangler motioned to the secretary and she took his glass for a large refill.

The Turncoat was on display, in person, close up, and each member of the program operation took full advantage of the situation.

Fran Patterson brought the drink and handed it to him politely.

"I'll stop by tomorrow with Tim Henderson," said Spangler. "We'll have lunch."

"And take a few pictures, if you don't mind," added the publicity man.

"We'll talk about press and publicity," Spangler continued. "I want everything controlled, for your sake as well as our own."

"I won't be here," said Hawthorne matter-of-factly.

The executive started to react, hesitated and then smiled.

"What do you mean, Gerald?" he asked quietly.

"I want to go out and look around," said Hawthorne, sipping his drink.

"You'll have plenty of time to look around," said Spangler.

"Not in New York," countered Hawthorne.

The program executive paused, searching for the safest approach to the problem.

"You'll be home soon, Gerald," commented Arnold Dorfman. "The people of Waverly are interested in every quote out of your mouth. You have to watch your step."

"Arnie is right," said Spangler. "And remember, you have an exclusive agreement with this company. Don't forfeit your passage home and a percentage of the television program revenue just to take a short walk."

"Mr. Spangler has a boss," Henderson reminded solemnly. "He won't be able to help you."

"Tell you what," said the executive after thinking for a moment. "Take an extra day in New York after the interview." He winked. "I'll give you a Spangler guided tour."

Hawthorne ignored the suggestion and put his glass down on

a small table near the chair. "I'm tired," he said. "Can I get some rest now?"

Spangler glared at the sullen expression on the character's face before answering.

"Of course," he replied, trying to control his irritation. He turned to the rest of his staff. "Come on, everyone. We're leaving."

A prison, thought Hawthorne, unable to sleep, as he stared up at the elegant ceiling and felt the silky smoothness of the sheets. A giant, flowery padded cell, complete with guards, bolted doors and various security devices. An American prison for very special cases.

SEPTEMBER 28, 1950
FORT POLK, MARYLAND

7 THE GENERAL APPEARANCE of this sprawling military installation was known to be very deceptive. The administration buildings and the barracks, for example, were constructed as impressive colonial mansions, spaced neatly on landscaped gardens. There were large shade trees and walks, even several luxurious fountains, and the grounds were spacious and immaculate.

The parade grounds were the finest in the military system and there were four modern motion-picture theaters, two stadiums, professionally equipped athletic fields and gymnasiums, a PX operation; in fact, Fort Polk was a beautiful, self-contained community and the pride of the United States Army.

However, six miles past the chrysanthemum display on the Northeast Mall, the recruits encountered the most strenuous obstacle course on the east coast of America.

The staff instructors at the fort were hand-picked World

War Two noncommissioned officers. Military perfectionists, with very little sympathy.

The training schedule at Fort Polk was considered to be the most exacting in the country and the results were always impressive.

Gerald Howard Hawthorne's frantic escape from Waverly, Michigan, had taken him to this base in the southern part of Maryland.

His previous fears were nothing compared to the outright terror involved in facing the daily requirements of the United States Army.

Hawthorne's physique and general carriage did not help the situation any. At nineteen, the recruit was five feet seven inches tall and weighed one hundred eighteen pounds. The uniform seemed to accentuate the worst features of his emaciated frame.

As usual, his appearance and morose personality set him apart and he was avoided from the first day of arrival. It was very quickly established that Private Hawthorne was the platoon freak. Once again, he was without friends.

As the pressures of training increased, Hawthorne realized that he did not have the strength or the endurance to meet the Army's rugged standards.

To make matters worse, his pathetic performances were anticipated and enjoyed by the rest of the platoon. The other recruits would band together as an audience, heckle, howl with laughter and then applaud wildly each time he pulled himself up and out of the dirt.

Hawthorne kept to himself, healed his own wounds and did not complain. He was determined to meet the challenges of his new life.

"Hey, buddy boy!" a voice called from an upper bunk at the far side of the barracks. "Hey, Hawthorne!"

It was B. G. Foulkes, a particularly obnoxious trouble-maker from Montgomery, Alabama. The stocky man had a thick Southern drawl. He was always one of the key agitators and the platoon adored his antics.

"I heard that Gerald was hung bigger and longer than Joe Louis," he squealed. "That's what I heard."

Hawthorne calmly turned his face to the wall.

"Yeah, I heard that too!" added another recruit. "Take it out, Gerald. We'll inspect it for you."

"I heard he was hung like a fucking canary," interjected a soldier with a New York accent, and the platoon responded with cheers and a round of applause.

A voice, cold and authoritative, cut through the barracks as the noise subsided. "Why don't you goddamn people shut up and leave the guy alone?"

There was silence as all eyes turned to a bunk located close to one of the exits. It was occupied by a muscular, six-foot-three-inch athlete named Harry Jarvis.

No one else in the platoon would have had the audacity to slap down B. G. Foulkes. Jarvis was a former Golden Gloves boxing champion from Baltimore, Maryland, and he had the complete respect of the barracks.

"Just having a laugh, Harry," said Foulkes.

The former boxer looked up as he continued to shine a buckle on his belt.

"I know that, B. G.," he said pleasantly. "But give the man a breather once in a while."

Jarvis went back to his belt.

The strong man of the platoon had stood up for Gerald Hawthorne, and for the moment, the session was over.

Training intensified and Hawthorne struggled.

His physical efforts continued to fall short of the required standards and the troops persisted in spoofing his disappointments, but he pushed forward and set his own goals.

One Sunday afternoon, after three strenuous weeks of basic training had passed, the young recruit met Harry Jarvis unexpectedly while walking in the administration area.

"This place looks like a goddamn plantation," said Jarvis as he fell into step alongside Hawthorne. "Remember the picture *Gone With the Wind?*"

Hawthorne had seen the film twice and it was one of his favorites. He wanted to talk about the beauty of Vivien Leigh and the fact that her delicate face had always reminded him of his mother. Also, he would have liked to mention the scene with Clark Gable, when the actor stood in the doorway and cursed. He remembered the dialogue, word for word.

But he was only able to nod as they continued to walk slowly around the Mall.

"Amazing," said Jarvis as they moved past one of the base movie houses. Neatly dressed recruits were standing patiently in line, waiting for entrance to a Sunday comedy double feature with Abbott and Costello and the Three Stooges. "We're in the Army!" he exclaimed as he turned to Hawthorne. "Can you believe that we're soldiers?"

"No," the boy mumbled awkwardly.

"I can't believe it," Jarvis went on. "We've been in the Army for three weeks. It's all like a dream."

It was like a dream, thought Hawthorne. It was less than a month since he had cleared the house on Elm Drive. He had searched briefly for his father, but had left without seeing him.

They approached his favorite corner of the Mall Gardens, where there were low-hanging willow trees, a picturesque fountain and a neat row of green benches.

"Let's sit," said Jarvis. "This is a beautiful spot."

They enjoyed the scenery in silence for a few moments and then the former boxer offered a cigarette and a light. Hawthorne accepted.

"When I have problems," said Jarvis, "I come here and sit. It clears my head."

"Me too," said Hawthorne.

Jarvis frowned. He apparently had something on his mind.

"They want me to go on the fort boxing team," he said quietly. "I don't think I'll do it."

"Why not?" Hawthorne asked cautiously.

"I've had it with boxing," said Jarvis. "I won't turn pro, so what the hell is the sense of busting up my face?"

Hawthorne noticed that the boxer had a thin scar over his left eye.

"Were you cut in a fight?" asked Hawthorne.

"Twice in the same place," answered Jarvis. "To hell with

boxing. I'm going into the grocery business. Select stuff only. Delicacy stock from all over the world. Not only gourmet items but authentic products from everywhere. Get it?"

Hawthorne nodded. "That's a very good idea," he said.

"The rich bastards in Baltimore love this kind of stuff," Jarvis went on. "My old man is putting up the money for the first shop as soon as I get out. I'll start a chain and try to move them all over the United States."

He took a long drag of the cigarette and then glanced at Hawthorne.

"What are you going to do when you get out?" Jarvis asked.

"I don't know," the boy answered candidly.

"Have you thought about it?"

Hawthorne hesitated. Ordinarily, he would have brought the interrogation to an immediate halt. This was the first time he had ever allowed himself to open up, even slightly.

"I know about plumbing," he said softly.

"How? Is your father a plumber?" asked Jarvis.

"Yes," answered Hawthorne. He ground out his cigarette butt and then threw it into the receptacle near the bench. "But he's a drunk," he added.

Jarvis looked away and they were silent once again. Two recruits from another platoon passed and waved to the former boxer from Maryland. He returned the greeting with a smile and a wink.

He turned back to Hawthorne and spoke very seriously.

"I've been watching you," he said. "People shit all over you and you don't fight back."

Hawthorne did not respond.

"Do you mind if I talk straight?" Jarvis asked.

Hawthorne felt confused. This was an unexpected invasion of his privacy.

"Foulkes and the other bastards are harmless," the boxer continued. "Stand up to them in any way, and they shut up and fall apart. I can do it everytime, because I'm bigger and stronger, and I can beat the hell out of them." He glanced over at Hawthorne. "You'll have to find some other way," he added.

Another lecture, thought Hawthorne, remembering the shallow, tiresome words of Beatrice Powell, or the drunken gibberish of his father.

"Get real good at something, Gerald," the boxer advised warmly. "Any damn thing. But be the best. You'll knock B. G. Foulkes on his ass without throwing a punch." He hesitated for a moment and then added, "I'll put my money on you anytime."

The following days at Polk were the most strenuous since Hawthorne's arrival. The fort had its own methods of developing soldiers and physical conditioning was the order of the day, every day, during this phase of basic training.

Hawthorne threw himself willingly into the arena. He stumbled, fell and came back for more.

The taunts and the burlesque continued but Hawthorne never fought back. Now, more than ever, he was proving to be a very stubborn victim.

For the first time in his life, he had established a relationship with another human being. There was a strong possibility that Harry Jarvis was becoming his friend.

One night, after his work detail, Hawthorne was given an hour break before reporting back to the barracks for taps. He decided that he would stop by the "slop house" for a hot dog and then take a leisurely walk around the Mall.

The garden area was nearly deserted as he approached his favorite bench near the fountain.

"Hey, Gerald!"

He turned and saw Harry Jarvis stumbling toward him. His uniform was disheveled and he seemed to be staggering. The boxer reeled past him and then flopped crazily down on the nearby bench.

"Wow!" he exclaimed. "I'm swacked!"

Hawthorne reluctantly took a seat next to him. He could smell the whiskey and it reminded him of his father.

Jarvis surveyed the recruit for a moment and then grinned broadly.

"What the hell are you doing in fatigues?" he asked.

"I had a work detail," he answered.

"Anterio?"

"Yes."

Jarvis laughed loudly. "I was just with the bastard. He got me into the NCO Club."

"How was it?" asked Hawthorne, trying his best to sustain a conversation.

"Typical military gin mill," Jarvis answered. "Combat bullshit and hot pussy stories."

"He was at Anzio," said Hawthorne.

"Anterio? He sure as hell was," slurred Jarvis. "The crazy bastard was busted four times but he's a damn good soldier."

Jarvis fumbled for his cigarettes and Hawthorne took out a pack of his own and offered him one.

"We took Pyongyang," mumbled Jarvis as he accepted a light.

Hawthorne looked puzzled.

"The gook capital," said Jarvis.

Hawthorne had never thought about the American police action and he had certainly never discussed the situation with anyone. It was not his business. The United States Army represented escape only and had nothing to do with patriotism and warfare. He had blocked it all out from the very beginning. Korea and combat and possible death.

"Right smack up to the Yalu River," Jarvis was saying, "on the border of fucking Manchuria."

He took Hawthorne by the arm and leaned close to his face. "The guys will be home for Christmas," Jarvis whispered confidentially. "MacArthur said so."

Hawthorne was suddenly aware of the pressure on his arm. Jarvis's face was still close to his own and it was beginning to make him feel uncomfortable. For some reason, the boxer seemed to be exaggerating his drunken condition.

"Gerry," he whispered, moving his face even closer. "I want to ask you something."

Tactfully Hawthorne attempted to move his arm but the boxer continued to apply pressure.

"Do you like me?" Jarvis asked softly.

"Yes," answered Hawthorne.

"How much do you like me, Gerald?" His voice was husky.

Hawthorne did not answer. He studied the athlete's face.

Jarvis rested a hand on his knee.

"I know you like me," the voice was muttering, "and I like you. There's nobody around," the voice continued to babble in his ear. "Give me your hand, Gerry."

Hawthorne's world was exploding and falling to pieces. He had been tricked. God and Harry Jarvis had played a game. He had exposed himself to another human being and now he would be punished for trusting and annihilated for believing.

His fingers touched the stiff hardness of the man. He pulled away as repugnant lips slobbered on his cheek.

"Suck me," the voice whispered. "I know you want to."

Hawthorne jumped to his feet.

It would have been easy to kill, he thought, to erase the loathsome apparition sprawled on the bench, to eliminate the ugliness and the humiliation of the experience.

Instead, he looked down at Harry Jarvis with an expression of disbelief and sadness.

Then, he walked slowly away.

On the following morning, the officers supervising the training at Fort Polk, Maryland, evaluated the progress of the new recruits and then approved the commencement of phase-two basic.

Rifles were issued.

His face suddenly flushed with excitement as he held the weapon for the first time. Hawthorne was not prepared for the strange churning of emotions as he stroked the gun and then signed for possession.

The devastating incident with Jarvis had just drained him of all feeling, and now, unexpectedly, he was bursting with new strength and confidence.

Instantly, he knew that the rifle would change many things in his life. It would serve as an equalizer in his struggle against the animals of the world. A smooth trigger and an accurate eye would certainly lower all the odds and he would now have a chance in any contest.

Hawthorne smiled as he thought of Harry Jarvis and his friendly advice. Yes, he was certainly going to be good at something. In fact, he was going to be the best, at something very important.

The new recruit became totally obsessed with the standard M1 rifle which was issued by the United States Army for basic training at Fort Polk.

He oiled and cleaned and cherished and studied the weapon, and in a short time Private Gerald Howard Hawthorne had become the first member of his training platoon to qualify as an expert marksman.

A medal was presented to mark the feat and the boy had his first taste of recognition and accomplishment.

That night in the barracks, Foulkes and the operators had a field day with the new sharpshooter and Jarvis made no attempt to interfere.

This time, however, Hawthorne did not turn toward the wall. He watched and listened and touched the rifle near his bunk, thinking how he could shoot them all dead.

AUGUST 31, 1961
NEW YORK CITY

8 AMALGAMATED BROADCASTING Television was a profitable division of an expanding empire which included theaters, radio outlets, a high-powered advertising agency, two magazines and a diversified real estate syndicate.

At the top of this lucrative network was Mr. Frederic G. Bateman, the Chairman of the Board, a bombastic fifty-year-old tycoon who was determined to establish Amalgamated Enterprises Inc. as a major force in American big business.

Bateman spent most of his corporate time in sensitive, complicated growth transactions and was seldom seen by members of his working staff. However, it was a known fact that he had his eye on every button in the organization.

He had a very special interest in the television operation of the company and every program news release carried his name.

Bateman had delayed a trip to Bermuda in order to fly to New York for a meeting with his program chief, Robert C. Spangler.

"I am not happy with this Hawthorne situation, Bob," Bateman said sourly. "I spoke to Wineburg this morning."

"I have other points, Mr. Bateman," said Spangler.

The chairman held up his hand.

"First of all, I don't know if this damn news-buying technique of yours is worth the trouble," he said frankly. "If the networks pick up the practice, they'll sure as hell outbid us on every breaking item. And I'm not ready to compete with these boys for news. They're too damn far ahead and I want our money spent in other program areas."

"May I say one thing, Mr. Bateman?" asked Spangler.

"I've arranged a corporate program policy meeting," said Bateman, ignoring the request, "for radio and television. Talk about it then."

"Yes, sir."

"Bob, several members of the Board and the corporate legal department are concerned about this program with Hawthorne. You have arranged for this company to enter into a commercial agreement with a man who is considered by many to be a traitor."

"Although not proven, Mr. Bateman," interjected Spangler.

"If nothing else, his loyalty to this country is certainly in question."

Spangler nodded agreement and Bateman continued.

"We have advanced him funds and he is in a position to make a financial profit because of our arrangement."

"That is correct, Mr. Bateman," said Spangler.

"This company has associated itself with a defector and soon we will make air time available which could be used as a platform for a man who has renounced his country in order to live under communism."

"He will not have a platform, Mr. Bateman," said Spangler quickly. "I can assure you."

"This company is pretty damn active in many areas," said Bateman, "and growing every day." He paused. "We are on a schedule and we cannot afford trouble. For example, we are now involved in a license renewal for the Detroit radio station. Our counsel in Washington has told me that the Federal Communications Commission is taking a close look at our business arrangements with Mr. Hawthorne."

Spangler shifted in his chair.

"And there is something else," Bateman continued. "I have it on reliable authority that the government is concerned about this strange character and they would like to see him get home as quickly as possible."

"I know that, Mr. Bateman," said Spangler.

"Do you know why?"

"No, sir," answered Spangler. He paused and then added, "Maybe they can watch him better in Waverly, Michigan."

"Why would they watch him?" Bateman persisted.

"A known collaborationist," answered Spangler. "Eight years with the Communists in Red China. I'm sure it's standard operating procedure."

Bateman studied the program chief for a moment and then shook his head. "I think it's deeper and much more important than that. Frankly, it frightens me. I'm sorry we're involved."

"We'll have an award-winning television program, Mr. Bateman," Spangler answered calmly. "And I assure you, we will not be hurt."

"What time does Arthur Fremantle get here?" Bateman asked.

"Late tonight."

Bateman sat back thoughtfully.

"You know that I do not interfere with any division in this company," he said.

"I know that, Mr. Bateman."

"This time, however, I am demanding that you and Fremantle make certain that this traitor does not use our good facilities as a soapbox."

Spangler nodded.

"And furthermore, I demand that an accurate portrait of this man be painted for the American people. This program must be tough and provocative. Let the viewers take a good, long look at an American defector." He hesitated for a moment and then added, "It's your only justification for presenting Gerald Howard Hawthorne on Amalgamated Television."

"I understand, Mr. Bateman," said Spangler.

The chairman paused for a moment, leaned across the desk and spoke very softly.

"And if the Detroit license fails to go through, and I can trace it back to this program, I will personally fire you on the spot. Is that clear?"

"Yes, sir," said Spangler dryly.

"What is he like?"

"Exactly as you would expect," answered Spangler. And then he added, "Would you like to meet him, Mr. Bateman?"

"Absolutely not. Tell Henderson to get with me as soon as possible," he continued. "I'll give him a statement of corporate policy in reference to the program."

"Yes, sir," answered Spangler.

"And tell Henderson not to bring a photographer. I don't want any pictures with this man. Understood?"

"Yes, Mr. Bateman," said Spangler.

The Chairman of the Board stood up and stretched, indicating that the meeting was over.

Sleep was a waste of time, thought Hawthorne, as he rested calmly in his plush bedroom in the Carlton Hotel.

In the morning, he was scheduled to meet Arthur Fremantle.

The prisoner surveyed the rich furnishings in the magnificent bedroom and then he closed his eyes and allowed the bright colors to fade and then dissolve into the dismal gray of the Fort Upton combat briefing room.

"This is a very important date, gentlemen," barked Sergeant Calvin Shaw as he welcomed the new arrivals to the preparation center in North Carolina.

"October 27, 1950, is a date you boys will certainly remember," he continued. "As you know, we took Pyongyang, the North Korean capital, and we've driven up to the Yalu on the border of Manchuria. MacArthur is confident that everybody will be home for Christmas."

The Sergeant seemed to be evaluating each member of the new combat unit as he looked slowly around the briefing barracks.

"As of today, things have changed," he went on. "The Chinese Reds have moved in and everything has come to a dead halt."

He stepped down off the elevated platform and moved closer to the troops.

"You will be briefed frequently by experts," he continued. "You should know your enemy by the time you complete your training here at Upton." He paused for a moment and added solemnly, "I suggest that you pay attention to every damn word. It could mean your lives."

Hawthorne was beginning to grasp the true meaning of his military service. Now he realized that the United States Army was much more than part of his own personal escape plan and he was suddenly curious and interested.

The Army preparation center, located in the swamps of North Carolina, did not resemble the model military installation, Fort Polk, from which he had just been transferred.

Upton was crude and temporary. The makeshift wooden barracks and numerous tent areas were grim reminders that this squalid military dunghill had been designed as a jumping-off point into hell.

The constant movement of troops and equipment, the

abundance of supply depots, the dust and noise and determined activity, all indicated that time was running out.

The mood was reflected in the solemn faces of the American soldiers who were now preparing to face the Chinese Reds in a strange police action in Korea.

"Remember that you are dealing with a fanatical savage and you must act accordingly," the instructor was preaching.

These briefings aroused Hawthorne and his interest increased with each session.

"Realize that the Chinese Communist soldier is an animal," the instructor continued. "You must kill first and think about it later."

Animals, thought Hawthorne, animals without feelings, representing all the heartless animals on the earth.

"The man you will soon face in combat has been brought up with strange gods and freak customs," the instructor continued. "He is war-like and brutal. The Chinese Red soldier has been thoroughly and religiously trained in the art of torture and slow death."

Hawthorne studied the manuals, absorbed the lectures and waited anxiously for shipment and combat. He now had a reason for living. His purpose on earth was clear. The United States Army had whisked him safely away from Waverly, and he would use his new-found strength and ability to rid the world of animals.

His loneliness was always most painful during mail call each day. He often wondered about his father and even Beatrice Powell. The situation was frustrating and very sad. His exciting new mission was about to begin and he was unable to discuss it with anyone.

Mainly, he wanted to show someone his medal for expert marksmanship.

DECEMBER 6, 1950
COLFAX, NORTH CAROLINA

9 COLFAX, NORTH CAROLINA, was a small, dreary town, located slightly over six miles from the Army preparation center. It was the liberty area for Upton and the soldiers made the most of the limited facilities.

The streets were dingy, narrow and constantly patrolled by the military police. The decent, church-loving citizens of the community had long ago moved to more peaceful parts of the state, leaving the town to an organized band of professional Army-base blood suckers.

The town's facilities included two motion-picture theaters, a bowling alley, a small library, several off-limits restaurants, a gambling casino and two pornographic picture establishments.

Hawthorne remained on the base most of the time and seldom took advantage of liberty. Once in a while, he would go into town alone and walk on a particular street in a remote residential section. It was quiet and clean and it reminded him of his favorite lane in Waverly. Sometimes he would have a few beers in a run-down saloon which was located at least ten blocks from the busy main drag. The shabby establishment was empty most of the time and Hawthorne appreciated the solitude.

"Hawthorne," a voice called. "Gerald Howard."

The sound of his own name during afternoon mail call jolted him for a moment and he had a difficult time pulling himself off the bunk. As usual, he had been cleaning his rifle and trying his best to ignore the bothersome daily ritual.

He sat and studied the envelope and the handwriting,

realizing that he was reluctant to open the letter from his father.

Finally, he read it.

> My Dear Son,
> I am sorry that I was not around on the day that you left for the Army. You remember my old friend Bill Johnson? Well, he had a little plumbing job for me to do out at his house and I didn't have a chance to leave you a note.
> I'm damn proud of you, Gerald. You don't know what it means for a man to have a grown son in the United States Army. I think of you all the time and I miss you very much.
> I would have written to you sooner but I haven't been feeling so good lately. My back started up again and I get that same pain in my chest every once in a while. Your old Dad just ain't what he used to be.
> Gerald, you have a big job to do and I don't want to worry you with my troubles. But you know that I haven't been able to work much. Well, things are real bad right now, son. I mean to the point where I don't have money for food. Now, I know what you're probably thinking. That I'll take some money from you and go buy whiskey. Well, I swear to God and on your beloved mother's grave that I will not do that, Gerald.
> Can you let me have a few bucks? Whatever you can spare, son, but I need it right away. I'll get it back to you the minute I do my next job.
> Well, not much news here. I guess they'll be sending you over soon. I get worried everytime I think about it. That damn Korea might go on for years now that the Chinks are in it. Anyway, take care of yourself and write to your old Dad.
> And please remember to send me some money, son.
> Hey, take a picture in your uniform. I want to show off to all my friends.
>
> All my love,
> Dad

He slowly tore the letter into small bits and tossed the rubbish into a container near the wall.

Training became more rigorous and exacting and the reason was obvious to every potential combat soldier at the fort.

On November 30, 1950, the Red Chinese Army had launched a major offensive and the United States forces were pushed back off the line. This action shattered MacArthur's theory that the Korean conflict would be over by Christmas.

Gerald Hawthorne was getting closer to his personal military objectives. According to the shit-house information center, December 10, 1950, was the date set for shipment to Korea.

The troops were granted their last liberty weekend before the rumored shipping date and Hawthorne spent Saturday night alone in Colfax.

He managed to stay as far away as possible from the spirited, drunken invasion of the town. His usual beer joint remained unaffected; it was completely deserted.

He had already consumed his customary two beers as part of his own private celebration. He felt a flush of excitement at the thought that his expert marksmanship would soon be tested against the enemy. His bullets would now rip into flesh and bones and a bull's-eye would mean instant death.

Suddenly he felt a cold chill and his heart pounded unnaturally for a moment. The astonishing possibility that he might also die began to register, and he could not toss the thought aside as pure fantasy.

He gulped a third beer and hesitated before ordering another. The proprietor of the establishment, an elderly hunchback with a dirty apron, was limping toward his table, carrying a tall whiskey with ice.

"On the house," he mumbled, plunking the glass on the table.

Hawthorne was about to tell the cripple that he did not want whiskey but the man continued.

"The word is that you boys are going over," he said without a noticeable trace of emotion in his voice. "Besides, you've been a pretty good customer, kid."

He started to drag himself back toward the bar. "Drink up," the man added.

A few years back, he had vowed to stay away from the evil alcohol which had poisoned his father but he nodded a polite thanks to the proprietor and took a large gulp of hard liquor for the first time.

Hawthorne could feel a tingling sensation in his legs and he had difficulty focusing on various objects in the saloon.

He cursed his father and blessed his mother and sneered at Beatrice Powell. After the fourth straight drink of Scotch whiskey, he pictured his mother's face and longed to tell her about the dangerous mission to Korea. His loneliness increased as he fondled the medal for marksmanship in his jacket pocket. His mother would have kept it under her pillow.

She was dead and he was alone on the earth, with no one to tell or to touch. He would leave without a goodbye and the thought was beginning to infuriate him.

He slammed his fist down hard on the table and called for another drink.

The bartender pulled himself over to the table and placed a large Scotch and a scribbled tab in front of Hawthorne. He pointed a scrawny finger.

"You'd better make this last, kid," he said. "Eighty-six and out after this one."

Hawthorne gulped the drink and maneuvered himself out of his chair and away from the table. He wobbled and swayed but managed to keep his balance while moving toward the door.

"Good luck, kid," the proprietor called, and Hawthorne waved clumsily without turning around.

He had to navigate around a putrid mound of fresh vomit but made steady progress up the dark, narrow stairs leading to the floor above the strip theater he had noticed a few weeks earlier. A photograph on the garish billboard outside had attracted his attention.

The girl ("Marlene" was the name under the photograph) had a delicate look about her, and in spite of the provocative pose, he thought she looked kind and understanding.

The climb was even more difficult because Hawthorne didn't dare touch the worn, splintered handrail, fearing that syphilis or gonorrhea would certainly rub off and contaminate his system on the eve of departure.

He paused at the cramped landing, took a deep breath, adjusted his uniform and prayed for courage.

The door buzzer was situated next to a neatly engraved card which read, "Mrs. L. B. Travers." Hawthorne pondered over the name for a moment but then pressed lightly and waited.

He was finally admitted to the dingy waiting room by a matronly woman with glasses. She motioned for him to take a seat on a soiled red divan near the window.

"You waiting for Sugar Baby, honey?" she asked.

The whiskey was beginning to numb his senses. He had a difficult time answering through a pickled mouth.

"I came to see Marlene," he managed.

"She's onstage downstairs, soldier," said the woman as she moved closer to the divan. "Have you had Sugar Baby?"

Hawthorne's head was throbbing and he felt the first frightening tug of acute nausea. His answer was inaudible.

"What do you like, honey?" she inquired softly.

The woman moved closer and her image was now becoming slightly hazy and unreal.

"You won't get kink stuff with Marlene," she advised. "A straight fuck, soldier, and not even a blow job."

Hawthorne turned away and suppressed an urgent desire to heave his upset guts all over the whorehouse floor.

"Sugar Baby will make it for you in any pocket," she continued. "And you look as though you need a good draining, son."

"I came to see Marlene," he mumbled almost incoherently.

"Suit yourself," she replied.

He stared straight ahead as she left the room, feeling the dizzying effects of the whiskey in his system.

"She's ready," said the lady of the house when she came back to him several minutes later.

He stared at the woman with a pained and bewildered expression.

"Marlene is waiting, soldier," she repeated impatiently. "Can you make it?"

Hawthorne nodded and pulled himself up on very shaky limbs.

"Want to make it another night?" she asked.

"No," he answered quickly, making a ludicrous attempt to smooth out the wrinkles in his uniform jacket.

She smiled and led the way. He followed.

Marlene, obviously weary from her exotic downstairs performance, was nude and comfortably spread-eagled on the large bed as Hawthorne entered the room.

Her long black hair was draped neatly over one breast and her trim middle was partially covered with a clean hand towel.

"Hi, sweetheart," she sighed.

Hawthorne squinted in the dim light and tried to bring the vision into sharper focus.

"Hello," he muttered.

"What's your name?" the girl asked.

"Gerald."

The girl twisted on the bed and then yawned lazily.

"I'm so goddamn tired, Gerald."

Her voice was soft and gentle, he thought, and she could not be blamed for profanity after being around animals for so long. He took a timid step closer to the bed.

"Take your clothes off, honey," she whispered.

The stripper kicked the hand towel away, leaned back on the pillow and closed her eyes.

He took a slow, careful look at the young woman on the bed. She was slim and beautiful, he thought, but not as delicate-looking as his mother. He could not see the color of her eyes but he still imagined that they were moist and deep blue. Her skin was pale and smooth as velvet, he noticed, although she did have a long, thin surgical scar on her left side.

Hawthorne studied the wide, firm nipples, the flatness of her stomach and the sharp curve of her hips. Then he allowed himself to survey the soft hair between her legs and he longed to touch it.

The girl yawned again and turned on her side away from him.

"I'm an expert marksman," he blurted as he moved another step closer to the bed.

"That's wonderful, darling," she murmured drowsily without opening her eyes.

"I've got a medal," he added.

"Good." She was dozing. "You must show me sometime."

He stopped at the edge of the bed, reached into his jacket pocket and brought out the rifle range citation.

"Here it is," he said proudly, dangling the medal over her head.

Marlene opened her eyes and glanced up at the swaying object.

"Interesting," she breathed. Then she closed them again and added, "Get your clothes off, soldier."

The sickness had gone and the pounding sensation in his head had softened and mellowed into an almost pleasant throb. His legs felt unsteady—the effect of the whiskey, so he took a seat on the edge of the bed.

He wondered how to proceed. Vital military information must never be divulged and therefore he was not in a position to tell Marlene about the December 10 departure date for Korea.

"I won't be seeing you again," he said softly.

The girl was nearly asleep and did not respond.

"I'm going to kill more goddamn Red animals than any other American soldier in history," he continued. "You'll be proud of me and very glad that you knew me."

He leaned forward and his hand touched her bare leg. His immediate instinct was to pull away quickly but even so, he took a deep breath and stroked the smooth skin.

"Will you write to me?" he asked quietly.

The girl's eyes opened as Hawthorne took her hand. She looked at him curiously as he moved forward and began to stroke her hair.

"I'll answer every letter," he said. "And I'll read them over and over again."

He put the medal down on a table near the bed, nearly knocking over a bottle of mouthwash.

"That's for you," said Hawthorne. "I hope you sleep with it under your pillow every night while I'm gone."

The girl rubbed her eyes and glanced sleepily at the table.

"Listen to me, soldier," she commented seriously. "You're very sweet, but I don't have all night. Either you take off your clothes and get to it or we'll have to break this up right now."

Hawthorne drew back in disbelief.

"I have to talk to you," he insisted.

She tried to roll away from him but he held her firmly by the shoulders.

"I want to kiss you and say goodbye," he whispered.

She continued to struggle. "Now, take your goddamn hands off me, you idiot."

He pinned her down again, leaned forward and tried to kiss her gently on the mouth.

"I need somebody," the boy mumbled, forcing himself on her unwilling lips.

"You freak!" she screamed. "You goddamn sick freak!"

In that instant he knew. She was the same as all the others. They were all the same, except for his mother.

"You dirty whore!" he bellowed.

And suddenly her face was hard and cruel and she belonged with the rest of the female scum, groveling and squirming under his drunken father.

He struck her hard with his fist. She screamed and he struck again and again.

Marlene was quiet.

He bit his lip and backed away. The girl was unconscious and bleeding from the mouth. Hawthorne watched for a moment as the thick red blood trickled slowly down her pale neck and then soaked into the bedsheets.

Suddenly he was aware of a noisy commotion in the outside hall. He snatched his medal from the table and the bottle of mouthwash fell, smashing to bits on the floor. He ran to the door, pulled it open, stormed past a rescue party and plunged down the dark, narrow stairway three and four steps at a time.

"Shit!" he muttered as both feet landed squarely in the large pool of vomit at the bottom, but Hawthorne did not break his stride as he ran out the door, down the street and all the way to the Colfax liberty bus station.

Later that night in the barracks, he erased the disturbing image of Marlene, the whore, by concentrating on the peaceful beauty of his mother's picture.

He also thought about the news bulletin which had been posted on the information wall at the main gate.

On December 1, 1950, the United Nations forces had retreated and Pyongyang had been abandoned.

Gerald Hawthorne cleaned his rifle and waited for combat.

SEPTEMBER 1, 1961
WASHINGTON, D.C.

10 SENATOR EDWARD ATKEN, the Chairman of the Foreign Relations Committee, took a seat opposite Roger D'Allesandro's desk and noticed that the Secretary was not smiling. "What the hell is the matter with you?"

D'Allesandro sat down and then nervously drummed his fingers on a wooden cigarette box. "I want to talk to you," he said quietly.

"You've got the floor," replied the Senator. "But no filibuster, please. I've got a dental appointment."

"I'll get right to the point," said D'Allesandro. "I have some information and I'm afraid to process it."

"Like what?"

"Like I smell rats at a very, very high level."

"I thought you were getting to the point."

D'Allesandro leaned forward and spoke softly and confidentially. "This Turncoat, Hawthorne, is being worked over by some very bad characters."

"So? What the hell does that have to do with anything?"

"Hector Rambeau is involved again."

"So?"

"Oh, goddammit, stop it, Ed!" he shouted. "I'm trying to be serious."

He stood and walked around the desk to the Senator.

"I have reliable information that Rambeau and his thugs were hired for the job."

"Nobody hires Hector Rambeau."

"All right, not hired. Let's say that he was enlisted again by the Vice President of the United States."

"That's quite an accusation, Mr. Secretary," said Atken as he lit up a small cigar.

"I understand that substantial Rambeau bribes have already been paid to certain television people at a broadcasting company in New York," he went on. "And there is plenty more to come."

"Bribes for what, Roger?"

"I don't know exactly," said D'Allesandro as he sat on the edge of the desk. "It probably has a great deal to do with the electronic miracle of video tape."

"Meaning?"

"The commentator, Arthur Fremantle, will obviously smear this boy from one end of the screen to the other."

"Doesn't he always?"

"Yes, but this is a very special case," answered the Secretary. "I'm sure he'll do it in a unique way."

"So?"

"So, if the Fremantle assassination doesn't work properly, and it should, the producer is still in a position to cut and edit anything that remotely refers to the blunders in 1953."

D'Allesandro walked back to his chair behind the desk without looking directly at Atken.

"Is that how you see it, Mr. Secretary?" Atken inquired.

"Something like that."

"Do you believe that these broadcasting people will purposely concoct a dull, one-sided television program?" the Senator asked. "Designed not to make any noise or impact?"

"They will," answered D'Allesandro flatly. "Rambeau pays very, very well."

He took a cigarette from the wooden box on the table and continued.

"They'll present a twisted case and destroy the man's credibility. Hawthorne will be shipped back to Michigan branded as either a traitor or a lunatic. Our trusted leaders will continue to sail the good ship of state without a blemish," D'Allesandro added solemnly.

"I thought you said no filibuster," prodded Atken.

The Secretary of State pulled himself up from the chair and walked to the window.

"I could blow the whistle on this whole goddamn affair," he said.

"You could," the Senator said calmly. "But you won't. Roger, regardless of the circumstances, this government must be protected at all costs."

"Don't make me laugh," said D'Allesandro without turning around.

"We've got the Wall," the Senator went on. "The Russians are blasting over fifty megatons in November, we've got Cuba and the Congo, and so damn much more. And what about domestic?" He snuffed out his cigar in a large gold tray on the desk. "At this moment, we have to sustain the honesty and integrity of our leaders or they won't be able to operate effectively in these critical areas."

D'Allesandro turned from the window and faced the old man.

"I thought you had a dental appointment," he said impatiently.

"I know more about this mess than you do, Roger," said Atken, ignoring D'Allesandro's remark. He lowered his voice to a near-whisper. "These men are prepared to go to any lengths in order to protect the Presidency, the Vice Presidency, the Party, the government and, in the long run, the people of the United States."

"Even murder?" D'Allesandro asked as he slowly took a seat behind his desk.

Atken leaned forward and his face was grim.

"The unfortunate predicament of one confused soldier must be weighed against the sensitive state of this Union."

"What about injustice, civil liberties, premeditated criminal acts?"

"Meaningless."

"Punishment of the guilty?"

"Meaningless."

"Gerald Howard Hawthorne's life?"

"Weighed against the problems facing our great nation? Meaningless, Mr. Secretary."

The anger built quickly and the pressure had to be released. D'Allesandro crashed his fist down violently on the desk.

"I'm sick and ashamed!" he fumed.

Senator Edward Atken stood and looked down at his old friend.

"Roger," he said softly, "you are eight years late for the blow of a whistle."

D'Allesandro met the old man's eyes and then rose to his feet. "A slight twinge of conscience, Mr. Chairman. I can assure you that I will not forget myself again."

They walked to the door.

"Fill me in," said D'Allesandro.

The Senator glanced at his watch. "Hawthorne is being interviewed right now in New York. Two of Mr. Rambeau's associates are in the studio and they'll report back as soon as the project is completed. And this fellow Spangler will deliver a copy of the tape tomorrow afternoon. I don't think we'll have a problem, Roger."

"The President?"

"The idea is not to bother him with this anymore."

"The Vice President?"

"Same."

The Secretary of State sighed and then smiled broadly. "Everybody is very lucky so far."

"Except me, goddammit," said the Senator as he opened the door. "I made a vow that they would have to bury me with at least one real tooth in my head."

He hurried out the door.

SEPTEMBER 2, 1961
NEW YORK CITY

11

FREMANTLE: Can you recall the approximate population of Waverly, Michigan, in 1950, Gerald?

HAWTHORNE: About fifteen thousand people.

FREMANTLE: It was a prosperous community, I understand.

HAWTHORNE: I guess so.

FREMANTLE: You certainly were not brought up in a poor environment.

HAWTHORNE: I guess not.

FREMANTLE: (smiles) So, we can't blame the usual evil influences, can we?

"Stop it, right there," ordered Spangler.

The exhausted video tape operator stopped the machine and reached for his cup of black coffee.

The prolonged studio interview with Hawthorne had lasted over four hours, and as usual, on the dot of completion, Spangler had stormed into the tape room, demanding instant editorial work and to hell with dinner breaks and overtime.

"Roll back to Hawthorne's line . . . about fifteen thousand people . . . cut there," said Spangler, consulting a lengthy draft transcript. "Then roll ahead to his father and the crap about the plumbing business. It should be about six minutes in."

"Christ, Bob," protested a bleary-eyed Fred Schroeder, "you've cut a big segment of early childhood."

Spangler suddenly twisted on the stool and pointed angrily to the door of the video tape room.

"Please, shut up or get the hell out," he barked. "This is very delicate work."

"I happen to be the director of this program, Mr. Spangler," said Schroeder.

"OUT!" screamed Spangler at the top of his lungs.

All engineering eyes in the room riveted on the young director. He moved slowly to the door.

"You can take my name off the credits, Mr. Spangler," said Schroeder, but the executive had already turned back to his transcript and his words had been drowned by the whir of the fast-forward rolling video tape.

Tim Henderson, Arnold Dorfman and Morris Wineburg were sprawled over the set, cursing and waiting impatiently for further instructions.

"Well," said Dorfman, "I have to admit that it was a much slower death than by hanging or the guillotine."

"And much more painful, Arnie," said Wineburg.

"Bullshit," countered Henderson. "The bastard didn't feel a thing. Now I'm convinced that this man does not have blood in his veins or a brain in his head."

"He can read and write Chinese," said Dorfman, "and that takes a brain, Timothy."

"It takes time, patience and instruction, Arnie. This guy had plenty of all three."

"What do you think, Morris?" asked Dorfman.

"We sure as hell witnessed a death on video tape this evening," said the lawyer. "But I can't make up my mind whether it was murder or suicide."

"What do you mean?" asked Henderson.

"As usual," Wineburg went on, "Fremantle used his research effectively and managed to intimidate, demoralize, unnerve and finally paralyze his victim."

"So that's the murder part," said Dorfman. "What about suicide?"

"The man openly admitted his friendship and association with the enemy in the prisoner-of-war camp and he did live with them in Red China for eight years," said Wineburg. "These are facts."

"Suicide?" interrupted Henderson. "That's treason."

"That isn't my point," the lawyer continued. "Gerald Hawthorne did not act like a guilty man on that video tape. He certainly didn't hang his head in shame, crawl, or beg forgiveness."

"True," interjected Dorfman.

"He stood by his own actions and convictions," Wineburg continued, "as though they were perfectly normal, legal and justified."

"Hawthorne does have a brain, Tim," said Dorfman. "In fact, the man looks shrewd and very dangerous to me."

"Then why doesn't the government lock him up?" asked Henderson.

"It's obvious that they don't have a case at the moment," said Wineburg. He stood and walked to a nearby table for another cup of cold black coffee. "One thing is certain," he added. "The American public is in for a shock when this tape is played."

Arthur Fremantle, a connoisseur of food and beverage, enjoyed New York's East Side bars. His particular favorite was the Sheridan Arms, a small, quiet, very discriminating hotel cocktail lounge between Third Avenue and Lexington in the midtown area. The lights were soft, the booths were plush and comfortable, and the management was unusually discreet.

Ordinarily, the commentator's dates were wined and primed here in preparation for more serious advances in the privacy of Suite D-11 upstairs. In fact, a private hotel elevator was located close to his usual booth and this made the operation smooth and swift.

On this particular night, however, Arthur Fremantle was not interested in sex. His two guests at the Sheridan were imposing-looking men, and the commentator's serious expression was an indication that the special booth was not to be disturbed by anyone, for any reason.

Both men were tall, lean and conservatively dressed in dark gray business suits. One man was dark, possibly a Latin, and the other had short blond hair and a bronzed, weatherbeaten complexion. They seemed to operate in a firm but quiet manner.

"Relay this information to Mr. Spangler as quickly as possible," said the Latin.

"First thing in the morning," answered Fremantle.

"Tonight," the other man snapped. "As soon as you get back to the studio."

Fremantle studied the serious features of the two visitors. "Very well," he said.

Both men nodded politely and prepared to leave.

"We're big fans of yours," said the dark one. "It was a thrill watching you work in person."

"Thank you."

"Don't lose your package, Mr. Fremantle," the other man warned.

Fremantle frowned for a moment and then touched his jacket pocket. "I won't," he said grimly.

The men stood and the Latin extended his hand. "Thank you for the hospitality, Mr. Fremantle," he said. "We appreciate it very much."

"Where can I reach you?"

"You can't at the moment," the blond man explained. "We'll be in touch with you and Mr. Spangler."

He watched the men leave the lounge, and then ordered another drink.

HAWTHORNE: They allowed me to live. Without pushing me.
FREMANTLE: Were you being pushed here in America?
HAWTHORNE: It was tougher for me here.
FREMANTLE: Where?
HAWTHORNE: Waverly, Michigan, when I was a kid.
FREMANTLE: The people of Tsinan, China, were nicer to you

than the people you knew as a young man in Waverly, Michigan?

HAWTHORNE: Yes. They were nicer to me.

The operating pace had been hectic and Robert Spangler was beginning to feel the strain. He sat wearily behind his desk without bothering to switch on the main office lights. The soft glow of the reading lamp was soothing after the hot glare of the studio and the fluorescent burn in the control room and the video tape center.

Spangler needed a drink and a shave and a few hours' sleep.

Arthur Fremantle entered the dark office without knocking.

"What the hell is this, a seance?" he asked.

"I'm tired, Arthur," said Spangler as he leaned his head back on the chair and closed his eyes.

Fremantle moved slowly and cautiously out of the shadows and made his way to a comfortable leather chair. He sat opposite Spangler, removed his shoes and propped both feet on the edge of the desk.

"How was the tape?" he inquired.

"Interesting."

"Our friends don't think so."

"That's too goddamn bad," said Spangler.

Fremantle pulled his feet off the desk and leaned across it.

"Robert," he said very quietly, "I have a detailed critique and I suggest that you listen."

"I'm listening," said Spangler with his eyes closed.

"For example, they want certain edits made," said Fremantle.

"Too late," answered Spangler. "The editorial work on the Hawthorne interview has already been completed."

"Bob," said Fremantle firmly, "let's not play games. These people mean business."

Spangler opened his eyes, turned and faced the worried commentator. "So do I, Mr. Fremantle," he said just as firmly.

Fremantle reached into his jacket pocket and removed his

reading glasses and a small black notepad. He thumbed through several pages and then stopped. He put on his glasses and adjusted himself properly in the large chair.

"They want to kill all references to the people of Waverly, Michigan," said Fremantle as he studied the notepad. "They want to soften the killing of the five American soldiers. They want to eliminate . . ."

"STOP IT!" yelled Spangler.

Fremantle watched carefully as his boss rubbed his chin nervously and tried to prevent a further emotional outburst.

"I don't want to listen to detailed instructions, Arthur," he said. "Just give me the top of the criticism."

"I think we made it too good, Robert," Fremantle said. "The Rambeau boys think the program will provoke thought and attract too damn much attention in this country."

"Marvelous," said Spangler. "Our first review."

"It could be our last," commented Fremantle.

"Don't count on it," said Spangler. "What else?"

"It seems that you neglected to fill me in on all the rules, Robert."

"I did fill you in."

"Not properly."

"Balls."

Fremantle's plastic smile faded and his face appeared hard in the dim light of the small desk lamp.

"I honor deals, my friend," he said soberly.

"And I don't?"

"You don't seem to be doing it this time."

Spangler opened the bottom drawer of his desk and removed a nearly empty fifth of whiskey. "Want a drink?"

"No."

He twisted off the top and took a swig straight from the bottle.

"Go ahead, Fremantle," he said, swallowing hard. "Get it off your chest."

"I understood that the plan was to confront the man with the published facts, squeeze a soft confession, and then send him home without stirring up a commotion of any kind."

"And?"

"The people involved want this character forgotten as quickly as possible," said Fremantle.

Spangler held the bottle of whiskey up. "Want a small one?"

"I said no."

"He'll be forgotten, Fremantle," said Spangler. He took another long swallow of Scotch. "As soon as I'm finished with him."

"They don't want any noise, ratings, awards or trouble," said Fremantle. "In other words, Robert, your assignment is to kill the Turncoat and bury him without a funeral, and without a ceremony of any kind."

Spangler finished the bottle and tossed it into the waste-paper basket under the desk.

"I think we killed him, Fremantle."

"We did, but my two companions are concerned about the manner in which the victim died." He paused while he slipped back into his shoes. "They feel that millions of disturbed Americans might come to the funeral in order to spit on his grave. And that, my friend, is exactly what they do not want."

"It's too damn late," Spangler asserted. "The program is practically in the can."

"Edit the interview, Robert," said Fremantle. "And I strongly suggest that you follow the rules this time."

"I'll do it my way," Spangler said coldly.

The commentator leaned closer and lowered his resonant voice to a near-whisper. "These people bought the program from you, Spangler. You can't have it both ways."

Spangler picked up the clipboard and flipped through the interview transcript. "This project is too goddamn good to throw away." He sat back in his chair and thought for a moment before speaking.

"Let me tell you something, Fremantle," he said smoothly. "With effective promotion, this television program will capture a massive audience and we are certain to walk away with another Emmy or Peabody. In addition, we'll perform a major public service by exposing and destroying a traitor to this country. As a conscientious programmer and as a loyal American citizen, I cannot allow this magnificent opportunity to be wasted."

Fremantle laughed loudly.

"You crazy bastard," he said. "You made a deal and you took the money. Doesn't that count?"

"I thought the proposition had to do with national security."

"I think it has."

"No," said Spangler. "I'm sure that it has to do with one particular official in Washington, D.C. This elaborate plot was devised to cover up the shady actions of one man and it certainly cannot have the approval of the United States government."

"What man?"

"I don't know," said Spangler. "Somebody close to the top."

"What actions?"

"I don't know exactly," he said, "but I can sure as hell make a good guess."

"What are you going to do?"

"Proceed with my project as planned, Mr. Fremantle," said the program executive. "I'll take Gerald Hawthorne to the airport at eight o'clock this morning and then I'll proceed with my scheduled press conference at eleven-thirty."

"*Your press conference?*" Fremantle asked incredulously.

"We will tease and promote by releasing certain stimulating quotes from the interview," said Spangler. "Such as this bastard calling you an American pig, Arthur."

Fremantle shook his head in disbelief. "You must be out of your goddamn mind. I should never have agreed to go along with you."

"You might be right."

"You intend to double-cross these men?"

"Yes."

"Do you happen to know who they are?"

"I do."

"Do you realize that they are capable of murder?"

"Yes," said Spangler, smiling, "but in this case, they will do nothing."

He leaned his head back on the chair again and closed his eyes.

"Rambeau's client is certainly one of our respected leaders," he said. "If I remember correctly, this money manipulator is a close friend of the Vice President of the United States. Don't the Veep and his family spend vacations with Rambeau on his estates in South America?"

"Yes."

"This particular client cannot afford a publicized Mafia-type association, that's for damn sure," Spangler continued. "In addition, if they screw around with me, I intend to dig a bit deeper into Gerald Howard Hawthorne and I have a feeling that I might come up with some startling revelations." He paused. "If they leave me alone, I will do nothing more than present my original television program."

Spangler laughed and then opened his eyes. "This Turncoat could have been open game for every irresponsible reporter in America. I have exercised complete control over his statements and movements. That alone is worth the contribution from Rambeau. And besides, I have a contract with Hawthorne for one year. These people will need my cooperation and my expertise. Get the picture?"

"I don't want any part of it," said Fremantle. He was unusually pale and looked shaken.

Spangler laughed again and pointed to a bulge in the commentator's jacket.

"What's that?"

Fremantle touched the inside pocket self-consciously. "I'll give it back."

"Arthur," said Spangler, still laughing, "Hector Rambeau doesn't take refunds."

Fremantle settled back in his chair, grimaced and nervously removed a cigarette from a thin gold case.

"You are one of the most despicable characters I have ever come across in my entire life," he said bitterly.

"Probably," replied Spangler as he reached for the clipboard. "But I'm honest with myself."

He stood and moved around the desk.

"Be smart at the press conference, Arthur," he said coldly. "Or I'll set you up for a real execution."

Fremantle looked startled as Spangler leaned over the chair, very close to his face.

"I'll tell your wife about your Swedish research broad," he whispered, "and Edna will cut your balls off."

SEPTEMBER 1, 1961
NEW YORK CITY

12

A FEW MORE HOURS of anxiety and sleepless agony and then peace, thought Hawthorne as he paced the bedroom suite. The ordeal with Robert Spangler was nearly over and he longed for the privacy and security of his own home on Elm Drive.

He removed his shoes and sprawled on the luxurious bed.

The lengthy interrogation under the hot studio lights had been tiring and painful but it was a very familiar experience and Hawthorne was quite satisfied with the results. In fact, he had prepared himself for much worse.

The small, evil man they called Fremantle was soft, he thought, and a novice compared to K. M. Wing and the other expertly trained interrogators at Camp Six in Korea. Practical experience had taught Hawthorne the advantages of caution and patience. He felt that his commitment to the television people had been honored without a serious loss of face. Information of a sensitive nature had been withheld and it would be protected forever, regardless of the pressure or circumstances.

He removed his rumpled shirt and ran his hand slowly over his stomach. The sudden transition to luxurious surroundings, rich food and vintage wine was beginning to bloat his stomach and poison his mind. The details of the interview had jogged his memory and he recalled the days of combat and his friendship with Robert Bean.

December 16, 1950
A routine patrol
Korea

The moment had arrived for Private Gerald Hawthorne of the United States Army to put his training and conditioning to the test for the first time, under actual combat conditions, and the soldier was ready.

It was scheduled to be a routine patrol, close to the base, but heavy enemy sniping had been reported in the area for over two weeks, and Lieutenant Thomas Gavin had briefed the squad so somberly that many thought they were heading for a major clash with the entire Chinese Army.

Robert Bean, a quiet, intelligent man from Columbus, Ohio, who was several years older than the others in the outfit, also seemed edgy and disturbed. Understandable, reasoned Hawthorne, because the man had a wife and child.

He made the same justification for a very agitated soldier by the name of Frank Coe, who was in the middle of divorce proceedings in the States.

Gerald Hawthorne told himself he was the coolest and most determined of them all. At last, he had been given an opportunity to prove that he was the best marksman on earth. His courage and exploits would be recorded in the American history books.

Sergeant Ernest Donica, a World War Two veteran, had expertly checked and adjusted their gear and they had moved out to face the possibility of ambush and capture, or simply being incapacitated by the running shits.

Hawthorne had prayed for action of any kind but the patrol had been routine for nearly an hour. The area seemed quiet and secure as they moved into a thick grove of trees.

"Keep your eyes and ears open," shouted Donica as the soldiers moved cautiously out of the grove into an exposed area. "Get down fast and chew dirt if I give the word," he added.

The bright sunlight exposed a moderate but rugged elevation to the left of the clearing, and from the troops' position on the plateau, it was impossible to observe conditions on the top of this rocky ridge.

"Hold it up, men," shouted Donica. The patrol halted and waited for instructions. "Foulkes and Boulting," the Sergeant called, "get up there and take a look."

Hawthorne watched enviously as the two men zigzagged to the base of the incline, flattened, and then began to crawl on knees and elbows until their heads were level with the rocky crest.

"We should have stayed in the grove," mumbled Coe as he studied the reconnoitering action of Foulkes and Boulting.

"Worse," said another man. "These gooks love the branches. You can't see a goddamn thing in the grove."

"I just don't like it out here," Coe muttered as he watched Foulkes and Boulting double-time back to Donica.

Hawthorne had wanted to interject his own feelings about safety and the enemy but decided that there would be ample time later, after he had proven himself to be an able and courageous combat soldier.

"All clear up there," reported B. G. Foulkes to the Sergeant.

"It's flat," added Boulting, slightly out of breath. "No place to hide."

"Good work, men," said Lieutenant Gavin.

Both soldiers smiled broadly as they returned to their positions in the patrol.

"All right, move out!" shouted Sergeant Donica. *"Keep to the right of that ridge and stay awake!"*

Hawthorne felt the unpleasant tug of jealousy. He frowned and clenched his fist tightly as he started off with the rest of the patrol. The world suddenly shifted into ethereal slow motion for Gerald Howard Hawthorne.

He heard the loud, sharp crack of a rifle and felt a warm,

wet spray on the side of his face. Anxiously he reached up and smeared it with his fingers and came away with blood. He wondered how badly he had been hit and why he had not fallen.

The Sergeant's voice was yelling urgent instructions and Frank Coe was sinking to the ground directly under Hawthorne's feet. The left side of Coe's face had been torn away and pieces of bone were protruding out of the eye socket.

A putrid, sour taste in his mouth was beginning to make him retch and he spat blood, and a sickening mixture of flesh, bone and teeth.

"Take cover!" a voice shrieked over the confusion. *"Back to the grove! On the double! Back to the grove! Take cover!"*

Three additional rifle cracks sounded in rapid succession from the same area, close to the ridge, and Private William Snyder of Trenton, New Jersey, was a corpse with a large fragment of lead lodged deeply in his throat.

He had spun in a complete circle like a circus clown, thought Hawthorne, except that his eyes had nearly popped out and his hands could not stop the gush of blood from a deep opening in his neck.

He suddenly felt a strong grip on his arm.

"Come on, Hawthorne," shouted Robert Bean as they ran. *"Back to the grove, on the double!"*

He ran, with the older man beside him, realizing that most of the others had already taken cover in the grove.

As he glanced back over his shoulder, another rifle shot split the air and Robert Bean staggered and fell forward. Hawthorne made a futile lunge for the wounded soldier but Bean tumbled to the ground as several other shots were fired in the direction of the retreating patrol.

Hawthorne slowed up automatically as he moved past the crumpled figure. Donica and Lieutenant Gavin, who were crouched near the grove entrance, frantically waved him on.

"Not now, Hawthorne!" screamed Donica. *"Shag-ass! Take cover!"*

Continuous rifle fire urged him forward and he stumbled into the protection of the trees and collapsed close to Donica's position.

"We're covering Bean from here," the Sergeant shouted as Hawthorne positioned his rifle. *"We'll pull him back when we can!"*

Suddenly the sporadic rifle fire ceased and the patrol area was deathly still. Even the slight breeze had dropped.

A groan broke the silence as Robert Bean twisted in agony on the rough terrain. Although the gunfire had been persistent, the enemy had managed to remain completely concealed and the area still appeared to be deserted. The wounded soldier was positioned midway between the grove and the ridge, which had been declared free of enemy troops by the rookie scouting party.

Hawthorne concentrated on the exchange of dialogue between Sergeant Donica and the officer-in-charge. Lieutenant Gavin was very upset.

"The man is badly wounded, Sergeant," he was saying. "He seems to be losing a lot of blood."

"It's an obvious trap, sir," Donica insisted. "They'll cut down anything that moves."

"We know that, Sergeant," said the Lieutenant coldly. "But what the hell do you intend to do?" He suddenly raised his voice. "Let the man die there in front of our eyes?"

"I suggest we wait until dark, Lieutenant," said Donica firmly.

"We'll be rescuing a corpse by then," said Gavin. "Besides, I want these men back at the base before dark." He glanced around quickly at the strained faces. "Do you realize that these men are on their first patrol out here?"

While the brass argued, a dramatic plan of action was rapidly taking shape in Hawthorne's mind and another moan from Bean convinced him that he must execute it immediately. He jumped to his feet, took a firm grip on his rifle and bolted past the astonished men of the Korean patrol.

"Cover me!" he yelled as he ran a fast, twisting pattern out of the grove and into the exposed area.

"Who the hell was that?" yelled the Lieutenant.

Donica made a quick visual check of the men. "Hawthorne," he said, shaking his head in disbelief.

"Cover him!" ordered the Lieutenant.

"On your toes!" barked Donica. "Cover the crazy bastard from every angle!"

Hawthorne knew that the men behind him in the grove were watching and this drove him forward without fear or hesitation. He crouched low and snake-hipped toward the broken body of Robert Bean. There was still no sign of the enemy.

"Hang on, Bean!" he gasped. "I'm coming!"

The wounded soldier groaned and lifted his head slowly, staring in amazement as the small, frail figure plunged head-long across the dangerous terrain.

Suddenly Hawthorne heard the sharp crack of an enemy rifle and he slammed down hard to the ground as a bullet whined and ricocheted off a nearby rock.

He remained motionless, but at the same time he pinpointed a large rock which jutted close to the top of the elevated ridge.

Another shot rang out, almost simultaneously. From his prone position, Hawthorne twisted, aimed and fired at the jagged boulder.

A shriek cut through the echo of gunfire and an enemy soldier reached up wildly and then tumbled over the front of Hawthorne's rocky target. The Chinese sniper rolled down the incline and finally came to a dead stop, close enough for the American to observe the results of his handiwork.

Hawthorne took a quick, guarded look and felt a warm flush of excitement. He had hit his first animal. The upper part of the face was red pulp and the mouth was contorted and frozen in the shape of the soldier's death cry.

Hawthorne reluctantly turned away from his bull's-eye and concentrated on the rescue mission. He listened and scanned the area carefully for a moment. It was quiet. Yet he knew that other snipers were probably dug in and waiting somewhere in the vicinity of the ridge.

To crawl, flat and low, would take too much time, and besides, the odds would probably be the same no matter how the operation was executed.

Hawthorne pulled himself to his feet, surveyed the area

quickly, crouched low, held the rifle at ready and then moved briskly toward the wounded American soldier.

Robert Bean was lying in a pool of blood and the wound in his side was gaping. He groaned but said nothing as Hawthorne dropped beside him.

"I'll have to drag you back," said Hawthorne. He was out of breath. "I can't carry you."

Bean nodded and Hawthorne noticed that the man's eyes were glassy and out of focus.

He would have to move quickly. He squinted and checked the ridge area once again and there was no sign of the elusive enemy.

In the grove, all eyes and guns were trained on the area around the two men. The anxious members of the patrol found it hard to believe that the principal player in this display of combat heroics was the silent, weak jerk-off from Waverly, Michigan.

"He'll need some help," said the Lieutenant as he watched Hawthorne try to position Bean for the difficult withdrawal.

"They'll open up the minute anyone makes a move out of this grove, Lieutenant," said Donica. "That's what they're waiting for." The Sergeant hesitated for a moment and watched Hawthorne grip the wounded man tightly at the back of the collar. "Besides," he added, "that crazy kid might make it."

Hawthorne started the slow and painful process of dragging the bleeding soldier toward the protection of the grove. With one hand locked on the man's collar and the other firmly gripping his rifle, Gerald Hawthorne faced the ridge and pulled back slowly.

The exposed ground was dry and rugged. Hawthorne proceeded cautiously, a few inches at a time, in order to protect the man's wound as much as possible.

Suddenly Bean screamed and the shrill, agonizing sound carried throughout the area. Hawthorne quickly released his grip and dropped beside the injured soldier.

"I can't help it, Bean," he said hoarsely. "We've got to get back." And then he realized that the wounded man was either unconscious or dead.

At that precise moment, there was a suspicious sound of movement just ahead and slightly to the right of their position. Again Hawthorne made an instant mental calculation. Without hesitating, he whirled, aimed, fired and brought down another Chinese soldier, who had been concealed behind a small mound of rocks. The enemy sniper had been pierced cleanly through the throat.

Hawthorne maneuvered the leather sling over his head and then adjusted the rifle securely across his slim shoulders. He put both hands under Bean's arms and locked his fingers around the man's chest. And then he proceeded to drag the wounded soldier swiftly across the rugged terrain regardless of the dangers, the wound and the trail of thick red blood.

Heavy rifle fire suddenly exploded from several concealed positions near the ridge but Hawthorne did not take cover. The patrol finally opened up and the two men were caught in a dangerous cross-fire but still he did not slow down or try to adjust his course.

He was breathing heavily as they neared the entrance to the grove. Hawthorne could feel the strain in his arms and chest. Both legs were numb and his head was spinning as he continued to pull Robert Bean to safety.

Hawthorne could hear the excited voice of Sergeant Donica screaming something about taking cover and hitting the dirt but he ignored the commands.

Suddenly he was grabbed hard and low, around the knees, a rough and professional football tackle. He was down and being dragged rapidly across the rocky ground by the veteran Army sergeant.

"Stay down!" Donica screamed close to Hawthorne's ear as he pulled him violently toward the protection of the grove. *"Go easy with Bean!"* the Sergeant blasted. Boulting and Foulkes had taken over the completion of the rescue mission. Under a heavy cover barrage, the two men had lifted the wounded soldier slightly off the ground and were now covering the short distance to the trees on the double.

In the shelter of the grove, Gerald Hawthorne had been

propped against a moss-covered trunk. Sergeant Donica was in the process of studying the exhausted young soldier with a mixture of contempt and consternation.

Lieutenant Gavin also left his position and crawled over to Hawthorne. Other members of the patrol, although they were exchanging rifle fire with the hidden enemy, managed to glance over their shoulders and catch a quick glimpse of the platoon's first Korean combat hero.

Hawthorne's head lolled back and his eyes were tightly closed. His short black hair was wet and matted to his forehead. Dirt and blood smeared his thin face and he was breathing heavily.

"Is Bean alive?" he asked.

"Yes," Lieutenant Gavin replied.

Donica rubbed his unshaven chin and continued to stare at the boy in amazement.

"Who the hell do you think you are—John Wayne?" he asked.

Hawthorne slowly opened his eyes and blinked.

"Oh," he mumbled. "Yeah, I guess."

And then he fainted.

The rescue of Robert Bean was recognized, by the proper military authorities, as a genuine act of heroism and Gerald Howard Hawthorne was promoted to the rank of Private First Class. In addition, Lieutenant Thomas Gavin had submitted Hawthorne's name to the appropriate department along with a glowing personal recommendation and a detailed account of the soldier's heroic exploits while on a routine patrol on December 16, 1950. The young officer felt certain that Gerald Hawthorne would be awarded the Silver Star for gallantry in action.

The members of the platoon continued to avoid the strange, morose character from Waverly, Michigan, but now the evenings were quiet. The bullets which had killed the two Chinese snipers had also put an end to the constant heckling and cruel harassment.

His rifle had brought him a taste of recognition and respect and it was now much easier for him to accept his loneliness.

Love and friendship were still impossible dreams. But he was no longer concerned. A man could live a good enough life with respect only, he decided.

He had rescued Robert Bean, and a small part of his own soul.

11:30 AM
SEPTEMBER 2, 1961
OFFICE OF ROBERT C. SPANGLER
NEW YORK CITY

13

"IT'S A LITTLE EARLY, gentlemen," said Spangler, "but I've got booze here, as usual." He smiled warmly and winked at several of the arriving press representatives.

"So I'm an alcoholic," said Tony Rivers, a columnist for *Tele-Pace,* the popular New York television magazine.

"Help yourself, Tony," Spangler suggested, pointing to the bar at the far side of his spacious office.

He studied his guests very carefully and tried to analyze the attendance. The basic turnout was much better than he had anticipated, although one local newspaper had failed to send any representative and another had delivered a very junior man.

Pete Drummond of the *Times* was present and that was a pleasant surprise. Drummond, a Pulitzer Prize winner, was known for his authoritative, in-depth Washington political reporting.

With smooth professionalism, Spangler officially welcomed his guests and proceeded with the next delicate phase of his Hawthorne operation.

"Our chairman, Mr. Frederic Bateman, has issued a detailed statement in reference to the program," said Spangler. "Miss Patterson will be happy to give you a copy at the completion of this conference. She will also make available a complete bio on Fred Schroeder, this genius on my right." He put a hand on the man's shoulder. "Freddy directed this masterpiece and I predict an Emmy for him." Schroeder looked up at his boss and grinned broadly.

"Ladies and gentlemen," Spangler continued, "we're going to release a few important quotes from the interview with Hawthorne and then we'll try to field some of your questions. Tim Henderson, our director of publicity and promotion, will release the excerpts," he explained. "We have purposely not made copies for distribution. So please make notes if you have an interest in any of the material."

He took his seat at the table, while Henderson stood and assumed control of the press conference.

"Gerald Hawthorne was quite derogatory whenever he referred to his hometown of Waverly, Michigan," said Henderson as he consulted his notes. "The man deplored conditions there and gave the impression that he was grossly mistreated by most members of the community." He paused for a moment while the press made notes, and then went on.

"Hawthorne felt that the Red Chinese were much nicer to him in Tsinan and that he had more freedom and better opportunities under communism. He has admitted to the killing of five American soldiers but claims that an American officer had given the command to open fire."

"He says he was never disturbed by the act of killing. In fact, he found it exciting, and this he has so stated on the video tape," Spangler cut in.

"Are you saying that Hawthorne assassinated five American soldiers because of a twisted desire to kill?" asked a reporter from a New York State weekly.

"No, sir," Spangler replied. "I'm saying that his candid statement should be taken into consideration whenever we try to analyze Hawthorne and his actions. And his actions speak for themselves."

Arthur Fremantle, pale and shaken, leaned close to his boss's ear and whispered, "How dare you?"

"Noise, Arthur," Spangler replied softly with his hand partly covering his mouth. "We're going to make noise."

Fremantle stared at Spangler's profile for a moment but could not make him react or turn toward him.

Fremantle leaned even closer. "You are a dead man, Mr. Spangler," he whispered hoarsely.

The executive rubbed his jaw and continued to look straight ahead.

"Worry about yourself, Fremantle," he replied in a whisper.

Mary Minter of the *News* raised her hand.

"Many American prisoners of war died of starvation at Camp Six," she said. "Survivors in 1953 claimed that Gerald Hawthorne was always well fed and well taken care of by the Chinese. Was he asked about this?"

"Yes, Mrs. Minter," Henderson replied. "He admits that he was very well treated by his captors."

"He was also charged with informing on a fellow prisoner," she continued. "The man was later tortured and then executed by the Reds. Did he answer this accusation?"

"He informed."

"Hawthorne admits to this charge?" asked Pete Drummond.

"Yes, sir," answered Henderson.

Drummond settled back in his chair and looked at Spangler curiously. "I think you'd better play this amazing tape for a Federal grand jury."

"They'll see it, Mr. Drummond," said Spangler casually. "With millions of other Americans."

"Do you think he's an enemy agent?" asked another reporter.

Spangler laughed lightly. "That's for others to decide."

"Are you working with the government on this case?"

Spangler glared at him. "I work for Amalgamated Broadcasting Television, young man."

Then he stood and addressed the others. "Tim will move into the Tsinan, China, phase of the interview in a few minutes." He smiled and winked at Tony Rivers. "I think we all deserve a break and a few swallows of some civilized refreshment."

The Michigan Inter-State Transit bus was nearly empty and making excellent time on a direct route out of Detroit. The driver had made a very few suburban stops and now Gerald Hawthorne was in open country, speeding toward his destination. He was very anxious to get home.

The flight from New York to Detroit had been swift and uneventful and he had gone unnoticed at both airports. Several passengers had stared curiously at his colorful Chinese traveling bag but there had been very few comments and no disturbances.

He adjusted the reclining seat and made himself comfortable as the familiar Michigan countryside whizzed by his window. Particular landmarks jogged his memory and stirred his emotions.

He shoved his hand deeply into his jacket pocket and pulled out the crumpled bills which had been given to him earlier by Robert Spangler. He smoothed them out and counted twenty-five dollars.

The highway was broad and smooth and the motion of the bus was soothing. He leaned back and closed his eyes.

He thought about the various people in his life and how death had forced such drastic changes. His mother, Ling Yu, the plumber and even Robert Bean.

If enemy airmen had missed their designated targets on January 9, 1951, he might now have been living in Columbus, Ohio, and China would have remained as remote as Mars.

JANUARY 10, 1951
KOREA

14 A SHOWER OF LETHAL bombs had been dropped with incredible accuracy at exactly 3:50 AM on the morning of January 9, 1951.
The raid on Hawthorne's base was considered to be the most devastating enemy action since the start of the conflict and most of the troops believed that seasoned Russian

pilots were responsible for the destruction. Damage was extensive and the casualties were high.

The official report listed the total destruction of five supply depots, twenty-eight vehicles, including thirteen jeeps, the newly constructed annex section of the senior officers' quarters, and the south wing of the main base hospital.

Identification had already been established for fifty-seven American dead and eighty-five wounded. It was rumored that the statistics would climb even higher as the difficult rescue operations continued.

Hawthorne, who had been blasted out of his bunk, managed to disentangle himself from a pile of shattered timber and mangled bodies. Miraculously, he had sustained only slight cuts and a few minor bruises.

His concern for Robert Bean had prompted him to stumble through the debris in search of the burning south wing of the base hospital.

Hawthorne had finally experienced friendship. He had visited Bean nearly every day and they had talked openly about their lives and their futures. Hawthorne was cautious at first but soon he discovered that Bean was all right—there were no twisted desires or devious schemes in him.

It had been his first chance to observe the healthy influence of a loyal wife and devoted child and he had envied the Bean family.

Veronica Bean had mentioned Hawthorne in every letter to her husband and once she had sent him a large food package, including jars of homemade preserves and candy. A small card was enclosed: "You are always in our thoughts and prayers."

Robert Bean's father owned a small factory which manufactured engine parts. It was located in the suburbs of Columbus. Robert was slated to join the organization and begin working his way up from the floor assembly line. He had asked Hawthorne to come to Ohio after discharge in order to take advantage of the same opportunity and his father had confirmed the offer in a formal note.

By five forty-five in the morning on January 9, 1951, the

south wing of the main hospital had burned to the ground and Private First Class Robert Bean of Columbus, Ohio, was pronounced dead.

Sadness mixed with bitterness and anger, and Hawthorne drifted back into his brooding, solitary existence. He pledged to avenge the death of his friend by using his rifle and annihilating every animal on the earth.

A brief letter from Veronica Bean had driven him deeper into his melancholia. She had accepted her husband's death courageously. "Fate," she had written. "You saved his life but God was determined to take it. This is destiny, Mr. Hawthorne. We can cheat it a little but we cannot alter it permanently."

A few days later, another letter arrived. He scanned it without emotion. His father was destitute and desperate. He was ill and in no position to obtain assistance of any kind. Hawthorne was unmoved by the childishly scribbled appeal. Bean's death had left him stunned and temporarily immune to emotion.

The following morning, he made arrangements with the base paymaster to send thirty dollars a month to his father. He did not answer the letter.

During the early-morning hours of January 19, 1951, Gerald Hawthorne finally had another opportunity to face the enemy. His outfit was involved in the drive to recapture Seoul from the Chinese Reds.

The important American thrust was being slowed down by a sizable force of enemy troops. The Communist soldiers were strategically positioned on the route to the South Korean capital and Hawthorne's platoon was participating in a complicated flanking operation, designed to cut off and destroy the paralyzing opposition.

A thick blanket of fog had smothered visibility to zero.

Private First Class Hawthorne was in a forward position waiting with other troops for an order to advance or pull back. All firing on both sides had ceased and the silence seemed to increase the tension and the feeling that death was imminent.

Hawthorne could barely distinguish the outlines of several American officers who were huddled nearby. He could hear their whispered voices and prayed that their orders would call for an immediate move forward.

He squinted into the dense fog and prepared himself for action as he heard the officers begin to disperse. Foulkes was crouching low to his left and Boulting was lying prone on his right.

Suddenly he heard muffled sounds coming from somewhere in the distance. There was silence again for a few moments and then he detected movement ahead and to the left of their position.

Hawthorne glanced in the direction of the officers but could not locate them in the haze. He turned back, slid flat to the ground and maneuvered himself into his most effective firing position.

He patted the rifle paternally and brought it up to his cheek. Regardless of the nearly insurmountable obstacles, Private First Class Gerald Howard Hawthorne's gun was loaded, cocked and ready for the enemy.

The unknown noises in the shadows were increasing and becoming more distinct.

"What the fuck is that?" blurted Foulkes. He sounded terrified.

"The goddamn gooks are attacking!" yelled Boulting.

"*Shut up!*" a harsh voice ordered. The Captain, a tall, severe West Point graduate named Matlock, was positioned directly behind B. G. Foulkes. "*Keep quiet,*" he barked. "*Keep down and hold your fire.*"

A patch of fog dissolved slightly and most of the outfit caught a distorted but horrifying glimpse of rapidly advancing troops. Possibly several hundred men, still partially concealed by the opaque mist, were running a frenzied and jagged course toward the American position.

Hawthorne's finger was resting on the trigger and a dim figure was squarely in his sights. He started to squeeze but then decided to wait with the others as the attacking silhouettes plunged forward. He twisted around and managed to spot

Captain Matlock. The officer was waving his arms and screaming a frantic, garbled message to a runner.

Total confusion at the top, thought Hawthorne, as he turned
back to his rifle and quickly aligned another bull's-eye possibility. He cursed under his breath and waited.

"OPEN FIRE! OPEN FIRE!"

The order was given suddenly and with great excitement.
It was a gruff voice, either that of the Captain, or possibly
the Colonel, thought Hawthorne, as he brought down a running, screaming shadow.

The steady chatter of machine guns mixed with the spontaneous burst of rifle fire and once again Hawthorne's bullets
tore into the distant human targets.

Four, he counted, four.

The deafening blasts of grenades blended with the other
sounds of war and Hawthorne was caught up in the delirium.
He screamed at the top of his lungs and fired wildly.

His bullet dropped another approaching shape. *"Five!"* he
yelled. *"Five!"*

The shrill voice of Lieutenant Gavin cut through the bedlam. *"Cease fire! Hold your fire!"*

There was silence, except for the groans and agonized cries
of the wounded.

"Oh my God!" shrieked Gavin. The young officer suddenly
burst into hysterical tears.

The smoke screen was slowly lifting and the grotesque pano-
rama of death was exposed. Hawthorne turned away from the
scene. His mind refused to register what he saw.

In a daze, he watched two medics care for the First Lieutenant who had fallen to the ground in a state of shock.

"Jesus Christ, we shot our own guys!"

"I can't believe it," muttered Boulting, rubbing his forehead
nervously. "What a horrible fuck-up."

A dream, a disgusting hallucination, thought Hawthorne.

"On the double, men," the Captain said in a monotone.
"Move up and work with the medics." He went down the line.
"On the double," he repeated. "Come on, get it together.
Move up, men. Work with the medics. On the double."

The Captain's open hand slammed hard against Hawthorne's back and he followed the others lethargically into the nightmare of blood and flesh.

He tried to isolate the sights and sounds. The massacre was fantasy, unreal.

The terrain was painted red. Mutilated corpses and the ruptured parts of the dying were scattered in a bizarre pattern.

He stared dazedly at an untouched head which had rolled clear of its body. The hair was blond and the eyes were blue and Hawthorne shuddered. Its mouth was contorted into a broad grin.

He was suddenly aware that a soldier was waving and motioning for him to approach.

"Over here!" the man was shouting. *"Give me a hand, over here!"*

The medic was kneeling over a pile of broken bones and lacerated flesh.

Hawthorne stumbled toward him and then stood mesmerized as the medic struggled with the mortally wounded soldier.

"I can't get a goddamn needle into him!" the medic shouted, attempting to get a firm grip on the body.

The dying man was twisting and jerking violently and his squeals reminded Hawthorne of a stuck pig.

The medic looked up and bawled angrily, *"Come on, goddammit! Help me!"* He was holding the hypodermic in one hand while battling the man desperately with the other.

"Straddle his chest and hold him down."

Hawthorne fought down nausea and panic and managed to sit on the convulsing figure. He leaned forward and gripped the mangled arms as the medic prepared the needle for injection.

He could feel the man's chest heaving furiously and the steady gush of blood was beginning to soak his pants and run down his legs. Hawthorne watched as the medic jammed the needle into the pathetic body.

A sudden thought flashed across his brain as he stared at the soldier's twisted face.

One of his own bullets might have hit this man and set him up for machine guns or grenades. He had meant to demonstrate his expert marksmanship and courage by helping to destroy every Chinese animal on earth. Instead, he had chopped down five American soldiers.

"Thanks, buddy." The medic slapped him on the shoulder and moved off quickly to attend to other victims.

Hawthorne did not respond. He could not move from his position. His eyes were expressionless as he calmly watched the soldier die.

Then he cursed his rifle. Once again he had been deceived by a friend. Like everything else on earth, he thought, the weapon had let him down. Now he was completely alone, exposed, incapable of any action.

Tears began to stream down his cheeks.

He took a deep breath and pitched forward into the blood.

His face rested next to the mutilated head of the dead American soldier.

"I'm sorry," he mumbled to the corpse.

The darkness engulfed him.

Hawthorne was unable to erase the haunting memory of the carnage. Bean's sudden death and the slaughter which followed combined to rob his life of what meaning it had. His bitterness and frustration drove him even deeper into his own solitary world.

He could not sleep. It was often impossible for him to breathe sufficient air into his lungs, and on several occasions he had choked and vomited because of imagined asphyxiation.

His appetite was gone and a drastic loss of weight had shriveled his thin frame into skeletal proportions. Cold sweats, chills, a pounding heart, sudden attacks of weakness in his limbs, vertigo and a churning stomach plagued him constantly. Hawthorne was not prepared for the demanding military action which was rapidly approaching.

On the twenty-seventh and twenty-eighth of January 1951, the United Nations forces attacked the Chinese Reds in the capital city of Seoul. A day later, Hawthorne and his platoon faced the enemy in a bitter engagement near Usan, North Korea.

He crouched low against a large rock and calmly watched the frantic activity explode around him.

An enemy machine gun spewed hot lead into B. G. Foulkes and his blood spurted in every direction. Boulting had been shot in the stomach and his intestines were dangling from his body. He was screaming and running in a grotesque circle.

Suddenly a fist crashed into the side of Hawthorne's face and he looked into the piercing eyes of Sergeant Donica.

"Pick up that fucking rifle!" the Sergeant yelled angrily.

And at that precise moment, Hawthorne saw a bullet penetrate the soldier's forehead. The wound was clean and neat and Donica dropped slowly to the dirt without uttering a sound.

Hawthorne rubbed his jaw. The blow had shocked him out of his reverie. The din of battle was now audible to him and he could see that the screaming figures on the ground were real. His platoon was being wiped out by the Chinese Reds. He heard the chilling battle cry of the enemy and knew that they were storming the position.

Hawthorne peered cautiously around the rock. The sight which met his eyes forced him to reach for his weapon.

His hand was trembling as he brought the heavy piece up to his cheek. A charging Red was soon in the sights and he moved his finger slowly to the trigger.

Cold perspiration flowed down his face but he blinked and followed the attacking soldier.

A violent stomach cramp caused him to cry out and the pain moved swiftly to his chest. Tears were beginning to fill his eyes and mix with the stinging sweat as he desperately traced the movement of the advancing Red.

Finally, he ordered his finger to squeeze.

All the loneliness and the bitterness of his life seemed to come to a head. Hawthorne was frozen and unable to fire. His arms and legs began to tremble furiously and the rifle fell to the ground. He sat with his back propped against the large rock, powerless to control his convulsions.

As the enemy neared the position, Hawthorne took a last look at the pitiful remnants of his platoon. Then he buried his head between his legs and clamped his hands tightly over his ears.

Gerald Howard Hawthorne was captured by the Chinese Reds on January 29, 1951. He was taken to Prison Camp Six near Pyuktong.

SEPTEMBER 3, 1961
WASHINGTON, D.C.

15 THE COLUMBIA WAS A small, exclusive hotel, located close to the Capitol, in Washington, D.C. Clete Hardigan and Santo Morales, two trusted members of Hector Rambeau's velvet mafia, sat in the bar talking quietly.

"Senator Brewster has arranged everything in Waverly," Morales said.

"Is Brewster aware of the entire package?"

"Absolutely not," answered Morales. "The Senator has agreed to hire some men for legitimate staff work in the Detroit area. They'll be keeping an eye on Hawthorne for us."

"Is Spangler being spanked?"

"Not at the moment, Hardigan."

"Why not?"

"The plan is to deal with Mr. Fremantle."

"Why?"

"Any direct move against Spangler now will provide ammunition," Morales continued. "He might blow the whole damn thing sky high."

"He'll do it anyway."

"Maybe. But we feel that we can convince Fremantle very quickly and he should be able to put the skids on Spangler before the tape is played on television."

"That will never happen, Morales," Hardigan replied. "This man Spangler is going for all the marbles." He paused for a moment as the customer moved past the table. "I know my people," he added.

Morales checked his watch and cut the meeting short. "I'll have to be getting back soon. Are you prepared to leave in the morning?"

"Yes."

"Do you need any additional information?"

"No."

The men left the bar separately.

The long journey from China was over for Gerald Hawthorne. He was finally home at 12 Elm Drive, Waverly, Michigan.

As usual, the small local bus depot had been noisy and crowded and he was able to slip through easily without being noticed.

However, he had been recognized by an elderly taxi driver during the short ride back to the house. The old man had been watching him curiously through the rear view mirror from the start of the trip.

"Are you Gerald Hawthorne?" he had asked without turning around. The driver continued to stare into the mirror until Hawthorne nodded.

"I'll be damned," he muttered. "Saw your pictures in the Detroit press."

They were entering the quiet street with its cool ceiling of interwoven leaves and branches. Hawthorne tried to ignore the inquisitive eyes as the cab took a right turn and then a left and came to a jolting stop in front of number 12.

He sat for a moment and allowed the sight to sink in. The house seemed much smaller and less dignified and the neglected grounds certainly did not resemble the landscaped property in his memory. The white paint was chipped and faded, two of the porch steps were broken and the screens were damaged.

The cabbie had turned completely around in his seat and

was now studying Hawthorne with a sour expression on his face.

"I'll be damned," he repeated. "Gerald Howard Hawthorne." He shook his head in disbelief. "My wife won't believe me."

Hawthorne stepped out of the taxi while the old man remained inside, muttering to himself.

"How much?" asked Hawthorne through the window.

The driver scratched his head and thought for a moment.

"One dollar," he demanded coldly.

The cheating bastard, thought Hawthorne. He regarded the driver with contempt for a moment and then tossed a dollar bill into the taxi. The driver caught the crumpled note and smoothed it out as Hawthorne hauled his Chinese traveling bag out of the back seat.

"Don't the Chinks tip?" the man snorted.

Hawthorne slammed the car door and walked slowly toward the house. He controlled himself, realizing that his survival in Waverly depended on a cool and tolerant approach to every distasteful confrontation.

The taxi's engine had started as he mounted the battered wooden steps. Hawthorne sighed with relief as he heard the driver curse loudly and then pull away.

He started to unlock the front door but paused for a moment to examine the porch. The swing was no longer positioned near the far railing, in the shade close to the elm branches. It had been his mother's favorite spot.

Hawthorne shuddered as he entered the house on Elm Drive.

He sat stiffly on the sofa, avoiding his father's worn leather armchair. The living room had a musty smell and the stillness in the large house was beginning to aggravate his nerves.

It was early evening and Hawthorne could not generate an appetite or relax enough to take advantage of a cool, upstairs bedroom.

He spent the first afternoon of his home-coming on a hasty inspection tour of the dilapidated premises.

The spacious kitchen was in need of a good scrubbing and a fresh coat of paint. The round wooden table in the center of the room would have to be varnished, he decided. He tried to block out the recollections of his father's drunken mealtime tirades.

He noted that the drapes in the downstairs study were badly worn. A mirror was cracked and the ancient rug looked terrible. He leaned heavily against the closet door. Certain objects in the room forced him to remember the days and nights of humiliation and punishment. His familiar anxiety symptoms seemed intensified as he moved quickly from one location to another in the lonely house.

He opened the creaky door leading to the basement stairs but then decided to postpone this particular survey until his strength and confidence had returned.

The upstairs rooms were an even more traumatic experience for him. He spent a short time in his old room but managed to avoid looking over items which were certain to cause further emotional stress, such as photographs and documents, and especially things which had been given to him by his mother.

He opened the door of his father's room but was unable to step inside.

Cold perspiration moistened his hair and forehead as he moved down the hall. He glanced to his right and observed that the door to his mother's room was still chained and bolted.

His legs felt weak as he descended the stairs and walked unsteadily into the living room at the front of the house. He sat on the windowsill overlooking the porch and tried to control his breathing.

His eyes had begun to haze and burn and he needed a drink badly. He was glad that he had stuffed three bottles of Scotch into his bag at the Carlton Hotel while waiting for Robert Spangler.

But he decided to honor his own pledge and stay away from whiskey until conditions became unbearable. There were going to be challenges to face, and he would have to exercise complete control at all times.

After the inspection, he moved to the sofa.

*   *   *

This was a taste of the peace and quiet, the independence and solitude, which he had thought about so often. He was determined to make the most of his surroundings, deciding that for a few days he would block out the disquieting echoes of the past.

Soon he would have to analyze his present position and begin to formulate a practical plan of action. Before long, he would have to face the past.

Hawthorne debated whether to go upstairs, unpack, wash and prepare for his first sleep at home in eleven years.

The decision was suddenly made for him when a loud and unexpected crash shattered the stillness of the house. Jagged bits of glass sprayed in every direction as a large rock smashed through one of the front windows.

Hawthorne fell to the floor behind the sofa. There was silence for a moment. He stayed undercover and waited.

"HAWTHORNE!"

The drunken shout came from the yard in front of the house.

"COME OUT, YOU YELLOW BASTARD!"

Hawthorne did not move or respond. He planned an immediate dash for the light switch in order to plunge the room into darkness.

"HEY, YOU GODDAMN COMMUNIST!"

This was a different voice, a younger sound, shriller, and obviously also influenced by alcohol.

Hawthorne kept his head low as he started to crawl slowly across the room to the lamp in the far corner.

"WE'LL WAIT FOR YOU, CHINAMAN!"

It was another voice. A street gang, thought Hawthorne. They were gathered close to the front porch steps.

"YELLOW GOOK BASTARD! COME OUT AND SAY HELLO!"

Hawthorne suddenly jumped to his feet and managed to switch off the light as another rock smashed a second window, sending glass flying all over the room.

The room was dark and the moonlight enabled Hawthorne to see that his assailants were now assembled on the porch close to the shattered windows.

He crouched low in the corner, breathing heavily, praying

that the band of hoodlums would tire of the operation and scatter without a serious fight.

"I suggest you get your ass on the first train out of this town," a mature voice instructed through the smashed window.

Hawthorne suddenly realized that the men in front of his house were not ordinary street bums. This group was older and more determined and they seemed to be dedicated to a common cause.

"Traitors ain't welcome in this town, Hawthorne," said one of the drunken characters. "We'd better not catch you outside."

"We were all in Korea," said another. "And we can't wait to get our hands around your gook neck."

Hawthorne closed his eyes tightly and pressed his forehead into the wall. This position, in the corner of the room, was painfully familiar. He could almost hear his father's tirades and his mother's screams.

Something was tossed through one of the broken windows and he thought immediately of a bomb or a grenade. He covered his face with both hands and waited for the explosion. There was only silence as the object hit the floor hard and rolled toward him.

"We'll move on now, Hawthorne," the same voice continued. "Next time you won't get off so easy."

Raucous laughter rattled the stillness of the night, quickly followed by the smashing of several bottles against the porch steps. He listened as the group moved down the front path, through the yard and out of the gate. His foot touched the object which had been thrown through the window. It was a rock covered with a piece of newspaper.

He waited until the voices had faded away. Then he picked up the rock and pulled himself to his feet. He moved cautiously through the dark house to the downstairs study.

The shutters were still firmly secured and the windows were shut and locked. He bolted the door and then turned on a small reading lamp.

He unraveled three turns of string and the front page of

the *Waverly Evening Express* explained the actions of his welcoming committee.

He spread the newspaper on a card table and sat close to the lamp.

The headline announced the return of the Turncoat. Hawthorne was amazed at the statements, editorial comment and pictures, and he suddenly realized how ruthlessly Robert Calhoun Spangler had exploited him.

"The Chinese Reds were nicer to me than the people of Waverly, Michigan," the Turncoat had stated, and the quote was carried prominently in the upper right-hand corner of the page. *"They gave me an opportunity to live my life in Tsinan, China, without pushing me."*

It was all there. The delicate work of the professional assassins. Each of Spangler's points at the New York press conference had been well taken by the local journalist.

Nervously Hawthorne lit a cigarette and read the twisted account of the interview, which highlighted his hatred of America and love for Red China, the slaughter of his comrades and collaboration with the enemy.

A cleverly devised editorial at the bottom of the page featured a flashback to 1953 and the article captured the mood of the Waverly citizens at the time.

An appropriate series of quotes and pictures, including a vicious comment by his former teacher Beatrice Powell and a pathetic statement from Mr. Howard Hawthorne, the Turncoat's father, recalled the citizens' blind rage and hostility toward the defector.

"Now he has returned to Waverly," the editor summarized. *"He admits his guilt but feels no shame. He embraces communism and denounces our American flag. Gerald Hawthorne will ask this fine community for hospitality and consideration after informing Mr. Arthur Fremantle that he would do it all again if the circumstances were the same.*

"Many of our boys have not returned from foreign wars. The Turncoat is home . . . and he has blackened the name of patriotism. I cannot bid him welcome."

Hawthorne decided to have a drink.

Spangler, Fremantle, their helpers and the press had created an infamously distorted portrait of him. He was now hopelessly trapped in a blind alley.

Later that evening, Gerald Hawthorne managed to drink himself into unconsciousness.

SEPTEMBER 4, 1961
NEW YORK CITY

16 ARNOLD DORFMAN, AMALGAMATED'S news director, sat with Morris Wineburg at the Nosh Delicatessen on Lexington Avenue near 56th Street. Wineburg nudged him and then pointed to a table in the corner of the crowded and noisy restaurant. "There's Henderson," said the lawyer. The Amalgamated publicity director was eating alone at a small, cramped table near the front entrance.

Dorfman waved and motioned for him to join them.

Henderson greeted them and took a seat. The waiter brought over the remains of his sandwich and a ginger ale.

Wineburg studied the publicity director for a moment before speaking. "How are things going?"

"Good," answered Henderson, sipping the ginger ale.

"Trouble with Spangler?"

"No more than usual."

They continued with their lunch in silence for a few minutes.

"I understand that the interview is set for next Friday night," commented Wineburg.

"New York and Los Angeles only," Dorfman confirmed. "At ten o'clock."

Wineburg wiped the corners of his mouth with his napkin. "He'll leave you alone, Tim, as soon as he gets Hawthorne out of his system."

"Really?" Henderson pushed his plate to one side without

finishing the sandwich. "That man will never get Hawthorne out of his system."

There was an uncomfortable silence once again at the table as the men proceeded to finish their lunches.

Henderson stared solemnly at his plate, absently tracing one finger along the circular pattern of the bright tablecloth.

"Have you heard the news?" he asked without looking up.

"About Hammarskjöld? asked Dorfman.

"No. About Fremantle."

They indicated that they had not heard and Henderson finally looked up and stared at Morris Wineburg.

"He had an accident last night," he said bluntly, and his voice had a sharper tone.

Wineburg leaned across the table. "What do you mean?"

Henderson took out a cigarette and lit up. "The porter in his New York apartment found him in the lobby early this morning."

"Oh my God," muttered Dorfman.

"What happened?" asked Wineburg, shocked.

"They think he fell down the steps."

"The building has two elevators," Dorfman commented.

"Is it serious?" Wineburg asked, ignoring the statement.

"Yes," said Henderson calmly. "Concussion, broken ribs and facial lacerations."

They were quiet for a moment.

"Jesus Christ," said Dorfman. "Was he drunk?"

"I don't know," Henderson replied. "Spangler is at the hospital now."

"He must have been drunk," Wineburg insisted.

"Shut up, goddammit!" Dorfman barked angrily. "Why drunk? It could have been anything."

"That's true, Arnie," said Henderson as he looked at the glowing tip of his cigarette. "It could have been anything."

"Morris is right," the publicity director continued. "He was probably drunk." There was a pause and then he added slowly, "If he wasn't drunk . . . well . . . somebody threw him down two long flights."

"What the hell are you talking about?" Wineburg asked sharply.

"This Hawthorne business," Henderson replied quietly. "That's what I'm talking about."

"What about it?" Wineburg was becoming irritated.

"I don't know exactly, but I have a feeling that Spangler has finally stuck his finger into the wrong pie."

The waiter arrived and Dorfman paid the check.

"I've got to get back," said Wineburg. He glanced at his watch and started to pick up his briefcase.

"You shouldn't talk that way, Tim," said Dorfman. "It causes trouble."

"It's my own opinion," snapped the publicity director. "I have a right to my own opinion."

"Hell, yes, man," countered Wineburg. "But why don't you keep it to yourself?"

Henderson regarded him with contempt. "Maybe I will and maybe I won't."

Dorfman rose to his feet and Wineburg moved close to the publicity director.

"If you think you have a case, Tim, don't brood about it. Go to the authorities. Otherwise, keep it to yourself. It's a lot safer."

Henderson did not raise his head or react. The men said goodbye and left the restaurant.

"Get them up here." Spangler spoke wearily into the desk intercom. He closed his eyes and leaned his head back against the chair.

It was nearly five o'clock in the afternoon and he had been on the go since his six-in-the-morning arrival at Columbia Presbyterian. The elderly superintendent at Fremantle's Fifth Avenue apartment building had called urgently the moment the ambulance had pulled away.

He had paced the drab hospital corridors for nearly four hours without receiving a proper medical report on Fremantle's condition.

Finally, at ten o'clock, Dr. Louis G. Tolkin, Amalgamated's company physician, had disclosed the details of the man's injuries. The concussion was slight, but the broken ribs, facial lacerations, severe bruises and sprains, combined with shock, would require Fremantle's hospitalization for an extended period.

The doctor had also confided that Fremantle had been drinking at the time of the accident and that the fall had probably occurred because of his intoxicated condition. Alcohol had been found on his breath, in his system and on the front of his clothing.

Fremantle had regained consciousness at two o'clock in the afternoon, and at three Spangler had been allowed to visit him for a few minutes.

The patient was an unrecognizable mummy, bandaged heavily from head to foot. Two small slits in the white mask allowed his eyes to stare out. They registered an expression of panic. Only his mouth was exposed.

Tolkin and a nurse had stood quietly with Spangler at the foot of the bed. They had watched as the pale lips struggled to form a word. The doctor had motioned for Spangler to leave the room.

Later, in the hospital corridor, Dr. Tolkin had commented on the incident. "I had to give him a strong shot and put him to sleep. Arthur cannot afford any strain at the moment."

"Did I disturb him?" Spangler had asked.

"Yes, you did. I think he was trying very hard to say something to you."

"Really?"

"I put my ear close to his mouth when I gave him the injection," Tolkin had continued. "It was difficult to hear. Only a hoarse whisper. But it sounded like Rimbo or Rainbow."

"What?"

"He repeated it three times."

"Rambeau?"

"Yes," Tolkin had replied. "That could be it. Rambeau. He repeated it three times and then he went under. Is it a name or a place?"

"It's a name, Doc," Spangler had replied grimly. "But it isn't important."

The program chief opened his eyes and positioned himself properly behind the desk as the Amalgamated production staff entered the office. They took seats silently and their expressions indicated that they were prepared for the funereal tone of Spangler's voice.

"I want to report about the Fremantle accident before we make a detailed statement to the press later this evening."

"What have they got so far?" asked Dorfman.

"A straight hospital bulletin," Spangler replied. "Sometime between three o'clock and five this morning, Arthur Fremantle fell down two long flights of stairs in the lobby of his apartment building on Fifth Avenue."

He got up and paced nervously in front of the group, then stopped close to Tim Henderson. The publicity director was staring out of the office window.

"I read the draft of your release at the hospital, Henderson," said Spangler sourly. "I was not satisfied with the contents."

"I didn't have all the facts this afternoon, Mr. Spangler," Henderson protested.

"Fremantle did not have an accident on the stairs, Henderson," Spangler barked. "He fell down the steps. I want it put just that way. Is that clear?"

"What's the difference?"

"Plenty," snapped Spangler. "And you know it."

The program chief moved back to his desk and sat on the edge, facing the members of the staff.

"The press will continue to insinuate that Arthur Fremantle was drunk at the time of the accident," Spangler continued wearily. "We can't stop this approach but let's not help it along."

"Why the hell didn't he use the elevators?" asked Dorfman.

"I had a long talk with the building's super today," Spangler answered patiently. "He will verify that he has had some trouble with both elevators for the past two weeks. This information will be passed on to the press this evening as well as the disclosure that Arthur Fremantle has always suffered from claustrophobia. He detests elevators and the slightest indication of trouble could have put him off."

"Logical," muttered Dorfman.

Morris Wineburg proceeded cautiously. "If we deny the whiskey theory, Bob," he said, "what could have caused the accident on the stairs?" He caught himself. "I mean, the fall down the steps?"

Spangler leaned his head back against the chair and paused thoughtfully for a moment before speaking. "Arthur Fremantle has been tired and overworked," Spangler finally lectured. "He is in the process of preparing several difficult and important documentary broadcasts and I can verify that the man has gone without sleep and proper food for the last three weeks. I have personally warned him on numerous occasions."

"He probably lost his balance on the stairs because of sheer exhaustion," commented Schroeder.

"That's exactly what I mean, Freddie," said Spangler, winking at the director.

"What's the latest on his condition?"

"He's bashed up pretty good, as you know," Spangler responded. "But he'll pull through after a long period of convalescence."

"Did you see him today?" asked Wineburg.

"Yes, I did."

"Was he conscious?" Dorfman queried.

"Just barely."

"Did he recognize you?"

"How the hell do I know?"

"I mean, did he talk?" Dorfman was quietly insistent. "Did he say anything?"

"NO!" It was practically a scream. The group was stunned by Spangler's unexpected outburst and Arnold Dorfman's face had gone from red to gray in a matter of seconds.

Spangler managed to bring himself under control.

"I'm sorry, people." He sighed and then continued softly. "I've had quite a day today. I guess I'm on edge." He looked at Dorfman. "Forgive me, Arnie."

Dorfman nodded nervously. Spangler continued with forced calmness.

"Fremantle did not say anything when I visited the room." He paused and then added, "He was under heavy sedation and unable to speak."

"Is the Hawthorne program still set for September 16?" asked Henderson.

Spangler looked at the publicity chief strangely for a moment.

Then he turned to the others and scanned their faces before speaking.

"The Hawthorne interview will be transmitted as scheduled on the sixteenth of September. New York and Los Angeles will have the initial play. The other Amalgamated stations will air on a staggered basis during the same week. I've scheduled a meeting at ten tomorrow morning. We'll discuss advertising and promotion."

Spangler looked slowly from one member of the staff to another.

"This project has become more than just another television program to me," he commented bitterly. "This is an important attack. Part of a campaign to rid this country of undesirable citizens who take liberty and justice for granted."

He paused and looked around him.

"I intend to bury Hawthorne." Spangler was now perspiring freely. "And I want every person in this country to come and spit on his grave."

SEPTEMBER 7, 1961
WAVERLY, MICHIGAN

17

IT WAS MORNING. Hawthorne had finished two of the three bottles of Scotch and the whiskey had eased him through one full day and one night. Now he was sober, upset and empty, and it was obvious that hunger would soon force him out on the dangerous streets of town.

He had locked himself in the study, refusing to make use of the upstairs facilities. He had slept, cramped and twisted, on a small sofa and had not washed, shaved or removed his clothing since arriving.

His face was pale and drawn and his eyes were embedded in deep, dark sockets. His beard was heavy and his short black hair was tangled and matted to his head.

He had left New York wearing a white shirt with sleeves rolled to the elbows and now it was badly wrinkled and whiskey-stained. His ill-fitting gray slacks, which had been purchased hurriedly in Hong Kong, were in the same shabby condition.

He tried a few painful and unsteady steps across the room but quickly flopped back on the crumpled sofa, unable to keep his balance. His bones ached and his ribs were sore and his stomach was growling for food. And then he remembered the crazy lady and wondered if she was still alive and in business.

Hawthorne got up and stood for a moment trying to conquer the sway and the sickening tilt of the room.

Out the back door of the house, he recalled, through the yard, down the cluttered alley to the left for two blocks and then the short-cut to the woman's place on the next street. Her name was Mrs. Foster and she used to stock supplies and sell them in a small garage under her rickety old house on Oak Place. No one had ever heard the crazy lady speak. Her wiry gray hair and bony fingers had made her appear witch-like. The local kids had concocted wild tales about sinister doings in her basement and several had seen the old woman taking midnight strolls through the cemetery on Pine Hill. The crazy lady was certainly the answer to his predicament. He hoped she wasn't dead.

Hawthorne opened his travel bag and removed the last bottle of whiskey. He took three long gulps for courage, braced himself and then left the house.

He returned from his mission twenty minutes later. It had been a complete success. He had moved quickly and expertly over the emergency route, managing to avoid contact and trouble.

Mrs. Foster was older but still silent, still evil-looking. He reasoned that his meager purchases of food and essential household items would be enough to keep him alive for at least a week. He could always go back for more.

The canned soups, tuna and sardines would have to take the place of meat for a long time to come, he figured. And besides, a daylight trip to the A&P would be the same as asking for a split skull.

He counted his money very carefully and shrugged off the splurge on a half bottle of wine and two Milky Way bars. He promised himself to stay away from luxury products in the future.

Hawthorne unpacked the precious groceries and stored them neatly in the kitchen cupboard. It made the large room seem a little warmer.

He sat at the table for the first time and opened his wine. He tilted back the bottle into his mouth and closed his eyes. He was halfway through before his stomach began to heave.

Hawthorne stumbled to the stove and proceeded to put together a hurried breakfast consisting of two fried eggs and a few slices of white bread.

He devoured the food quickly and felt a little stronger. He left the dish and frying pan on the table and carried the remainder of the wine into the study.

After bolting the door and inspecting the windows, he sprawled on the rug with his head resting on one of the sofa cushions.

Hawthorne sipped the wine slowly and thought about his humiliating return to Waverly, Michigan. He glanced at the heavy bolt on the inside of the study door and realized that he was a prisoner once again.

February 2, 1951
Camp Six
Near Pyuktong
Korea

The Fort Upton briefings had prepared him for the worst. Hawthorne had anticipated bright yellow faces with sinister slant eyes and sharp, pointed teeth.

He expected to be ruthlessly mangled by torturers who

feasted on unborn mice, monkey brains, and snakes cooked alive and served with boiled rice.

The enemies' crazed, shrieking voices would disrupt all sleep and the eyes of stubborn prisoners were undoubtedly destined to be scooped out by long, razor-edged fingernails.

"We give these gooks name, rank and serial number. Nothing more. Understood?"

Sergeant Alvin Proctor of New York City had established himself immediately as the strong man of the slovenly unit. He was also the ranking noncommissioned officer in the hut.

Proctor was short and stocky, but according to a craphouse legend, his bullneck, massive shoulders and powerful arms had pulverized various giants on numerous military compounds around the world.

He was a career soldier with a foul mouth and a belligerent attitude. His thin dark hair was beginning to recede and spots of gray were developing on his shaggy mustache. Proctor had managed to squeeze the start of a puffy paunch up and into the chest area by applying painful pressure around his waist with a thick belt.

"This hut will be pure," he announced. "I'll deal personally with any gook-loving progressive."

There were one hundred ninety-two prisoners in the camp and this group was divided into four platoons. Each platoon was separated into squads of approximately eight. The men lived in thatched huts which were inadequately heated by unreliable stoves. The rooms were small and bare and one overhead bulb supplied all the light for the cramped quarters.

Hawthorne's Fort Upton briefings had not prepared him for the first stage of the psychologically devised Chinese indoctrination. First of all, the guard assigned to the hut was about as menacing as a five-year-old child. His skin was not bright yellow, his eyes were soft and most of his teeth were missing. The beefy giant was round and flaccid. A broad, asinine grin gave him a permanently jovial expression. His name was Chow Chow.

Hawthorne was perplexed; however, after studying the man carefully on the first day of captivity, he had decided that

Chow Chow was some kind of a Mongolian slave and not truly one of the Red Chinese savages. He also reasoned that the sloppily uniformed soldier would instantly become a killer the moment an American agitated him or defied an order.

On the third day of imprisonment, the new arrivals were told that they must write a detailed autobiography. The Chinese officials asked them to express themselves freely.

The prisoners were not aware that the Reds were following the Russian method of patient indoctrination. This simple exercise was designed to help the camp supervisors "select" and "categorize" the captured American soldiers.

"My fist and a firing squad to any bastard who turns in a paper," Proctor had declared to the men on the night before the scheduled filing date. The entire hut, including Hawthorne, had cooperated with the Sergeant and the requested material was not submitted to the Chinese.

Hawthorne and the others were amazed that the enemy did not retaliate for this open act of defiance. Late that evening, Alvin Proctor explained to an attentive audience the reason for the surprisingly lenient attitude.

"These Chinks respect men who stand up to them as American soldiers." He paced around the hut. "They admire strength and courage and they shit on cowards. This should be a lesson for all future dealings with these yellow pricks."

After two seemingly uneventful weeks, the prisoners were settled into a fixed camp routine and the formal indoctrination periods began. There were lectures and discussions from nine in the morning until noon, and then again from two to four. All prisoners were forced to attend.

Proctor and other combat veterans had organized an effective campaign designed to disrupt the daily sessions and they were able to drown out the various speakers with American songs and loud hand-clapping. The Chinese anticipated the reaction and once again they were lenient for several weeks.

Hawthorne was silent and curious. He studied the speakers and the guards and decided that the briefings at Fort Upton exaggerated the general appearance of the enemy.

At the end of the first month, the Chinese Reds began to tighten the rope and demand more attentiveness and obedience. It started almost imperceptibly. Three noncommissioned officers were expelled from an afternoon lecture and confined to a special hut without exercise privileges for two weeks. The punishment for "immaturity and ignorance" became more severe as the weeks passed. Food rations were reduced and hard-labor details were organized. Eventually the defiance ceased and the indoctrination sessions were strictly controlled by the Chinese.

"Let them waste their breath," Proctor rationalized. "We'll let it go in one hole and out the other."

The prisoners smirked but remained quiet as they sat back with arms folded and pretended to listen.

An elderly Chinese lecturer had attracted Hawthorne's attention. The man was small and thin. He had a kind voice and he moved with great dignity. Hawthorne felt that the old man must surely be very intelligent, cultured and wise. He did not resemble the crude, blood-sucking gargoyles described in the Fort Upton briefings.

The enemy speaker was obviously spouting lies and propaganda, he realized, but he presented them in a civilized manner. The teacher was a soft-spoken man who could not be classified with murderers or assassins. However, he was certain that the elderly Communist was another exception just as Chow Chow was, and soon the enemy would reveal its true face at Camp Six and bear out the description he remembered from Upton.

During the early part of the second month of captivity, a notice was circulated, stating that the camp library would be open from six to nine every evening. Each prisoner would be allowed to use the facilities for a period of two hours. The Chinese considered the library offer a very special privilege and attendance was not enforced.

The small wooden structure, which was located close to the administration shacks, remained empty for the first few weeks, and this too was anticipated by the Chinese. Any prisoner of war accepting the generous enemy offer would obviously be branded a camp progressive and this tag guaranteed a thoroughly miserable existence for the duration of imprisonment.

"Any son-of-a-bitch who takes a walk in that direction will find himself crippled for life or worse." Alvin Proctor was establishing squad policy in reference to the camp library notice. "These gook books are supposed to follow up their goddamn lectures. If a soldier is found in that shack, it means that he's interested in buying what these yellow bastards are selling. The library is off-limits to this hut. Take my advice and keep it that way."

Gerald Hawthorne had read very little in his lifetime. Outside of the required reading of school textbooks, he had managed to complete a few detective stories and one or two science fiction novels. He did not have the patience to concentrate on printed pages for lengthy periods of time. His own daydreams were infinitely more exciting and immeasurably more satisfying.

But the Camp Six proposition, at the time, had very little to do with reading. More than anything else, it presented an opportunity to leave the hut for a few hours each evening and escape Proctor's ranting oratory and the constant stories about broads and battle. It was also an excuse to take another close look at the barbarous Chinese.

One evening, after a full day of careful thought, Gerald Hawthorne decided to defy the squad leader and visit the library.

The wooden shack was warm, comfortable and surprisingly pleasant. The camp officials had made certain that the room was a perfect snare for any potential customers.

They had even spread a few worn but colorful scatter rugs over the roughly planked floor and a tall vase of flowers decorated the center of a long reading table. Several chairs were placed near lamps which provided adequate lighting and the painted shades were welcome luxuries after the glare of overhead bulbs. Makeshift shelves lined the room, well stocked with old and new volumes, selected magazines and various folders.

A small, inconspicuous desk was strategically placed on an elevated platform toward the rear of the library shack. The librarian had a quiet manner, a neat uniform and a pistol strapped to his waist.

Hawthorne observed that there were three prisoners present. Two at the table and one in a chair close to a reading lamp. They did not appear to be aware of each other, nor did they look up as Hawthorne entered. The only sound in the room was the frequent sniffing of one of the prisoners, who evidently had a cold.

Hawthorne walked slowly past the shelves, scanning titles and avoiding eye contact with the guard. The books were strange and without meaning to Hawthorne.

Titles such as *Marxism, Leninism, Mao Tse-tung and the New China, Revolutionary Culture and Scientific Thought, The Battle Against Imperialism, The Peasant and Contemporary Chinese Poetry,* among many too long and complicated to register, struck his eye.

He was more interested in the librarian-guard. This soldier did not resemble Chow Chow or the camp lecturers. He was young with alert eyes and a cold expression. This man might certainly be classified as one of the savages described by the Fort Upton briefing officers. In fact, Hawthorne recalled killing a similar type of Chinese soldier on the ridge while rescuing Robert Bean.

A book title caught Hawthorne's eye as he neared the shelf closest to the desk. The slightly tattered volume was nearly hidden by other publications but he recognized the name of Mark Twain.

Hawthorne was aware that he would have to make a selection of some kind in order to fill his allotted time in the new camp facility. He took the Twain book from the shelf and sat in one of the chairs near a reading lamp. The guard studied him carefully for a few moments, made a note on a desk pad and then turned away.

Hawthorne settled back in the comfortable wooden chair and placed his elbows on the armrests. Cautiously he glanced at the two prisoners at the table. One was an emaciated-looking character, slightly bald, with thick, black-framed spectacles hung low on his nose. He alternated by looking through them and over them every few seconds. He was absorbed in the thickly bound volume he was reading. The younger, heavy-set soldier was coughing, sniffing and wiping his bulbous nose with a dirty brown handkerchief which he held crumpled in his right hand.

The third prisoner was seated on the opposite side of the room nearly hidden from Hawthorne's view by the vase of flowers. He could easily see the bold black title of his book, however. *A History of American Aggression.*

Hawthorne turned back to his own book and flipped through the dog-eared pages of the famous classic. A few interesting passages caught his eye and he took the time to read them. Then out of curiosity, he went back to the beginning and forced himself to focus on the words and homespun style.

After a while, it was evident that for the first time in his young life Hawthorne was caught up in the world of literary fantasy. He read slowly and absorbed every word and the time passed swiftly.

When the library period ended, Hawthorne went to the desk, listed his squad and hut number, signed a small white card, nodded timidly to the guard and left the shack with the book under his arm.

He entered the hut and walked directly to his bunk. The members of the squad were strangely silent. He stuffed the book into a locker box and tried his best to ignore the increasing tension and growing antagonism of the men, who were quietly beginning to surround him.

"Been to the library?"

Alvin Proctor's tone was even more threatening than usual. Hawthorne, with his back to the hut leader, removed his heavy shoes and placed them under the bunk.

He stretched full-length on the worn blanket and stared up at the ceiling. Hawthorne knew that the men were moving closer but still he refused to react. He could picture their faces as they assembled in a tight circle around him.

"I asked you a question, Hawthorne." Proctor's voice was

calm but ominous. "Did you enjoy the library? You'd better answer, you Communist son-of-a-bitch." Hawthorne could sense the group preparing for action.

The Sergeant leaned forward and Hawthorne was forced to look directly into his eyes.

"Are you going to hand over your little book peacefully?" he asked with quiet menace, "or do we have to take it ourselves?"

Hawthorne was silent. Proctor suddenly clamped his hands around Hawthorne's neck, yanked him violently to his feet and slammed him hard against the wall of the hut. The wind was momentarily knocked out of his frail body and he began to choke and wheeze.

Proctor pinned him to the wall with one arm and then smashed him viciously across the face with his opened hand. Hawthorne did not struggle or attempt to retaliate.

"Get the book, Talbot!" he ordered, and his small Southern lackey instantly reached for the lid of the locker. He rummaged for a few seconds, lost patience and then turned the box over, scattering Hawthorne's belongings on the floor of the hut.

Hawthorne looked bitterly at Proctor and then at the jumble of personal items, which included an expert marksman's medal and a small collection of colorful rocks and pebbles. He was thankful that his mother's picture was face-down and out of sight.

"I've got it!" Talbot exclaimed, and then he tossed the book to Martino, who was standing close by.

Sergeant Alvin Proctor slid his muscular arm up to Hawthorne's neck and applied more pressure. "Read the title, Martino," he ordered, glaring into Hawthorne's eyes.

The Italian studied the book cover and hesitated.

"Read the goddamn title!" screamed Proctor. He pushed harder and Hawthorne was finding it more and more difficult to breathe properly.

"The Adventures of Tom Sawyer," said Martino softly.

"What?" Proctor bellowed.

"The Adventures of Tom Sawyer," the Italian repeated. "By Mark Twain."

Proctor released some of the pressure on Hawthorne's neck. "What the fuck are you talking about?" he asked. His face was beginning to flush with anger.

"The title of the book, Sarge," Martino replied.

Some of the other members of the squad moved to the Italian prisoner and glanced over his shoulder.

"Let's see that book, Martino," Proctor growled as he released Hawthorne.

Martino handed the novel to him and then went toward his own bunk.

The Sergeant checked through the pages suspiciously and then inspected the cover. Finally, he threw the book into the disarranged contents of Hawthorne's locker box.

In a sudden rage, Proctor kicked the pebbles violently, scattering them in every direction, all over the hut.

"You arrogant little bastard!" he screamed. And then he turned to the others, who were preparing to climb into their own bunks.

"Listen to me. All of you! I don't give a shit whether it's Karl Marx or Huckleberry Finn! The fucking library is off-limits to the men in this hut!" He looked down at Hawthorne, as the others prepared for lights-out. "Try one more time, you little bastard," he growled. "You'll read your own obituary while I break your fucking neck!"

SEPTEMBER 8, 1961
WAVERLY, MICHIGAN

18 WAVERLY HIGH SCHOOL had been built in the spring of 1925 by the Palmer Corporation, a prominent and reliable Detroit construction firm. The two box-like red-brick buildings were still in excellent condition and the neatly landscaped grounds and compact stadium were frequently displayed in Chamber of Commerce advertising.

Closely trimmed shrubs surrounded the area and large shade trees with thick low-hanging branches stood at precise intervals along the school's sprawling boundaries.

In the late afternoon, on this cloudy day in September, the broad trunk and dense foliage of one of the spreading elms was serving as an excellent hiding place for Gerald Hawthorne.

He had been waiting for nearly an hour. The former Waverly High student had forgotten that Beatrice Powell was usually the last member of the teaching staff to leave the premises.

Most of the money was gone. He had spent the largest portion on whiskey, which had become much more of a necessity than food. Instead of the study, he now locked himself in his own upstairs bedroom each evening.

Hawthorne pounded his fist into the dirt and cursed under his breath. He had always resented Beatrice Powell and now he was being forced to crawl and beg for mercy.

She had once written to the prison camp explaining that a job had been arranged with Allen Porter at Anderson's Hardware. The position would be available as soon as he returned to Waverly, the woman had promised.

Steady work could mean the difference between total annihilation and survival and only the teacher was in a position to arrange the opportunity.

He heard the tap of her heels on the cobblestones. His heart was pounding as he stood up cautiously and tried to conceal himself behind the tree trunk.

"Mrs. Powell," he called in a loud whisper.

The woman was startled. She gasped and stopped abruptly.

"Over here," directed Hawthorne.

The teacher moved closer to the tree. "Who's there?" She was slightly alarmed but curious.

"Gerald Hawthorne," he murmured.

There was complete silence and eventually Hawthorne was forced to step out of his hiding place and face the woman.

Mrs. Powell was glancing around anxiously. "Gerald," she stammered. "What are you doing here?"

"I want to talk to you, Mrs. Powell," he said in a low voice.

"Impossible," she blurted. "You shouldn't be here."

"I have to talk to you," he insisted.

The teacher seemed extremely distressed. She continued to look back nervously at the school building every few seconds.

"Not here," she said finally. "Come to my apartment at ten tonight." She started to walk away and then she added curtly, "Try not to be seen."

Hawthorne watched as Mrs. Powell moved quickly down the path without looking back.

"Why did you want to see me?" Beatrice Powell asked. She was evidently very uncomfortable.

"I need some help."

"There is very little that I can do."

"I don't have any money and I need a job," he said candidly. Mrs. Powell checked her watch and fidgeted on the sofa.

"You must be joking," she responded dryly.

"I'm not." He lit a cigarette and attempted to steady his voice. "What about Mr. Porter at Anderson's Hardware?"

She shook her head in disbelief. "Listen to me, Gerald Hawthorne," she lectured. "You will not get a job with Mr. Porter at Anderson's Hardware or anywhere else in this town. Don't you understand? What you said in the national newspapers about this town, Gerald, will never be forgotten."

Hawthorne took a long, final drag, inhaled deeply and crushed the cigarette out in an ashtray on the floor.

"I don't want to cause you any trouble, Mrs. Powell," he said without looking at her.

She studied him for a moment before speaking. "I can give you some very good advice." Her voice lowered to a stage whisper. "Why don't you sell the house on Elm Drive and leave?"

He looked at her and could not conceal his growing irritation as the woman leaned forward and spoke in a professorial tone of voice.

"You are not welcome here," she said. "And for good reasons. Waverly is a very special town. The people are clean, sensible, hard-working, patriotic and religious. Life here is serene and predictable. In 1953 you disrupted the normalcy of this town. The citizens are going to make certain that you *do not do it again.*"

Hawthorne stared at her grimly.

"I won't sell my house," he announced. "And I will not leave Waverly."

"That's your business," Mrs. Powell replied solemnly. "I'm merely advising you as an old friend."

She stood and walked to the door and Hawthorne followed. She turned to him and her tone was sincere. "You were always an unhappy boy. It breaks my heart to watch your life being destroyed completely. Leave this town and begin again somewhere else."

Hawthorne thought of the day when he had decided to leave school.

Now, so many years later, he was still obliged to turn away from the teacher, bite his lip and stare at the bolt on the door. He could feel the tears beginning to well up inside and it was difficult to check his emotions.

"Wait a moment," Mrs. Powell whispered.

He continued to stare at a spot on the door as she moved away and then returned with her purse. She opened it and took out several bills and pressed them into Hawthorne's hand.

"It isn't much, Gerald," she sighed. "But believe me, this is all I can do for you."

He turned and faced her.

"I don't want to see you again," she said with finality. "I'm certain that you will understand." She opened the bolt. "As a teacher I must protect my special standing in this community. I must also think about my students."

She opened the door of the apartment and Hawthorne left quickly.

He was still clutching Mrs. Powell's donation when he walked slowly out of the apartment building and into the dimly lit street.

He was too disillusioned and upset to worry about the shadows in the park or an emergency short-cut to Elm Drive.

The small iron garden gate was closed and he stood for a

moment under the street lamp. A quick inspection revealed that his working capital had increased by ten dollars. He smoothed out the two bills, folded them carefully with his own five-dollar note and stuffed the wad deeply into a trouser pocket.

He pulled down his bulky tan sweater and stretched it over the precious bankroll. Then Hawthorne started his walk toward home.

MARCH 10, 1951
CAMP SIX
KOREA

19

HAWTHORNE HAD MANAGED to keep to himself since the camp library incident and there were no further acts of open hostility from the inhabitants of Hut Three.

Sergeant Alvin Proctor considered the young prisoner to be a "man on the list" and a potential pushover for special enemy propaganda and indoctrination. He kept a constant eye on Hawthorne's actions and treated him with quiet contempt. The others, however, ignored him completely. They had all been prisoners for nearly six weeks.

Life consisted mainly of indoctrination, a few strenuous work details, minor punishment for most camp offenses, bland food, some trivial harassment, and the usual frustrations and boredom of confinement. The men had not been subjected to formal interrogation or harsh treatment of any kind by the enemy.

Proctor explained that the reasons for the leniency were simple and quite obvious. On February 27, 1951, the Chinese Reds had retreated from Seoul and the capital was now a demolished city. "The yellow bastards are on the run," according to the squad leader.

One afternoon, Chow Chow, who could speak some English, brought a visitor to Hut Three. The man was a Chinese officer, small, neatly uniformed and absolutely silent. He was not introduced to the prisoners.

Chow and the official stood in the center of the hut and the Americans pulled themselves off their bunks and stood at comical attention after the jovial, potbellied guard had squealed the appropriate command.

He placed a large box on the floor of the hut.

"These papers you study," Chow Chow yelled. The official, standing beside him, grimly studied the face of each prisoner very seriously as the guard continued with his instructions in halting English.

"Read them good," Chow Chow went on as he reached into the cardboard box and removed a stack of printed booklets. He handed a folder to each man in the squad.

"In two days," he held up his fingers to indicate the number, *"important men will come. You will tell what you learn."* He looked at Proctor and the permanent, toothless grin had still not faded. *"Understand, Sergeant?"*

"Yes, teacher," said Proctor dully. He thumbed quickly through the printed material. "Any pictures of Chinese broads?"

The crudely printed propaganda material became the basis for lewd comedy in the evenings before lights-out.

"What the hell is it all about?" asked Guzman seriously after one particularly boisterous round of jokes.

Proctor quickly flipped through the pages of a folder. "This is all part of a Communist plan." He looked at Hawthorne. "Anyway, *everybody* in this hut knows how to handle the situation. Right?"

The men nodded and the Sergeant added, "Name, rank and serial number. Or screw them up with some pig latin or baby talk. Suit yourselves."

While Proctor's comedy session was in progress, Hawthorne allowed himself to glance at some of the forbidden phrases in the Communist information booklet.

It was a concentrated, simplified, almost child-like briefing on Chinese history and Hawthorne could not help being fascinated by the achievements of that ancient civilization.

The pamphlet reported that a thousand years before the birth of Alexander the Great, the Chinese people were growing wheat and rice and weaving silk. They were casting bronze and carving jade, fighting with chariots and writing in an alphabet which consisted of over two thousand characters. During the first thousand years before Christ, they were constructing armor and using crossbows and Hawthorne was awed by dates like 240 B.C. and the birth of Confucius in 550 B.C. He wondered how fanatical savages could have accomplished so much.

Two days later, the Chinese Reds arrived at Hut Three to test the American prisoners of war. The squad was not aware that this was the formal beginning of their true indoctrination at Camp Six and the Communists were no longer prepared to tolerate disobedience.

This particular experiment was elementary but it was the start of an important phase of the Red conditioning process: Always trade on the ignorance of the American prisoners.

Gerald Hawthorne had studied and absorbed the enemy pamphlet. He had practically memorized every fact and figure. It was a feat that he had never been able to accomplish in school in Waverly, Michigan.

Chow Chow, with his sloppy tunic buttoned properly for the first time, stood formal guard duty at the entrance while two Red officers moved to the center of the hut. One of them was familiar to the men in Hut Three as the small, silent man who had accompanied Chow Chow on a previous visit. He surprised the squad members by speaking perfect English.

"You may rest at ease, gentlemen," he ordered.

Proctor and the others smirked as they took seats on bunks and on the floor of the hut.

Most eyes were focused on the other officer, a tall slim man of about twenty-five, or thirty at the most. His features were clean-cut and refined but still there was a cold ruthlessness about him that subdued even Proctor. This man was Kwen

San, the camp disciplinarian. His somber expression remained unchanged as he took the measure of each prisoner in the squad. Meanwhile, the small official, paced slowly around the center of the hut as he continued to address the American prisoners of war.

"You people were given special reference material and I assume that you are now prepared for your examinations." He stopped in front of Proctor. "Is your squad prepared, Sergeant?"

The hut leader glanced quickly at Martino, winked, and then smiled at the Red official.

"We're ready," he announced.

"Excellent," said the officer. He motioned to Chow Chow and the guard brought a leather pouch into the hut and handed it to the officer. The friendly giant, on his best military behavior, then returned to his position at the door.

"I will give each of you a prepared test form and you will have exactly one hour in which to complete the answers."

He removed the papers from the pouch and handed one to each man. "We wish you to separate, gentlemen, so that you will be able to think and respond individually." He turned again to Proctor. "Sergeant, have each man return to his own bunk and work from there. The forms will be completed in this manner."

Proctor thought for a moment, grimaced, and then with much exaggerated blustering, shouted his instructions. *"To your bunks, men! On the double!"*

Kwen San muttered a brief statement in Chinese to his colleague, turned around and left the hut. The small officer then spoke to the inmates of Hut Three slowly and very seriously.

"You have exactly one hour in which to complete your test papers," he said crisply. He glanced at his watch. "I suggest that you begin now."

He removed a package of cigarettes from his jacket, lit up, and watched the Americans begin the first serious phase of Communist indoctrination.

The questions were phrased simply and the forms provided ample space for complete and detailed answers. Hawthorne concentrated on the examination and tried to block out the chuckles and frivolous remarks of his fellow prisoners and the frequent calls for silence by the Red officer.

The fascinating names of the great Chinese dynasties had been etched into Hawthorne's brain and he was able to supply the requested information on Han and Tang and Sung and Ming.

He recalled with ease that the Great Wall was more than sixteen hundred miles long, that it was twenty-four feet high and that there were forty-foot towers along the way, that in the seventh century China had built a Grand Canal which linked the Yellow River to the Yangtze.

He enthusiastically replied to every question about the Tang dynasty and its accomplishments, which included the invention of printing, the making of porcelain and the effective use of whale and seal oil. The fact that the Chinese had discovered the principles of fingerprinting had amazed him more than anything else.

He supplied the necessary information on the Sung dynasty and continued to fill out the form until he finished the last question.

He was proud and excited. It was an academic achievement unknown in his young, muddled life. His memory had never been acute, especially where figures and statistics were concerned, and yet he had been able to state that the population of China in the year A.D. 754 was approximately fifty-three million. He had added, without being asked, that by 1762 there were two hundred million Chinese people.

He had completed the test in less than thirty-five minutes.

"Your time is up, gentlemen," the camp official announced.

Chow Chow entered the hut and collected the papers. He handed the forms to the officer and then returned to his guard position at the door.

"I sincerely hope that you did well," the official said sternly. He had taken notice of the men's indifference as well as the obvious attempts to treat the test as a joke.

"These papers are extremely important to all of you." He

placed them carefully inside the leather case and then fastened the strap. "We will discuss the results very shortly."

The Red officer turned and walked briskly out of the hut as the giant guard snapped to attention and made a feeble gesture of assuming a military bearing by pulling in his paunch.

When the official had left, Chow Chow turned to the men of Squad Three and shook his huge head sadly.

"You are stupid," he squealed. *"Now you make bad trouble."*

Late in the afternoon of the following day, the small Chinese officer returned to Hut Three to read a directive which had been signed by the camp disciplinarian, Kwen San.

He announced grimly that the squad had submitted the worst test papers of any group in the entire camp. Smirks and attempts at bravado faded very quickly as the prisoners suddenly realized that the Chinese Communists had stopped playing games and that the punishment outlined in the official camp order was serious. The hut grew quiet.

"All mail, incoming and outgoing, is hereby suspended until further notice. This squad will perform hard labor from six in the morning until the first indoctrination period at nine in the morning."

"What kind of hard labor?" Guzman asked.

"Quiet!" the officer barked and again there was silence in the hut.

"Hard labor will again be assigned to this squad from four in the afternoon until seven o'clock in the evening. Hard labor will continue each day, including Sundays, until the order is adjusted or rescinded by the camp disciplinary authorities. Food rations for this squad will be reduced as of tomorrow morning."

There were curses and groans from the disgruntled American prisoners of war.

"Silence!" the officer shouted. "I warn you to be quiet or you will suffer severe consequences."

He motioned for Chow Chow and the guard moved solemnly

to the center of the hut and stood directly behind the camp official.

"This drastic reduction in food rations will continue for the complete duration of the squad's punishment period. It is also decreed that admittance to the camp library and all other special privileges are hereby suspended until further notice. This order is signed by Kwen San and the camp commandant. It is effective as of this very moment."

The official placed the document into a thin cardboard folder and handed it to Chow Chow. He then addressed Proctor sternly.

"The party is over, Sergeant. I can assure you that Kwen San has been lenient this time. Do not test him further with nonsense or you and your men will discover the true meaning of discipline at Camp Six."

The officer turned and marched abruptly out of the hut, followed by Chow Chow.

There was silence for a few moments as the impact of the visit began to register. Hawthorne lay on his bunk, staring at the wall. The others faced the Sergeant and waited anxiously for his reaction.

"Like I told you before," Proctor said smoothly, "we take whatever these gooks give and we face them as American soldiers. They can't break us."

He swung himself onto his bunk. "Soon, we'll find some interesting ways to get back at these yellow bastards," he said thoughtfully. "I promise you."

Knowing that he had answered every question on the form and in detail, Hawthorne was both surprised and disappointed at the Chinese reaction.

He closed his eyes and thought about his newly acquired knowledge of China. The material in the folder had taught him something new and it was beginning to stimulate his interest in the world around him. This was certainly better than dwelling constantly on a miserable past and present while vegetating with a group of prejudiced military automatons.

He was determined to learn more about China and he was sorry that Kwen San and the camp commandant had closed the camp library.

20

THE CAMP SIX punishment order for the American prisoners of war in Hut Three had lasted for four grueling weeks and the camp officials were more than satisfied with the results.

The consistent hard-labor details combined with a drastic reduction in food rations had effectively sliced the edge off the arrogance and defiance of Sergeant Alvin Proctor and his squad. The suspension of incoming and outgoing mail had also undermined the already deteriorating morale of the American soldiers.

The Red authorities had finally decided that the American prisoners of Squad Three were ready for formal interrogation, and Camp Six, which was considered to be a very special penal institution, was reputed to have the most persuasive and efficient staff in the entire camp system. Each member of this elite staff had attended college in the United States and three had graduated with honors. They were young and aware and they understood the American prisoners very well.

By remaining in contact with various people in the United States, they were well informed on all current American affairs, including politics, entertainment and sports.

The Camp Six interrogation staff had an impeccable record of success with their prisoners and each man on the team was considered to be an expert in his own field. A young official named K. M. Wing, from the town of Tsinan, was no exception.

The interrogation rooms remained open around the clock and they were in constant use. Various methods were used on prisoners, including the "stack" treatment, as it was called in English.

An official-looking pile of documents was usually faked by

the interrogator and placed prominently on the desk during each session, giving the anxious prisoner the impression that his complete background was already well known to his inquisitor. And there was always a pistol lying conspicuously on the desk.

The special rooms at Camp Six were equipped with various listening and recording devices. The prisoner was watched at all times by means of six one-way mirrors which had been installed in each interrogation chamber.

After each session, the captive was ordered to complete a detailed form. This information was used during his next interrogation in order to minimize his chances of concocting a false story.

Conflicting reports had spread throughout the camp in reference to these frightening interviews. Hawthorne remembered his briefings at Fort Upton and he was prepared for the worst.

A particularly horrific account of one session had been circulated recently among the prisoners concerning a soldier from Butte, Montana. Sergeant Proctor informed his men of the gruesome details.

"The bastards wanted some special information about troop movements from this kid," he told the squad. "The boy refused and the gooks strapped him in a chair and slowly sliced off one of his ears with a fucking razor blade."

"Jesus Christ," Landau gasped.

"The kid fainted," Proctor continued, "then they shook him awake and kept up the questioning."

"Did he talk?" asked Talbot.

"Name, rank and serial number is all they got," the Sergeant replied. He bowed his head and paused for a moment before continuing. "The gooks took off his other ear."

There was complete silence in the hut until Hymie Landau asked, "Is the kid dead?"

"No," Proctor replied, "but he sure as hell wants to be."

"Where is he?" asked Gordon.

"The camp butcher shop," Proctor answered. "I hear the Chink doctors have been cutting him up a little at a time.

They want that information real bad and I guess this kid knows something."

"Dirty, rotten yellow bastards," Page cursed bitterly.

"The gook interrogator was called K. M. Wing," said Proctor. "I won't forget that name. Nobody in this goddamn Army should."

"The kid rates the Congressional Medal," Guzman announced.

"No, he doesn't, Pancho," Proctor replied. "He doesn't rate anything special. The kid was doing his job as an American soldier and every man in this hut will do exactly the same when the time comes." Once again the Sergeant glanced at Hawthorne and their eyes met. "American soldiers. Right, Corporal Hawthorne? Whether they cut off your ears or your balls."

Hawthorne turned away without responding.

On March 7, 1951, General Douglas MacArthur had predicted a stalemate in Korea, and on March 21 the Chinese Reds were continuing their retreat to the 38th parallel. March 24 marked the date when MacArthur became unpopular with President Truman for suggesting an attack on China.

On April 2, 1951, the United Nations troops followed the Reds back over the line and on April 11 MacArthur was dismissed by the President because of his China attack theory.

In the late afternoon of April 17, Chow Chow entered Hut Three and announced that Sergeant Alvin Proctor and Corporal Gerald Howard Hawthorne were both scheduled for immediate interrogation and that they were ordered to accompany him without delay.

Both men were marched to the camp administration sector, which consisted of three wooden barn-like structures surrounded by six smaller planked and thatched sheds.

Proctor was pleased when he discovered that he was being deposited at Building Two, which was known to be supervised by one of the most lenient interrogators on the camp staff. Hawthorne was hustled to Building One, which was the domain of the infamous K. M. Wing.

He was told to wait outside the door of a small room in the

crudely built structure. Hawthorne sat on a low wooden bench under the watchful eyes of Chow Chow and another armed guard who was positioned in the hall, close to the entrance of the busy building.

The young prisoner thought of the sadistic tortures awaiting him and he pledged to resist the interrogator with more strength and courage than Alvin Proctor or any other member of his squad.

Chow Chow checked his watch and then tapped Hawthorne lightly on the shoulder.

"*Get up,*" he ordered with his usual grin. "*You go in now.*"

The room was much larger and more comfortable-looking than Hawthorne had imagined. In fact, there was a rug on the floor, a well-stocked bookcase and two small reading lamps. A low, round wooden table was located in the center of the room and it was surrounded by several comfortable leather chairs.

A young man was seated behind a desk in the far corner of the office. Oddly enough, he was not wearing a Chinese Army uniform. Hawthorne observed a stack of official-looking documents in front of the man and a pistol resting on the top of the pile.

Chow Chow closed the door very quietly behind him and Hawthorne heard the guard settling on the bench in the hall.

"Come in and take a seat, Hawthorne," the man said in flawless English. He stood behind his desk, smiled warmly and motioned to one of the leather chairs.

He was trimly built, of average height with good looks and an elegant manner. He was wearing a stylish black turtleneck sweater and snug-fitting gray slacks and seemed to be in his late twenties or early thirties. Hawthorne stood transfixed, completely confused and bewildered as he took note of the man's collegiate-American appearance and behavior.

The official politely waved Hawthorne to the chair again. With an effort, Hawthorne walked over and sat down awkwardly.

"I don't think we'll be needing this," the man chuckled as he carefully placed the pistol into the bottom drawer of his desk. Then he walked to one of the chairs facing Hawthorne and took a seat.

"My name is K. M. Wing and I've been waiting to meet you." He took out a pack of American cigarettes and offered one to the startled prisoner of war.

Hawthorne shook his head, and the interrogator tossed the pack on the table, pretending to ignore the boy's nervousness and apprehension. He lit up and relaxed against the comfortable leather.

"I understand how you must feel," he said gently, "and I can assure you that I will not be offended by your silence or uneasiness."

He paused and studied Hawthorne for a moment before continuing. "You are not here today for standard interrogation, Corporal. Consider this an introductory meeting but please understand that you will be required to tolerate much more formality in the future."

Hawthorne was stunned by the unexpected atmosphere of the interrogation room. He was certain that the suave and cultured gentleman sitting opposite him was an impostor and that soon a brutal and impressively uniformed K. M. Wing would step into the office.

"The result of your test was excellent, Hawthorne," the man was saying. "One of the most impressive I've seen here at the camp. Are you interested in history?"

The boy hesitated and then nodded.

"I showed your work to a few of my superiors and they were very pleased with your enthusiasm and intelligence."

Wing leaned forward and pushed the cigarettes toward the prisoner. "Hell, have a smoke." He smiled broadly and held the pack up for Hawthorne. "I wouldn't call it collaboration with the enemy," he added.

Hawthorne had not anticipated this recognition of his work on the examination paper, and the sudden praise combined with a burning desire for a cigarette was enough of an inducement. The interrogator lit it for him with an unusually designed gold pocket lighter. Hawthorne caught a glimpse of a dragon breathing fire and there were initials engraved on both sides.

"I instructed Kwen San to ignore your fine efforts on the test," he apologized. "I'm sorry that you were forced to participate in the punishment program with the rest of the squad but I did not want you to have problems with Proctor and the other men in the hut." He looked carefully at Hawthorne. "The sergeant *is* a problem. Am I correct?"

Hawthorne did not respond and Wing took a long drag of his cigarette. "You don't have to answer," he said quietly. "I have had a great deal of experience in dealing with men like Alvin Proctor. Your staunch patriotic leader will undoubtedly be the first member of the squad to betray his country. You will soon see that I am correct."

The interrogator stood, walked to his desk and studied one of the papers at the top of the stack.

"I have a copy of your citation for winning the Silver Star." He waved the paper and then placed it back on the desk. "I respect bravery as well as intelligence. Especially since I have not participated in actual combat."

Wing sat behind his desk and motioned for Hawthorne to take a seat in a chair across from him. "I must say that I am very happy to have missed the experience."

Hawthorne moved apprehensively to the desk, holding the butt of his cigarette, and the interrogator pointed to an ashtray next to the chair. The prisoner used it and then sat rigidly facing K. M. Wing.

"I am also aware of the unfortunate blunder in which you participated as a combat soldier when your own men were killed." He paused and checked several papers on his desk. "Another shocking incident in the utter stupidity of war." The man sighed wearily. "I hope that you do not feel any personal guilt for this slaughter. We always have to trace this sort of thing straight to the top."

He inspected another document. "Speaking of war, I have some distressing news for you. The United Nations forces are being pushed back again, which means that we will all be involved in this struggle for a very long time."

Wing sat back in his chair and smiled.

"If you knew more of our Chinese history you would understand why it is so difficult for your wealthy and powerful military tacticians to end this affair quickly and successfully. Have you ever heard of Sun Wu?"

Hawthorne shook his head. He could not conceal his interest.

"All warfare is based on deception and Sun Wu was the tactical master. His teachings were passed along through the years and today my people have been proving the brilliance of his military principles."

Hawthorne suddenly realized by the expression on Wing's face that he was a good deal more oriented toward prison-camp mentality than might have been suspected at first.

"For example," he explained, "when the enemy advances, withdraw! When the enemy halts, harass! When the enemy avoids battle, attack! And when the enemy retreats, pursue! Interesting?" Hawthorne nodded. "Someday, if you are truly interested, we'll talk about Sun Wu and even the Taoist philosophy which was developed before him."

The interrogator stood and then walked to his bookcase and pointed to the contents. "I understand that you admire the works of Mark Twain?" He turned to Hawthorne. "Am I correct?"

"Yes," Hawthorne answered softly.

"I also appreciate this particular author," Wing continued. "There are several books here by Twain and I will have them transferred immediately to the camp library."

He checked several volumes in the ornate wooden case. "Do you like Robert Louis Stevenson?"

"I haven't read much," Hawthorne replied.

"Look carefully in the library and you will find some interesting and informative material. Read for enjoyment and read what you like."

He walked back to his desk and took a seat facing Hawthorne.

"You have intelligence and curiosity and you seem to have an open mind. The camp library is at your disposal and I can assure you that you will not be limited to required reading." He smiled. "If you know what I mean."

The interrogator began to place the stack of documents into several official-looking folders marked: *"Hawthorne, Gerald Howard. Corporal, United States Army."*

"I am also a curious man," he said, putting the material neatly into one of the desk drawers.

"I am fascinated by suburban America, for example. I used to live just outside of Los Angeles in a very small community. I'd like to know more about Waverly, Michigan, and the people and the way of life. Perhaps you would be interested in my hometown called Tsinan. Quite a contrast. We'll exchange stories some other day."

He pointed to the remaining cigarettes in the pack. "I'd give these to you, Hawthorne, but I don't want you to go back to the hut looking as though you have been bribed for delivering the detailed secrets of American rocket power." He laughed, started to get up and then hesitated.

"I told you at the beginning that your silence and apprehension would not offend me. It is understandable. We will have further talks in the future." He stood. "Remember, you can always ask me questions and I will be happy to answer them. Is there anything that you would like to ask me now?"

Hawthorne wondered if he had the courage to ask. He decided to put K. M. Wing's honesty and sincerity to the test.

"Did you ever talk to a boy from Butte, Montana?" Hawthorne inquired in a voice which had come close to trembling.

"Wayne Cunningham?"

"I don't know."

"Yes," said the interrogator. "His name was Wayne Cunningham. Why?"

"Can I ask what happened to him?" He was trying desperately to control the sound of his voice.

K. M. Wing sat down again and stared at Hawthorne thoughtfully. "I do not ordinarily discuss other prisoners," he said sternly. "Is this man a friend of yours?"

"No."

"Do you know him at all?"

"No."

"Then why is his particular situation important to you?"

Hawthorne thought for a moment before answering and then he took the plunge. "Proctor said that something terrible happened to him after he met with you."

The interrogator nodded knowingly. "Oh, I understand," he said. He hesitated and then reached into a drawer and removed a thick folder. "I will make an exception in this case," he said, removing a document and placing it on the desk.

"Proctor is correct," he said. "Something did happen to Private Wayne Cunningham shortly after he had a brief visit with me in this office. A ruptured appendix had turned gangrenous and the young prisoner was rushed to the camp hospital. He is still gravely ill."

Wing returned the folder to the desk drawer and then addressed Hawthorne very seriously.

"You will hear many reports in reference to prison indoctrination, interrogation and camp disciplinary action." His face was grim as he studied Hawthorne. "Most of the information will be pure fantasy and fabrication."

He lowered his voice. "However, understand that you will also find that some of this talk will be true." He paused and put out his cigarette in an ornamental tray on the desk. "After all, this is a prisoner-of-war camp and not an American mountain resort in the Catskills. Do you understand, Hawthorne?"

The prisoner nodded.

"You will go back now and we will talk again at another time," Wing said. "Once again I want to congratulate you on your excellent test paper and urge you to make good use of the camp library."

Hawthorne rose to his feet as Wing spoke quietly and almost confidentially. "We will have scheduled meetings in the near future but you can arrange an informal session with me at any time by mentioning it to your hut guard." He nodded politely. "Good afternoon, Hawthorne."

K. M. Wing shouted for the guard in Chinese and Chow Chow entered the interrogator's office.

That evening Hawthorne remained on his bunk, face to the wooden wall of Hut Three, and listened to the dramatic account of Sergeant Alvin Proctor's interrogation session in Building Two.

"Name, rank and serial number, you Red bastard," the squad leader was reporting. "That's exactly what I told him."

The Sergeant glared at Hawthorne's bunk. "These people wait for the easy targets and I have a strong feeling that this character they call K. M. Wing has already hit a bull's-eye."

The group immediately turned their attention to Hawthorne, who still had his back turned.

"Word gets around fast in this place," Proctor warned. "Are you listening, Hawthorne?" Hawthorne did not move or respond. "We'll know every time you kiss a Chink's ass and I promise you quick and very personal attention."

The boy from Waverly ignored the threat. He resolved to learn more about China and the Chinese people by using the camp library. Regardless of the risks involved.

SEPTEMBER 19, 1961
NEW YORK CITY

21 FRAN PATTERSON, WITH the able technical assistance of several members of the engineering staff, had transformed Amalgamated's Studio B into a shimmering midnight fun factory. She had created a festive orgy of fine cuisine, flowing wine and booze, and had hired some talented jazz musicians to provide the entertainment. The Hawthorne tape had been well received by the press and the public, and this favorable reaction would of course help to prime the Amalgamated syndicated sales force as the men prepared a hard-hitting sweep across the nation.

Station switchboards in New York, Los Angeles and other key markets had been inundated with calls and this certainly reflected the extent of the public's interest and indignation about the unrepentant traitor.

Mail response had reached an all-time peak in New York and Los Angeles and the other local operations had already reported that similar records would probably be achieved by the end of the week.

A few of the letters and telephone calls had expressed a certain amount of sympathy for the returning veteran, but this reaction was triggered mainly by a general dislike for Arthur Fremantle and his overpowering, obnoxious approach to television interviewing. The veteran broadcaster had been recently discharged from the hospital and was now recuperating at his ranch in Palo Alto, California.

Spirits were high at Amalgamated Broadcasting, amid much self-congratulation at their handling of the Turncoat affair.

At precisely one forty-five in the morning, Fred Schroeder approached his program boss, who was in the process of offering formal congratulations and personal thanks to the engineer for his creative video tape editing of the Hawthorne interview.

"Can I see you for a minute, Mr. Spangler?" He motioned urgently.

"Why?"

"You have a telephone call in the control room," Schroeder replied. "The man said that the call is urgent. And it sounds that way to me."

He took Spangler by the arm and the unsteady executive grunted and pulled away.

"What man?" Spangler asked. "What the hell are you talking about?"

"His name is Hector Rambeau," Schroeder replied.

Gerald Howard Hawthorne was rapidly sinking into a world of apathetic fantasy. Insanity was an imminent possibility, perhaps even death by starvation unless he could come up with a positive and realistic plan of action.

He sat nearly stupefied in a corner of the Elm Drive living room and stared at the thin shaft of sunlight glancing off the window ledge, warming his pale features.

A few days earlier, he had discovered several light wooden planks under the kitchen sink which he had nailed firmly over the broken windows at the front of the house. He had left a slight opening between the boards in order to provide a peep-hole for constant vigilance. It afforded a narrow but ade-quate view of the overgrown front yard.

He leaned back against the wall and proceeded with an inventory of his circumstances. His deteriorating health was a major factor. Lack of nourishment was making him weak, list-less and practically bedridden.

His rations were now severely depleted and he was now existing on a few potatoes and a large box of stale biscuits. If he had any money, of course, he could subsist on food pur-chased from the crazy lady.

He had spent most of his time in the downstairs study. He still had not been able to bring himself to explore the base-ment of the house or his father's room on the floor above.

His mother's quarters remained locked and bolted. He knew now that he would never have the courage to enter this shrine.

Several days earlier, during a particularly depressing period of pain and hunger, he had scribbled a pathetic note to Robert Calhoun Spangler at Amalgamated Broadcasting Television in New York City. He had mailed it in the early hours of the morning at the corner when the street appeared to be deserted.

He had asked about the possibility of arranging a loan from the company and had stated his willingness to sign a "written and legal" promise to repay the debt *with interest* as soon as Spangler's pledged compensation arrived in Wav-erly. Or, "if it is more convenient," the company could deduct the amount from his initial television earnings.

Ironically, an answer arrived from the New York program executive on the day after the taped interview had been trans-mitted on the corporation's Detroit station.

The reply was brief and business-like. The executive stated that the recorded television interview had not as yet been assigned to the corporate syndicated sales force for national distribution and therefore contractually the company was not required to compensate Mr. Hawthorne for his participation until all program costs had been recouped.

Spangler had been kind enough to enclose a current account-ing of these expenditures and the list was lengthy.

At the close of the formal declaration, Spangler had added the following paragraphs.

"I am very sorry to hear about your unfortunate financial situation, Gerald. Your request for assistance has been thoroughly explored by our Corporate Legal Department and I must inform you that this company, for many reasons, technically and legally, cannot advance funds for program participation and will not consider the granting of loans to anyone.

"I can assure you that this decision has nothing to do with you personally. It is based entirely on corporate policy and the ruling holds for every employee of Amalgamated Broadcasting Television."

Five crisp, new ten-dollar bills were folded neatly with the letter. There was a brief handwritten note on a small sheet of white paper:

"This has nothing to do with my company. And do not consider this a loan or an advance. It is a personal gesture of thank you for your cooperation and participation."

It was signed "Bob Spangler."

He had smirked and counted the money carefully before shoving the bills into his back pocket. Then, he had read the television executive's document at least three times before tossing it into a wastepaper basket in the study. He felt sad and disappointed, then angry.

A cheerful ray of sunshine was piercing the crack between the two protective wooden panels which covered the front windows. It was inviting. He got up and moved toward the makeshift peephole.

What he saw forced him to pull back abruptly and he nearly fell over backwards. He blinked and peeked out once again and this time he allowed the incredible scene to register.

An orderly crowd, perhaps fifteen or twenty people, was gathered outside his fence. They were quietly and curiously gaping at the house, like Sunday tourists inspecting an important monument of special historical significance. The men were pointing and the women were nodding and several children seemed to be receiving serious lectures from a group of elders.

Hawthorne stepped back, shaking his head in disbelief. He managed to navigate his way back to the large kitchen at the rear of the house.

He cautiously moved aside the shade on one of the shuttered windows and glanced through a narrow opening.

Once again he was startled by the sight. There was another crowd on this side of the house. His astonishment grew as he realized that some members of this group were standing in the tall grass *inside* the yard, close to the wire fence and gate.

They too were quiet, inquisitive and nonmilitant.

Hawthorne released the blind and flopped into a chair near the kitchen table. He was dazed and confused by the unexpected activity around his house.

After a period of reflection, he realized that days and nights must have slipped by and his television interview had at last been transmitted in the United States. His face and voice and actions were now known to millions of American people, and the curious visitors were staring at the Turncoat's suburban prison.

SEPTEMBER 20, 1961
NEW YORK CITY

22

SPANGLER COULD NOT SLEEP.

He reached for the alarm clock on the night table, drew it close to his face, squinted, and cursed at the illuminated dial. It was four o'clock in the morning, and he had been twisting and pounding hell out of his pillow for three restless hours.

The executive sat up, pressed a light switch and removed a cigarette from a pack on the night table. His pajamas were damp around the collar. He could not get the hotel meeting out of his mind.

Hector Rambeau and his associates had been effective.

Very few human beings were able to upset Spangler's equilibrium, causing him to break out in a cold sweat and pass a sleepless night. He ran the scene back through his mind.

The telephone contact at the studio party had set up a four o'clock afternoon session at Rambeau's Warwick suite.

Spangler had been greeted rather coolly by two gentlemen who were in the process of packing several suitcases. Shower water could be heard running in the bath and it was apparent that the group was preparing for departure.

The taller of the two men had short blond hair and a bronzed, weatherworn complexion. He stopped his work for a moment and motioned to a chair.

"Sorry, Mr. Spangler," he said apologetically. Then he nodded in the direction of the bathroom. "Mr. Rambeau is getting ready for an unexpected flight back to Washington. He'll be with you in a few minutes."

Spangler took a seat by the window without responding and the man pointed to a bar. "Please help yourself to a drink."

"No, thank you," the executive replied curtly. He studied both men as they resumed their duties for one of the world's wealthiest and most influential operators.

Spangler prepared himself for his first personal meeting with Hector Rambeau. He had seen the South American tycoon at various functions in New York, Washington and Los Angeles but several requests for a formal introduction had been denied by the members of his permanent entourage.

Rambeau walked briskly into the room. He was barechested and wore a towel wrapped around his neck. His hair was still wet and uncombed and he was wearing dark slacks and red slippers.

He moved directly to the shorter, dark man without acknowledging Spangler's presence.

"I changed my mind, Morales." He pointed to a neatly packed shirt in one of the cases. "Give me that one."

"I'll pack the other one," the subordinate replied.

"Later," Rambeau snapped, "when I finish."

Santo Morales nodded obediently and the tycoon headed back into the bathroom, still dripping water on the ornate Warwick rug. He left the door open as he completed his toilet. Rambeau's voice blasted out from the bathroom once again.

"Ordinarily, I have better manners, Spangler." It sounded as though the man was brushing his hair vigorously. "But in this particular case I refuse to acknowledge scum."

The program executive was startled by the words and the tone.

"I have another appointment," he said hesitantly to the two men opposite him. "Mr. Rambeau will have to excuse me."

Santo Morales and Clete Hardigan glanced toward the open door as their employer entered the room.

He was buttoning the sleeves of an expensively tailored silk shirt and his thick, wavy black hair had been carefully combed, brushed and conditioned.

"I will never excuse you, Spangler," he said coldly, disappearing into one of the bedrooms.

His two agents watched the television executive as he slowly and cautiously started to rise to his feet.

In a moment, Rambeau had reentered, carrying a small glass container. He moved directly to the far side of the room and inspected himself in a full-length mirror. Then he began to pat lotion on his face. Spangler gradually lowered himself back into the chair.

"I detest two things on this earth," said Rambeau. He continued to adjust his appearance in front of the glass. "Midgets who want to be giants and whores who accept fees and then refuse to complete the act."

He tossed the small glass container to Santo and turned to Spangler. "You fall into both of these categories, mister."

Rambeau moved to a comfortable-looking overstuffed armchair and sat facing Spangler and the two associates. As Spangler opened his mouth to speak, Rambeau held up his hand. "I'll talk," he said quietly. "You listen."

Spangler was still astonished by the unexpected treatment. He was outraged to find himself on the receiving end of such insults and open contempt.

"I have to catch a plane," said Rambeau smoothly, "so I'll be as brief as possible." He turned to Morales. "Better check the car and pick up that package for my wife."

The man nodded and left the room quickly. Rambeau turned back to his visitor.

"Years ago, a few mistakes were made by some dear friends of mine," the financier stated levelly. "The pressure of the times had caused a particular blunder and this blunder was clumsily covered up with a slight indiscretion. This slight indiscretion soon developed into outright stupidity."

He studied Spangler for a moment before continuing. "It was a shame because these acts were committed in good faith by competent and dedicated public servants."

"May I ask one simple question?" Spangler ventured.

"Let me finish," Rambeau replied sharply. "We finally managed to smooth out these problems so our government could get on with important affairs of state."

He took a cigarette out of a case but did not offer one to Spangler. Hardigan leaned over and lit it for him.

"All of this *started* with Gerald Howard Hawthorne at the time of McCarthy," he continued. "This man was and *is* the key to the entire affair for many reasons."

Rambeau stood and walked to a wardrobe in the corner of the room. He selected a jacket, slung it over his shoulder and returned to the chair. Spangler's attention was riveted at the mention of the Turncoat's name.

"As years went by, several of my friends moved into more prominent positions in the government and today their accomplishments stand as a matter of historical record. One particular friend is . . . ," he paused and selected the correct wording, "nearing the pinnacle of his political career."

He put on his jacket and adjusted it carefully.

"Gerald Hawthorne," he continued, "is an insignificant man who spent eight years in Red China. God knows what else he did—I am not particularly interested in the story of his life. I *am* concerned about his actions since he returned to this country."

Rambeau walked back to the mirror and inspected the jacket and trousers. He continued, "If this man is given the opportunity to enlist the aid of attorneys in order to take some kind of action or if his case is taken up by some lunatic, crusading organization . . ."

He walked back to the chair. "If there is an investigation *of any kind,* my friends and the government of the United States will face many serious problems."

Rambeau glared at Spangler.

"You agreed to help us."

Spangler was growing weary of the lecture and was less intimidated than he had been at the start of the meeting.

"I think I've heard just about enough, Mr. Rambeau," he interrupted firmly.

The room was silent. Hardigan continued to stare at him coldly and Rambeau's expression did not change.

"Please get to the point." Spangler glanced mechanically at his watch. "I do have another appointment."

Rambeau continued with his smooth declaration as though Spangler had not spoken.

"You accepted a part payment of ten thousand dollars and agreed to follow our instructions in reference to the treatment of Gerald Hawthorne."

Morales entered the suite, placed a small gift-wrapped package next to the suitcases and sat down quietly.

"You purposely failed to fulfill the terms of our agreement," the tycoon continued slowly, "and instead you reversed your position completely and tried in every way to work against the basic conditions of our understanding. And you are still doing this."

He paused and turned quickly to Morales. "Everything okay?"

The man nodded and pointed to the parcel. Rambeau smiled. "Grace will love it." He nudged Hardigan with his elbow. "For that kind of money I'd wear it around my own neck."

He turned back to Spangler and his expression was cold and scornful once again.

"I am in a position to do several things at the moment,

Spangler," he went on grimly. "I don't have to draw pictures for you."

Rambeau glanced at his wife's present. "It must be very obvious to you that ten thousand dollars will not break me. But, as I told you, I refuse to pay a prostitute without getting something for my money."

He leaned forward and his voice took on an even sharper edge.

"Let me put it this way. Your career and your health will now depend on Gerald Howard Hawthorne."

Spangler was taken aback by the warning. "How dare you threaten me? I'm not one of your goddamn trained monkeys."

"I'm not threatening you, Spangler," Rambeau replied firmly. "I'm *promising* you." He stood, walked to the suitcases and inspected the special wrapping on his gift. "You happen to be lucky so far," he continued. "Your television program has attracted some attention but to the best of my knowledge no one has come forward to cause any important trouble."

He handed the box to Morales. "Pack it in the small case when we leave," he ordered.

The man nodded and Rambeau walked back to Spangler. "It seems that Hawthorne is a mixed-up drunk who will probably keep to himself until he hits the gutter and drains down the sewer with the rest of the world's garbage. You had better hope so."

Rambeau stopped abruptly and glanced at Hardigan. "I'm going downstairs for a few minutes. Mr. Hardigan and Mr. Morales will explain exactly how this game will be played from now on."

He made his exit and Santo Morales sat down with his colleague in the chair opposite Spangler.

"We'll only keep you for a couple of minutes, Mr. Spangler," Hardigan said. "I know that you have another appointment."

He offered Spangler a cigarette.

"No, thank you," the executive snapped. "Just get this crap over with as quickly as possible."

Hardigan smiled and handed the pack to his friend.

"I'll do my best, Mr. Spangler," he said, purposely taking his time. "We understand that you are now preparing a special program with veterans' organizations, former government officials and a group of legal authorities. Is this correct?"

"It's a program segment, not a program," Spangler replied impatiently.

"I'm sorry, Mr. Spangler," said Hardigan, with an exaggerated smile. "I don't know too much about television production."

"Some stations have demanded more program balance. We'll tack this segment to the interview for syndication." He did not attempt to hide his irritation. "Does that answer your question?"

"Yes, it does."

"Anything else?"

Morales handed the pack of cigarettes back to Hardigan and entered the conversation, speaking softly but with authority.

"Mr. Rambeau feels that a feature of this kind could be troublesome and he wants you to forget it."

Spangler shook his head in disbelief and then lost control.

"Fuck Mr. Rambeau," he bellowed. *"And fuck you! Both of you!"*

He stood and faced the two calm but grim-faced men.

"You people are jerking with the wrong man," Spangler blasted. "I'm not Arthur Fremantle. If you try to push me around in any way, I'll have you and your goddamn boss put away for life. *Do you understand?"*

"Yes we do, Mr. Spangler," Hardigan replied politely. "But we're afraid that *you* don't understand."

"I understand more than you think." Spangler walked back to his chair and took a seat. His confidence was building now that he was on the offensive.

"Now I'll talk and you listen," he ordered. "Take this message back to your boss. Hector Rambeau paid me ten thousand dollars. I did not ask for or receive the two remaining payments. I knocked the hell out of Hawthorne's credibility and I kept him away from the press. I have him under an exclusive contract for one year and he cannot grant an interview or make an appearance of any kind without my approval."

He paused and lit a cigarette. The two men listened, making no attempt to interrupt.

"As far as I'm concerned, my actions justified the money," he continued. "Everything else from now on will be my business. I consider the obligation to be paid in full." He lowered his voice. "Frankly, I don't want Hawthorne to vanish quietly into the sticks of Michigan. I want the dirty bastard to pay for his crimes."

"Are you finished, Mr. Spangler?" Hardigan asked politely.

"Yes, I am," Spangler replied. He checked his watch again. "It's late and I have to leave."

"Just a few more minutes," Morales said. "I think my colleague here analyzed the situation very clearly."

"What do you mean?" asked Spangler.

"You truly do not understand."

"Understand *what?*"

"You will not tape an additional segment for your interview and you had better hope that Hawthorne fades away very fast."

Morales spoke very softly, savoring each word.

"This meeting is over, gentlemen," Spangler said hesitantly, getting to his feet.

"Sit down!" Morales ordered. *"Don't be a damned fool!* We have a file on you as thick as your head," the agent continued. "Everything from petty tax-return manipulating to the suspected rape of a twelve-year-old girl in Allentown, Pennsylvania. You were employed at a radio station there. *Everything,* Spangler. *Every* indiscretion, *petty* and *grand,* is detailed in our special folder."

Spangler sat back stupefied as Hardigan came to his chair and put a hand on his shoulder.

"Ever heard of a man called Ellsworth Plant?" he asked. "Ellsworth Plant is a former convict, a man who has been booked and accused of just about every crime on earth, with the possible exception of cattle rustling." He smiled and shook his head. "Most of the time this slippery character has been able to beat the conviction and get right back into business again."

Spangler shifted nervously in his chair. "Very interesting," he commented hesitantly. "But what the hell does it have to do with me?"

"He gave you the money," Morales responded matter-of-factly.

"*What money?*" Spangler gasped.

"Ten thousand dollars, Mr. Spangler." Clete Hardigan grinned.

"You people are crazy," he stammered, trying to compose himself.

"Plant made a pay-off to you in the Barbary Room on East 63rd Street and we have the date and the time."

"You're lying!" blasted Spangler.

"What a scandal," Hardigan drawled calmly. "Amalgamated's glamor boy associated with a convicted extortionist."

"You are both liars," Spangler repeated with shaky conviction. "This is a con job and I won't fall for it."

Santo Morales looked at his watch and tapped Hardigan on the shoulder.

"It's getting late," he said. "Let's wrap this thing up."

They stood and Hardigan reached into his inside jacket pocket, and brought out a sealed brown envelope. He handed it solemnly to his partner.

"We have to pick up Mr. Rambeau in a few minutes," Morales explained. "You might be a sharp television producer, Spangler, but as a man of the world, well, you've got a lot to learn."

He waved the envelope.

"This package contains a very special present for you from Mr. Rambeau." He tapped it with his finger. "Don't worry. No money. Just photographs."

Spangler watched the man anxiously but did not respond.

Morales dropped the parcel onto Spangler's lap and then turned to his colleague. "Pack the small bag, Hardigan, and don't forget Mrs. Rambeau's package."

Hardigan stared at Spangler for a moment, smirked and then went into the bathroom.

Morales stood quietly by the chair and watched the program executive tear open the envelope. Spangler grimly studied three snapshots, the indisputable evidence of his misconduct.

Hardigan did not gloat over Spangler's discomfort. "This Hawthorne affair is very important to Mr. Hector Rambeau and to several prominent American officials," he explained softly. "We intend to do everything possible to eliminate serious trouble."

He held the door of the suite open and Spangler left hurriedly.

Spangler gave up the idea of sleeping, got out of bed, opened the bedroom door and yelled down the hall.

"*Nora!*"

It was still difficult to take in the incredible details of the Rambeau conference.

A drowsy Jamaican maid entered the room, wearing a negligee.

"Call Fran Patterson," he ordered.

"It's six-thirty in the morning, Mr. Spangler," she reminded him.

"*I don't give a damn!*" he howled. "*Wake her up!*"

She watched him walk over to the bed and sit down.

"Do you want me to switch it in here?" she asked.

"No," he answered sharply. "I don't want to talk to her. Tell her to call Dorfman, Schroeder and Henderson. I've decided to cancel the Hawthorne discussion segment." His voice was bitter and hostile. "We'll play the exact tape in syndication."

"What time are you leaving for the office?" the maid asked.

"I'm not going in at all today. Tell her I had a bad night." He thought for a moment. "Ask her to arrange a full program meeting with all department heads tomorrow at ten in the morning."

Spangler turned his back to Nora and she shook her head slowly. "Man, you certainly are in a state."

"I'll survive," he mumbled. "Go call Fran Patterson."

23 THE FIRST MEETING with K. M. Wing had occurred on April 17 and Hawthorne soon realized that the interrogator had told the truth about many things, including the skill and tactics of the Chinese Red Army. On April 22, 1951, the United Nations forces had been pushed back once again and the futile war was obviously destined to continue for quite a while.

The boy from Butte, Montana, still had both of his ears and on April 29 he had been discharged from the prison hospital after recovering from a case of acute appendicitis.

K. M. Wing had kept his promise and donated several of his own books to the camp library so that Hawthorne had been able to continue with his new interest in reading.

He had visited the library on four occasions and this questionable conduct had resulted in a steady campaign of hatred and persecution by the other members of his squad. Hawthorne had limited his reading to American novels, although his interest in the Chinese people had been growing with each passing day.

He had been very careful not to handle any library book or periodical which appeared to contain information about communism or even about China.

Two weeks had passed slowly and Hawthorne wondered why he had not been called back for any further interrogation. Proctor and the other men had been summoned on numerous occasions and their accounts of the grueling interviews were always the same. Name, rank and serial number only . . . American military bravery in the face of possible torture and death . . . patriotism and honor . . . and screw the yellow Chink bastards.

Hawthorne was being ignored both by the Americans and the Chinese Reds and he was baffled.

One evening in June, four selected squads of prisoners were summoned to the main indoctrination hall, where they were subjected to a complicated and repetitious lecture by a visiting Communist dignitary from Peking. The official preached in glowing terms about Mao Tse-tung, his mandate from the masses and his exemplary government of the people.

As usual, Gerald Hawthorne listened with keen interest and tried his best to absorb every detail.

The Communist official glorified Mao's sweeping policy of socialization. In shrill, faltering English, the man described China before and after its rescue by Mao, the almighty scholar, poet and warrior. He depicted a country full of misery, division, unrest and ignorance which had changed when Mao Tse-tung's personal brand of communism established schools, work, food and security for all. Communism had created a proper balance between poverty and riches and all men and all women were equal and free.

The dignitary had closed the session by reading a poem about the skill and courage of the peasant workers. The clumsily translated piece had made very little sense to anyone, including Hawthorne, but the official had tears in his eyes as he announced that the author of the poem was the great leader Mao Tse-tung.

Two evenings later, Hawthorne had visited the camp library in order to return a Sherlock Holmes mystery. He deposited the detective novel with the guard-librarian and was about to leave when a title caught his eye: *A History of Chinese Poetry and Painting*, by O. G. Wyatt-Stone.

It was a large, beautifully bound volume and Hawthorne was tempted to remove it from the shelf for closer inspection. He had never touched anything in the library other than American novels, and a driving desire to learn more about the Chinese and their customs was beginning to produce a feeling of guilt.

Still, Hawthorne had removed the book from the case and for nearly an hour he had read about Li Po, the Chinese poet, who was born in A.D. 701. The text of the poems had been simplified and the verses were illustrated with landscapes, fish, birds and flowers. Hawthorne was entranced. This Oriental art form had created a new avenue of escape for the lonely young man.

He had decided that he would not remove the book from the library, but he had returned several times in order to continue his exploration of this newly discovered treasure.

By June 20, 1951, the Chinese Reds had lost their stronghold in Korea. The United Nations forces had captured the area around Pyongyang, Chorwon and Kumhwa.

There had been great rejoicing by the prisoners on July 8 when word was passed that cease-fire talks were being arranged. There had been some anxiety on July 12 when Russia had intervened and disrupted the discussions but the prisoners' jubilation resumed on July 15 when the truce conferences had continued.

On July 25, 1951, a load of garbage and fish oil had been accidentally deposited on "Kwen San's passage," a stretch of roadway located a short distance from the official's bedroom windows. The men of Hut Three were assigned to clean it up.

Only seven members of the unit were present and accounted for. Sergeant Alvin Proctor had been called to Building Two for extensive interrogation at four-thirty in the afternoon and had not returned. The squad, with the exception of Hawthorne, was beginning to worry about the leader when the camp floodlights were turned on at seven-thirty.

It was understood that the outspoken sergeant had been giving the Chinese interrogators a very rough time and Kwen San had vowed to break the man.

The men worked silently in the harsh glare of the prison spotlights. Their movements were now almost mechanical and exhaustion had eliminated the usual wisecracking banter and sarcastic grumbling.

Their welcome ten-minute rest break was over and Hawthorne pulled himself to his feet and joined the others with shovels and pails as the work continued.

It was getting colder and the men were not dressed properly for late-night activity. They had not been told to bring their bulky winter jackets, but it was evident that they would be needed. The guard in charge of the detail decided to dispatch the dump truck with Chow Chow and one member of the squad in order to bring back the garments from the hut.

Chow Chow selected Hawthorne as his personal helper and the men took off in a roar of backfiring as the battered vehicle rattled over Kwen San's road.

The truck finally screeched to a halt in front of Hut Three and Hawthorne was nearly thrown through the cracked windshield.

Chow Chow climbed out of the back and walked to the prisoner's door and motioned for him to get out.

"You get coats," he ordered, pointing to the hut.

Hawthorne stepped down from the truck and the grinning giant towered over him.

"Don't run away," he admonished, moving his rifle playfully in front of the prisoner's face. *"I shoot you in head!"*

The guard roared with laughter and the little driver joined the merriment. Chow Chow removed a pack of cigarettes from his tunic and turned to the driver as Hawthorne made his way to the hut entrance.

The young prisoner heard the sounds of hurried movements inside and knew that something was going on the moment he approached the door. He entered and stood motionless in the dimly lit shack as the scene began to register.

Sergeant Alvin Proctor was crouched next to his bunk in a corner of the barracks. He was frantically packing various articles into his locker box. Hawthorne caught a brief glimpse of cigarette packages, small cans of food, two bottles of wine, and several unidentified items which had been shoved down into the wooden case.

The Sergeant slammed the lid shut and stood in the shadows facing Hawthorne. Sweat was dripping from his forehead and he seemed to be trying desperately to regulate his rapid breathing. His face contorted into a grotesque expression of fury and contempt.

"You keep your fucking mouth shut," he threatened in a hoarse whisper. "Or I'll have your goddamn throat slit from one ear to the other."

Hawthorne stared into the man's eyes for a moment and then turned away. The Sergeant moved a few steps out of the shadows and stood with powerful fists clenched at his sides.

"If you open your sick mouth to anyone," he warned, "I'll have your ass tortured and then shot full of holes. Do you understand?"

Hawthorne thought of K. M. Wing's evaluation of Alvin Proctor, the dedicated and patriotic voice of the United States Army.

"I understand, Sergeant," Hawthorne replied. For once his voice was strong and steady.

He took another quick look at his leader, grabbed the winter jackets from the wall pegs, and then wheeled about abruptly and left the hut.

In the truck, as he was bumped and jolted wildly on the return trip to the work area, Hawthorne came to an important decision. He twisted in the seat, steadied himself by holding on tightly to the door handle and watched Chow Chow as the giant tried to sleep in the lurching truck.

"Chow Chow!" Hawthorne shouted.

The guard turned in his direction and he took a firm grip on the rifle.

"Chow Chow!" the prisoner repeated. *"I want to see K. M. Wing!"*

The guard squinted and seemed puzzled.

"I want a meeting with K. M. Wing. The interrogator."

A grin slowly replaced the perplexed expression and it was evident that the message had been comprehended.

"Wing!" screeched Chow Chow. *"K. M. Wing!"*

"Yes!" yelled Hawthorne as the truck swayed dangerously and nearly tipped over. The giant beamed happily.

"I fix!" he squealed.

Then he glared at the drowsy truck operator and blasted angrily in shrill Chinese.

The ancient truck slowed down as it approached the bright lights illuminating "Kwen San's passage."

24

ESTELLE MANNING POURED another cup of coffee for her husband.

"From now on," she chided jokingly, "I intend to have my Sunday breakfast with Rollins in his quarters downstairs."

Charles Manning's face was completely hidden behind a newspaper and he did not respond.

"Did you hear me, Charles?" the woman asked.

"Yes." The voice was pleasant but disinterested. "Affairs with handsome chauffeurs are no longer frowned upon, darling," he said, putting the paper down with a smile. "In fact, it has become quite chic."

The *Detroit Sunday Express* moved up slowly and Charles Manning, sixty years old and one of Michigan's wealthiest and most prominent industrialists, disappeared behind it.

Four separate manufacturing operations were now producing a variety of Manning products, from plastic toys to armaments, and a recently developed chain of retail outlets had prompted numerous national trade magazines to publish front-page color portraits of the mogul with the caption, *"Manning is Michigan."*

He had inherited a very successful automotive parts factory from his father in 1939. Shrewd management, foresight, hard work and a basic gambling instinct had resulted in a rapid and phenomenal growth pattern for his company.

Estelle Manning, fifteen years younger than her husband, had married him in 1936, three years before the inheritance of his father's business, and the wedding had been one of Michigan's most publicized social events. The prosperous manufacturer's son had won the hand of Detroit's most beautiful and intelligent debutante. In addition, the girl's father, Andrew G. Darwell, was a former governor of Michigan and the President of the State Law Society.

Estelle Darwell Manning's good looks, sharp wit and intelligence had made her an able helpmate over the years. Charles Manning had shown his appreciation by showering her with love and respect and affording her an unusual degree of independence.

She was active in various political, civic and philanthropic organizations and her particular favorite was the Michigan Chapter of the American Civil Rights Association. She had refused the national vice presidency of the society in 1959 because of her many other interests and affiliations.

Middle age had softened and improved her classic beauty, and her trim and elegant figure was envied and admired by every fashion designer in the area. She had simply-styled, jet-black hair with a few streaks of gray, lively blue eyes, a radiant complexion and a soft but animated voice and manner. Her appearance had inspired the Mayor of Detroit to comment during a Chamber of Commerce banquet, "The Mannings are the richest, smartest and best-looking damn couple in the world."

They lived in the exclusive Winchester Estates section of the city and their sprawling mansion and spacious grounds were familiar to every member of the town's high society.

The Mannings had everything. Or nearly everything. Early in the marriage Estelle had suffered a miscarriage and serious complications had prevented any further opportunity to build a family. Charles had talked frequently about adoption but Estelle was always opposed to the suggestion "for her own personal reasons."

"I'm serious, Charles," she frowned. "Put the damn paper away."

This time the tone of her voice prompted immediate action and he folded the journal, smiled and placed it on the table.

"Sorry, darling."

"Charles," she said, "have you been following the Gerald Hawthorne case?"

"The Turncoat?"

"Yes."

"In the papers," he replied. "I missed the television interview."

"I saw it," she stated. "You were in Wilmington that night."

"So?"

"That man has certainly received a raw deal," Mrs. Manning continued. "The interview was absolutely atrocious. Arthur Fremantle deliberately cut the boy to ribbons."

"That's his job, honey."

"There is something haunting and pathetic about that young man," she continued. "I just cannot get him out of my mind."

"It's an interesting case," Manning said. "Eight years in Red China."

"He's been thoroughly abused since his return to this country," Estelle Manning went on. "Did you know that the government refused to pay his passage out of Hong Kong?"

"Yes."

"Was that fair?"

"It's difficult to say, honey," Charles Manning replied evasively. "I don't know enough about the actual facts involved."

"I was discussing the case with Alan Purvis at the Civil Rights Association the other day. He agrees that there is something very strange about this Hawthorne affair."

"Is the association going to investigate?" he asked.

"Not officially," she replied. "It's premature." She thought for a moment. "If nothing else, perhaps the boy needs some help. Financially or otherwise. Hawthorne might have a strong case against the United States government for back pay and an illegal dishonorable discharge. We could assist him with competent lawyers if Larry Goldenson thought we had sufficient grounds for court action."

"Goldenson?"

"The association's general counsel in Washington."

Manning bit into a piece of toast and washed it down with coffee.

"What do you intend to do?" he asked.

"There is only one man in the world who knows the entire story," she said. "Gerald Hawthorne. And he lives in Waverly."

Estelle Manning hesitated and then leaned across the table toward her husband.

"*I* want to talk to Hawthorne, Charles," she said. "He is

clearly an odd character and anything remotely resembling an official contact by the association might scare him off forever."

"How do you know the man will talk to you?"

"I don't," she responded. "But I want to try." Estelle Manning paused and smiled warmly at her husband. "With your permission," she added softly.

Her husband posed in mock deliberation for a moment. Then he pounded his fist down on the breakfast table.

"Permission granted," he announced. "When do you begin your crusade?"

She leaned back in the chair and relaxed. "I want to go to Waverly as soon as we get back from the cruise."

"November 25," he calculated. "Good." He wiped his mouth with a napkin and then reached for the newspaper. "Now my beautiful humanitarian, I am retiring to the study in order to scan the filthy pages of my Sunday sporting news."

Estelle Manning put her hand gently on her husband's arm. "Thank you, Charles," she murmured. "You are a kind and considerate man and I appreciate you so very, very much."

He looked at her lovingly for a few seconds and then grinned. "Maybe it will get your mind off Rollins," he kidded. "That ugly little devil in Waverly is no competition at all."

He patted her hand and Estelle Manning returned his smile.

SEPTEMBER 25, 1961
WAVERLY, MICHIGAN

25 HAWTHORNE BREWED A CUP of strong coffee in his kitchen. He was about to take it into the study but decided instead that he would drink it in his own room and perhaps read a book or even explore some of his personal belongings for the first time since his arrival.

He climbed the stairs, holding the cup and saucer, and then walked down the quiet corridor leading to his bedroom.

He paused reverently at his mother's door and stared at the strong padlock.

Perhaps one day he would find the courage to smash it to pieces and enter the shrine and look and touch and remember and love her all over again.

Nothing in the room had been disturbed since the night of her death and he felt that to enter there would be the same as bringing her back to life. It would be frightening and wonderful at the same time. Perhaps in a week or two, he would be able to find the strength to do it.

Hawthorne continued down the hall to his own room, switched on a lamp and sat on the edge of his bed, sipping the hot coffee.

He looked up at a red and blue pennant which was tacked to the wall. It read, "Waverly High." His father, in a drunken rage, had insisted that every "normal and healthy" boy ought to decorate his room with his school colors.

Hawthorne recalled the baseball gloves and track shoes which had never been worn and pictures of college and professional football heroes who were totally unfamiliar to him.

His father had nailed two large, full-length color portraits of Betty Grable and Rita Hayworth on the wall over the bed. They had shared his bedroom until he had torn the garish photographs to shreds on the day of departure for Fort Polk, Maryland, and Army basic training.

He remembered hiding a colorful assortment of pebbles in a cigar box under his bed and a glass-enclosed butterfly collection in a closet under a pile of old sweaters.

Hawthorne opened the desk drawer and removed a snapshot of his mother which had been taken during one of the family's rare Sunday picnics in Silver Springs Park. She was so beautiful, he thought, staring at the photograph which showed her climbing a large rock. Her long black hair was flowing gracefully behind her and he could almost hear the sound of her laughter. He placed the picture back in the drawer of the desk and rose to his feet.

His eyes moved slowly and carefully around the room, inspecting every piece of furniture and each personal item. At last he decided that he would unpack the rest of his belongings on Sunday and put the mementos of his life in China with Ling Yu around him.

Hawthorne closed his eyes and thought of K. M. Wing's first description of Tsinan, China.

July 29, 1951
Camp Six
Korea

"My town is located about two hundred twenty miles from Peking," the interrogator explained. Hawthorne and K. M. Wing were studying a large map of China which was spread on a dining table in the official's living quarters.

"Look here," he pointed. "Tsinan is situated at the base of the great Northern Plain. See?"

The young prisoner leaned forward and squinted at the map. He was fascinated and very thankful that Chow Chow had been able to arrange this afternoon's meeting.

"The plain extends from this ridge of hills immediately south of the city and it goes right up to the Great Wall." Wing slid his finger along the chart. "Five miles to the north of Tsinan . . . right here . . . the Yellow River."

He looked up at Hawthorne, smiled and then motioned the prisoner to sit at the table. He folded the map and put it on a small table near his bookcase.

"I miss my home and my family," he commented somberly. "It is a pity that the cease-fire talks have broken down. This trouble will now continue."

"It must be very old," Hawthorne said as though Wing had not spoken.

The interrogator looked at him curiously for a moment.

"Tsinan," Hawthorne repeated, "it must be very old."

Wing continued to stare. Finally, he answered. "Inside our

town we have the Old Walled City dating back to the sixth century."

"That's when they built the Grand Canal," said Hawthorne proudly.

"No," Wing corrected. "The Grand Canal was started in the seventh century." He noticed the look of disappointment on the prisoner's face. "The Grand Canal is just a short distance west of my town."

"Do they still use it?" Hawthorne inquired.

"Not much now," Wing replied. "Most of the traffic moves on the Shantung and Peking-Pukow railways." He hesitated. "You truly are interested in China," he commented.

"Yes."

Wing sat back in his chair and folded his arms. "The Old Walled City is very picturesque. The water from the 'one hundred springs' pours into a canal and this canal empties into the Gulf of Chili."

"Do they still use *that* canal?" Hawthorne asked.

"Yes," Wing replied patiently. "Long, narrow boats are pushed slowly up the canal with crude wooden poles. It is very primitive. The boats carry provisions from the countryside and . . ." He paused and his expression changed. "And sometimes Korean lumber for coffins."

"How many people are in your town?" Hawthorne asked.

"Many, Hawthorne," the interrogator answered. "Too many for a city of its size. Perhaps eight hundred thousand people."

"What do they do?"

K. M. Wing laughed. "Well, Tsinan is primarily an industrial center. We produce flour and matches and cement and paper." He thought for a moment. "My town is also known for cotton weaving and oilseed milling. Traditionally, however, Tsinan is noted for silk goods and imitation precious stones."

Wing stood and walked to his bookcase.

"We also have a university located just outside the south wall of the city."

"A large university?" Hawthorne asked.

Wing opened the ornate case and removed several thin hard-covered books.

"Cheloo University is big and modern and respected by educators all over the world."

He walked back to the table and sat, still holding the three volumes.

"I understand that you would like to learn the Chinese language, Hawthorne."

"Yes," the prisoner answered. "Very much."

Wing placed the books on the table and fingered them as he spoke. "It is very, very difficult," he said. "Thousands and thousands of complicated characters and associations are involved. However, our new movement is attempting to simplify the written language and reduce the number of characters to three thousand. This difficult and ambitious program is part of our drive for literacy and culture."

Hawthorne glanced inquisitively at the books and the interrogator opened one of them.

"Don't be offended," he smiled. "These are designed for very young children. But it is new basic Chinese prepared by our specialists in Peking. Perhaps you will learn something from these simple books."

He pushed them across the table to Hawthorne. "A beginning anyway," he added.

The prisoner flipped through the illustrated pages quickly and then picked the books up from the table.

"Thank you, Mr. Wing," he murmured.

The official's expression was serious and he seemed to be genuinely concerned. "I will arrange to have these three books placed in the camp library and made available to you whenever you visit." He watched for Hawthorne's reaction. "It might avoid a problem in your hut," he added.

"No," Hawthorne answered immediately. "I'll keep them."

"Very well." The interrogator smiled warmly. "Study hard and perhaps we will be able to graduate you from the kindergarten level."

On September 8, 1951, the Korean war was stepped up by the United States. By the twenty-seventh, heavy air battles were reported and the Americans had asked for a "no man's land" conference. September 30, 1951, marked the date of a fresh, major attack by the United Nations forces.

Hawthorne had not seen K. M. Wing since the last requested visit and he had not been summoned by any other camp official.

The food was getting worse, the prisoners were grumbling more, and the indoctrination sessions were being intensified. The repetitious daily propaganda lectures were now accepted as a normal way of life.

Hawthorne spent all his free time studying the set of language books, and he was becoming able to recognize many of the strange characters and form certain necessary associations.

One late evening, on a special work detail with Chow Chow, the giant had encouraged him to speak several words in Chinese and he was enormously pleased that they came out clear and understandable. Hawthorne was even more excited by his phenomenal progress when the huge guard uttered two or three very basic expressions and he was able to comprehend and then answer.

On several occasions after that, Chow Chow had allowed the prisoner to "read" letters which the guard had received from his seven-year-old daughter in Peking.

Hawthorne was unable to decipher the contents but several of the childish characters were understandable, and he spent hours each evening trying to work out the general meaning of two or three lines.

After nights of studious endeavor in the library and in Hut Three after lights-out, he was able to solve the latest dispatch to Chow Chow from his daughter. The young girl stated that she loved her father more than the sun and the moon and the stars and the deep sea.

Hawthorne cautiously relayed this translation to the camp guard, and as a gesture of friendship, Chow showed the boy from Waverly a rather faded and crumpled picture of his daughter. Hawthorne was amazed at the remarkable family resemblance. A miniature, female Chow Chow was pictured standing awkwardly in a small garden. The stout little girl had the same friendly but asinine grin and several of her front teeth were missing. Her school or Communist Party uniform was disheveled and several buttons on the tunic were open. A few others appeared to have popped and vanished around the waistline. The proud father beamed and kissed the photograph tenderly before putting it back in his pocket.

Chow Chow suggested that Hawthorne prepare one or two simple expressions in Chinese and promised that he would send this private message to his daughter. He also informed Hawthorne that this very special privilege had been granted by K. M. Wing.

Hawthorne appreciated the interesting proposition and considered it to be a challenging test of his newly acquired ability to concentrate, and absorb and retain knowledge and information. He sat at the library table with books, paper, pencils and firm determination.

Gerald Hawthorne was writing a message in Chinese and it would soon be approved by his guard and then addressed to the Communist capital of Peking.

While the young prisoner labored at the library the members of Squad Three were receiving an important American visitor.

Colonel Roland Fawcett was the senior officer in charge of the Camp Six prisoners of war. Ramrod-straight, West Point-trained, and the personification of military discipline and tradition, the forty-six-year-old former Airborne Division hero had been awarded some of the nation's highest honors for bravery and leadership during World War Two.

Fawcett, who was attired in a neatly pressed uniform complete with swagger stick, called for "at ease" as he entered Hut Three and positioned the squad members in a semicircle on the floor of the hut.

He accepted a small wooden stool from Proctor and then used it as a footrest as he stood facing the men.

"First of all," he began, "I have some encouraging news. As you probably know by now, Panmunjom has been selected as the center for the truce talks."

He took his time and studied the prisoners as most of them nodded their heads. "We have reliable information that these important negotiations are now in progress."

The spontaneous comments of "great" and "terrific" stopped abruptly as the Colonel held up his hand.

"I said encouraging," he admonished. "This action will take time and no one can be certain of the results. However, Panmunjom is now being considered a legitimate starting point for peace and this is certainly good news indeed." He paused for a moment.

"Now I will get to the main purpose of my visit this evening." He lowered his voice, and his tone was both solemn and confidential.

"It is no secret that many of our American comrades have been guilty of collaboration with the enemy. Numerous cases have been reported and confirmed here at Camp Six."

The Hut Three inmates exchanged knowing glances and turned their attention back to the Colonel.

"I will not discuss the details or the extent of this collaboration," he continued gravely. "Nor will I dwell on our specific investigations, charges or plans for disciplinary action."

Fawcett turned to Alvin Proctor. The commander's voice was now almost a whisper. "One particular American soldier in this camp is being briefed and prepared for assignment as an enemy broadcaster."

The men looked puzzled and the officer explained.

"Broadcasters are American prisoners of war who are especially trained by the Chinese Communists to deliver enemy propaganda on radio to our own people."

Again Alvin Proctor and his subordinates exchanged meaningful looks.

"This effective Chinese weapon has been in operation for quite some time," the Colonel went on. "In fact, we have substantiated information that an American prisoner from the 24th Infantry Division had broadcast a speech on behalf of the enemy exactly four days after the outbreak of this Korean conflict.

"I consider the broadcasters to be more despicable than any

other kind of traitor. These men hide behind enemy microphones. They are not even exposed to the danger and sacrifice of an act of espionage."

Fawcett paced for a moment and then returned to the Sergeant.

"Are you Proctor?" he asked.

"Yes, sir," the soldier replied crisply.

"We have good reason to believe that this particular prisoner is a member of your squad here in Hut Three."

There was silence. The prisoners watched Proctor and waited for his response.

"With your permission, sir," he barked in a military fashion, "we can give you the name of this traitor right now."

Fawcett stood stiffly and tapped his boot with the metal end of the swagger stick.

"You cannot, Sergeant," he replied. "*We* will give *you* his name in a few days."

Proctor was confused by the statement and looked inquiringly at the senior officer as he continued.

"This is a very serious offense and we must have all the facts. There can be no guesswork or presumption when an American soldier is accused of treason."

"Sir," the Sergeant insisted, "we have facts."

"Good," Fawcett replied. "We'll call on you when we need your testimony."

The Colonel looked intently from one man to another as he scanned the semicircle. "Mainly," he stated, "we want you to be aware of our suspicions."

He hesitated and then spoke directly to the squad leader.

"Demand maturity from your men, Sergeant," the officer ordered. "I do not want this unpleasant visit to turn one good American soldier against another. You have received an official alert and I will expect intelligent conduct from the members of this squad."

"Sir," Talbot ventured, attempting to control a quiver in his voice.

"What is it, soldier?" the officer demanded impatiently.

"Not all of us are here."

"What?"

"One member of this squad is missing," Talbot explained hesitantly. He looked at Proctor and his eyes pleaded for support. The Sergeant took over.

"Corporal Gerald Howard Hawthorne, Colonel," Proctor announced grimly. "The man is at the camp library."

"He goes every night, Colonel," Landau interjected.

The officer lifted the sleeve of his uniform very carefully and glanced at his gold watch.

"The soldier is within the specified time limitations established by the camp officials," Fawcett replied with irritation.

"That's true, sir," Proctor interceded. "But there are plenty of other things about this man Hawthorne and . . ."

"*Proctor!*" the officer shouted. "We know about Corporal Hawthorne and we know about you, Sergeant."

He glanced quickly at the other men, who were squatting around him. "We are familiar with all of your military records as well as your conduct and attitudes during this period of internment." The officer composed himself and his tone was now cold but level once again.

"Maturity, Sergeant," he advised strongly. "As a squad leader I suggest that you set the example and make absolutely certain that your men conduct themselves in a sensible manner. Remember that this particular prison camp is special. Part of the elaborate scheme is to play one prisoner against another. Stay alert, Proctor, and avoid being outsmarted by the enemy."

"Yes, sir," the Sergeant mumbled. His irritation was evident as he watched the Colonel move slowly toward the door.

"This has been a difficult period for all of us," Fawcett said thoughtfully as he turned back. "Let's pray that peace becomes a reality at Panmunjom. In the meantime, we must conduct ourselves as loyal members of the Armed Forces and citizens of the United States of America."

He opened the door and added, "Captain Kilburn will visit this hut sometime during next week. Thank you, gentlemen."

He moved out militarily.

"*Attention!*" Talbot yelled.

"Oh, fuck off, Talbot," said Proctor.

Then the Sergeant spat twice on the floor of Hut Three.

Hawthorne stopped abruptly as he neared the front door of the crude wooden shack. His time at the library this evening had been particularly profitable.

The overhead lightbulb had been switched off suddenly and the entire hut was in darkness.

Hawthorne checked his watch and it indicated 9:10 P.M. There was no logical explanation for the blackout or the unfamiliar silence; however, he decided that his uneasiness was due to an overactive imagination. He opened the door and stepped inside.

The chilly room was pitch-black and silent. He stood at the entrance and waited for his eyes to grow accustomed to the darkness and then he slammed the door shut behind him with his foot.

He listened anxiously. There was not a sound. Because of the blackness in the shack he was forced to move slowly and carefully and feel his way down the line of bunks until he reached his own at the end of the row.

After much touching and probing, he was able to locate his locker box. He stooped, opened the lid, placed his language books neatly inside, closed it and then leapt to his feet, blinded by the glare of the flashlight. He gasped and tried to shield his face with his hands.

A moment later, a vise-like grip from behind pinned both arms painfully to his sides and the pressure of the stranglehold choked the breath out of his lungs.

Not a sound was uttered by the invisible assailants as several rags were stuffed into his mouth. He could not scream or swallow or breathe properly.

The light was suddenly switched off but the grip around his waist seemed to be immovable.

The silence and darkness were frightening, and Hawthorne was beginning to feel the effects of the pressure on his chest.

The flashlight was snapped on again and this time his face was lit from a different direction. Still, there was not a sound nor a movement. It was impossible to distinguish the shadowy figure behind the torch.

Suddenly a fist smashed against the illuminated right side of his face and the pain of the impact forced him to cry out. But there was no sound.

The light was switched off again and the arms of steel tightened around his body. Hawthorne tried desperately to breathe through his nose.

The light came on again from another direction. The left side of his face was bashed by something made of wood and there were splinters and Hawthorne felt an excruciating pain in his temple and ear. The cloth in his mouth was now moist.

Immediately there was darkness and the grip was strengthened to hold the victim erect.

The light again. This time, straight in front of his face. He anticipated the blow but was still stunned by its power and force. It came from a metallic object. Warm liquid began to flow from his forehead.

His knees buckled, but the arms held him rigidly as blood from the facial wounds covered his eyes and clogged his nose. Hawthorne was suffocating, he felt himself drifting into an abnormal sleep.

The flash went out and the grip loosened slightly, allowing his body to sag as a hand pulled the blood-soaked rags from his mouth.

Hawthorne took a breath and then vomited as two bright beams penetrated the darkness of the hut and lit both sides of his beaten face.

Then the silence was broken by heavy breathing as someone leaned close to him. He could not see and he was barely able to hear the husky whisper.

"Now, broadcast *this*, you Communist son-of-a-bitch!"

A fist or a hammer finally completed the job and it was almost painless, an explosion without noise. There were lights and colors and a floating sensation and he was wet and relieved as a numbness began to overcome the unbearable pain. He remembered pondering over the word "broadcast" just before sinking into oblivion.

26

THE HOSPITAL IN the administration area of Camp Six was called the "butcher shop" by the American prisoners of war and the designation was nearly correct.

It was a large wooden structure with paper-thin partitions separating the various wards, operating rooms, laboratories and staff quarters.

The building was always unbearably overheated and Kwen San had ordered the few small windows to be sealed shut for security reasons.

The wards and operating rooms were seldom clean and a variety of foul odors from patients and strong medication produced a chronic nausea in all the patients. A "vomit bucket" was strategically placed by each bunk and the container was always full by the end of the day, regardless of the prisoner's illness. Most of the patients were suffering from pneumonia, dysentery, malnutrition and scurvy.

It was a known fact that the majority of the Chinese doctors on the hospital staff were incompetent and inexperienced. They were all concerned with relief rather than cure. Many prisoners had already experienced the horrors of the unsanitary operating rooms and most of them were convinced that a serious disease or even death was preferable to another torturous surgical procedure where no anesthetics were available and most of the instruments were improvised. The screams of patients undergoing surgery, whether it was an appendectomy or an amputation, could often be heard and these sounds blended with the continuous moans of the sick and dying.

Corporal Gerald Hawthorne was slowly recovering from his injuries in Ward Two. He had not been handled badly by the hospital personnel. A young doctor from Peking had tried his best and seemed qualified and dedicated to the medical profession. The physician had treated his wounds quickly and efficiently, without displaying any resentment or hostility.

Hawthorne was left alone to rest, recover and try to subdue his growing hatred for all American prisoners of war.

His bitterness and confusion seemed to increase daily and the thought of Alvin Proctor and the other members of Squad Three forced him to examine his own beliefs and feelings honestly, setting aside pride and fear, patriotism and politics.

On November 14, 1951, Gerald Hawthorne was called to a small visiting room in the Camp Six hospital.

His face and head were still bandaged but the wounds were healing satisfactorily. He had been told by his doctor that his release was scheduled for November 18 or 19, if there were no further complications from an injury to his left ear. K. M. Wing was waiting, seated behind a table, and he greeted the prisoner warmly.

"You had a very good doctor," said Wing. "He is my dear friend and I told him to pay particular attention to your condition."

"Thank you," Hawthorne replied. "He was very good."

The interrogator took a cigarette, offered one to Hawthorne and then lit them both. He studied the prisoner's bandaged features.

"Sergeant Alvin Proctor is no longer a member of your squad," said Wing. "Did you know that?"

"No," Hawthorne answered, showing little concern.

"In fact, Proctor has been transferred out of Camp Six."

"Why?"

"Sergeant Proctor is helping us with a particular assignment elsewhere." The interrogator inhaled deeply. "The squad assaulted the wrong man and Proctor participated, of course."

Hawthorne was not used to the cigarette and the smoke irritated his throat, and he coughed. The inside of his mouth was still sore and infected from the cloth gag and the brutal attack.

"The men of your hut know that Proctor is now working

for our cause," Wing continued. "They were told by Colonel Roland Fawcett."

Hawthorne took shorter drags and tried not to inhale the smoke. He did not respond.

"Are you shocked by the news of Proctor's collaboration?" Wing asked.

"No."

"The members of your squad are stunned by the revelation. They find it very difficult to believe."

"I knew about it."

"How?"

"I saw him hiding things in his locker box one night," said Hawthorne.

The interrogator watched carefully as the prisoner adjusted a bandage which was beginning to loosen on his forehead.

"Caught him in the act," Wing commented.

"Yes."

"Why didn't you tell the other men in your hut or Colonel Fawcett?"

Hawthorne smoothed the plaster on his head and did not answer.

"Proctor threatened you," Wing stated flatly.

"Yes."

"Were you afraid that he would kill you?"

"No," said the prisoner firmly. "I'm not afraid of Proctor." He hesitated. "Or anyone else," he added.

"I believe you, Hawthorne," said Wing. "Then why didn't you tell the others about him?"

Hawthorne sighed heavily and looked out of the tightly secured window.

"Because I don't give a damn about Proctor or the others," he said. The statement was barely audible and it was spoken to himself.

There was silence in the room as the young man continued to stare out of the window. The interrogator watched for a moment and then spoke briskly.

"Corporal Martino has assumed the hut leadership. He will probably give you more trouble than Proctor. Especially if you continue with your studies about China. Are you still interested?"

"Yes," he answered without hesitation. "Very interested."

"Then I strongly suggest that you consider a transfer to a different squad. With perhaps nicer people. There are many good men in this camp, Hawthorne," he explained smoothly. "Chinese and also American." He turned to the prisoner. "Hut Two in particular."

The boy watched attentively as Wing moved back to the table. "The men of Hut Two are intelligent and cultured. They read and discuss and conduct themselves as civilized human beings." The interrogator leaned on the table and lowered his voice.

"You belong with these men, Hawthorne. Martino and the others are vulgar, ignorant and dishonest. Proctor is the perfect example. The American soldiers of Hut Two do not have to open their mouths wide and pound their chests constantly in order to prove themselves. Don't be fooled. Obscenity, narrow-mindedness, bigotry and loud, patriotic poppycock have nothing to do with courage or manliness or being American."

Their eyes met and this time Hawthorne did not turn away. He seemed to be searching for something in the other man.

"I will introduce you to the men of Hut Two and then judge for yourself. Make your own decision about the transfer," said Wing. He glanced at his watch. "I have to be going now."

He nodded politely and started to move out the door of the small room.

"*Mr. Wing!*" Hawthorne called.

The official halted abruptly and turned to face the prisoner, who was now standing awkwardly beside the table.

"I don't want to meet the men of Hut Two," he said softly. "And I don't want a transfer."

Wing stared at him curiously and then took a few steps back into the room.

"May I ask why?" the interrogator queried.

Hawthorne glanced down at the table and spoke in a voice so low that Wing was forced to step closer.

"I want to learn about China and the Chinese people but I want to do it on my own," he spoke hesitantly, "not with special guys in Hut Two."

"Suit yourself, Hawthorne," the interrogator replied somberly.

Then he wheeled about and left the room as the Chinese escort entered.

Hawthorne's return to the hut had been treated with silent contempt by the members of Squad Three and there were no apologies for the assault on October 26.

Life became an unbearable nightmare for Hawthorne and he wondered how long his mind and body would be able to withstand the constant pressure from the other members of his squad.

He opened his locker box one morning and found that the set of language books had been slashed to shreds and stuffed into several of his socks. On another occasion, he discovered that someone had urinated on his bunk during the night. There were frequent verbal attacks as well.

In the evenings, weakened by the lack of decent food and weary after hours of hard labor, he would lie on the bunk with his face turned toward the wall, trying to ignore the other prisoners.

Winston Talbot's shrill imitation of the Chinese would usually begin the sessions.

"Hey, Hawthorne!" he would squeal. "You speakee Chinee? Ming Tong! Ping Pong! Ding Dong!"

And the others would then pick up the chant and the juvenile performance would continue until the nonsensical words began to irritate and madden him.

Then, on the evening of December 18, 1951, a member of the squad finally stepped over the line. At ten forty-five that evening, Hawthorne returned to the hut with Guzman and Hyman Landau after completing a particularly exhausting hard-labor assignment on the punishment rock pile near the west parade grounds.

He sat on the edge of the bunk and removed his boots. He heard a snicker and then a muffled laugh. It sounded like Winston Talbot.

There was complete silence in the hut once again and Hawthorne continued his usual preparations for lights-out at eleven.

He opened his locker box and tossed his heavy socks inside. Then he noticed that the picture of his mother was not in its usual place but on top of a book entitled *Chinese Poets and Philosophers*. Hawthorne stared in disbelief and his hands began to tremble on the lid of the box.

He heard the snorting laugh again.

An unknown intruder, with charcoal or dried mud, had painted a crude penis on the photograph and the tip of it was resting against his mother's lips.

He removed the picture and closed the box.

Then he walked to the center of the hut and stood holding the photograph at his side.

Winston Talbot was the first to react. He raised himself up on one elbow and stared at Hawthorne and in a few minutes he was joined by Martino and Gordon.

Talbot suddenly burst into hysterical laughter. *"Ming Tong! Ping Pong! Ding Dong!"* he screeched.

Guzman and Landau also got themselves up to take a look at this strange character who was standing pale and rigid, and facing the entire squad.

Talbot's inane chant was not picked up by the rest of the squad and the man's laughter slowly faded as the prisoners studied the unfamiliar expression on Hawthorne's face.

There was something diabolical about his appearance and even Martino glanced down at his bunk when he saw the expression in Hawthorne's eyes.

Finally, Hawthorne held the photograph up.

"This is a picture of my mother," he said bitterly.

Not one man looked up.

"Look at it," he stammered, nearly choking on his words.

Landau and Guzman stared at the photograph and then they turned slowly to Martino, who seemed to ignore their attention.

"My mother is dead," Hawthorne said softly. "Did you men know that?"

He took a firm step toward Winston Talbot's bunk. The man tried to force a smile but Hawthorne's penetrating expression forced him to turn his head away.

"I intend to find the man who did this," Hawthorne vowed. "Then I'll kill him," he added with cold sincerity.

The eyes of every member of the squad were riveted on him as he lowered the photograph and bowed his head.

"Then I'll pray that *his* mother dies and rots in hell."

He walked very slowly back to his bunk and Hut Three was silent.

DECEMBER 22, 1951
CAMP SIX
KOREA

27

ON THE EVENING OF the twenty-second of December, 1951, Gerald Hawthorne received his first official summons to appear at the camp's main interrogation sector in Administration Building Two.

The room was damp and bare except for a wooden table and several straight-backed chairs. There were no windows and the harsh lighting was furnished by three overhead bulbs and a table lamp without a shade. There were eight doors and Hawthorne assumed that each led to one of the camp's torture chambers.

Hawthorne had entered with Chow Chow and he was very surprised to see K. M. Wing standing behind the table. There was also a distinguished-looking official seated next to the interrogator, and the man's hostile manner unnerved the prisoner for a moment until he realized that Wing was smiling warmly and motioning to a chair.

Hawthorne sat facing the men. Chow Chow was dismissed by K. M. Wing, and the uniformed officer was formally introduced as the third-ranking official in the prison camp.

"I do not have time," he announced without the slightest change of expression. "Mr. Wing will say fast."

The interrogator took a seat and proceeded.

"I was not in favor of your return to the squad and my feelings were expressed very clearly at the time of your hospitalization," Wing said. "Do you remember our discussion?"

"Yes."

"Do you agree now that my evaluation of the situation was correct?"

Hawthorne glanced at the official and saw that the man was glaring suspiciously.

"You are going to be transferred out of the Third Squad immediately," said Wing. "I can assure you that your life will be much easier and more productive."

Seeing that Hawthorne was about to interrupt, Wing held up his hand.

"You are not going to Hut Two," the interrogator said quickly, and then he paused, allowing the important statement to register.

Hawthorne narrowed his eyes but remained silent as the man went on.

"That was your main worry, wasn't it?" Wing asked.

"With the gracious approval of my superiors," he continued, nodding in the direction of the camp official, "I have been able to arrange a very special situation for you, Hawthorne. You are going to be allowed to work in the camp's administration building every day from eight in the morning until seven in the evening."

Hawthorne was too dumbfounded to react.

"Your normal duties will be very simple," Wing went on. "Probably menial cleaning tasks will be included in your daily routine. We have not as yet worked out the exact details of the assignment. Mainly, this will be an excellent opportunity for you to progress with your study of Chinese language, history and culture. Your employment will bring you into daily and direct contact with the entire staff and perhaps you will begin to know and understand our people."

"You first and only prisoner," the Chinese official interjected. "No one else ever in camp."

"This is true," Wing continued. "Now listen and you will realize the importance of the opportunity. In exchange for your daily services in the administration buildings, you will be allowed to live in a small private hut of your own. This shack is located in the staff area near Building One. It will be supplied with adequate heat, food, cigarettes . . ." he paused and smiled, "and reading material of every description."

The tall officer suddenly stood up and K. M. Wing jumped to his feet while motioning for Hawthorne to do the same.

The prisoner pulled himself up to a sloppy form of attention as the officer spoke.

"I go now," he stuttered, searching for words. "You smart American. Curious and quiet. You like China and Chinese." He finally smiled. "Work in buildings and maybe you be Chinese too."

Hawthorne stared at the officer and debated whether to accept the interrogator's suggestion and offer his thanks for the gracious privilege.

The awkward problem was soon solved as Wing bowed to his superior and muttered something in Chinese. The officer returned the bow, smiled broadly at the prisoner and then marched briskly out of the interrogation room.

"I told the General that his imposing presence had caused you to lose your tongue temporarily," said Wing as he took his seat at the table. "I also explained that you were thanking him silently. You are a very lucky man, Hawthorne. I hope that you appreciate the generosity of the camp officials."

The prisoner was stunned by the entire proposition but he started to consider the obvious pros and cons as Wing talked excitedly about the advantages of leaving Hut Three.

"Have you heard any news?" He became aware that Wing was asking him a question.

"They fixed a cease-fire line," the prisoner replied.

"That was on November 27, Hawthorne," said Wing. "The talks fell apart again on December 12."

The interrogator hesitated, realizing that the boy did not seem particularly interested in the disappointing news.

"The negotiators are now involved in a major dispute over the handling of prisoners of war," he added.

"Oh."

"We will all be confined to this camp for quite some time," the man went on. "I intend to make things as interesting as possible for myself and I suggest that you do the same."

"Can I ask a question?"

"Go ahead."

"Will I be a broadcaster?"

"A what?"

"A broadcaster," the prisoner repeated.

Wing seemed puzzled for a moment and then he laughed loudly.

"No, Hawthorne," he said, trying to control himself. "You definitely will not be a broadcaster."

"Then why am I needed in the administration buildings?" the prisoner asked innocently.

"No one said that you were needed," the interrogator replied bluntly. "We said that we were granting you a special privilege and a unique opportunity because of your sincere interest in China and the Chinese people. It's a favor, Corporal."

Hawthorne thought for a while before speaking.

"Why would you do me a favor, Mr. Wing?" he asked quietly.

The Chinese interrogator shrugged. Then he stood up and began to pace around the table. He seemed to be debating whether to answer the question or simply walk out of the room.

"We do not need your political collaboration at the moment. Is that blunt enough?" He leaned on the chair and spoke softly. "Your fellow prisoners have been weak, poorly trained, inadequately disciplined and completely lacking in loyalty and character. We have had a very easy time with the American soldiers here at Camp Six and I can assure you that our recruitment record has been incredible."

He took a seat and faced the prisoner.

"We have discovered that your interest in our country and our people is pure and honest and it was stimulated here at Camp Six without excessive pressure, favored treatment or the use of specialized indoctrination techniques."

One of the doors in the room opened as a soldier spoke a few words of Chinese to the interrogator. Wing smiled, replied, and the soldier withdrew, closing the door quietly behind him.

"We must finish in a few minutes," said Wing. He motioned toward the eight doors leading to the adjoining rooms. "There will be quite a bit of activity here in a very short time."

Hawthorne glanced around the room and shivered.

"Take the job and move into your own hut," Wing said with finality. "Do it tomorrow."

Hawthorne sat slightly dazed as the interrogator stood and prepared to leave.

"Can I think about it?"

"No." The reply was stern and very final.

"If I work in the buildings," Hawthorne persisted, "can I refuse to obey an order if I think it's wrong or against my country?"

"You have my promise, Hawthorne," Wing replied impatiently.

The prisoner rubbed the back of his neck nervously. He was floundering and deeply confused.

"The stuff in my own hut," he said. "I don't want any more than the other guys and I don't want cigarettes or special things."

"That's entirely up to you."

"Except for books," he added quickly and Wing smiled.

"Chow will help you move early tomorrow morning," he stated. "Perhaps one of Kwen San's men will accompany him in the event that Corporal Martino disapproves of your transfer."

Hawthorne rose to his feet.

"I don't give a damn about Corporal Martino," said the prisoner bitterly.

K. M. Wing looked over to the door where Chow Chow was standing. The man straightened up and made an effort to button his tunic.

"Chow," said Wing pleasantly, "Corporal Hawthorne will leave Hut Three in the morning." The interrogator spoke slowly and carefully in English. "He will move into the small hut and work in the buildings."

A grin of sincere delight spread quickly over the guard's face.

Wing glanced at the prisoner. "The big boy was truly worried about you. He likes you very much." He smiled and extended his hand.

Hawthorne hesitated for a moment but finally accepted the friendly gesture.

"Good luck," said the camp interrogator.

"Thank you, Mr. Wing."

The interrogator left the room. Hawthorne sighed deeply and then started to move toward Chow Chow, who was waiting to escort him back to the squad for the last time.

At that precise moment, there was a commotion in the building entrance and Chow Chow stepped aside quickly as two American prisoners were shoved violently into the interrogation room. Both men hit the floor hard, close to Hawthorne's feet.

He stood dazed in the center of the room, staring at them. *"We go now!"* Chow Chow called. *"We go!"* he repeated.

The guard beckoned and Hawthorne managed to pull himself together and walk slowly out of Camp Six's main interrogation sector.

November 10, 1961
The Main Ballroom
Waldorf-Astoria Hotel
New York City

"Mr. Chairman Rutledge, ladies and gentlemen, I accept this important honor with mixed emotions."

Robert Calhoun Spangler, formally attired and modestly diffident, was in the process of thanking the selection committee of the Stanhope Fund for its unanimous decision to present a special award to Amalgamated Broadcasting. The company's outstanding contributions to American television journalism had merited the prize.

The unique presentation had marked a drastic change of policy for this philanthropic institution. Ordinarily, it reserved its coveted citations for newspaper reporters, photographers, editors and publishers, but Amalgamated's Vice President of Programming had scored another television "first." The Emmy and Peabody presentations were yet to come.

Robert Spangler was almost at the end of his well-rehearsed acceptance speech.

"The Turncoat was a team effort. I must publicly convey my personal thanks and deepest appreciation to Mr. Arthur Fremantle for his expert handling of the Hawthorne interview."

There was spirited applause for the commentator and several members of the fashionably groomed audience turned toward the Amalgamated tables in the hope of catching a glimpse of him.

"I regret that Mr. Fremantle is unable to be with us. He is now in California hard at work on another important assignment," Spangler explained. "We certainly cannot and will not ignore the essential contributions made by our professional Amalgamated Broadcasting production staff and technical crew. We are *all* honored and appreciative. However, it is my personal feeling that this award has been presented to the wrong man this evening."

He allowed the statement to register.

"This marvelous trophy should grace the office of our company's Chairman of the Board."

Courteous response followed and Spangler held up his hand dramatically.

"This man has a very bold approach to television programming and his particular brand of leadership has allowed the creative members of our industry to flourish. Always free of inhibitions and unnecessary restrictions."

He paused.

"Chairman Rutledge, ladies and gentlemen, may I present Mr. Frederic G. Bateman."

Applause again as the Amalgamated Corporation leader rose to his feet and walked energetically to the Waldorf dais.

MARCH 16, 1952
CAMP SIX
KOREA

28

NEARLY THREE MONTHS had passed since Hawthorne's acceptance of the transfer, and the move out of Hut Three had altered every aspect of his prison life.

The young soldier had even admitted to himself that his present existence as a captive was now more exciting and far more productive than all his dreary and troubled years in Waverly, Michigan.

The small wooden shack in the camp administration section had been furnished with care and inventiveness.

The room contained a round table, two straight chairs, a standard bunk and a crudely constructed bookcase. Hawthorne knew the luxury of privacy for the first time in his life.

An overhead lightbulb dangled from the ceiling but Hawthorne had managed to appropriate a shaded reading lamp from his employers in Building One. This lamp could not be issued without the personal approval of Kwen San but, as usual, Wing had managed to arrange the permission.

The unpainted bookcase had been presented to Hawthorne by one of the senior staff officers in Building Two after he had renovated his own private living quarters. The same man had donated a fascinating collection of Oriental bric-a-brac.

K. M. Wing had contributed several colorful reproductions of Chinese art which Hawthorne had tacked around the roughly hewn walls of his hut. Chow Chow had located a worn rug in the camp storage depot and this, together with the other gifts from his captors, had turned the dreary prison shack into a moderately comfortable and attractive home.

K. M. Wing had kept his word, and Hawthorne's bookcase had been stocked with literature of every style and period. There were American fiction and selected poetry, as well as numerous volumes in English devoted to Chinese history, philosophy and the arts. Wing had also managed to assemble a large collection of books and material on the Chinese language and Hawthorne valued this particular treasure enormously.

In addition, there were books, magazines and special pamphlets on the Communist Party, Mao Tse-tung, Marxism and Leninism, the New China and the New Society, and a whole range of information explaining the truth about the Korean conflict and other wars and the role of Red China in relation to America and Russia and the rest of the world.

Hawthorne had spent every moment of his free time reading and studying. He was not forced to limit himself to specific material for fear of threats or possible condemnation. He selected and read, absorbed, retained or discarded and did not give a damn about conformity or patriotism or political rules and regulations. His mind was becoming more active and alert as the exposure to the diversified literature helped to expand his interests.

He had repaired the picture of his mother and he was now able to display it prominently on his table. This factor had added to the boy's growing contentment and self-respect.

The job appraisal which had been initially presented to him by K. M. Wing had turned out to be an accurate description of Hawthorne's daily routine. He was stationed in a cluttered stock room in Building One and his duties were basically menial.

A young Chinese soldier called Yang was his immediate supervisor. He had been severely wounded during the early stages of the Korean conflict. Ugly burns had completely disfigured the left side of his face and neck, and a mangled leg and spine had partially paralyzed him from the waist down.

He managed to stay active by dragging himself around the work area on two homemade crutches which frequently collapsed under him, throwing him to the ground. This pathetic sight had become so familiar in the administration section of the camp that no one ever bothered to assist him.

Yang appreciated this lack of pity and attention and had screamed hysterically at Hawthorne for attempting to help when the American had first seen the crude supports begin to buckle and collapse and had rushed to his rescue.

The prisoner had been assigned hall and office cleaning details in both buildings, and he also performed a variety of servile tasks for various officials, including messenger work and boot polishing.

In the beginning, the camp officials had treated Hawthorne with quiet contempt. It was soon apparent, however, that the American was honest, sincere and determined to learn everything possible about China and the Chinese people including their difficult language.

By March 1, 1952, many of the Chinese Communists in the administration section of Camp Six were actively assisting the strange prisoner in his quest for knowledge.

Wing, Chow Chow and Yang had encouraged others to help Hawthorne whenever possible and he was slowly being accepted as a very interesting project, with a great deal of potential. The English-speaking Communists cooperated by discussing history, customs and language with the soldier while others donated books, magazines and newspapers from home.

Hawthorne began to develop companionship and for the first time, a touch of normalcy entered his wretched and lonely life.

On March 16, 1952, Hawthorne was called unexpectedly to the main interrogation room in Building Two.

Ordinarily, Chow Chow or Yang would relay K. M. Wing's summons to a meeting and these sessions were usually pleasantly social if they did not pertain to specialized assignments in the administration area.

This time, even Yang was slightly startled when one of

Kwen San's armed guards marched briskly into the cramped stock room and ordered Hawthorne to accompany him at once to the special interrogation section.

Most of the time in his work details, Hawthorne had strolled leisurely through the administration area with Chow Chow as his guard, and he had never been treated as an enemy security risk or a potential escapee. Now, however, he was marched at a military pace across the open field which separated the two buildings, accompanied by an expressionless guardsman who had a ready hand poised on the holster of his revolver.

Hawthorne was not particularly alarmed at the situation, assuming that Chow was busy on another assignment and that Wing had probably recruited one of Kwen San's troopers as his messenger.

They entered the large wooden building and stopped abruptly in front of the interrogation room door. The guard motioned for him to sit on the low bench in the busy hallway and Hawthorne obeyed.

While they waited, several familiar Chinese staff enlisted men, some civilians and a few officers nodded and smiled at him as they passed, but Kwen San's guard stood grimly at attention next to his prisoner.

Suddenly the door of the interrogation section was opened from the inside and Hawthorne was ordered to enter.

The prisoner stood rigidly for a moment as he heard the door close quietly behind him.

He recognized Kwen San, the disciplinarian, but the other three men were unfamiliar. He was certain that they were important visiting officials and not members of the Camp Six administration staff.

The young man in the center was a civilian and the other two were obviously high-ranking Army officers.

Three pistols and several stacks of official-looking documents had been placed on the desk in front of the committee, and it was evident that this particular session had nothing whatsoever to do with social amenities or generous offers of executive camp employment.

"Come here and sit down, Hawthorne," the civilian ordered.

The prisoner walked to the table and took a seat opposite the officials.

The man who had spoken studied several documents and Hawthorne noticed that he had a nervous habit of pulling on his earlobes.

Hawthorne glanced quickly at Kwen San and the jailer nodded without smiling.

"I must compliment you," said the civilian in crisp English as he put the papers back on the pile. "Your camp reports are excellent. We are all very pleased with your progress."

Hawthorne took a look at the other members of the group, who were now smiling. It was evident that they did not speak or understand English.

"We need your cooperation in a matter of great importance," the civilian explained. "You have been granted privileges in this camp that no other American prisoner has ever received. You have a private hut, correct?"

"Yes," Hawthorne answered quietly.

"Is it comfortable?"

"Yes."

"You have a special reading lamp and an impressive library?"

The prisoner nodded.

"Weekly favors have been granted and your work in the administration section is less strenuous than the strict hard-labor details which are normally assigned to prisoners of war. Do you agree?"

"Yes," Hawthorne replied, beginning to shift uneasily in his chair.

The civilian then turned to the two officers and an animated exchange of Chinese followed. Hawthorne realized that Kwen San had begun glaring at him ominously. He shifted his gaze down at the floor, suddenly anxious, and waited for the conference to end.

Finally, one of the officers handed a document to the civilian, who moved his pistol to one side and placed the paper on the table in front of him. He pulled on his right earlobe and looked up at Hawthorne.

"The peace talks at Panmunjom are now in a chaotic state

but our people are not responsible for this unfortunate situation. Are you aware of the problems?"

"No."

"We have absolute proof that our soldiers have been subjected to bacteriological warfare in Manchuria," he announced bitterly. "Your country was officially accused of this atrocity during the talks on March 7. Were you aware of these formal charges?"

"No," the prisoner answered.

"Do you understand the seriousness of the crime?" He waited for a reply but Hawthorne was silent. "Do you know what this is all about?" he asked with mounting irritation.

"Germ warfare."

"Correct," growled the civilian. "It is one of the most heinous acts ever perpetrated by one human creature against another. Inconceivable in a civilized world and yet your country is guilty."

"I don't know anything about it," the prisoner stated very quickly.

The pressure was beginning to build and Hawthorne was now certain that the interrogation was rapidly leading to one of the eight doors and the Camp Six chambers of horror.

"You are interested in China and the Chinese people," the civilian continued. "The importance of truth is stressed in the works of every great Chinese writer and teacher. Surely you have discovered this fact by now."

One of the officers leaned toward the speaker and whispered earnestly and the civilian nodded several times before proceeding.

"Your country is guilty of bacteriological warfare in Manchuria and we have proof," he declared. "Many of your fellow American soldiers have already testified that your government has committed these hideous crimes against humanity."

He tapped a stack of papers.

"We have hundreds of confessions and more are being received daily. These papers will be inspected at Panmunjom and we will then present them to the International Red Cross for inspection and official certification."

The civilian picked up a document and handed it to Hawthorne.

"What is this?" the prisoner asked.

"A statement of your condemnation as a sensible and civilized human being."

"Condemnation of what?"

"Bacteriological warfare. Read it and perhaps you will understand the situation a little better," the civilian suggested harshly.

"I don't want to read it."

"Then sign it." The man had raised his voice to a shout. "Don't try my patience, Hawthorne."

The young prisoner glared at the interrogator for a moment and then looked down at the floor and reflected.

"I don't know anything about my country using germs."

The senior officer leaned toward the civilian once again, and as they talked, it was obvious that the younger man was translating the prisoner's reply. The Communist officer suddenly turned scarlet with rage and screamed in Chinese, pounding the table furiously. The civilian pushed the paper closer to the prisoner and placed a pen close by.

"You are typical, Hawthorne," the man snarled. "An ungrateful American pig. We have tried in every way to favor you and cultivate your understanding and friendship. You have lived in comfort as a prisoner of war."

He pulled on both earlobes.

"Have you killed Chinese soldiers, Hawthorne?" he asked with increasing resentment.

"Yes," the prisoner replied, avoiding the civilian's eyes. "Three."

"Three," the interrogator repeated. His pockmarked face was now contorted as he lifted the pistol and pointed it directly at the prisoner's head.

"I could blow your skull to pieces and the act would be justified," he announced brutally.

Hawthorne's heart seemed to stop momentarily. He waited for the explosion and the sensation of instant, violent death.

Instead, the man lowered the weapon and replaced it on the table in front of him.

"I advise you to sign the document, Hawthorne," he said hoarsely.

Silence descended over the interrogation room as the prisoner stared from one member of the panel to the other.

Finally, he pushed the pen back to the Communist official and the point touched the handle of the black pistol.

"My country would never use germs or things like that." Hawthorne pointed to a stack of documents. "Those bastards lied and you know it and I won't join them."

"You have deceived our people with your artificial display of interest and allegiance," the civilian fumed. "If it were up to me, I would have you executed for hypocrisy and ingratitude."

Hawthorne managed to suppress a shudder as the spokesman proceeded to discuss the situation with the two officers. He turned back to the prisoner.

"Once again you are a very lucky soldier," the civilian went on. "You will not be executed and my personal methods of persuasion have been rejected by my superiors."

He glanced at the senior officer and then at Kwen San as he gathered up his papers.

"You will vacate the private hut before seven o'clock this evening and you will be returned to Squad Three by armed members of the camp prison force. You will obviously leave all furnishings, including your library and the special gifts which were presented to you by the gracious but gullible members of the Camp Six staff."

The civilian picked up the pen as he continued.

"Your special employment in the administration section is hereby terminated and you will now follow the camp's standard schedule and regulations for all prisoners of war."

Hawthorne felt a fleeting temptation to sign the document. He tried to ignore the thought.

"All camp privileges are suspended as of this moment," the civilian was saying. "This suspension will include incoming and outgoing mail and the use of the library and other facilities. Food and clothing rations will be reduced and special hard-labor details will be assigned immediately."

He reached for the document.

"It is possible that further disciplinary action will be taken against you at a later date," he said, folding the paper. "We shall wait and see."

"Can I speak to K. M. Wing?" Hawthorne blurted without thinking.

The young Communist scowled.

"Mr. Wing has been temporarily furloughed," the civilian announced. "He is in Tsinan."

He placed his briefcase on the table.

"Do not count on his attempts to minimize your punishment, Hawthorne. We have all heard your patriotic declarations this afternoon. Let me assure you that Mr. K. M. Wing is a loyal Chinese citizen."

The senior officer suddenly stood up and the others jumped to attention.

"On your feet, Hawthorne!" the civilian screamed.

The boy got up very slowly and kept his head bowed as Kwen San shouted in Chinese for the armed guard.

Gerald Hawthorne was reunited with his former squad members in Hut Three at seven-thirty on the evening of March 16, 1952, and he was shocked by what he saw. Appalled, he stared at the apparitions who had once been such spirited American soldiers.

Martino, Guzman and Landau were sprawled listlessly on their own bunks while Talbot and Gordon were stretched full-length on the wooden floor. The hut was cluttered with trash and garbage and the stench was overpowering. Hawthorne tossed his possessions into the locker box and then placed the photograph of his mother deep inside, making sure that it was protected by an old pair of work fatigues. He flopped wearily on the bunk and then discreetly examined each of his fellow prisoners of war. He soon realized that their silence and the lack of movement had nothing to do with trickery or vicious pranks.

The boisterous members of Squad Three had somehow been transformed into apathetic zombies.

Martino and Talbot were both obviously in better condition than the others. The health of Landau and Guzman had deteriorated markedly and Private Lawrence Gordon appeared to be close to death.

Hawthorne settled back in his bunk and prayed for strength and endurance. He wondered about his own chances of survival and about his ability to resist the temptation to commit treason.

Private and Confidential.

From: Senator Samuel Brewster
  To: Hector Rambeau

November 27, 1961

We are interested in a lawyer who is now practicing with a local firm called B. M. Rifkind and Partners.

His name is Lawrence A. Goldenson. He is the general counsel for the American Civil Rights Association.

Can your organization compile a detailed dossier on the gentleman as quickly as possible? *All facts please.*

We understand that Mr. Goldenson has proceeded with a private investigation into the Red Watch affair.

A priority please.

Brewster

Private and Confidential.

From: Hector Rambeau
  To: Senator Brewster

December 9, 1961

Subject: *Lawrence A. Goldenson*

Preliminary examination has been completed.

Recommend an immediate conference in reference to the Red Watch affair.

Suggest lower-level participation for this briefing.

Secretary D'Allesandro and your colleague Senator Atken will be briefed on all forthcoming information.

Rambeau

The six months since Hawthorne's return to Hut Three had crawled by as Hawthorne's bitterness and frustration had grown.

All negotiations at Panmunjom had come to a standstill, mainly because of prisoner repatriation problems and charges of germ warfare against the American forces in Manchuria. In addition, there were rumors of sporadic raids on the Red capital of Pyongyang.

At times Hawthorne wondered why he had deprived himself of all privileges in order to remain loyal to his nation's questionable cause. His daily rations had been reduced to the lowest in the hut and he had been assigned regular work details while the others had lazed through the days and nights of imprisonment. During the long evenings, he would turn his face to the wall and try to ignore Corporal Martino as the man held regular court, outlining impossible and at times maniacal plans to procure food, whiskey, cigarettes and freedom.

The plots frequently included the use of tunnels, hidden explosives, disguises or organized resistance and revolt against the Chinese. None of the insane proposals was ever attempted and Hawthorne had managed to close his ears to most of these rambling sessions.

On the night of September 5, 1952, Hawthorne returned exhausted from a grueling labor detail on the punishment rock pile. He stumbled wearily across the room and flopped face-down on his bunk without glancing in the direction of the other men, who were huddled together as usual, listening attentively to another imaginative Martino scheme.

The muffled whispers sounded almost soothing as he adjusted his position and turned toward the wall.

Hawthorne was beginning to doze as he heard Martino mention Chow Chow and food and something about an unauthorized nightly delivery to an officer in the administration section. Chow was the answer to their food and cigarette problems, he heard Martino preach softly.

Details of the special delivery were mentioned once again and Martino whispered something about a shirt and a surprise. Talbot agreed to take the box while the hut leader tightened the noose.

"Not too tight," Hawthorne heard Guzman interrupt, and then Martino jabbered on about his own expertise with silent weapons.

"My special technique will keep him out and under for about an hour. He wakes up to an empty food crate and he can't do a damn thing about it," Martino said.

"Just don't pull that fucking thing too tight," cautioned Guzman.

Somebody laughed and then another voice talked quietly about food and whiskey and Chinks as Hawthorne floated into a welcome sleep.

SEPTEMBER 5, 1952
CAMP SIX
KOREA

29

SUDDENLY HE WAS jolted awake by the crushing impact of a fist against the side of his head.

He sat up abruptly and stared into the angry face of an unfamiliar guard.

After a moment of shock and total confusion, he realized that the soldier was pointing a pistol directly at his chest.

Hawthorne glanced quickly around the hut and was amazed to see five other camp guards with revolvers drawn and aimed at the heads of the other squad members who looked dazed.

Hawthorne blinked several times and then tried to shake

himself awake as Kwen San burst into the squad room accompanied by another high-ranking official.

"One of our prison guards is killed by men in this hut!" he stammered. *"Chow is dead. The man who killed Chow will confess tonight or all in this hut will die by morning!"*

The announcement stunned Hawthorne and he was forced to repeat the statement slowly to himself in order to take it in. His eyes moved slowly from the officer to the terrified faces of the American prisoners of war, and then he remembered what he had overheard of Martino's latest plot.

The camp jailer wheeled about and marched out of the hut while the other officers remained at attention in the center of the squad room.

There was complete silence.

The ranking officer unfolded a document from his tunic and squinted at the contents for a moment.

"First Class Private Landau Hyman," he shrieked.

The prisoner gasped as a guard yanked him out of the bunk and held his weapon against the side of his face. Another officer pointed to Landau and shouted, *"This man go first for questioning!"*

Then he nodded to the armed guard, who gripped Landau firmly by the back of the collar and shoved him across the room with the revolver pressed between his shoulder blades.

When the prisoner had stumbled out of the hut, the official stood at ease and addressed the remaining prisoners of the Third Squad.

"We now wait!" he shouted. *"He come back and next man go. No talk and no move!"*

Grief for Chow and a deep sense of loss began to replace Hawthorne's feelings of resentment and hatred for Martino and the others but then he shook off these emotions and decided he would not give way to sentimentality. Corporal Martino was a fellow American soldier and a prisoner of war. So was Winston Talbot and the other three members of Hut Three.

Chow was a Chinese Communist soldier. A guard. The enemy. He had not been murdered. The man had been killed in action by captive members of the United States Armed Forces.

Hawthorne knew that this self-imposed emotional clamp must remain secure during the rest of his confinement. He must continue to think and act as a dedicated soldier and a loyal American citizen. If he allowed his emotions full rein, he would surely make it his business to find the sharpest knife in the administration section kitchens and then slice strips of flesh from the bodies of the American pigs in Hut Three as personal revenge for the death of Chow . . . his very dear friend.

Private First Class Hyman Landau was hauled back into the squad room by two of Kwen San's elite troopers and tossed violently across his bunk. The other hut members gazed fearfully at the first victim of the interrogation.

Landau appeared to be semiconscious. He had been beaten severely about the face and on various parts of his body. His nose was bleeding profusely and it might have been broken. There was a deep gash over his right eye and both cheeks were puffed and badly scratched. It also seemed that he was unable to move his left arm properly.

Landau turned slightly on his side, screamed in agony and then passed out.

"Can we wipe the blood off his face?" asked Guzman.

"*Quiet!*" the Chinese official demanded. "*Talk or move and you die!*" He referred to his list once again.

"*First Class Private Winston* . . ." He peered closer at the document. "*Talbot,*" he added.

The soldier turned deathly white. The officer motioned with his head and Private First Class Winston Talbot was booted across the room and out the door of the hut.

In a short while, he was hauled back to his bunk with blood flowing from his mouth but it was obvious that he had endured a far less severe interrogation session than Hyman Landau. He had a few reddish welts on his neck and the beginning of a black eye, but he was conscious and able to navigate back to his bunk without assistance.

Corporal Pancho Guzman was next on the list. He walked out confidently, without protesting.

His return was rather peculiar.

There were no outward signs that he had taken a beating and yet the man seemed to be in a state of total shock. He moved slowly through the hut with both arms held rigidly at his sides, and this trance-like condition was more startling than the obvious injuries of Landau and Talbot. He had to be directed to his bunk by the guard, and when he sat down, he glanced at the two wounded squad members. He remained in a daze. His lips began to tremble and in a moment tears were streaming down his cheeks but he made no sound or movement.

"*Corporal Martino!*" the officer shrieked. "*You go next!*"

Hawthorne had been waiting for this moment. He watched the hut leader climb defiantly out of his bunk, ignoring the guard's pistol which was positioned a few inches from his head.

Talbot suddenly raised himself up slightly and spluttered through his broken mouth. "Give those Chink bastards all kinds of hell."

"*Silence!*" screamed the officer.

Corporal Martino marched stiffly out of the hut with his eyes straight ahead.

Landau was still unconscious when Martino returned to the hut an hour later.

Guzman was too detached to pay any attention to his arrival but Hawthorne inspected the hut leader with intense curiosity and suspicion as the Chinese guard prodded him through the door.

The Corporal's body was bent forward and he appeared to be suffering from pain in his groin. His movements were slow and unsteady and his face was contorted in an expression of agony. Martino was unmarked and Hawthorne had a strong feeling that the man was exaggerating the severity of his ordeal. He groaned as he was pushed across his bunk.

"*Corporal Hawthorne!*" the officer shouted without glancing at his list. "*Hawthorne go now!*"

The assigned guard moved the pistol a few inches closer as Hawthorne slid calmly off the bunk and started his walk to the front door.

"We will dispense with formalities, Corporal," the civilian stated grimly. "Sign this document now and you will save four American lives."

Hawthorne faced the panel of Kwen San, the civilian, and a small officer in the main interrogation room and did not look down as the document was shoved across the table with a fountain pen. The atmosphere in the room was unusually tense. An armed guard was posted at attention in front of each of the doors leading to the private interrogation chambers.

"Your last refusal to cooperate was merely an insult," the interrogator went on in perfect English. "This time the matter is of the utmost gravity. I can assure you that your vacation is now officially over."

He lifted one of the pistols and aimed it threateningly at the document on the table.

"This piece of paper has nothing to do with cooperation," he snarled. "A Chinese soldier has been murdered and the killer or killers will die in a few hours."

He slowly raised the muzzle of the weapon until it was pointed directly at Hawthorne's head.

"Sign the confession, Corporal," he ordered coldly. "You will spare the lives of your fellow American soldiers."

"I did not kill Chow," Hawthorne stated firmly without flinching from the revolver. "He was my friend."

"You had confidential information because of your work in the administration buildings," the civilian continued, ignoring the prisoner's statement. "You planned and executed this crime with the help of one or two others."

He moved the pistol closer until it was nearly touching Hawthorne's forehead. The interrogator proceeded to squeeze lightly on the trigger. "Confess at once and name your accomplices."

"Chow was my friend," Hawthorne repeated. "I did not kill

him." He lowered his eyes. "His death has made me very sad."

"You refuse to sign?"

Hawthorne continued to stare at the table without answering.

"Have you anything else to say, Hawthorne?" the civilian asked.

"No," the prisoner whispered. "I don't have anything else to say."

Kwen San leaned close to the civilian and spoke softly in Chinese. Finally, the interrogator nodded, slowly withdrew the weapon and placed it on the table. He settled back in his chair as Kwen San barked an order which instantly activated two of the guards.

The men lifted the prisoner out of his chair in one sweeping motion and he was hauled swiftly through the first chamber door. Hawthorne had expected an array of sinister-looking tools but was amazed to find himself in a small, square, windowless room.

This cubicle was furnished with a plain wooden table and a straight-backed chair, and there was soft padding on the walls and ceiling. There were no weapons or special instruments of torture anywhere in sight.

One of the guards motioned to the chair and Hawthorne sat down.

Suddenly a total eclipse transformed the small room into a black pit. The effect was more than just an absence of light. This was pitch-blackness, thick and impenetrable. Instant blindness, he thought.

At the same moment, both hands were locked securely behind his back and his legs were clamped to the sides of the chair.

He tried to move an arm but stopped instantly when he realized that the restraining device had been designed to tighten painfully each time he made an effort to struggle or to shift his position.

Hawthorne sat motionless and waited.

There was absolute silence and it was impossible to determine whether he was alone or surrounded by the guards. At the time of the unexpected blackout, he had remembered hearing a heavy door clang shut but there had been no other sound since.

The abnormal stillness was soon broken by the resonant tones of an unfamiliar voice. It could have been an American or an expertly trained Chinese interrogator.

"You'd better sound off, Hawthorne," the voice warned. "These boys play very rough."

He did not respond.

"Four innocent guys will be slaughtered unless you have the guts to take your punishment," the voice continued. "This is your last chance."

The small room was completely still as the hidden interrogator waited for a reply.

Finally, Hawthorne heard a bolt being drawn and the metal door swung open and then quickly slammed shut again.

There was a strange shuffling noise, and without a word of warning the prisoner felt a cold, thin wire being adjusted around the top of his head. It was tightened firmly by someone who had obviously been standing behind him since their entrance into the room. There was no pain or discomfort of any kind. A metal halo, Hawthorne decided, and he nearly smiled.

At that moment, a blinding beam of light was flashed directly into his face and he was forced to close his eyes.

"Confess! You are killer of Chow!"

Another voice. Unfamiliar but definitely Chinese.

"I did not kill Chow." He responded quietly. "He was my friend."

It all happened very quickly and unexpectedly and at first he could not establish the source of the trouble.

The sensation began in his mouth. At first he experienced an ache, which developed quickly into severe pain and soon his teeth were splitting and crumbling into chalky powder.

His tongue and gums were beginning to swell and he could not swallow. Hot prongs were forced deeply into his nostrils and he could not breathe.

A shrill and piercing tone increased in volume until it was

bursting his eardrums and he was forced to scream hysterically.

The prisoner opened his eyes and stared insanely into the glaring ray of light but could not locate his assailants in order to beg for mercy.

A razor-sharp steel object was being hammered through the back of his skull, slowly cutting and slicing through the inside of his head.

Unbearable pressure of some kind was forcing his eyes to bulge and he knew that in a short time they would pop from their sockets.

A steady flow of sour vomit swirled inside his nose and throat and he was unable to heave it out of his mouth.

Then a high voltage lightning bolt struck his brain and the shock created weird patterns and strange colors. He watched with fascination as a thick knife hacked painlessly through his neck.

In a moment, his head had fallen to the floor of Chamber One and the excruciating pain vanished.

Gerald Howard Hawthorne was unconscious.

The odor was very strong. It choked him and jolted his senses each time he was forced to inhale.

In a while, he was able to lift his head and stare blankly at the three hazy figures who were sitting across the table in the main interrogation room.

He quickly ran his tongue around the inside of his mouth and was relieved to find that his teeth had not turned to powder. The steel wire had been removed from his skull and there were no signs of permanent injury.

"You will survive," said the civilian. "For the moment anyway."

Hawthorne managed to bring the man into focus although his hearing was still temporarily impaired by the ordeal in the special chamber. His head ached and he knew by the stains on his scattered clothing that he had not imagined the swirling green sickness.

"That was a very mild example of our persuasive techniques," the official was saying. "We have been lenient with you again, Hawthorne." He paused as the prisoner leaned forward in order to hear properly. "Will you now confess to the murder of our camp guard?"

"No."

"You will find the next chamber even more convincing," he promised coldly. "Not just a slight shock treatment, Hawthorne. That second door leads to permanent injury."

The fuzziness had cleared completely and the prisoner was now able to take in the entire scene. He calmly observed Kwen San and the small, bespectacled officer. He was aware of the pistols, documents, chamber doors, guards and the grim face of the interviewer.

"I will not confess," Hawthorne declared in a shaky voice. He turned to Kwen San. "*You* should know that Chow was my friend. I didn't kill him."

The camp jailer glared at the prisoner and remarked, "You stupid American. Tell or die with the others." Then, changing his tactics: "Help Chow," San suggested gently. "Confess for Chow."

The civilian interjected, "Let us suppose that you may be telling the truth. *Someone* in the Third Squad killed Chow. Will you give us the name of your Chinese friend's murderer?"

"I can't do that."

"Do you know the name of Chow's killer?"

"I think so."

"But you will not divulge the information?"

"No," the prisoner whispered. "I can't."

"Why not, Hawthorne?"

"I can only say that I didn't kill him."

"You refuse to inform on your fellow Americans." The civilian smiled. "Correct?"

"Maybe."

"But Chow Chow was your friend and his death has saddened you."

"I'm a soldier and an American citizen."

"Admirable, Hawthorne," the civilian said sourly. "But a complete waste of time and effort."

The prisoner looked bewildered as the official leaned back comfortably in his chair.

"We have the name of Chow's killer already," the man announced grimly. He glanced at his watch. "The murderer will be executed in exactly thirty minutes. These are signed statements, Hawthorne. We do not ordinarily spend so much time trying to elicit official proclamations of guilt. In this case, we have taken special precautions to observe the conditions of the Geneva Convention because of the delicate situation at Panmunjom."

He shoved the documents toward the prisoner.

Hawthorne scanned the confessions of Squad Three and felt the bitterness and hatred welling up inside him.

"Corporal Gerald Howard Hawthorne," the small officer announced in surprisingly good English, "this special camp tribunal finds you guilty of murder and orders that you be executed by an assigned firing squad at precisely seven o'clock this morning."

The accused seemed neither startled nor afraid as he gazed steadily at the officer. His eyes then moved slowly to the interrogator and finally they came to rest on the cold, chisled features of Kwen San.

Hawthorne turned back to the civilian and pointed to the neat pile of official papers. "Every statement is false," he said quietly. "I did not kill Chow."

Kwen San picked up the documents and placed them in a folder.

"It makes very little difference now," he remarked casually. He put the folder in a leather briefcase and snapped it shut. Suddenly he pounded his fist on the table and the unexpected action startled the interrogator as well as Hawthorne.

"Stupid American!" he blasted. *"You not kill Chow. Why you die for pigs?"*

He lowered his voice and leaned closer to the prisoner. "Who kill Chow?" he asked again.

They had set him up for execution, Hawthorne realized. Martino and all the others. And then he thought of the huge giant and the little fat girl in Peking.

"Corporal Albert Martino devised the plot and strangled Chow," Hawthorne confessed. "I didn't see it happen but I heard them talking."

Kwen San leaned back in his chair.

The civilian opened his briefcase, removed the signed documents, and tore them to shreds as Kwen San shouted a crisp order in Chinese. One of the guards left the main interrogation room. The civilian removed another piece of paper from his briefcase and picked up a pen.

"Give me a complete and truthful statement," said the interrogator. "Name Martino and then sign this document."

"I'll do it," Hawthorne replied in an unsteady voice. "But you have to promise me something."

The Communist glanced up suspiciously.

"Only Martino should be punished," Hawthorne stated very firmly. "You have to promise that none of the other guys will be hurt." The prisoner paused. "Only Martino," he repeated somberly.

The civilian thought for a moment and then nodded. "You have my word. Only Martino."

He turned to Kwen San and explained in Chinese. The camp jailer also indicated that he was in agreement.

"Tell true story!" San commanded. *"Only one pig then die. Martino!"*

Gerald Hawthorne paused thoughtfully as his eyes focused on the small pile of torn documents in the center of the table.

"Proceed," the civilian ordered. "We must complete your statement as quickly as possible."

At eight-thirty in the morning on September 6, 1952, Corporal Albert Martino of Newark, New Jersey, was removed from Hut Three for additional questioning in reference to the killing of a Chinese prison camp guard.

The American soldier did not return to his squad.

At precisely 11:45 A.M. on this date, the prisoner of war was executed by a Chinese firing squad and buried in the cemetery section of Camp Six, which was located at the far end of the exercise field.

The following squad members participated in the morning burial detail: Private First Class Winston Talbot of Virginia. Corporal Pancho Guzman of New Mexico. Corporal Gerald Howard Hawthorne of Michigan.

Private First Class Hyman Landau of Maryland had been excused by a member of the Camp Six hospital staff because of his weakened physical condition.

The burial was personally supervised by Kwen San and three of his most proficient troopers.

The American prisoners of war cooperated without the usual complaints and excuses.

There were no incidents of any kind.

October 7, 1952
Camp Six
Korea

The days and weeks and months of confinement were beginning to claw at Hawthorne's sanity and he was forced to muster all his strength and determination in order to separate himself from the others. They had already surrendered to the filth, boredom and deprivation of life as Korean prisoners of war.

Martino's death and burial had never been discussed in Hut Three. It was apparent to the others that Hawthorne must have put the finger on the actual murderer.

Winston Talbot was a twitching bag of bones and Pancho Guzman had evidently suffered some kind of permanent brain damage. His movements were unsteady, and his reactions were slow and unpredictable.

Hyman Landau was blind in both eyes and spent much of his time crouching on the floor next to his bunk, sobbing bitterly.

The Communists had ceased to assign heavy work details to the three prisoners and adequate food and clothing rations had been provided for the hut on a steady basis. Hawthorne assumed that the leniency and special attention had something to do with the peace talks at Panmunjom.

At times, he wondered how he had managed to survive the ordeal of imprisonment without suffering the same physical and mental breakdowns as the others. The stench and silence and the feeling of human decay in the hut were slowly affecting his sensibilities, but he had not lost his will to survive. The others were dying and he was alive because of his early conditioning. All his life, and especially since the death of his mother, he had been subjected to indifference, beaten, humiliated, starved and sadistically tortured in every possible manner. He had already experienced prolonged silence and only in isolation had he known peace and tranquility. For years, he had been the butt of other people's aggression and unpredictable outbursts and he was used to the pain of hopelessness.

Whereas the three other prisoners in Hut Three were totally unprepared for the rigors of their present existence, and they were destined for oblivion.

All three men, Talbot, Guzman and Landau, had quickly signed numerous documents condemning the actions of the United States in the Korean war. Hawthorne despised them for their weakness and open collaboration with the enemy, but mainly he cursed himself for his own decision to hold out and thereby eliminate every opportunity for study, contact and productive activity in the administration buildings.

He had not been summoned to the interrogation area since his formal charges against Corporal Albert Martino. K. M. Wing was still in Tsinan and the other Chinese officials ignored him completely. The library was still out of bounds and all other camp privileges had been suspended.

The war seemed never-ending, and he was beginning to question the motives and tactics of the United States government. Distressed and confused by the lengthy peace negotiations, he wanted desperately to discuss the situation with someone—anyone—American or Chinese or Korean. Friend or foe. He needed so many answers and explanations.

30

ON NOVEMBER 10, 1952, Trygve Lie resigned as Secretary General of the United Nations and on the fourteenth India submitted a compromise plan in connection with the repatriation of prisoners of war.

Russia rejected the proposal on November 21, 1952.

On the twenty-sixth of November, Gerald Hawthorne received a brief note from his father.

Dear Son,

Sorry for not writing sooner but I've been real sick.

Doc Beaton told me that the old pump is weak as hell and I've got to take things smooth and easy from now on.

God bless you, boy, for having the United States Army send me money every month. It sure has saved my miserable soul.

It must be hell for you over there but the thing is almost finished now.

Don't try to be a big war hero. Just do the best you can and come home to Waverly where people love you.

I'll make damn sure that all these terrible years are made up to you properly.

I think about you all the time and can't wait to see you.

All my love,
Dad

Hawthorne thought for a while about the sick plumber and Elm Drive.

Then, instead of tearing the note to pieces, he placed it neatly in a corner of his locker box.

On December 1, 1952, Hawthorne was officially summoned to the main interrogation area.

For the first time, the prisoner snapped to stiff and immediate attention as he entered the large room. He was momentarily shocked by the scene. Colonel Roland Fawcett was sitting ramrod-straight in the center of a dignified group of senior Chinese officers.

"At ease," the officer ordered. "Take a seat over here, Hawthorne."

The prisoner sat nervously facing the men at the table. This was completely unlike any of the other interrogation sessions and the expressions on the faces of the panel members testified to the importance of the occasion.

There were no pistols or documents on the long table.

The Chinese participants were all high-ranking military men, smartly uniformed and unfamiliar to Hawthorne.

Colonel Roland Fawcett appeared to be presiding. The tall American officer looked as crisp and commanding as ever. His uniform was immaculately pressed and his dark crew-cut hair had been neatly trimmed. He was the personification of strict West Point leadership and Hawthorne marveled at the man's ability to endure the pressures of confinement without showing the slightest change in manner or appearance.

"I'm glad to see you looking fit, Hawthorne," the officer remarked in his clipped fashion. "It's the sign of a good soldier."

Slowly the scene began to make sense to the prisoner. Since Fawcett was obviously in complete charge of the session, the only explanation was peace at Panmunjom.

"Have you been in a position to receive reports from Panmunjom?" the officer asked quietly.

"No, sir," Hawthorne replied, feeling certain now that his reasoning was accurate.

"The conflict is nearly over," Fawcett explained. "A plan in connection with prisoner repatriation was proposed by India on the fourteenth of this month but it was rejected by the Russian government."

Hawthorne sat at attention and absorbed every word with interest.

"It seems now that the plan will be accepted by the United

Nations in a day or two." The Colonel paused. "It's certainly good news for all of us."

"Yes, sir."

The American officer leaned back in his chair and glanced up at the ceiling thoughtfully.

"We have gone through a terrible ordeal," he said. "This political and military insanity cannot be allowed to happen again."

The prisoner watched closely and was fascinated by the officer's lack of constraint in the presence of the silent Chinese Communists. Suddenly Fawcett stared directly at him and his expression was grim and angry.

"There is only one way to prevent further barbaric acts of this kind," he snarled. "Every man involved must have the courage to speak the truth, regardless of the consequences."

Hawthorne stared for a moment and felt puzzled.

"Do you have courage, Hawthorne?"

"I hope so, sir," the prisoner replied uneasily.

"It has nothing to do with being a soldier or an American," he explained. "I'm talking about the duties and responsibilities of human beings. Do you understand?"

"I think so, Colonel."

The man leaned across the table and lowered his voice.

"As a corporal in the United States Army you are at a disadvantage," he explained somberly. "You are not in a position to know, understand or judge the workings of your high command."

"No, sir."

"As a good soldier you take orders and obey your superiors and in this way the military can function effectively."

"Yes, sir."

"I also obey *my* superior officers, usually without question or hesitation."

Hawthorne studied him and waited for him to get to the main point of his lecture.

"As a human being I am ashamed of my blind obedience and you must also bear the burden of guilt."

"I don't understand, Colonel," the prisoner replied.

"We have been using germs in Manchuria, Hawthorne," the officer responded bluntly. "I have signed a statement to this effect."

Hawthorne's expression remained unchanged as the officer confided quietly. "This has been the most difficult action of my life. As a loyal American officer I could have helped to conceal this monstrous act against humanity. But as a civilized human being I must join those who will make certain that it never happens again."

The officer leaned back and picked up a briefcase from the floor. He removed a document and placed it on the table.

"The Chinese have many detailed confessions already in their files but we feel that additional statements from American combat heroes in Korea will arouse public outrage and make an impact during the talks at Panmunjom."

He twisted his mouth slightly into what Hawthorne assumed to be a smile. "Your Silver Star for gallantry in action carries a lot of weight back home. America loves heroes and the press exploits them cleverly."

The officer pushed the document across the table and the prisoner accepted it without glancing down.

"Were you in Manchuria, Colonel?" Hawthorne asked very politely.

"No," the officer replied. "I rely on very dependable eye-witness accounts and we have our special Army intelligence information." He handed Hawthorne a fountain pen. "Read the statement if you wish."

"I don't have to read it, sir," the prisoner replied dutifully.

"Then sign at the bottom right-hand corner." He pointed. "Add your serial number, age, place of birth and date of enlistment. Several of the officers here will witness the signature."

Hawthorne stared at him without making a move to inspect or sign the official paper.

"How can you confess to germ warfare when you didn't see it happen?" he asked resentfully.

"Are you questioning me, Corporal?"

"Yes, sir."

"How dare you?"

"You see, Colonel," the prisoner continued as Fawcett's face hardened. "I once signed a murder charge against a man in my squad. I didn't actually see him kill the guard called Chow." Hawthorne noticed that the officer was furious but he decided to continue anyway. "The Chinese executed him and I was responsible for his death."

Hawthorne touched the document in front of him. "This is much worse, Colonel," he went on. "At least then I heard some talk during the night."

"Sign the paper," the officer ordered in a low voice. "I'm warning you."

The prisoner stared at him silently with cold contempt.

"Sign the paper, Corporal," Fawcett repeated sternly. "I will disregard your impudence and give you this last chance."

Hawthorne did not move and the Colonel suddenly reached across the table and gripped him tightly by his shirt collar.

"*Sign the paper, Corporal!*" Fawcett shouted. "*That's a direct order!*"

The young prisoner glared with uncontrollable hatred for an instant. Then he pulled back slightly and spat into the face of his superior officer.

"You goddamn pig!" Hawthorne forced the words out as the Colonel's hold became a vise of steel on his neck. "You make me hate my country."

The two figures seemed to be frozen in their positions for several seconds. Fawcett released his stranglehold and removed a handkerchief from the pocket of his uniform. He dried his face quickly and then put the cloth away.

"You had better pray to God that these people kill you, Hawthorne," the Colonel said with surprising restraint. "If for some strange reason you happen to be alive at the time of repatriation . . ." He paused, lifted the document and placed it back in the briefcase. "Then I suggest very strongly that you take your own life before you board the trucks for home."

The officer closed the case very quietly and glanced at Hawthorne.

"I am quite certain that the Chinese will accommodate you after witnessing your exhibition this afternoon," he added.

On the evening of December 1, 1952, Hawthorne was placed in solitary confinement by official order of the Camp Six commandant. It was a cold black box, located deep underground at the west end of Kwen San's prison compound. It was known as the "coffin" and very few prisoners had ever survived in the hole for more than two or three days.

Even those who had been subjected to just a short spell in solitary were transferred to the base hospital immediately after release, and not one man had ever been reassigned to his original squad.

The "coffin people" had most frequently just disappeared from Camp Six.

It was always the same dream. Exact in every detail. Night after night for months and years.

Only this time the antiseptic smells were sharper than ever before and the muffled sounds of suffering were now more distinct. This time the narrow white bed was not floating in space and the smiling Chinese face had developed eyes and ears, a nose and a mouth.

Hawthorne felt himself sinking slowly back into the cold, rat-infested darkness and he gripped the sides of the hospital cot.

"Try very hard to stay awake. You will feel much better in a few days."

Hawthorne squeezed the edges of the bed even tighter and forced his eyes to focus on the source of the soothing voice.

"We have already made very good use of deep sleep. Now you must not be lazy."

There was someone sitting on a chair close to the hospital bunk and Hawthorne finally grasped the fact that he had somehow been rescued from insanity and probably from death.

"My name is Dr. Liang Yu."

The physician was thin and appeared to be elderly although it was difficult for Hawthorne to see him properly because of the slight haze which marred his vision.

He had white hair and a kindly face and Hawthorne was immediately impressed by the man's sincere manner. His English was impeccable and Hawthorne assumed that the man must have spent a considerable amount of time outside of China.

"You are a very lucky man, Corporal," the voice spoke gently. "I have seldom seen a patient recover from so many complications without suffering prolonged and serious illness."

He rose wearily to his feet and Hawthorne observed that the man was wearing a clean white medical uniform.

The prisoner remembered his last visit to the "butcher shop." This dignified doctor seemed to be the only professional-looking member of the entire hospital staff. Hawthorne had not seen him in the camp before and wondered if he had recently arrived from Peking. Dr. Yu stood at the edge of the bed.

"I will visit again later this evening," he said pleasantly. "Your progress has been remarkable. I attribute your strong recuperative powers to youth and obstinacy."

The man smiled and Hawthorne raised his hand as though requesting permission to speak.

"Use your throat, Corporal," the doctor ordered professionally. "The sensation of dryness is quite temporary."

The prisoner swallowed hard several times before attempting to speak.

"What's the date?" he asked. The harsh sound of his own voice startled him for an instant.

"January 6, 1953."

Hawthorne looked stunned and the doctor explained.

"You were imprisoned on the first of December 1952 and the ordeal continued until the twentieth." His expression changed abruptly and he spoke with a touch of bitterness. "A few more days and Wing would have rescued a corpse."

"Wing?"

"K. M. Wing returned from Tsinan on December 19 and asked about you on the following day. I do not know the details of your release but you were brought to me on the evening of the twentieth."

Hawthorne studied the doctor very carefully as the haze began to clear. He estimated that the doctor was sixty or perhaps sixty-five although he appeared to be older because of his stooped posture and a wrinkled complexion. However, his eyes were young and bright and they sparkled with vitality and alertness.

"Is the war finished?" the prisoner asked.

Dr. Yu frowned and seemed to adopt a more formal attitude as he replied.

"No. The talks are deadlocked." He glanced at his watch and looked uneasy about discussing the situation. "In fact, some of the fighting has increased," he added. Then his features softened into a smile. "Wing can tell you more about these things. I'm concerned with medicine."

"Is he coming to the hospital?" Hawthorne asked.

"Wing has visited you on two occasions already."

"I didn't know that."

"He ordered certain important antibiotics and brought them to me personally on the twenty-third of December." The doctor paused and seemed to reflect for a moment. "These particular drugs are not usually available at this hospital. They probably saved your life, Corporal."

The prisoner looked up at the ceiling. "We used to talk a lot about China and things. I haven't seen him in a long time."

Dr. Yu watched as the boy closed his eyes and turned his head away.

"Wing is my very close friend," said the doctor. "I am also from Tsinan. We have talked about you at various times."

"I'm interested in China," the prisoner said without opening his eyes.

"I know."

The doctor started to leave but then hesitated as Hawthorne stirred and propped himself up on one elbow.

"When is he coming to the hospital?" the prisoner asked.

"Wing will be here in a week or two."

"Oh."

"My friend has been waiting to talk to you about something very important but I have refused to allow the meeting until your condition improves considerably."

"I'm all right now."

"We'll wait another week, Hawthorne," the doctor said seriously. "Wing's visit is a little more than social and I don't believe that you should be subjected to a serious discussion which will probably result in a critical decision."

Hawthorne stared at him curiously. "What does he want to talk to me about?"

Dr. Yu smoothed his white uniform. "My business is strictly medicine, Corporal. I do not question K. M. Wing. Continue to improve and you will know in a short time."

Hawthorne's progress was remarkable. He attributed his improvement to Dr. Liang Yu's care and kindliness. After a few days, he was well enough to leave his bed for short periods of time and he would sit in a quiet corner of the hospital ward and discuss various topics with his physician. Dr. Yu was impressed with the boy's intelligence and his almost obsessive interest in China and the complicated Chinese language. He told Hawthorne about medical superstition in the Sung dynasty and the history of Chinese drugs, herbs, moxibustion and acupuncture, and everything he spoke of seemed to interest the boy.

But he refused to discuss politics or the war in Korea.

On the evening of January 11, 1953, Dr. Yu took a photograph from his pocket and changed the life of Gerald Hawthorne.

"This is my daughter," he beamed. "Her name is Ling Yu. She is a teacher and I am very proud."

The man handed the snapshot to Hawthorne.

Liang Yu's daughter was sitting gracefully on a rock in the midst of a calm, clear lake, wearing a simple and conservatively styled dress. She had long black hair and delicately-formed features. She had her father's radiant smile and sparkling eyes but her expression suggested a certain shyness.

Hawthorne definitely wanted a closer look at the girl. He imagined her to be gentle and kind and very understanding.

Of course, she was intelligent. A teacher had to be well educated and clever.

"Ling teaches in a small school on the outskirts of Tsinan," the doctor commented as Hawthorne returned the snapshot.

"She's beautiful," said the prisoner.

The man smiled and put the picture back in his uniform pocket. He stood and Hawthorne did also.

"I forgot to mention that a meeting has been arranged with K. M. Wing," the doctor stated.

"When?"

"Tomorrow evening," he replied. "You will talk with him in the private visiting room downstairs at eight o'clock."

"I'm looking forward to seeing him."

"Yes," the doctor replied. Then he paused thoughtfully. "Wing has wanted to speak with you for a long time but I purposely delayed the reunion until I was certain of your complete recovery."

"I think I'm ready now, Doc," Hawthorne commented confidently.

"Yes, Corporal," the doctor agreed. "I believe that you are ready now."

The private visit with K. M. Wing started very pleasantly.

Hawthorne thanked him for the rescue and also for the special antibiotics which had saved his life.

"Liang Yu is a modest man and a brilliant doctor," Wing interrupted. "Thank him instead."

Wing then talked about his family and his extended visit to Tsinan. During the course of the conversation, Hawthorne had the distinct impression that K. M. Wing really wanted to talk about something else—about a very important matter. They finally settled back and the interrogator offered a cigarette.

"Smoke it cautiously," he warned. "The doctor might disapprove."

Hawthorne accepted and the official got to the point.

"I managed to secure your immediate release from the 'coffin' because you were very close to death." He lit both cigarettes and the prisoner was careful not to inhale the first drag. "It was, however, a conditional release," Wing continued. "I promptly accepted the stipulations outlined by the commandant because there were no alternatives and time was the important factor. You needed hospitalization immediately."

"I understand."

"You must now sign a statement for the camp officials," Wing stated firmly. "This is in exchange for your life and I have taken complete responsibility for your cooperation."

"What statement?" Hawthorne asked suspiciously.

Wing pointed to a fat briefcase beside his chair.

"Statements, Corporal," he said quietly. "From nearly everyone about almost everything."

"Germ warfare?"

"A stack of impressive American confessions."

"But not mine," Hawthorne responded quickly.

"No. Not yours. The talks are deadlocked over prisoner repatriation, but the problems will soon be resolved and it will all be over. Camp Six will be forgotten very quickly."

He took a long drag of his cigarette and blew the smoke toward the ceiling.

"What statement, Mr. Wing?" Hawthorne asked harshly.

"You will place your signature on a statement of truth," the interrogator replied.

"I'm not placing my signature anywhere."

Wing scowled and opened the case.

"You participated in an engagement which resulted in the slaughter of seventy or eighty American soldiers." The interrogator removed a document from the case. "It seems that this information has been officially withheld from the people of the United States. Rumors have filtered back but actual proof of the military blunder has never been presented to the American public."

He took out a paper and placed the case back on the floor.

"You were there." Wing waved the paper and faced Hawthorne. "We want a personal and detailed account of the incident."

"What the hell does it prove?" Hawthorne growled. He

tossed his cigarette to the floor. Wing glanced at him angrily for an instant but then ground out the butt with his heel as he replied patiently, "The talks are still in progress. An *honest* description of this war in Korea must be presented to the world. That slaughter is a valid statement of fact and you were a participant."

The interrogator handed the paper to the prisoner, who accepted it reluctantly.

"You have twenty-four hours in which to prepare your report." He indicated the paper and Hawthorne took a cursory look. "There is an official seal at the top and space for the witnessing and verification of your signature at the bottom of the back page. The rest is blank. Tell the story accurately and in your own words."

The prisoner sat holding the document and he was obviously disillusioned.

"There is something else," Wing added in a brighter tone of voice. "If your statement pleases the commandant and a few other officials, you will have all of your camp privileges restored immediately. I might be able to set up. the private hut again and get you back into the administration buildings."

"Suppose I refuse to cooperate?" Hawthorne asked grimly.

"You will be discharged from the hospital and returned to Hut Three to await further disciplinary action. Colonel Roland Fawcett and the senior American prisoner group will also be involved in the recommendation of punishment."

"Filthy bastard."

"I heard the story," the interrogator said. "Beware of this man, Hawthorne. He is evil but very influential in America."

"He's still a filthy bastard."

Wing stood and picked up the briefcase.

"Make the statement," he said, stepping closer to the prisoner's chair. "It has nothing to do with patriotism or enemy propaganda. These are not fabricated charges against your country. You can make the statement and sign it in good faith."

Hawthorne rose unsteadily to his feet and took a deep breath, but before he could reply, Wing went on:

"You are being treated by the best doctor in Tsinan, and one of the finest men you will ever meet. Liang Yu is a dear friend and he has given you very special attention."

"I know," said the prisoner. "He is a good man. We talk every evening."

"His daughter is a lovely and intelligent young woman."

"I saw her picture."

"She had dinner with us on the evening before my return to the camp," the interrogator said. "My family adores her. The girl is genuine and charming and very much like her father."

"Is she married?"

"No, Hawthorne," Wing replied with a broad smile. "Ling Yu is not married."

Hawthorne returned to the hospital ward and found a letter on the small table next to his bunk. It was from Mrs. Beatrice Powell.

He read about the new bowling alley on Front Street and the divine French restaurant next to the Tivoli Theatre. Arnold Simkins had returned from Korea after serving seven long months and he considered the place a hell on earth. Mrs. Powell was waiting anxiously to hear about his thrilling personal experiences and Mr. Porter of Anderson's Hardware had promised a job in the shipping department.

Hawthorne lay down on the bed with Mrs. Powell's letter still crumpled in his hand.

He wondered whether the people of the United States were truly concerned about the "conflict" in Korea. No one had even called it a war. He tossed the letter into a wastebasket next to the bunk and stared up at the ceiling.

Late in the evening of January 12, 1953, Corporal Gerald Howard Hawthorne of Waverly, Michigan, willfully collaborated with the enemy at Camp Six, near Pyuktong, Korea.

The prisoner wrote a vivid and detailed account of an American military blunder which resulted in the slaughter of nearly eighty soldiers of the United States Army. He personally accepted responsibility for killing at least five of them.

In order to emphasize his condemnation of the prolonged conflict in Korea, he added that all participants were to blame, including the United States and the members of the United Nations.

On January 13, 1953, this statement was signed by Corporal Hawthorne and his signature was witnessed and verified by three officials in the presence of Kwen San and K. M. Wing.

It pleased the commandant and the other officials, and when Hawthorne was released from the hospital on January 21, 1953, all his camp privileges were restored.

He returned to his private hut and resumed his productive daily schedule in the administration buildings. K. M. Wing had added several new American novels to the prisoner's treasured bookcase and Dr. Liang Yu visited the hut on the first evening in order to celebrate Hawthorne's recovery and escape from his long ordeal.

DECEMBER 20, 1961
PRIVATE BAR
BRENTWOOD COUNTRY CLUB
DETROIT, MICHIGAN

31

"I APPRECIATE THIS opportunity for a private chat, Mr. Manning," the short, dark-haired man was saying. "Although your wife will never forgive me if she hears about this meeting."

"We'll be in the same boat," Manning replied. "Don't worry about it. Look, I believe in getting straight to the point, Mr. Goldenson. Why did you request a private meeting with me? Is it in reference to the Civil Rights Association?"

"Yes," the other man answered hesitantly. "It has to do with the Gerald Hawthorne case."

"That's my wife's project," the financier responded with some impatience. "I have nothing to do with it."

"That's quite true, sir," Goldenson said. "But I want to speak with you confidentially before having a formal meeting with Mrs. Manning."

"I can assure you that my wife is quite capable of handling her own affairs."

"You don't understand, Mr. Manning."

"Well, explain the damn thing, counselor," Manning demanded. "Get to the point."

Goldenson finished his brandy.

"I believe that you should be made aware of certain developments in this case before you allow your wife to become directly involved."

"First of all, Goldenson," he explained coldly, "I do not *allow* my wife to do anything. Estelle is an intelligent, mature and responsible individual. Secondly, I don't know what the hell you're driving at."

"I have started preliminary research for Mrs. Manning."

"I know that."

"My firm has studied and analyzed the provisions of the Amnesty Agreement of 1955. Are you familiar with the document?"

"Repatriation of prisoners after the Korean war."

"That is correct," said the lawyer. "The United Nations had agreed to deliver five hundred prisoners a day in groups of approximately twenty-five each and the Reds . . ."

"Mr. Goldenson," the industrialist interrupted, "tell me straight." He poured another brandy for his guest and added a touch to his own glass. "What's on your mind?"

"We have been gathering the available facts on Gerald Hawthorne's experiences in the Army, the prison camp and in Tsinan, China," the lawyer proceeded in a clipped and professional manner. "On the surface he looks like a collaborator and a treasonable type who ultimately rejected the United States of America in order to remain with the Chinese Reds."

"We all know this story, Mr. Goldenson."

"However, we need proof that there's more to it than meets the eye," the man continued. "The task is almost impossible. I have never crashed into so many brick walls before. I think we might have poked our noses into a political hornets' nest." He had lowered his voice.

"What do you mean?"

"This Hawthorne case appears to be the cover for a very complicated Washington affair."

"Meaning?"

"Certain people want us to forget about the Gerald Hawthorne investigation," the lawyer whispered. "Important people."

"Who do you consider important, Goldenson?"

"Possibly the White House."

Charles Manning threw back his head and laughed heartily. "I'm sorry," he apologized. "But that's pretty dramatic stuff, isn't it?"

The attorney's face remained grim and he did not alter the somber tone of his voice.

"I'm not a fool, Mr. Manning. My legal experience is respected in Washington."

Manning's smile vanished. "Please forgive me. I am certainly aware of your background and your credibility, Mr. Goldenson. Tell me, what happened?" Manning leaned forward on the table.

"Every door has suddenly been slammed in my face. For example, certain nonclassified files are missing, I repeat, *missing* from Archives, and this material is usually available for public inspection at all times," Goldenson proceeded in an urgent tone of voice. "Even school children use these records for class projects."

"Which files?"

"Specific information pertaining to American prisoners of war in Korea during a particular span of time."

"Did you demand an explanation?"

"I contacted a friend at the Pentagon and that's when things started to become a bit strange."

"What did he say?"

"I was told, off the record, that several folders had been pulled and reclassified for reasons involving national security. In checking back I realized that nearly every damn one of these folders had some connection with the Hawthorne case."

"Did you go to the top?" Manning asked. "I know some of the boys at the Building quite well."

"Orders for the reclassification came from some of the boys at the top," the lawyer replied. "My friend told me confidentially that he had seen General Fawcett's name on one of the requests."

"*General Fawcett?*" Manning was astonished. "Why in the hell would a man as important as Roland Fawcett be interested in a few nonclassified files on a defecting corporal?"

"Exactly," Goldenson said. "I tried other sources and again I discovered a complete lack of cooperation and an unusual absence of detailed information. Bits and pieces, nothing more. It seems that selected records have been pulled, adjusted or concealed."

"But why the commotion over a corporal?"

"I don't know at the moment," said Goldenson, "but let me finish my story and then you might draw your own conclusions."

"Please, go ahead."

"I did a bit of detective work and located two former members of the Washington bar. Whiting and Barlow. These two lawyers had started a similar investigation years ago and then the case was dropped abruptly. Both men suddenly disappeared from the legal scene.

"I had a talk with Barlow and he agreed that Hawthorne's dishonorable discharge was not justified because of the Amnesty Agreement provisions."

"Other boys went to China," Manning interrupted. "They can make the same claim."

"True," said the lawyer. "But this soldier is different. He has been accused and convicted of serious collaboration with the enemy." He cleared his throat nervously. "His official records list acts of violence against fellow American prisoners. Even murder."

"Murder?"

"In the camp near Pyuktong," Goldenson answered quickly. "Gerald Hawthorne has been judged guilty without proof or a trial. There could be a strong case against the government for back pay and damages."

"I see." The industrialist paused. "Did Barlow have more sensitive information than that?"

"He had plenty, Mr. Manning," the lawyer replied.

"What was the gist of it?"

"He knew about a dedicated McCarthy investigator with proof about the Secretary of Defense. Pressure for Hawthorne's dishonorable discharge and public disgrace for reasons still unknown. Bribery, blackmail, theft, falsification of government records and testimony. The man even alluded to physical assault and attempted murder as part of a political cover-up."

Manning shook his head. "This Barlow sounds like a complete nut."

"I thought so too."

"How did the conversation end?"

"Barlow said he has absolute proof that Hawthorne is a key that could open certain high-level doors and they all lead directly to the White House."

"How much does he want for his fantastic proof?" Manning asked sarcastically.

"I don't know," the counselor replied. "He said he wanted to think about things for a few days and he told me to contact him on the fourteenth." He paused and took a slow sip of his drink. "I did."

"And?"

"A complete change. He seemed very disturbed and asked me to leave his apartment at once."

"A maniac."

"I asked about his information and proof and he warned me never to contact him again."

"What about the other lawyer?"

"Whiting?"

"Yes."

"Nobody can trace him. And I certainly tried."

"Amazing."

"I tried to see a man by the name of Robert Spangler of Amalgamated Broadcasting. He could have told me several things about the case and besides I wanted a transcript of the

Hawthorne interview. His secretary claims that Mr. Spangler is very busy and cannot find the time to see me."

"You certainly have hit a few walls, Goldenson."

"Two evenings ago I returned to my office for a package and discovered that some very important Hawthorne research was missing from a locked file cabinet."

"I'll be damned."

Goldenson studied Manning's expression. "What do you think, Mr. Manning?"

"Hold off your meeting with my wife until I've had an opportunity to digest these facts . . . or bits of dangerous fiction."

"Should I continue with my investigation?"

Manning absently reached up to smooth his thick gray hair.

"From what you tell me, Goldenson, I have a feeling your brick walls will become thicker and higher as you get more involved. I would like to have a personal talk with Mr. Gerald Hawthorne before you take any further exploratory steps. My wife is trying to contact him in Waverly."

"I understand that Hawthorne is even more difficult to approach than General Roland Fawcett."

"My wife is a very persuasive woman."

"I can vouch for that, Mr. Manning."

"In the meantime, report to her by phone or mail and say that you are still in the process of gathering information."

"Yes, sir."

"I might take advantage of a well-placed contact of my own and perhaps ask a few discreet questions."

"Very good."

"Don't do a thing until I get back to you, Goldenson," Manning ordered. "Sometimes the smart money is on the man who knows how and when to forget information."

"I see your point, sir."

"Let's try to get *facts* and make damn certain that we know where we're heading. I don't need a skeleton key to the White House. I've walked straight through that door many times and I happen to like the people who live there."

MARCH 30, 1953
CAMP SIX
KOREA

32 ON MARCH 30, 1953, an equitable plan for prisoner repatriation had been outlined at Panmunjom. The camp hummed with talk of peace and home and family and each new development pumped fresh hope and vitality into the prisoners. News of additional progress spread rapidly after April 11 although the exact details were unavailable.

Gerald Hawthorne's unique employment arrangement in the administration buildings had placed him in a position to confirm the report that agreement had been reached, at least on the sick and wounded. The prolonged and frustrating negotiations were drawing to a close and it was now time to think of home and freedom.

Hawthorne had made effective use of his camp privileges, had perfected his ability to concentrate and study, and he was now able to absorb and understand all sorts of books. His patience and determination to learn the Chinese language were beginning to show results. The camp officials were amazed at the American's progress.

His enthusiastic interest in China had impressed Yang and Wing and Dr. Liang Yu and most of the important Communists in the administration buildings.

His world now was the world of the Chinese Communists. His hours talking with Dr. Liang Yu and K. M. Wing about Tsinan and the Chinese way of life had been fascinating. They had discussed the great philosophers and artists and poets and all the beautiful things which Hawthorne felt had been missing in his life. Wing often discussed Communism and the new Chinese culture but never seemed to insist on Hawthorne's acceptance of the theories he spoke of. The prisoner felt certain that he had never been exploited by the interrogator.

Ling Yu had enclosed messages for him in English each time she wrote to her father and Hawthorne had answered on several occasions. She had described the school on the outskirts of town and certain students and her life at home in Tsinan. Hawthorne had written very tactfully about his childhood in Waverly, Michigan. She had sent a larger photograph and Dr. Yu had allowed him to keep it in his hut.

The majority of the American prisoners at Camp Six had ignored the fact that Hawthorne had private living quarters and that he openly associated with the Reds.

Now, however, their attitude was beginning to change as the prospect of release became a reality. No longer was the struggle to survive the prisoners' only preoccupation; with this boost of morale they were now ready to turn their attention to an American traitor who enjoyed his own private hut with his own bookcase.

By May 15, 1953, the revitalized heroes of Camp Six had returned to their patterns of flag-waving, rank-pulling and tough military talk as the negotiation at Panmunjom brought the end of the Korean nightmare closer.

Gerald Hawthorne sprawled on his bunk in his private hut and thought seriously about freedom and returning to Waverly, Michigan.

He thought of his father, trying to develop a feeling of compassion for him, but was disgusted at the prospect of supporting the sick and drunken plumber. He visualized the house and his mother's sealed room.

He stood up and went over to his bookcase. He glanced at various titles and thought of how much he had learned since his frantic flight from the house on Elm Drive. The prisoner ran his fingers slowly over some of the thick volumes and decided at that moment that he would never return to the world he had known and come to despise.

"Where will you go?" asked Dr. Yu.

"I've been thinking about Columbus, Ohio," Hawthorne replied.

The physician had completed his final evening rounds and

Hawthorne appreciated the chance for a friendly chat in the staff lounge of the camp hospital.

"I know of Cleveland but Columbus is unfamiliar to me," the doctor commented. "Is there a particular reason for this choice?"

Hawthorne slumped in the chair.

He shrugged. "I've never been there but I know some good people who live in Columbus and maybe they can find me a job and a place to live."

"Most important," Liang Yu stated. "Friends are always very necessary. Especially in unfamiliar places. Have you known these people for a long time?"

"I've never met them," Hawthorne admitted. "We used to write but it stopped when I arrived here."

"I see."

"A man named Robert Bean was shot and I pulled him back." The prisoner paused and stared pensively at the floor. "He had a wife and kid and his father owns a company there. They thanked me and wrote some very friendly things."

"You saved his life."

"I liked Robert Bean very much," he continued. "They told me to come to Columbus with Bean after this war. His father offered me a job in the company."

"An excellent opportunity for you, Corporal," said the doctor. "Have you remained in contact with your friend Bean?"

"He's dead."

The old man did not react to the information, but Hawthorne realized that Liang Yu would usually become very silent whenever the subjects of war or politics came up.

"They wrote to me afterwards," the prisoner continued calmly. "Mrs. Bean asked me to come anyway and his father said that the job was still mine."

"They must be fine people," the doctor remarked. "Your presence could be a comfort to the young soldier's family."

"Maybe," the prisoner replied. "I'll write to her and see if they still remember me."

"People do not forget the saving of a life, Corporal."

"I'll let you know what happens about Columbus, Ohio."

"Good." Then Liang Yu's face seemed to light up. "How forgetful I am becoming as the years pass." He reached into the inside pocket of his white uniform and removed a small, velvet-covered box.

"My daughter wrote to me about a very special class project of hers," the doctor explained proudly. "Her pupils created small, delicate objects of art out of shell and wood and a very unusual green plant which grows near our city."

He opened the box. "Ling sent one to me—a tiny doll carved from this plant—I have it in my room. The child was very imaginative."

Liang Yu handed the velvet box to the prisoner. "She told me to give this one to you." He smiled warmly. "This is truly a fine piece of work. My daughter has favored you, Corporal."

Hawthorne stared into the box and was spellbound by the sight of two fragile forms covered with tiny, glittering diamonds and several ruby-colored gems.

He looked up at Liang Yu and was too dumbfounded to speak.

"Allow me to explain," the doctor said. "A young boy in the class has created a very romantic Chinese symbol."

He pointed to the two small figures in the velvet box. "The boy has designed and constructed two birds. Each bird has one wing. They can only fly if they are together. You see?"

The prisoner studied the objects and he blinked and swallowed several times before he could reply.

"This is the most beautiful thing I've ever seen in my life," he whispered.

"Ceramics and imitation precious stones, Corporal," the doctor explained. "Traditionally, Tsinan is known for these things as well as fine silk goods."

Hawthorne could not take his eyes away from the contents of the box and Liang Yu smiled. "Ling tells me that the boy is the son of a local merchant and he is already a master craftsman."

Dr. Yu studied Hawthorne's face for a moment before speaking. "My daughter presents this gift to you in the hope that you will give it to someone who is very close to your heart in America. She excuses the boldness of her gesture."

Hawthorne closed the box slowly and smoothed the velvet covering with his hand.

"I'll keep it," he said. His voice was choked and nearly inaudible. "Forever."

"You will be leaving this camp soon, Corporal, and our paths lead in opposite directions." He paused and placed his hand gently on Hawthorne's shoulder as the boy stared at the gift from China. "I wish you health and happiness . . . and the joy of love and true companionship."

On June 8, 1953, full agreement was reached on all prisoners of war and the news raced through the camp. Most of the captives did not understand the complex provisions of the amnesty arrangement but no one was particularly interested, at this point, in receiving a detailed interpretation. The appalling nightmare of Korea was nearly over and the official document represented freedom and a ticket home to America. Nothing else was important.

K. M. Wing had spent several hours one evening attempting to explain some of the complicated conditions of the agreement. Hawthorne was interested and had listened very carefully although Wing admitted that certain phases of the repatriation plan were still rather vague. He allowed the prisoner to read a roughly translated version of the actual agreement, explaining that the American senior officer staff was scheduled to meet with all United States captives at Camp Six very shortly and that the complicated provisions would be explained and discussed in detail.

Hawthorne scanned the contents of the document.

"What does it mean?" he asked.

"It means that every prisoner who wants to be sent home will be exchanged as soon as possible. In any case, within sixty days after the cease-fire."

"Suppose a prisoner doesn't want to go home?" Hawthorne asked slowly.

Wing laughed. "They rush him directly to the nearest

insane asylum." He then noticed Hawthorne's somber look and realized that his question was serious. Wing reached for the document and examined it.

"A representative commission will take charge of any prisoners who do not exercise their right to be repatriated," he read.

"They can't force a man to go home?" Hawthorne probed with great intensity. "Every prisoner has a choice. Right?"

Wing placed the paper on his desk. "I refuse to discuss any other details with you, Corporal," he said in a friendly manner. "My superiors will have me shot for discussing repatriation with an enemy soldier."

The room was quiet until K. M. Wing spoke once again.

"Why do you have such an interest in the details of repatriation?"

"I'm just curious."

"Are you returning to Waverly, Michigan?"

"No," Hawthorne answered quickly. "I've written a letter. I think I'm going to Columbus, Ohio."

"Do you know the city?"

"No," he confided. "But I have good friends there and I want to start a new life in a different place."

Gerald Hawthorne received two very important letters during the weeks following the agreement at Panmunjom. One arrived on June 28, 1953. It was a very brief note and it was signed by a Mr. Rupert Hurn of Columbus, Ohio.

Mr. Hurn identified himself as Veronica Bean's brother and reported that she had moved to Los Angeles, with her child. Mr. Horace Bean, Robert's father, had passed away some time ago and the family business had been liquidated.

The man stated that he had forwarded the correspondence to his sister and was certain that she would be very pleased to hear from her husband's dear friend. Mr. Hurn added his own sentiments and very best wishes for a safe return to the United States of America.

Then a scribbled and nearly incoherent dispatch arrived from his father on July 1.

Dear Son,

I am sitting here now with tears rolling down my cheeks. I can't believe that you will soon be home and we can start our lives again.

The Chinese Communist bastards will soon be off your back and you'll never have to set foot in a Chink restaurant or even that stinking Chink laundry next to the tavern.

This great town can't wait for you to get back and you'll get the royal Waverly treatment from every man, woman and child. I'm real proud of you, son.

We can't do much plumbing together anymore and that's a damn pity. I'm flat on my back most of the time now. Doc Beaton says that my insides are in real bad shape. Mainly heart and liver but I just can't stop coughing up blood. Must be lung trouble too. I get bad pains in my chest and it makes me scream all through the night.

Enough of my troubles. You must have plenty of your own after spending so much time with those dirty Chink Communists. I can't wait for you to walk through the front door of this house.

God bless you, son. Hurry up home. Your old Dad needs you very badly.

All my love,
Dad

Gerald Hawthorne placed the letter on his bunk and thought of his mother. Then he walked to the small table near the bookcase and picked up the velvet box.

He opened it slowly, allowing the beauty of the contents to erase the image of his father.

33

THAT EVENING GERALD Hawthorne visited Dr. Liang Yu in his quarters near the hospital and persuaded him to discuss the terms of the Amnesty Agreement.

The elderly physician repeatedly emphasized the fact that he was not qualified to interpret the precise meaning of the complicated provisions.

"The American representatives will soon explain them in detail, Corporal."

"I know," Hawthorne answered as he paced up and down in the tiny shack.

He stopped in front of an unpainted shelf on which various Oriental figurines were neatly arranged. He studied the delicate doll which had been carved from the plant.

"I can't go to Ohio," he commented sadly without facing the doctor. "My friends moved to Los Angeles and Robert Bean's father is dead."

"That is a pity."

Hawthorne suddenly turned and looked directly at the doctor. "This agreement gives every prisoner a free choice. Did you know that?"

"I imagine that it does."

"A man can refuse to be repatriated," he pointed out. Then he lowered his voice to a whisper. "A man can refuse to go home."

Liang Yu watched him with great interest as he turned back to the fragile objects on the shelf.

"Is that what you have in your mind, Corporal?"

"I've been thinking about it," Hawthorne replied.

"I strongly suggest that you continue to think about it before you take any serious action," the doctor counseled.

The prisoner moved slowly back to his chair and sat facing Dr. Yu.

"I don't want to go home to Waverly," he announced softly. "In fact, I don't want to go home to America."

Liang Yu was silent.

"I've learned many things about China and the Chinese people. Maybe this agreement will give me a chance to settle in Tsinan."

The doctor looked concerned as Hawthorne continued.

"I don't hate my country," he said softly. "Maybe it's me and I shift the blame all the time. But I'm just not ready for a rat race and I truly don't give a damn about money and phony prestige." He finally raised his head. "I'll get squashed very fast if I go home."

Liang Yu rubbed his chin thoughtfully and commented, "You are now older and wiser and possibly better equipped to meet the challenges in America."

"I'd hate to take a chance on that," Hawthorne replied. "Besides, I have other reasons for not wanting to go home now."

The physician sat back comfortably and folded his slender arms across his chest. "Do you know anything about Tsinan, China, Corporal?"

"Only what you and Mr. Wing have told me. And I read a little about the town in one of my books."

"Tsinan is not a beautiful place," the doctor said candidly. "There is noise, confusion and too many people. In fact, it is probably one of the most densely populated cities in the world."

"Wing said that."

"The streets are narrow and cobbled. Most of them are dirty and uneven. Many of the houses are small huts made of mud and straw. There are donkey carts and wheelbarrows and vendors with fruit and vegetables. The shops open onto crowded streets and we certainly have nothing like your modern supermarkets."

"I'm sure."

"Work is strenuous and the hours are long. The pay is

meaningless if you compare it to wages in other parts of the world."

"I know these things."

The doctor hesitated and then spoke very quietly.

"I have lived in America and have studied the temperament of your people," he explained. "Your motives would never be understood, Corporal."

"I don't give a damn about the temperament of the American people," Hawthorne replied sharply.

"It is possible that you will never see your own country again as long as you live."

"That could happen."

"That *will* happen," the doctor stated bluntly. "I doubt very much if you will ever be allowed to turn back once you have decided to live in *our* China."

"I'll never want to turn back."

"It is also possible that you will never be accepted by our people, and your life could become a constant misery in an alien environment."

"The same thing might happen in Columbus or Los Angeles or anywhere in America."

Liang Yu shook his head slowly and then he smiled. "I have said too much already and I have truly said nothing. We must wait and see."

"Will you object if I refuse repatriation and ask to settle in Tsinan?"

"Object?"

"Vote against me."

"I doubt if the representative commission will consult with the medical staff of Camp Six," he chuckled.

"Will you welcome me?"

"Yes, Corporal," Liang Yu replied warmly. "I will personally welcome you." The old man hesitated. When he spoke again, his tone was very sincere. "And I will help you in every way that I can."

"GRAHAM. ALFRED. E. PRIVATE FIRST CLASS!"

The First Lieutenant looked polished and professional as

he stood straight facing the line of ragged prisoners who were scheduled for immediate release. Hawthorne remembered the starched soldiers in the recruiting window next door to Woolworth's.

The date was July 19, 1953, and another shipment to Panmunjom was going out in accordance with the conditions outlined in the repatriation agreement. A convoy of five heavy vehicles was positioned and ready at the far edge of the parade grounds and Corporal Hawthorne was standing at strict attention with the others while the official repatriation roll was called out.

He glanced cautiously out of the corner of his eye to catch a quick view of everything that was going on, and he wondered why the United States Army had insisted on so much pomp and ceremony. The prisoners were mostly sick and bedraggled, completely out of place in this attempt at West Point ritual.

A fierce-looking American captain was standing close behind the Lieutenant and there were three or four more senior officers huddled together near one of the United Nations' trucks.

Several civilians with armbands appeared to be inspecting something in the vicinity of the convoy area, and Hawthorne was surprised to see the Camp Six commandant and his deputy standing to the right of the American captain.

Kwen San and two other Red Chinese officials were directly behind their superior officers and they were both holding documents.

The prisoners who had not been scheduled for exchange that day were sprawled on the ground at the far edge of the parade area and watching attentively and listening with great interest as the Lieutenant called each name from the repatriation roster.

"GRAHAM. ALFRED. E. PRIVATE FIRST CLASS!"

The men of Camp Six had been briefed earlier on the formal procedures to be observed during the official ceremony of military release and exchange.

Private First Class Alfred E. Graham proceeded to take one military step forward and then snapped to attention again. He saluted and the salute was returned sharply by the First Lieutenant.

There was silence in the parade area. Official procedure decreed that the watching prisoners should not yell their congratulations until the soldier had actually boarded one of the vehicles. Graham walked briskly to the Lieutenant and stood at attention once again.

He was formally presented with his United Nations repatriation orders which he held in his left hand while he saluted again. The Lieutenant returned the salute and then smiled as Alfred E. Graham marched jauntily to the convoy area. He was handed a barracks bag by one of the civilian representatives and was then yanked aboard the vehicle by the soldiers who had already been processed for the trip to Panmunjom.

Simultaneously, the spectator prisoners burst out whistling, screaming and applauding as the truck horns joined the wild clamor for Private First Class Alfred E. Graham.

Meanwhile, the officers and civilian representatives of the repatriation detachment waited silently and did not join the demonstration. The prisoners who were scheduled for exchange remained at attention and in strict military formation as the Captain raised his hand for silence.

"GUTTMAN. SAMUEL. CORPORAL!" the Lieutenant bellowed as soon as the area was quiet once again.

Corporal Samuel Guttman, a short, crippled soldier, pulled himself forward and took his first step toward freedom. He saluted obediently and exercised his right to be repatriated.

Hawthorne saw the tears streaming down Guttman's cheeks as he hobbled toward the convoy area.

There was absolute silence in the parade area as Guttman was lifted gently in the truck by several of the waiting passengers, who carefully propped him into an upright position in the vehicle. Guttman waved feebly as the deafening noise of congratulations swept the area.

Guttman saluted his fellow prisoners and continued to cry unashamedly as the tumult mounted.

In time, the cheering died away and there was silence again as the Lieutenant continued.

"HAWTHORNE. GERALD. HOWARD. CORPORAL!"

The moment had finally arrived. Hawthorne felt the reaction cut through his body like a bolt of lightning. He remained frozen at attention with his eyes straight ahead and he did not react to the officer's command.

The Lieutenant checked the roster quickly and then looked up again at the rigid line of prisoners.

"HAWTHORNE. GERALD. HOWARD. CORPORAL!"

Hawthorne made no response. He knew that all eyes were focused on him, and he sensed a ripple of movement in the parade area.

The Captain was stepping briskly toward the young officer responsible for the repatriation roll call. All activity in the convoy area had halted abruptly and the senior officers and civilians were now watching the proceedings. The prisoners on the trucks were silent and the spectators began to stand to get a better view. Some moved in closer to watch this strange defiant reaction to an American repatriation order.

"HAWTHORNE. GERALD. HOWARD. CORPORAL!"

The command came again almost automatically but the Lieutenant seemed to be prepared for the lack of response.

He conferred briefly with the Captain and then moved forward to stand right in front of Hawthorne.

Hawthorne avoided the officer's gaze by concentrating on a distant spot near the administration building.

"At ease!" the Lieutenant ordered.

The prisoner obeyed the command and stifled a sigh of relief as he realized that most of the paralyzing symptoms of anxiety were gradually disappearing.

"Are you Corporal Gerald Howard Hawthorne?" the officer snapped.

"Yes, sir."

"Are you refusing to step forward, Corporal?"

"Yes, sir."

The Lieutenant checked several papers in his hand and then looked at the prisoner's calm and dispassionate expression.

"Are you officially refusing to exercise your right to be repatriated?" the officer inquired.

"Yes, sir," Hawthorne replied quietly.

"Stand at attention, Corporal," the Lieutenant commanded. Hawthorne snapped into position immediately.

All of the watching prisoners were now on their feet. They had formed an orderly grouping which completely encircled the parade grounds.

"Have you been properly briefed?"

"Sir?"

"The rights of repatriation?" the Lieutenant asked in a crisp and formal tone of voice.

"Yes, sir."

"Were the official spokesmen clear about all details and did you understand them?"

"Yes, sir."

"I assume that you understand the serious consequences of this move, soldier?"

Hawthorne swallowed. It felt as if a coating of thick dust had accumulated in his mouth, preventing him from replying.

"I asked you a question, Corporal," the officer growled.

The prisoner coughed and then cleared his throat loudly. "I understand the consequences of my decision, Lieutenant," said Hawthorne firmly.

The Lieutenant executed a sharp about-face and marched over to the Captain. After a few moments' conference, they walked back to the group of United Nations officials. There was a brief exchange of words, then the Captain, a foreign staff officer and a civilian representative moved over to the Chinese Communist delegation.

The civilian appeared to be doing most of the talking as various members of the group glanced in Hawthorne's direction from time to time.

After a while, the Camp Six commandant, his deputy and Kwen San seemed to reach an agreement with the Allied representatives. They inspected documents, nodded politely and then moved off together toward the administration buildings.

The Lieutenant again positioned himself in front of the military formation and ignored Hawthorne as he proceeded with the repatriation roll call.

"HOBART. CLARENCE. L. PRIVATE!"

Clarence Hobart was repatriated and so was William Jameson and Lawrence Jorgenson and Edward Kimball and Sanford Lehman and Mark Logan ...

The military formation in the center of the Communist parade grounds slowly dwindled while the crowded trucks in the convoy area were loaded, ready to deliver the camp's second quota of repatriates to Panmunjom.

The atmosphere had changed noticeably since Hawthorne had defied the senior military staff and refused to take the required step forward for liberation. The impact of his actions had cast a pall over the spirited demonstrations, and mild applause had now replaced the uproarious response given to each of the prison releases.

The spectators and officials had closed in around to the short line of American prisoners still standing at attention in the center of the Korean administration compound.

All eyes were fixed on Gerald Hawthorne, but the thin figure remained rigid, inexpressive and seemingly oblivious to the scrutiny.

Theodore Mapes climbed aboard and he was quickly followed by Harry Morgenthau and Fred Nolan and Obrinski and Otis and Pezzaro and Preston and Rosenberg and Sadler ...

And then Gerald Hawthorne was standing at attention alone.

The Lieutenant lowered the repatriation folder and seemed to be debating whether or not the solitary prisoner should be ordered to rest at ease.

Then he wheeled about and walked away toward the convoy area.

In a while, the Army Captain and the rest of the Allied and Communist arbitration group marched out of Building One and moved directly toward the prisoner. The special detachment halted at a particular spot and only the American officer continued on his way.

He faced the prisoner. "*At ease, Corporal,*" the officer snapped.

Hawthorne relaxed.

"Your papers have been processed in accordance with your own decision to refuse repatriation."

"Yes, sir."

"Do you wish to change this decision?"

"No, sir."

"Are you aware that this action may at some point become final and irrevocable and you will not receive another opportunity to change your mind?"

"I understand."

The Captain moved a step closer to the prisoner and lowered his voice.

"Do you wish to postpone this action and wait for the final Camp Six release operation?"

"No, sir."

"A marked convoy will arrive for the last time on the twenty-ninth of July."

"I know."

"This will give you a little more time to analyze the situation and perhaps reconsider your rights as an American citizen."

"My decision is final, Captain," the prisoner announced firmly.

The officer came closer and whispered hoarsely. "To hell with formalities, soldier. If you want to change your mind I'll destroy these damn papers and you can climb on that truck right now."

The prisoner glanced quickly in the direction of the convoy area and then turned back to face the officer.

"I'll stay, Captain," Hawthorne remarked flatly.

The man's eyes narrowed and his jaw muscles tightened.

"I'm sure you will."

"Sir?"

"Stay with the Chinese Reds."

"Yes, sir."

"Colonel Roland Fawcett has already briefed the members of the Representative Commission and every detail of your case has been accurately documented."

The prisoner did not respond and the officer continued with growing resentment.

"'Perhaps you have made a very wise decision, Corporal," he whispered. "Colonel Fawcett anticipated your move for many obvious reasons."

Gerald Hawthorne smiled.

"Do you find this information amusing?" the Captain growled.

"I find Colonel Roland Fawcett amusing, sir," said Hawthorne seriously.

The officer stared contemptuously for a moment and then turned and pointed to a staff car which was positioned directly in front of the waiting truck convoy.

"Colonel Fawcett is about to move out," the Captain stated dryly. "Would you like to express your personal feelings to the senior prisoner?"

"No thank you, sir," Hawthorne snarled. "I never want to see Colonel Roland Fawcett again as long as I live."

The Captain studied the prisoner with open contempt. "I should think not, Corporal," he concluded.

He took three steps back, executed an about-face, and then signaled to the First Lieutenant who was standing in the convoy area with several other members of the commission.

"Start them up, Gary!" the Captain yelled. *"Let's roll to hell out of here!"*

Corporal Gerald Hawthorne stood motionless and waited for the trucks to disappear. He continued to watch as the large wooden gates were closed and secured by Kwen San's troopers.

He suddenly realized that all of the remaining inmates of Camp Six were still circled on the fringes of the parade area and they were inspecting him with silent curiosity.

The dust of the departing convoy settled and the prisoner started a slow, deliberate walk toward his private hut in the Administration area.

The other prisoners stared thoughtfully as Hawthorne made his way across the camp. This strange character, with his head bowed, was no longer a progressive or a collaborator or an informer or a traitor. He was much more.

"Christ almighty," an Army staff sergeant mumbled, as he watched Hawthorne enter his private hut.

Gerald Howard Hawthorne had given up his country, the United States of America, in order to remain in Communist China.

DECEMBER 24, 1961
CHRISTMAS EVE
RAVENHURST
WINCHESTER ESTATES
DETROIT, MICHIGAN

34

CHARLES MANNING WAITED patiently in the living room while his wife finished dressing upstairs.

He was immaculately groomed and tailored, and it was obvious that the Mannings of Michigan were prepared to monopolize the social spotlight at the Governor's formal Christmas Eve charity ball.

Manning carefully checked his evening attire in a special dressing mirror which was located close to the winding marble staircase. A butler brought him a drink on a silver tray and he accepted it with a smile.

"Thank you, William," he said. "A very merry Christmas to you."

"The same to you, sir," the butler replied. "And to Mrs. Manning," he added, as the industrialist drained the contents of the small brandy glass and placed it back on the serving tray.

"Make sure you have a few stiff shots yourself tonight." Manning winked. "And spread some joy with the others."

"Thank you, sir," the man replied.

He moved away just as Estelle Manning began to descend the elaborate stairway.

Her gown and jewelry complemented her figure, and the effect was truly dazzling.

Her husband bowed low, with an exaggerated flourish as she reached the bottom step.

"A vision," he proclaimed.

Estelle Manning walked nervously to the sofa. She sat and looked up at her husband.

"I just cannot get the damn thing out of my mind," she stated irritably. "I'm sorry."

"Goldenson?" he asked, moving toward her.

"Of course."

He leaned over and kissed her lightly on the cheek.

"Darling," the industrialist whispered softly. "This is Christmas Eve. I refuse to spoil a beautiful evening."

"This man has acted in an irresponsible manner and I cannot understand his total lack of courtesy," she pouted.

"We'll talk about it tomorrow," said Manning. "It's getting late."

"I don't give a damn," the woman snapped.

Charles Manning moved to the bar next to the fireplace.

He poured two drinks and brought one to his wife. She accepted the glass and Manning then took a seat in a lounge chair facing her.

"We'll tease the Governor and his guests," he grinned, swallowing a large quantity of Scotch.

Estelle Manning was not amused. She sipped her drink pensively.

"I'm mad as hell, Charles," she nearly shouted.

"I don't blame you."

"All this time wasted," Mrs. Manning continued with growing indignation. "The man failed to contact me after accepting a substantial amount of money. And then he just disappears."

"It borders on theft."

She glared at her husband. "You should have taken an interest in this case, Charles. There's something damn funny going on."

"What do you mean, darling?" he asked, pretending to be as nonchalant as possible.

"Lawrence Goldenson did gather some important information before he left," the woman commented. "I happen to know this."

"How do you know?"

"Alan Purvis was in Washington and he had a talk with several friends." She sipped her drink. "Purvis heard that Goldenson had the start of a very explosive file."

"Explosive?" he chuckled.

She hesitated and then lowered her voice. "There is a possibility that I may need some help from you."

"Why?"

"I intend to convince Blanchard in Los Angeles that this is a very important case and the organization must become involved."

Charles Manning's expression changed abruptly and his tone became serious for the first time during the conversation.

"Don't turn this thing into a case of intrigue and drama."

"No, of course. But I do agree with Alan Purvis in our Detroit office."

"Alan Purvis is an infant lawyer. He's still wet behind the ears. I strongly suggest that you limit your interest to a man by the name of Gerald Hawthorne in Waverly, Michigan," he cautioned firmly.

"Are you telling me what to do?" his wife asked, with a touch of contempt in her voice.

"I am suggesting."

"Does Washington frighten you, Charles?"

"Political manipulations can become very devious and at times quite dangerous," Manning pointed out calmly. "Even seasoned experts have been squashed by the machine."

His wife glared at him. "Are you afraid?"

"Maybe."

"You lack courage, Charles. Perhaps an infant lawyer will tackle Washington with me."

She moved away and began to pace the room slowly while sipping the drink. "No wonder you hide behind a tennis racket at the club every day."

"That's enough!" he screamed.

Estelle Manning stopped abruptly in the center of the room and studied her husband, astonished.

The man had raised his voice to a shout and he rarely let himself get out of control. They faced each other again and she was unable to speak.

"Help the boy," Manning advised quietly. "But do it calmly and sensibly and don't take the advice of young fools."

She started to move away but he took her arm gently.

"I spoke to him," he said quietly, but did not look up.

"Goldenson was here?"

"At the club."

"Why didn't you tell me?"

"He requested a private meeting," the man replied hesitantly. "The discussion was very sensitive and I ask that you allow me to be a bit evasive for the moment."

Estelle Manning glared at her husband in disbelief. She then moved to the sofa and took a seat. "I'll be damned," she muttered under her breath.

There was silence in the room as Manning allowed his wife to digest the importance of the situation.

"I was right," she finally whispered. "And so was Alan Purvis. There *is* something to all this."

"Possibly," he answered.

"What are you going to do?" Mrs. Manning asked in a somber tone of voice.

"Proceed very cautiously," he replied. "Or drop it completely. I'll know more in a few weeks and then a firm decision will be made."

"What about Hawthorne?"

"This man will be the key to the case, if I decide to go ahead."

Estelle Manning looked interested. "You promised a decision in a few weeks. Either to proceed or quit."

"That's right."

"Based on what?"

The industrialist paused and seemed to be debating whether to answer or simply avoid the subject.

He answered. "Goldenson's files."

"The files?" Her bewilderment was apparent.

"His information," Manning stated. "The stuff you paid him for, darling. Your counselor gave it to someone for safe-keeping," he answered.

"And you know the person who has this material."

"Yes."

"Will you have to buy it or take legal action?"

Charles Manning turned to his wife and whispered softly. "The man who is now in possession of Goldenson's files cannot be tampered with in any way. This particular gentleman is wealthy, influential and deadly when he makes up his mind to take action. He is also very well organized."

"How will you get them?"

Manning smiled broadly. "I am also wealthy, influential and very deadly when I make up my mind to take action."

He stood and glanced at his watch. "Although some people believe that I do nothing but hide behind a tennis racket at the Brentwood Country Club."

Hawthorne stood at the window and watched the Christmas Eve snow fall and drift gently in the front yard. The soft porch light transformed the trees and shrubs into glistening white objects of art and he thought of Ling Yu and his mother.

He moved to the table and switched off the lamp, allowing the bright winter scene to create a variety of shadows and patterns on the walls and ceiling of the living room. He relaxed in a comfortable chair and enjoyed the warmth of a glowing fireplace.

The pop and crackle of the logs were friendly sounds and the small portable radio on the mantel supplied a pleasant musical background with Crosby and Como and all of the familiar carols.

Hawthorne stretched and sighed contentedly. He had decided to settle in, to rediscover this home he was now using as a retreat from the hostile community outside.

Suddenly, he remembered his father's private stash of liquor.

It would be appropriate, he thought, to treat himself to some holiday cheer. He would simply have to search the basement.

He removed a heavy key and a flashlight from the desk drawer.

The squeaky cellar door was opened and he reached for the cord attached to the overhanging bulb at the top of the stairs. It was no longer operative, however, and the basement remained in pitch darkness.

He directed the light down the wooden steps, making certain that the thin railing was still intact and able to support his weight.

He gripped the flashlight and moved cautiously downward, one shaky plank at a time, until he reached the bottom.

A vivid image of his father's uncontrollable drunken fury prompted him to twist the light in an attempt to locate the wall fixture. He reached out and flicked the switch.

The basement remained black, except for the thin beam of the flashlight.

He surveyed the area, scanning the pipes and the meters, an old Baldwin piano, the boiler and the walls and the ceiling, and a bolted iron door which led to the garage.

There were no cobwebs or trash or empty whiskey bottles, and the basement was immaculate.

Hawthorne was fascinated. His father had obviously changed some patterns in the last years of his life. He moved down a few steps and flashed back to the storage bin.

He balanced the flashlight on one of the metal cases and this arrangement provided enough illumination for his rummaging. He noticed a battered crate in the corner, and as he flipped up the lid, he discovered three unopened bottles of Scotch whiskey. Overjoyed with his find, he placed them near the door and moved on.

He noticed another small wooden crate just as the light was lifted. The scribbled marking on the side could not be ignored. "MY SON."

Hawthorne hesitated and then moved slowly toward the box. He removed a strip of thick black tape and opened the lid.

The sharp ray of light was focused on the contents. There was a set of carelessly shellacked and unevenly carved bookends. Hawthorne recalled that he had received a failing grade for this effort in woodcraft at Waverly grade school.

Hawthorne swung the torch and spotted two of his favorite toys and a kindergarten drawing of a house. There were birthday cards which had been given to him years before and a cigarette box which he had once purchased with his own allowance. There were trivial items which should have been thrown away by the cruel and unemotional man Hawthorne remembered his father to be.

The lid was slammed shut and tears began to cloud his eyes, but he managed to fight off all feelings of compassion for the plumber.

Hawthorne directed the flashlight toward a large metal chest in which he assumed that his father's tools were stored.

He sat rigidly on a wooden crate and faced the object, which resembled a bank safe. It had always been bolted and positioned in a distant corner of the storage area and Hawthorne remembered his father's pronouncements about how a man's personal belongings ought to be respected.

As a boy, Gerald's wild imagination had filled this mysterious box with shrunken heads and human bones and bottles of foaming liquid which could be used by his sinister father to turn children into rats and beautiful women into dead witches.

Several years later, when the plumber was drunk and preoccupied with a whore, Gerald had sneaked down to the basement and discovered a few interesting facts about the actual contents.

He walked excitedly to his father's private vault.

All of the plumbing and carpentry tools were situated in the top section of the partitioned chest and Hawthorne removed them and arranged a neat pile on the basement floor.

The metal separator was hauled out and his hands searched the contents of the second section, where he found a collection of pornographic material.

He removed another partition which was filled with official documents and personal papers.

Hawthorne groped feverishly at the bottom of the deep iron

vault in search of a particular treasure, and finally removed the false bottom of his father's secret hiding place. He reached apprehensively into the narrow compartment and his fingers touched a heavy wrapping of wool or cotton or some other material.

A cold sweat poured from his forehead and he was forced to wipe the wetness from both eyes as he lifted the object and excitedly removed the cloth wrapping. His legs were trembling as he examined the cold steel of a .45 caliber revolver.

He held the gun lovingly and caressed it and then pointed the weapon at an imaginary target on the basement wall.

He squeezed the trigger and after the click he went back to the iron case and reached inside.

Another brief search on the bottom produced the necessary ammunition and Gerald Hawthorne was armed once again and prepared for battle.

His face suddenly flushed with excitement.

He stuffed the revolver into his belt and filled in both pockets of his trousers with bullets.

He gathered the liquor bottles in both arms, picked up the flashlight and made the trip back up the narrow stairs.

In his room Hawthorne opened his Chinese traveling case and placed the gun inside along with the ammunition. Then he fastened his bag and put it in a far corner of the closet.

He gazed at a silk Chinese kimono he had hung on the back of the door, and then he watched the snow and thought of the paper factory in Tsinan and his first daily contact with working people in Communist China.

At the same time, he recalled his important visit to Dr. Yu's home and his first meeting with Ling Yu.

Dr. Liang Yu had recently completed his Korean tour of duty and was pleased to welcome Hawthorne to the family house on the southern outskirts of Tsinan.

"Ling will have three full days to spend with me," he said happily. "The school is being repaired. Students and faculty have been granted a brief vacation." He glanced at his watch. "She will be home shortly and you will have an opportunity to meet your Chinese correspondent."

Hawthorne sat nervously on the edge of a couch and tried to smile. "I'm looking forward to meeting her," he said, clearing his throat at the same time.

The doctor was sitting in a comfortable armchair, smoking a small pipe. The tobacco had an unfamiliar but pleasant aroma.

Though modestly constructed, the house was clean and orderly. In fact, it appeared to be surprisingly modern in many respects. Some of the chairs were covered with an attractive plastic or simulated leather and it reminded Hawthorne of the latest furniture styles in the store windows in Waverly. He had also noticed a Formica-like top on a kitchen table and there were several chromium-plated items in the living room, including a radio and record player.

This commercial American look was blended with hanging scrolls decorated with Chinese characters, a silken lantern, two large Ming-type vases and other objects which Hawthorne considered to be exclusively Chinese.

There was also a small portrait of Mao Tse-tung on the mantel but it was partially hidden by a display of ceramic horses and giant birds.

It was evident that Dr. Liang Yu was better off than most of the people in the Old City.

Hawthorne examined a large and rather ornate bookcase and thought of his own squalid quarters in a loft over the crowded and smelly market streets of Tsinan.

"Are you enjoying your work at the factory?" the doctor was asking.

"It's interesting."

"Long hours and very low pay. Remember? I advised you when we were together at the camp."

"I don't mind. I'm learning many things and I've made a few friends."

Liang Yu smiled warmly. "Sung Tsen Tson tells me that you have worked very hard."

"It was nice of Mr. Sung to get me the job."

"He was formerly the plant supervisor."

"I know," said Hawthorne. "Sometimes he comes to visit Mr. Yen."

"Mr. Yen?"

"The new boss of the whole factory," Hawthorne replied. "He came from Peiping."

"Oh yes," the doctor remembered. "Sung mentioned him to me."

"Everyone likes Mr. Sung."

"My old friend will soon become an important local official here in Tsinan," Liang Yu explained. "He respects you and I am told that the workers appreciate your attitude and conscientious efforts."

"Some of the people in the factory are very nice and helpful."

The doctor glanced around as the front door of the house was opened.

"I have a feeling that you will make a life for yourself here in Tsinan." He stood and grinned. "The school teacher is home."

Hawthorne jumped to his feet and coughed nervously.

Liang Yu took the boy by the arm and led him toward the door.

"You have nothing to fear, Hawthorne," the doctor said good-naturedly. "My daughter will certainly be feeling the same way—or even worse! My daughter is about to meet an American soldier. They are very scarce in this part of the world."

Ling Yu was standing in the hallway.

She was slightly taller than he had imagined and her tight-fitting "cheong sam," with its high collar and slit skirt, revealed a slim and appealing figure.

None of the photographs he'd seen in Camp Six had done justice to the delicate shape of her body and the shine and silkiness of her long black hair, or brought out the pale contrast of a complexion which was pure alabaster.

It was apparent the moment the girl smiled that she was genuinely happy to meet Hawthorne.

They talked for hours on this first evening and Hawthorne had a strong feeling that the teacher was unlike any woman he had ever known, with the exception of his mother.

Ling Yu spoke English and her voice was soft and melodious. Mainly, however, she listened with sincere interest and soon Hawthorne realized that he had been rambling on. He had described his dilapidated room in the Old City, the factory and his desire to learn much more about China and the Chinese people.

"I'm sorry," he stammered.

"For what?" asked Dr. Yu.

"Talking so much."

Hawthorne lowered his head as the elderly doctor smiled warmly and then turned to his daughter.

"Are you counting the words of our friend, Ling?" he asked. There was silence.

Hawthorne glanced up slowly and met her eyes. Her expression was warm and sincere.

"I am very interested in everything that you have to say," the girl assured him softly.

She did not turn away and it seemed to Hawthorne that they were looking directly into each other's hearts and that everyone else in the world had vanished.

Liang Yu walked to the door of the living room and then turned to face the American and his daughter. He smiled broadly and left the room.

Hawthorne looked at the girl and this time she turned away.

"Your father is a good man," he said.

"He is very wise," she answered.

The beauty and excitement of his new life in Tsinan was dreamlike and overwhelming at times.

He found his work at the paper factory to be interesting and productive and the workers and group leaders were beginning to accept him as a very able and interesting new member of the Chinese labor force.

His knowledge of the language was improving steadily with the help of his fellow workers.

Their friendly cooperation was a welcome change after his

unhappy years in Waverly and his humiliation at the hands of his compatriots in the American Armed Forces.

He had discovered equality in China right down to the uniformity of dress in the factory, and this had helped to build his confidence. He had gained weight and strength since his arrival and he now had flesh on his bones and a much healthier-looking complexion.

A growing feeling of contentment and pride had made him stand straight and look others in the eye when he spoke to them. The frequent compliments of the factory group leaders had given him poise and a new sense of responsibility.

In his new life in Communist China—a life which to some might have appeared crowded, dismal, and monotonous—Gerald Hawthorne was beginning to achieve normality.

At night, whenever possible, he would spend time with Ling Yu at her father's home and the elderly physician would usually find an urgent reason to use his small study while the young people talked in the living room.

The girl's work had resumed at school and most of her time in the evening was devoted to the marking of test papers and the preparation of lessons and special class activities.

Ling and the doctor appreciated the fact that Hawthorne would visit only by formal invitation and whenever the girl had advised him in advance that she would be free.

Their conversations revolved around her school and his factory and the students and the workers and the difficult transition from one way of life to another.

A worker at the paper factory had briefed Hawthorne about Chinese women and the code of manners expected of gentlemen callers.

Hawthorne was positive that Ling Yu was a very respectable young woman, and he was careful to avoid all references to personal and intimate feelings.

There was one occasion when Liang Yu was working in the study, and Hawthorne was telling the young teacher about Robert Bean.

She sat in a corner of the sofa and listened as he expressed his personal feelings for the first time.

"I liked Robert Bean very much," Hawthorne told her. "He was my friend. I haven't had many friends in my life."

She watched him thoughtfully but did not respond.

Hawthorne noticed that her unusual eyes were soft and moist and he could not take his eyes off the beauty of her complexion and her magnificent black hair.

"Do you have many friends?" he asked cautiously.

"I know and like many people," the girl replied. "But true friendship means something quite different to me." She hesitated for a moment. "No. I do not have many friends," Ling answered.

On this particular evening Hawthorne gambled with the fragile rules of Chinese social conduct and continued to discuss the private details of his early life in Michigan.

He described his mother and was able to talk about her unexpected death for the first time since the accident years before.

"I understand your feelings very well," she told him. "The sad loss of my own mother is still felt very strongly in this house and her memory occupies a special place in our hearts."

Hawthorne fought his desire to step over the line completely and confide his deep feelings to her.

"I hope that you'll always be my good friend," he ventured, "and let me visit here and talk to you . . . whenever you have spare time."

She was silent.

Hawthorne avoided her eyes and waited anxiously for a response to his obvious advance into an intimate and forbidden area of conversation. He cursed himself for being stupid and immature.

"I will certainly be your good friend," he heard her say. "And I hope that you will be mine."

The candid words stunned him and he raised his head slowly as she continued in a low and very serious tone of voice.

"I will always look forward to your visits and our interesting talks." The Chinese girl hesitated before speaking again.

"You are welcome in this house . . . at any time, and for all time."

At the doorway, this particular evening, Gerald Hawthorne took another calculated risk before leaving for his loft in the Old City.

"I forgot to thank you for the beautiful gift you sent me when I was at Camp Six."

"The project of my student?"

"Yes," he replied. "The two birds. Each with one wing."

"It was very well done and the boy received an excellent grade," she said. "I am very happy that you appreciated the craftsmanship."

"I appreciated the gesture."

Ling Yu smiled and bowed her head politely as she opened the door for Hawthorne. He stepped outside and then turned abruptly and faced her.

"There was nobody to give it to in America," he confided. "Can I keep it in my room for you?"

They looked deeply into each other's eyes.

"I will be honored," she whispered.

One evening, after working late at the paper factory, Hawthorne was summoned to the large, drab executive office on the top floor of the old building.

He was unsettled by this unusual order to visit the restricted quarters of Mr. Yen, the new manager. All contact with supervisory personnel was ordinarily limited to the group leaders or, on very rare occasions, the factory labor administrator.

A young Chinese girl led him into the room and then left immediately.

Mr. Yen and Liang Yu's friend, Sung Tsen Tson, were seated at a wooden conference table. They both smiled politely as Hawthorne entered. Sung motioned to a chair.

"It is good to see you again, Hawthorne," he said. His voice was unusually high-pitched.

Sung was a round-faced, stockily built man with a jovial manner. He appeared to be much younger than his forty years. The doctor had frequently spoken of Sung's intelligence and popularity.

"Mr. Yen has been looking forward to meeting you," he added, glancing at the manager.

The executive nodded pleasantly. Hawthorne fidgeted awkwardly, but succeeded in returning the gesture.

Ho Yen, a short, thin man in his early fifties, had very little hair and a pale, sickly complexion. His left hand trembled slightly as he opened a folder.

"Your performance record is impressive," said Yen in perfect English. "We are all very pleased with your conduct and progress."

Sung Tsen Tson beamed. "Congratulations, Hawthorne." He moved several papers over to the manager and sat back in his chair, still grinning proudly. "The factory labor administrator has delivered excellent reports to Mr. Yen."

Hawthorne forced a nervous smile.

"We are now prepared to show our gratitude," the manager stated, closing the folder. His expression became serious. "Special approval has been received from Peiping."

The American was puzzled by the statement. He stared at Sung, waiting for an explanation.

"A new work unit is being organized here at the plant," Sung announced in a business-like manner. "It will be unique in every respect."

Mr. Yen leaned forward and spoke quietly. "Substantial government funds have been allocated." His tone was now confidential. "There will be many benefits for this group, including extra pay and comfortable living quarters."

"I don't understand," said Hawthorne, looking again at Sung Tsen Tson. "Why?"

"This is an official reward from the government," he answered. "You will supervise this important new unit. Our factory will participate in a series of very confidential projects," he continued. "We are honored."

Yen grunted in agreement. Hawthorne continued to stare. "What projects?" he asked with growing curiosity. "Military projects?"

Yen motioned with his head, indicating that the question should be answered.

"We will be responsible only for certain elements," Sung replied. He seemed to be choosing his words with great care. "Five selected plants will manufacture the essential parts."

"Each responsible only for its own," Yen interrupted quickly. "The official government blueprints will be distributed in five sections." He stretched the fingers of his left hand. "We will never see the overall plans."

"All parts will be delivered to Peiping for the actual completion," Sung added. "It is a complicated affair."

There was silence in the room as Sung and the factory manager studied Hawthorne, waiting for a reaction.

He glanced from one man to the other before speaking. "Secret military weapons," he proposed somberly. "It must be a hydrogen bomb."

Hawthorne's blunt accusation did not seem to surprise or irritate the men at the table. In fact, Sung's features softened and he grinned. The manager was expressionless.

"I will not speculate," Sung commented good-naturedly. "We are only concerned with our designated participation."

Ho Yen gathered up several documents and placed them in a neat pile on the table. "Think in terms of the personal advantages," he advised. "You will be advanced to a position of unusual trust." Mr. Yen paused, but as Hawthorne gave no response, he continued. "The other benefits will be extremely difficult to come by in this country, Hawthorne."

Hawthorne avoided their eyes as he struggled with his own conflicting thoughts and emotions.

"We have presented you with a fascinating challenge and a rare opportunity," Sung reminded him. "The details will be explained in Peiping."

The implications of all this raced across Hawthorne's brain. A factory supervisor, responsible to the Chinese government. Prestige and recognition. Respect and acceptance in a new land. An opportunity to better his standard of living. His apartment was cramped and too close to the factory's noise and pollution. He was concerned about Ling Yu's health. She did not look well. The long hours at school were tiring and the bus trips each day added to her burdens. Additional income after their wedding, which was to take place in three days, would allow them to . . .

"I will need an indication of your interest within one week," the manager was saying. "We must arrange for your trip to Peiping."

Hawthorne thought for a moment and then spoke frankly to Sung Tsen Tson. "I can't work on bombs or missiles." He glanced down at the table. "I'm still an American citizen."

Yen continued to arrange his files and place them into several large envelopes. Sung assisted the manager, ignoring the boy's statement.

"I want the job," Hawthorne admitted. "But I need more information."

"We can say no more." Sung picked up the last of the documents, indicating that the meeting was over. "Peiping will discuss it further."

The manager stood and prepared to leave. "One week," he repeated firmly. "We must have an answer." Yen nodded to each man and left the room.

"Will it hurt my country, Mr. Sung?" Hawthorne asked as soon as the door had been closed.

"Which country?"

"The United States."

Sung turned to him and glared. "You do have some obligations over here," he snapped.

The room was silent once again as Hawthorne watched the official rise to his feet. Sung appeared to be debating whether to continue with the discussion. He moved slowly toward the door, paused and returned to the conference table.

"Mr. Ho Yen is responsible for manufacturing on a local basis," he confided quietly. "There are other sensitive aspects which have not been mentioned this evening."

Hawthorne looked up, caught off-guard by the confidential tone of Sung's voice.

"The official in charge of these projects will explain everything during your visit to Peiping." He placed both hands flat on the table and leaned closer. "This is a very unusual opportunity for a person of foreign birth."

"There has to be a damn good reason, Mr. Sung."

"Exactly."

"Propaganda?"

"No," Sung replied. "Friendship."

"What?"

"The official in charge is Mr. K. M. Wing." Sung grinned at the astonished expression on the face of the American. "Your old friend is waiting anxiously to see you in Peiping."

Sung Tsen Tson straightened up and walked briskly to the door of the executive office. He suddenly turned and faced Hawthorne.

"My humble respects to Dr. Yu and his beautiful daughter," he said warmly. "I understand you are to marry, and I am most happy to hear this news. I will instruct Mr. Yen to proceed immediately with your travel arrangements to Peiping."

Gerald Hawthorne opened his eyes and stared blankly at the cracked plaster on the ceiling. The sofa was hard and uncomfortable. He had been sleeping, fully clothed, for over three hours. A sharp pain in his shoulder forced him to moan and change position.

"Are you feeling better?"

The gentle sound of Ling Yu's voice was a comfort. He turned on his side and tried to blink away the drowsiness. The sight of his packed traveling bag on the floor reminded him of the long and exhausting trip from Peiping.

"I'm just tired," he replied. "When did I pass out?"

"Ten minutes after your arrival." His wife smiled. "In the middle of a sentence and at the end of a yawn."

She was correcting test papers at a low table in the center of the room. A dim reading lamp accentuated her delicate beauty. Hawthorne studied her long black hair and pale complexion. She was dressed in a "Kam foo," a simple, pajama-like garment. It was his favorite.

"I have prepared some broth," Ling told him. "It will be good for you."

Hawthorne sat up and watched admiringly as she cleared the table and walked into the kitchen.

The tiny apartment had once been a storage loft for the owner of the dilapidated building. Thin partitions of varnished plywood separated the rooms. A narrow window, decorated with frayed curtains, offered a depressing view of a factory smokestack. It had to be securely shut at all times because of swirling black soot and revolting odors. Yet Ling Yu had managed to transform these bleak surroundings into a clean and orderly home.

The doctor had presented them with several gifts, including two well-stocked mahogany bookcases, a modern radio and a colorful assortment of wood and ceramic ornaments. These luxuries were out of place in a world of somber uniformity. The cramped rooms had been furnished many years before by the proprietor, a man of limited taste, and it was against the building regulations to replace or discard any of the items.

Gerald Hawthorne cherished his existence there, living each day as though the happiness and excitement would suddenly fade without a warning.

He stood and moved to the table as Ling Yu brought a cup of steaming hot soup.

"I'm not very hungry," said Hawthorne, taking a seat opposite his wife. "My stomach is still upset from the train ride."

"The broth will help," she advised.

Hawthorne toyed nervously with the handle of the porcelain cup. Ling studied his troubled expression.

"Your mind is also upset," she commented. "I have no remedy in our kitchen."

He massaged his aching shoulder and glanced thoughtfully around the room.

"Sung was right," he said, moving straight to the point. "They offered us a brand-new life."

Ling Yu watched and listened attentively.

"Extra money and one of the modern apartments," Hawthorne added. "Close to the university."

"It is a beautiful area," she interjected. "For very important people."

He stared and noticed that her eyes were unusually soft and moist. She looked unusually pale. Hawthorne shoved the heavy cup aside and frowned. "Trees and fresh air," he blurted.

He stood and walked pensively to the small window. He looked out at the factory and the crowded neighborhood rooftops before turning abruptly to face his wife. "I'll report directly to Sung here in Tsinan," he said. "But Wing is the top man."

"He is a very capable official," said Ling Yu. "Sung Tsen Tson is also well respected."

"They are my friends," he declared quietly.

There was silence. He walked to one of the bookcases and ran his fingers over the smooth wood. "I know everything," he whispered. "Wing trusts me. I was shocked at first, but I did a lot of thinking on the train."

"About trees and fresh air?"

"People," he replied quickly. "And obligations."

Ling Yu brushed the hair back from her forehead with a slender hand. "Has my husband become a factory supervisor?"

"Not yet." Hawthorne moved closer to her. "My situation is very unusual." He spoke in a confidential tone. "The government has special requirements."

"I am sure," said Ling.

"They have a right." He paused. "Mr. Wing explained all the reasons."

She raised her head slowly and waited for him to continue.

"I have to become a Chinese citizen," Hawthorne announced bluntly. "Foreigners can't work on these projects."

Ling Yu's eyes reflected the significance of the information but she did not comment. He finally took a seat at the table and faced her.

"We have to make a decision tonight."

She watched compassionately as her husband took a nervous sip of the broth, nearly spilling it.

"Are you anxious to participate?" she asked.

"I like the benefits."

"Have you solved the mysteries?"

"Yes," he answered. "I know more than Mr. Yen. And Wing and I have a personal understanding," Hawthorne explained. "I will never betray my friends."

Ling Yu picked up the cup and saucer. "It is difficult for me to discuss such complicated matters." She forced a smile. "I do not have the facts and you are obligated to withhold them."

He watched her stand and move to the flimsy red drape which screened off the kitchen.

"What about my American citizenship?"

"You must act on your own," she replied from the other room. "I will support your decision."

She came back with her test papers, sat down, and arranged them neatly on the table. Hawthorne studied the girl's dainty features.

"I belong in China," he said under his breath. "With you."

Ling reached over and touched his arm gently. "Someday you may wish to see your own people again."

"Never," he replied. "This is my home."

Her expression became somber. "Time and circumstances alter many things." She withdrew her hand but continued to gaze into his eyes. "Including obligations . . . patriotism."

"I'm now an expert on that subject." Hawthorne leaned toward her. "From phony generals to crooked politicians."

"I do not understand."

"It's very simple." His features hardened. "American officials are involved in these damn projects," he sneered. "They peddle government information like apples."

"Mr. Wing told you this?"

"Every detail," Hawthorne confided. "Along with a few personal things."

"He is very quick to reveal secrets."

"I've known him for years," the American replied. "We trust each other."

"My family is also acquainted with Mr. Wing." She picked up a marking pencil and prepared for work. "Perhaps his confidential information was intended to influence your decision."

"Part of it will," he answered bitterly. "The Army gave me

a dishonorable discharge. They call me a traitor and other lousy names." Hawthorne shook his head in a gesture of disgust. "Why the hell should I worry about patriotism and citizenship?"

Ling Yu looked at him solemnly. "I am your wife," she whispered. "Not your conscience."

He watched her return to the marking of the test papers. She seemed distressed and unusually tired. Her fragile beauty filled him with a disturbing mixture of love and apprehension.

"I have an obligation to you," he said quietly. "That's the important thing."

She stopped her work and looked up, motioning to the window of their apartment. "Will you trade your American citizenship for a change of scenery?"

"I want you to have a better life," Hawthorne replied. "To hell with flag-waving and allegiance. Anyway, we'll never get another chance."

Ling Yu put down the marking pencil and took his hand. "This home is richly furnished with love and companionship," she told him. "Mr. Wing has asked a high price for these additional comforts. Proceed with caution or you may forfeit our happiness along with your citizenship."

She released his hand. "I have expressed my thoughts," Ling said. "You will make the final decision." She turned back to her papers. "Please excuse my rudeness," she added. "I have an early class tomorrow."

Hawthorne watched in silence as she made notations on the students' tests. He weighed the importance of her reactions to the Peiping visit.

"I'll talk to Sung in the morning," he announced. "Mr. Yen has to organize his unit by the end of next week."

She raised her head and they gazed deep into each other's eyes. Then Hawthorne picked up one of the test papers and scanned the childish inscriptions. "I can read this," he said proudly.

"Excellent." Ling Yu smiled. "Perhaps you will help me with my secret project tonight."

"What's it about?"

"Mountains and lakes and birds and flowers," she answered. She held his hand and sighed deeply. "And other important things," she added with a touch of sadness.

JANUARY 10, 1962
AFTERNOON
WASHINGTON, D.C.

35

THE OFFICE DOOR SWUNG open and Robert Adler, Secretary D'Allesandro's assistant, stepped out and walked to the secretary's desk.

"Is he here yet?"

"Yes, sir," he replied. "He's outside."

"Good."

He walked briskly to a door at the far end of the outer office and entered the waiting room.

A tall and distinguished-looking visitor was standing in front of the spacious windows as Adler approached with his arm outstretched.

"Mr. Manning?"

Charles Manning turned away from the view and acknowledged the cordial greeting with a nod and a warm smile.

"My name is Robert Adler, sir," the man announced. "I don't know if you remember me."

"I certainly do, especially at Illinois Metals."

"Thank you, sir." Adler beamed. "The secretary is waiting to see you."

The two men had known each other for many years, in fact they had competed in various commercial areas prior to D'Allesandro's first appointment to a government post.

They had not seen each other for quite some time owing to the Secretary's heavy schedule, so D'Allesandro had made certain that their reunion would be uninterrupted.

After a few drinks, during which the informal conversation ranged from wives to sports and then to old times and departed friends and enemies, they at last got down to a serious discussion of Charles Manning's telephone request for a very special favor. He had refused to disclose the nature of the situation until he saw D'Allesandro privately.

The Secretary had heard reports earlier about Estelle Manning's abortive investigation of the Hawthorne case but knew that her husband was seldom directly involved in his wife's personal projects.

"Listen, Chuck," D'Allesandro said brightly, "I'll do anything but lend you money or lobby for your damn hula-hoops."

Manning laughed and settled back in a leather chair. The Secretary of State was relaxed on the office sofa with his shoes resting on a low coffee table.

"We'll skimp through even if the toys go out of fashion. I need information and advice, Roger," the industrialist grinned.

D'Allesandro smiled and gestured for his friend to proceed.

"Gerald Howard Hawthorne," Manning said quickly. "I need information and advice."

The Secretary sighed heavily and lifted his feet off the table.

"I was hoping that it was something else," he said seriously.

"Can you do it?"

"Do what?"

"Give me what I want."

"I'll give you some advice, Chuck. Leave it alone."

"Why?"

D'Allesandro stood and moved to a chair which was facing the industrialist.

"This is a very hot one and I can't say much more than that."

The room was silent for a while. Then Charles Manning leaned forward in his chair and spoke in a determined tone of voice.

"I don't want to place you in an awkward position," he stated. "You should know me by now. I'm not a candidate for any job and this is certainly not a crusade or a political witch hunt."

"Then why get involved?"

"Personal reasons," Manning replied. "I don't expect you to show me secret or classified files, but I want a few simple answers and you can supply them."

"And if I can't?" D'Allesandro asked. "Or if I won't?"

"I'll take the Goldenson files from your Hector Rambeau."

"Holy Jesus Christ!" the Secretary exclaimed as he jumped from his chair and headed toward his oval-shaped desk.

"I *will,* Roger," the industrialist assured him. *"And,* a few days ago I located another source of available Hawthorne material and it's supposed to be virgin. Very expensive . . . but I sell a lot of hula-hoops."

The Secretary of State took a seat and stared out of the window. His expression was grave. "What source?" he asked.

"A former Washington attorney."

D'Allesandro swiveled in his chair and faced Charles Manning. "He has nothing to sell."

"Really?"

"Others have tried, Chuck."

"And?"

"Barlow is a very quiet man."

Manning paused thoughtfully and then announced, "Not Barlow. The other one."

D'Allesandro's intense face thrust forward. "Whiting." It was a statement and not a question.

"Yes, Roger," Manning replied. "Thomas C. Whiting."

"Where the hell did you find him?"

"That's my business. I intend to respect his request for privacy."

There was silence for a few moments. Then Manning continued, "I want to make a deal with you. Answer a few questions and give me some time to think things over. I might forget the entire package and also make certain that my determined wife finds another project as quickly as possible."

D'Allesandro studied his friend for a moment and then nodded.

"This stuff is sensitive," he said. "Treat it all very gently."

"You have my word," Manning answered seriously.

"Okay. What do you want to know?"

"Was Hawthorne's dishonorable discharge from the Army a legal and proper act?"

"I don't think so."

"What happened?" the industrialist asked.

"Without names?"

"I know the names."

"A ranking official was coerced into making the move with Hawthorne and this forced a blanket edict for all the others at the time."

"All of the dishonorable discharges involved in this action could be considered illegal. Correct?"

"Possibly," the Secretary replied. "We don't know."

"They were certainly not investigated in detail by responsible military lawyers."

"No."

"There were no courts-martial."

"The actual details are still hazy," said D'Allesandro. "I became involved at a very late date."

"How late?"

"The roots go all the way back to the New Deal," he replied. "Crooked branches have been growing ever since."

"Meaning?"

"A government official resigned unexpectedly," the Secretary answered. "Later the man was accused of being an undercover Communist."

"The publicized case?"

D'Allesandro nodded. "He reportedly passed State Department files to an admitted Communist agent."

"That's sixth-grade history," said Manning. "A Congressional committee investigated and both men were tried, convicted and jailed. So what's the mystery?"

"The former official pleaded innocent all the way, and the committee took a very famous bow. But it was an overrated performance."

Charles Manning's puzzled expression prompted the Secretary to proceed. "It seems that five characters were involved in this particular game." He leaned back in his chair. "Only two were squashed, and the other three remained in the service of our government," he confided. "The code of silence prevailed and the three gentlemen suspended all covert operations."

"Are they around now?"

"No comment."

"Did they have important jobs?"

"Sorry, Chuck."

"What the hell does this have to do with coercion and dishonorable discharges?"

D'Allesandro stood and walked to the elaborate globe. "Let's examine a different branch," he suggested.

"The former Secretary of Defense?"

"No," he answered. "But a very prominent American. He was involved in some very bizarre financial manipulations." He spun the world map. "Everywhere."

"Who was he?"

"I said no names."

"Another Washington department head?"

D'Allesandro turned and faced the industrialist. "One of our most distinguished ambassadors, until his retirement."

"Stevens?"

The question was ignored. "Our three hidden characters made contact with the Ambassador as soon as the glare of publicity started to fade, and eventually they joined his firm," he added.

"Did they continue in government?"

"One of them did," the Secretary answered. "We're not certain about the other two."

"Tell me about this company."

"Not a chance," D'Allesandro replied bluntly. "Besides, I'm not familiar with all of the products myself."

"Commercial and harmless, I hope."

"Stevens was a mercenary operator but he respected the flag."

"More than gold?"

"As far as I know." He turned and saw a smile beginning to take shape on Charles Manning's handsome face. "What the hell is so funny?"

"It's quite a rotten tree," he answered. "How does an Army corporal fit into this complicated piece of work?"

D'Allesandro moved to the oval desk. "It seems that Gerald Hawthorne stumbled across some information about the Ambassador and his employees while he was living in Red China."

"Was he a member of the club?"

"Possibly."

"What kind of information?"

"We don't have the complete story," D'Allesandro admitted. "Speculation is easy and I intend to keep it at that."

Manning hesitated before speaking again.

"Can we get back to the former Secretary of Defense?"

"This conversation is getting . . ."

"Skip the details," Manning interrupted. "Just give me the surface."

D'Allesandro frowned and took a deep breath. "A junior clerk in the Patent Office caught an irregularity. Some secret plans were missing."

"When?"

"Shortly after Hawthorne went to China." The Secretary proceeded cautiously. "The Department of Commerce got involved at a low level but the details moved directly to the head of Defense and he took over the investigation."

"Did he discover the Ambassador's master plan?"

"No," D'Allesandro replied. "Just a few traceable items."

"Hawthorne's Chinese secrets?"

"A connection might have been made—with a little serious effort."

The industrialist stared and D'Allesandro turned away.

"I see," said Manning. "Who was the McCarthy investigator who 'persuaded' the former Secretary of Defense to cover up for Stevens?"

"I've gone far enough, Chuck."

"Was he one of the silent three on the Ambassador's payroll?"

The Secretary of State did not answer. Instead, he swiveled in his chair and faced the windows again.

Manning hunched forward earnestly. "A few more questions and I'll get off your back."

"Let's wrap it up right now."

"Not yet. What did the McCarthy man have on the Secretary of Defense?" Manning persisted. "I won't quit, Roger."

The Washington official met his intense gaze and finally decided to answer.

"Participation in a few questionable organizations," D'Allesandro replied. "Early in his career."

"Communist?"

"Mostly fringe but they were on Joe's list."

"That's all?"

"A few shady campaign contributions."

"Anything else?"

"He was linked to the convicted former official." The Secretary paused. "At the top of some ancient stationery."

Manning walked across the room to the globe. "You honestly don't know very much about this mess," he said thoughtfully. "And you should, Roger."

"Listen to me." D'Allesandro's sharp tone forced Manning to turn instantly. "I know one more thing."

Charles Manning walked back to the desk and studied the uneasy government official.

"The former Secretary of Defense was advised not to dig for worms. The state of the nation was more important. A friend and former business associate was quite adamant on this point. This man was a very powerful member of Congress at the time," D'Allesandro said, "and he got more powerful a few years later. He had also made a few innocent blunders at the start of a distinguished career."

"I'm sure," the industrialist said. "Is he still with us here in Washington?"

"Yes."

"How distinguished *is* the gentleman's career?" Manning inquired facetiously. "Don't tell me Cabinet rank."

"I won't tell you another damn thing. But I'm asking you to be smart."

Manning backed away from the desk and folded his arms.

"Christ almighty," he murmured. "You people are really up to your ears in skeletons."

"I honestly know very little about the original indiscretions," the Secretary of State explained quietly. "However, I do know a great deal about the efforts to cover them up."

"Bribes?"

"Yes."

"Theft?"

"Conceivable."

"Threats and political intrigue?"

"Maybe."

"What about physical violence and attempted murder?"

The Secretary of State checked his watch. "I have a meeting in a few minutes," he announced grimly.

"Why is General Roland Fawcett so damn interested in the case of an Army corporal?" Manning insisted. "Isn't he being considered for a move to the Joint Chiefs of Staff?"

"Yes."

"Do you condone all this crap?" Manning asked intensely.

"I sure as hell do not. Mistakes were obviously made in the past and I deplore a cover-up of any kind," he explained sadly. "But the world is in a mess and I love this country. Our leaders must have the complete faith and respect of the American people in order to function effectively."

He glared at Manning.

"Would you risk destroying this nation for the sake of one insignificant character in a town called Waverly, Michigan?"

The industrialist leaned on the desk.

"I might," he replied softly. "That's why I intend to take the research from Thomas Whiting and from anyone else who has information. I'm going to study it all until I have a more accurate picture of this entire affair."

He paused and straightened up.

"You can be sure that no further action will be taken if I feel that an investigation or a disclosure will destroy the United States of America. But as a citizen I demand to see for myself."

The Secretary of State rose to his feet and faced him.

"Roger," the industrialist added, "I love this country as

much as you do. But I want to know what the hell is going on before I close my eyes to any blanket edict. Do you know what I mean?"

D'Allesandro stared at him solemnly for a long moment and then put out his hand.

"Good luck, Manning."

"I'll be in touch, Mr. Secretary."

January 14, 1962
Waverly, Michigan

Hawthorne was surprised by what sounded like a scratching noise on the back door. It could have been his imagination, of course—he'd been imagining a lot of things lately—but he decided it was worth an investigation.

Slowly and carefully he moved toward the kitchen, crouching low as he passed the window. The noise came again. He remained immobile until he heard his name.

"Gerald . . . Gerald, please open the door. Gerald, it's Beatrice Powell."

He realized that this could be a trick, a conspiracy on the part of some of the more hostile residents of Waverly to lure him out of hiding. Nevertheless, he raised his head and peered out of the window. Mrs. Powell stood alone, shivering in her light coat. He opened the door a crack but left the chain attached.

"What do you want?"

"I shouldn't be here. But this could be important for you." She handed him a slip of paper.

Hawthorne glanced at it.

"What the hell is this?" he asked, still puzzled.

"It's Mrs. Charles Manning's private telephone number," said Mrs. Powell, stepping into the shadow of the porch. "She wants you to call her as soon as possible."

"Why?" Hawthorne asked.

Mrs. Powell leaned forward and spoke rapidly with great agitation.

"Last night I received a telephone call from the Manning estate in Detroit. I was astounded. Someone traced your old high school records and found my name. Mrs. Manning wants you to contact her immediately."

"I don't understand."

"Estelle Manning is very active in the American Civil Rights Association," Mrs. Powell continued. "She's probably interested in your case."

"Why would I talk about my life to a total stranger?" he persisted. "I don't know Mrs. Charles Manning and I sure as hell don't want to get involved with a civil rights group."

Mrs. Powell looked around nervously and took a deep breath.

"I don't know what it's about, Gerald," she answered finally. "But she's a very influential person."

Hawthorne folded the note and shoved it into the back pocket of his trousers.

"Everything that I have to say about my personal life has already been said on that bastard television program. Once is enough."

Mrs. Powell shrugged. "Well, you have the telephone number. The rest is up to you."

She stared at him, then turned and left abruptly. Hawthorne watched her leave the porch and disappear into the night. He finally closed the door and slid the bolt in place.

The January night was cold and the bitter Michigan wind swirled and slashed at him from every direction as he reached the empty lot near Hammond's Stables. The streets were deserted.

Hawthorne adjusted the collar of the warm leather jacket and shoved his chin deeper into the woolen lining. His pace was slow and unsteady, but he was on his own. His teacher's unexpected visit, the personal message from Mrs. Manning of Michigan, and a half bottle of his father's whiskey had convinced him that the time had come for a showdown in Waverly.

He had cautiously tested the front porch during his fourth drink and there had been no enraged citizens waiting in the dark. Perhaps an overworked imagination was partially responsible for his self-imprisonment. Six drinks had enabled him to stagger across the yard and down to the corner of Elm, without incident. He had even slammed the front gate loudly on his return. The demons were nonexistent. A few more swallows and a very warm glow had led him to the traveling case. K. M. Wing's present was delicately removed from a cloth wrapping. He was ready.

On this particular night Gerald Hawthorne was no longer a misfit and he intended to prove it by heading boldly and directly to Main Street. He grinned as his fingers touched the elaborately carved handle of the Chinese dagger in his pocket. An unusual weapon for an exploratory night patrol in suburban America, he thought. He had planned his itinerary so that he could make a brief exploration of the Chinese restaurant on Spruce Drive. The Tivoli Theatre, Anderson's Hardware, the Pizza Palace, and Woolworth's Department Store were also on the agenda, and he would surely take the time to walk slowly on Poplar, his favorite lane, where the trees on each side of the pavement seemed to grow together and form a ceiling.

Hawthorne wondered what would happen if he ended his nostalgic tour of Waverly with a civilized drink or two at Ted's Tavern, a saloon on Pike Place where the shots were unusually generous and the whiskey was the cheapest in town. The establishment was located on a desolate side street off Elm Drive and he remembered it to be a quiet haven for elderly and harmless neighborhood drunks.

He entered the gin mill and walked directly to the long wooden bar without taking any notice of the general layout or the clients. Hawthorne had never been inside this particular saloon.

His heart jumped momentarily as he realized that all conversation and laughter had stopped abruptly.

The aproned man behind the bar was small and hatchet-faced with thinning gray hair, bad teeth and a sardonic smile. His voice was high-pitched and raspy.

"Can I help you, sir?" he asked mockingly.

"I want a whiskey," Hawthorne managed, nearly choking on the words.

The bartender stared at him for a moment and then his artificial smile faded. "At your service, Mr. Hawthorne."

The man carefully poured a large quantity of bourbon into a glass and then looked up.

"Would you like water or ice, sir?" he asked.

"Ice."

The barman dropped two cubes into the glass and placed the drink in front of Hawthorne with a comical display of exaggerated service.

"Here you are, sir," he said with a flourish. "Only the best for our famous customers."

A few partially suppressed snickers from one of the side tables broke the silence in the room.

The tavern was a trap, thought Hawthorne, as he paid for the drink and took a slow sip of the contents. The tense silence convinced him that a long swallow was in order, and that this move should be followed by a very quick exit. He drained the glass and made an attempt to pull himself away from the bar. Then he decided against it.

"Another one, please," he said calmly, feeling that a fast move might be too conspicuous.

"With pleasure," the grinning proprietor answered. He poured the whiskey and placed the bottle close to Hawthorne. "Help yourself, sir." He glanced in the direction of the tables and winked. "We're always happy and proud to serve our returning war heroes."

He moved to the far end of the bar and took a seat on a high wooden stool.

Hawthorne concentrated on the glass and the bottle, trying to avoid looking into a large mirror directly in front of him. He sipped the drink and waited for the first reaction from the other customers.

He heard a few hoarse whispers at one of the tables behind him and then a harsh, grating voice cut the silence.

"Do you fellows notice a terrible smell in this joint?"

"Hell, yes," several voices chimed in unison.

"Is it you, Robertson?"

"Not me."

"Baker?"

"Not me."

"What about you, Sandy?"

"Hell no, Sarge. Not me."

The sound of raucous laughter filled the tavern. Hawthorne drained his second glass and poured himself another. The little bartender smiled sourly. "That one is on the house, General."

Hawthorne ignored the statement, lit a cigarette, took a drag and continued to stare into his whiskey.

"Maybe that damn smell is coming from across the room," the ringleader continued. "Do you guys stink?" he shouted to a group of older men who were quietly drinking beer at a corner table.

They shook their heads without answering.

"Well," the voice went on, "if it isn't at these two tables, it has to be coming from somewhere at the bar. Do you stink, Robie?"

The proprietor shook his head vigorously. "Not me, Sergeant. Not ever."

"What about you, Hawthorne?" the other man growled. "Do you stink?"

Emboldened by the whiskey, Hawthorne ventured a quick look into the mirror and he saw his antagonist for the first time.

The man was of medium height, stocky and nearly bald. Through the dirt-smeared glass, the man's eyes seemed to be slightly crossed. His soiled white shirt was opened to the navel exposing a thick neck and a hairy chest.

"Did the Chinks get your tongue, Mr. Hawthorne?" the man asked. "We want to know if you stink?"

He turned to a lanky youth who was sitting slumped and bleary-eyed to his right.

"What do you think, Robertson?"

"He stinks like a fucking sewer."

"Baker?"

"Like a dead rat."

"Sandy?"

"Like the inside of a fucking gorilla's armpit." The group laughed. "On a very hot day," he added, to even more boisterous mirth at the table.

"What do you guys think?" he yelled to the table of senior citizens.

"He stinks," the man mumbled without looking up.

"Robie?"

"Like a syphilitic whore," the proprietor giggled.

Hawthorne heard the sound of a chair being shoved back.

"I think he smells like a goddamn Communist. That's what I think."

The man swayed and then supported himself by leaning heavily on the table.

"I'll go over and sniff him," he muttered. "I never did smell an American gook before."

Hawthorne caught a glimpse of the burly figure in the mirror as the men started to move unsteadily toward the bar.

"Sniff him for me, Sarge," yelled Baker, and the others at the table roared their approval.

The man stopped a good distance away from Hawthorne and rested his elbows on the wooden counter.

"Get me a big drink, Robie," he ordered. "The smell is killing me."

The proprietor jumped down from the stool, poured a large drink and placed it in front of the troublemaker, who swallowed the contents in one gulp. Then he turned to Hawthorne.

"You can't go around stinking up places, Mr. Hawthorne. Clean folks don't like it." He took a step closer. "Especially here in this town."

Hawthorne stared down at his glass. He poured another long shot although his head was reeling and the room was beginning to blur.

The man slid his drink slowly down the bar and moved closer to Hawthorne. He lowered his voice.

"Weren't you married to a Chink?"

A sharp pain in his head and an almost unbearable throbbing sensation caused Hawthorne to rub his temples. He reached again for the bottle of whiskey; poured another drink and drained the glass. The other man moved further down the bar until his face was so close that Hawthorne was nauseated by the rancid smell of his breath.

"Tell me something," he said in a stage whisper. "Confidentially."

His appreciative audience at the table chuckled but he turned to them and motioned for silence.

"Gentlemen," he mumbled, "your minds are in the gutter." He swayed and nearly tripped on a brass footrail. After untangling his shoe and steadying himself, he continued. "We are all smart enough to know that the old story just ain't true."

He wiped spittle from the corner of his mouth with the back of his hand. "Chink girls are built the same as anybody else. Right, Mr. Hawthorne?"

He turned away from the entourage and directed his drunken words to the side of Hawthorne's face.

"I want to know if they eat dogs and screw monkeys."

The side table burst into spontaneous applause and riotous laughter. Two of the older customers from the other table had stood up and were preparing to leave as the leader pounded the bar and called for order.

"*Gentlemen—manners please.*"

He noticed the elderly clients and waved them back to their seats.

"Let's be courteous to our honored guest, Mr. Gerald Hawthorne." He stared menacingly at the quiet table. "We *all* stay until this special party is over."

The two senior citizens sat down again and stared at each other in silence.

The proprietor had stopped smiling when he realized that the drunken amusement might get out of hand. He brought another drink to the instigator.

"Here you are, Mr. Packard," he said. The man took the drink and nodded his thanks. Robie continued, "Don't you think we should let the old folks go, Sarge?" He laughed awkwardly. "Hell, they don't give a damn about Hawthorne anyway."

"*They stay, Robie,*" he ordered.

"But why?"

" *'Cause I said so.*"

The proprietor leaned toward Packard and spoke quietly. "I hate this bastard as much as you do, Sarge, but I still don't want real trouble in my place. Can you blame me?"

"There won't be no trouble, Robie," Packard promised, holding up his glass for a refill.

"With the law, I mean," the barman replied as he served a double whiskey.

Packard burst into loud laughter and nearly choked on the drink. "*The law?*"

He turned to his admirers at the table and joined them in a long laugh.

"Old Chief Crawford himself would love to come on over here and join us." He glanced at Hawthorne. "You can break his goddamn neck with a pipe and get a good conduct medal for doing it. You know that, Robie."

The proprietor forced a smile and walked back to his seat at the end of the bar.

Packard leaned forward to his victim and his tone was mock-friendly.

"I'm going to give you a break, buddy boy." He poured himself a large drink from Hawthorne's bottle. "All you've got to do is turn around to my good friends and tell them that you stink." He gulped the whiskey. "I'm doing this for good old Robie, who doesn't want trouble in his fancy saloon."

The proprietor giggled.

"Just turn around, Hawthorne, and tell the boys that you smell," Packard insisted. "It ain't a lie, you know," he added.

When there was no response, the man pushed himself clear of the bar and began to move slowly around Hawthorne.

"Ever hear of Peebles, Grey and Chester?" he asked.

There was some muttering from the men at the table.

"They were the three best fucking men ever produced in this town," he blurted out, and tears suddenly clouded his eyes.

"Hear, hear," the others shouted.

"Our best friends. Our brothers," he continued, moving clumsily to the other side of Hawthorne. He leaned on the bar and pointed his finger.

"The gooks took these boys apart at your fucking Camp Six. Did you know that?" His face was dangerously close. *"Did you know that, you Chink Communist bastard?"*

Hawthorne debated whether to step away but decided that the maneuver would be futile. He swayed, but held his ground and waited.

"They didn't get back," the man went on. His face was red and contorted. "But you did, Hawthorne. You got back." He paused for a moment and then stabbed his finger viciously into Hawthorne's chest. "And we know how you did it, you goddamn yellow traitor."

Suddenly and smoothly, Hawthorne reached for the bottle and smashed it violently against the edge of the bar. Whiskey and glass splattered in all directions and he jammed the jagged edge of the weapon hard against the man's stomach.

"Make one bad move and I'll rip you wide open," Hawthorne ordered.

The room was silent as the former sergeant glanced down and saw a few light trickles of blood begin to ooze out and dye his white shirt.

Hawthorne's face was ashen but there was no mistaking the almost homicidal expression in his eyes.

"Those bastards told me that I could go to China," he said. "Did you know that?"

Packard shook his head nervously and continued to stare at Hawthorne. He was obviously shaken by this unexpected explosion of temper.

"I didn't *run* to Tsinan. I *walked*." Hawthorne turned and faced the others, dropping the bottle from his hand. "Did you people know that I *walked* to China?" He shook his head trying to clear the alcoholic haze and get a grip on himself—it was as if something had snapped in his brain.

The men were silent and motionless.

"You guys in this hut gave up," he babbled. "You all make me puke."

He lunged forward but managed to prevent a fall by

catching the edge of a chair. He had begun to tremble violently. An icy sweat trickled down his spine, and he could not seem to focus his eyes, still less control his movements.

"You bastards did broadcasts and signed papers for a few cigarettes." His eyes were now expressionless and he seemed to be talking to himself. "I *studied* and *walked* to China."

"I think you should sit down and take it easy, Hawthorne," Robie, the bartender, interrupted.

"Fuck you, Proctor!" he screamed. *"Wing told me plenty!"* His voice lowered to a confidential whisper. "He was a *big* boss in Peiping and Sung was a *big* boss in Tsinan and I know *everything* about you bastards."

The men watched silently and cleared a path as he spun away from the bar and floundered crazily across the room.

His body slammed hard against a wall and the impact forced him to cry out and gasp for air.

"Fuck you, Proctor!" Hawthorne howled. *"And the same to you,* Fawcett!"

"I'm no goddamn traitor!" His voice trailed off as he stumbled around toward the windows.

The men stared in awe. Tension was reflected in all their faces.

"Proctor is a traitor!"

Hawthorne clutched the knife in his pocket. *"Fawcett* is a goddamn traitor!" He took the razor-sharp dagger by its handle and turned to Packard.

"*Ambassador Stevens* is a traitor!"

Hawthorne lashed out savagely with the knife, then hurled it. The blade pinned Packard's arm to the wall behind him. It had penetrated the center of the muscle without tearing the flesh or causing immediate pain. The shocked victim stared at his own bizarre crucifixion as blood began to trickle down the peeling plaster of the wall. Then as the reality of the situation hit him, he shrieked and began to sob. The bartender rushed to his aid.

Hawthorne suddenly twisted and faced the other men. "Did you guys know that Ambassador Stevens is a goddamn traitor?" he muttered, swaying.

Most of the men had taken shelter behind various pieces of furniture.

"Answer me!" he screamed. "Confess, you dirty bastards!"

"We don't know any of these people, Hawthorne," a small voice explained timidly. The man was hidden from view.

"LIARS! Beatrice Powell is a traitor! Estelle Manning is a traitor!" Hawthorne stopped abruptly and there was silence in the room. "My father is a traitor," the men heard him whisper. "Just leave me alone . . . and . . . let me live in peace."

"We'll let you go, Hawthorne." It was the bartender. He had made a tourniquet of a towel and was holding Packard's arm.

"You'd better. Or . . . I'll blast you all to hell."

"Just get moving," one of the men told him.

"I love my wife," Hawthorne mumbled as he walked to the door. "Did . . . you guys know . . . that my mother . . . is a saint?"

"You can take off, Hawthorne," Packard said, looking up from his wounded arm. "We'll meet up again."

Hawthorne stumbled to the door, exhausted, and staggered out into the night.

It all happened very quickly and without warning. The patrons of Ted's Tavern had taken a short cut to the house on Elm Drive, and were waiting in the shadows of the porch for Hawthorne's arrival.

On a given signal from Packard, the men pounced from all directions while the wounded leader watched and directed the proceedings.

The tavern hooligans conducted their business silently and efficiently with several thorny tree branches, an old bicycle chain, fists and feet, and finally a large empty bottle of Robie's best Scotch.

It shattered against the side of Hawthorne's head and he staggered up two steps and then collapsed in a pool of splintered glass and blood.

The group stood around their battered victim and inspected the damage while Packard looked down from his position at the top of the porch steps.

Hawthorne was unconscious and bleeding badly from a wound just above his right ear. His face was badly scratched and several welts were beginning to develop on the back of his neck.

"Good job," Packard complimented his subordinates. "He'll get the message fast enough."

"Should we pull him up on the porch?" asked one of the men.

Packard shook his head. "Want to tuck him under the sheets and tell him a fucking bedtime story?"

The others laughed and the man tried to join them but he was obviously disturbed by the blood and Hawthorne's seemingly lifeless body on the steps.

"Tell you what," Packard proposed. "I'll solve your problem."

He suddenly stepped back and then crushed his heavy boot against Hawthorne's bleeding head and the body tumbled crazily down the two steps and landed face-up on the gravel path.

"That should wrap it up for now," Packard announced.

The good citizens of Waverly, Michigan, had successfully completed their mission.

JANUARY 15, 1962
WAVERLY, MICHIGAN

36 HAWTHORNE TRIED SEVERAL times to open his swollen eyes but they seemed to be glued shut. Then, with a great effort, he managed to run his hands along the edges of a narrow and uncomfortable slab and thought immediately of a hospital, a prison or a morgue.

He reached up apprehensively and touched his forehead.

His fingers inspected a thick bandage which had been taped securely over his right brow and sharp pain registered as he touched it. He pushed his tongue cautiously against several loose teeth and he could feel clots of dried blood on both lips.

The familiar results of a drinking spree were adding to his general discomfort and the thought of whiskey and Ted's Tavern forced him to groan loudly.

"How do you feel?" the police chief asked. His tone was cold and unpleasant.

Hawthorne forced his voice through a hoarse and irritated throat. "Lousy."

"Can you eat?"

"I don't think so."

Police Chief Cyrus Crawford examined the man's battered features, unmoved.

"What time is it?" Hawthorne asked.

"Four o'clock."

"AM or PM?"

"Afternoon."

"Christ," mumbled Hawthorne, and then he closed his eyes again. "What happened?"

"You don't remember?"

"Something in Ted's Tavern," Hawthorne replied huskily. "After I left. Some guy called me a dirty Chink bastard and then I remember . . ."

"Listen to me," Crawford interrupted.

His unfriendly tone prompted Hawthorne to pry open his aching lids and watch as the other man sat down in a chair next to the bed.

"I frankly don't give a damn what you remember about last night. But you had better remember what I'm going to tell you right now."

"I can't hear too well in my right ear," Hawthorne murmured faintly. "Part of the bandage is covering it and there's a funny humming noise."

Crawford pulled his chair closer to the bed and continued impatiently.

"Assault and drunk and disorderly conduct. We hauled you off your porch."

"Oh Christ," Hawthorne mumbled.

The room was no longer out of focus and Hawthorne was

suddenly wide awake. He tried to pull himself up into a sitting position but the pain forced him back on the pillow.

"I'm sorry," he moaned, twisting his head from side to side while Crawford looked at him with disgust.

The chief picked up a local newspaper and started to read an article on the front page.

"The Turncoat, Gerald Howard Hawthorne, was arrested and charged with assault and drunk and disorderly conduct last night after a brawl in Ted's Tavern on Pike Place.

"Mr. William Semple, the owner of the popular Waverly meeting place, who was not present at the time of the incident, claimed that this was the first distasteful incident in his establishment since the doors were officially opened by Mayor Calvin R. Blake on March 3, 1940.

"Mr. Semple stated, 'This man Hawthorne viciously attacked one of our regular customers without provocation.'"

Crawford stopped reading and looked up solemnly. "And so forth, and so forth. All the lurid details."

He tossed the newspaper and it landed in disarray on the floor beside the bed. "There's also a picture of you being dragged off your steps and shoved into a police car."

Hawthorne avoided Crawford's eyes as the police chief moved back to the foot of the cot and glared down at him once again.

"An editorial on another page refers to you as Waverly's curse and it recommends a formal citizens' petition calling for your immediate transfer out of this model community."

"Bullshit," Hawthorne retorted. Anger was beginning to replace his feelings of shame and humiliation.

"Packard, the man you attacked, happens to be a respectable and very prominent citizen in this town," said the police chief grimly. "And an Army veteran."

"I don't give a shit who he is," Hawthorne responded.

One of the blood clots on his lip opened and he dabbed at it with the sleeve of his rumpled shirt.

"The word 'Chink' doesn't call for a . . ."

"I'll kill any man who calls my wife a Chink whore," Hawthorne interrupted fiercely.

"You shouldn't have been there in the first place," Crawford snarled.

Pain contorted Hawthorne's face as he managed to pull himself up into a sitting position. "Why not?" he asked belligerently. "This is a free country, isn't it? Why the hell should I be restricted and hunted and treated like a goddamn dog? Who the hell do these people think they are?" He paused and caught his breath. "Why shouldn't I be in Ted's Tavern like anybody else in this town?"

"Because as far as this town's concerned, you're not fit to live," Crawford snapped. "You'll be cooling your heels here at my station until we take you to court. Just protective custody, you understand. And then it'll be a nice long jail sentence, I hope. I don't mind telling you, Hawthorne, I'm glad to get you off the streets of my town." He left the cell and locked the door after him.

The Puebla Lake district in the Sandia Mountains of New Mexico is rugged, breathtakingly beautiful and almost uninhabited. The closest thing to civilization is a small Indian pueblo and this community is inaccessible because of a deep gorge and the lack of reliable trails leading from the secluded lake area. Santo Salinas is out of reach and Albuquerque is even further.

There is a grouping of several crudely built mining shacks and a dilapidated general store located in a canyon called Little Monterrey. Basic provisions can be purchased here if the proprietor receives the written requirements at least one month in advance of one's arrival.

A trip from the center of the lake section to the bottom of the canyon is slow and dangerous, and only veteran cliff dwellers are capable of navigating safely over the jagged mountain terrain.

The air in the Puebla region is healthy and the scenery is magnificent.

But above all, the isolated lake area is quiet, peaceful and very, very private.

*　　*　　*

On January 25, 1962, a sturdy jeep station wagon, loaded with a month's supply of basic provisions, left the general store in Little Monterrey and started the climb to Puebla Lake, New Mexico.

It was apparent that the driver was a mountain resident and familiar with the route. He guided the vehicle expertly over the narrow, winding roadway just as the shadows of twilight were beginning to create stunning patterns on the rocky slopes of the Sandias.

He was a tall, stocky man in his middle fifties with thinning black hair and a scraggly gray beard. His features, carriage and general manner suggested intelligence and refinement, completely out of place in the raw surroundings of the Sandia hills and canyons.

The steep incline forced him to slow the jeep to a near-standstill on the approach to the summit. There were no protective barriers on certain turns and there was a sheer drop into the canyon.

The road leveled out at a point near the top and he turned off and proceeded along a bumpy trail which cut through a densely wooded section of the Puebla district.

After bouncing past the shimmering blue water of the mountain lake, he descended for a short distance and then veered away from the path. He continued over an open stretch of pebbled land until the trees closed in again and forced him to slow down and maneuver cautiously. It was beginning to get dark, so he switched on his low beams.

Soon he reached a clearing and could see his ranch house in the dim glow of the headlights. The wooden structure was small and compact but some expense had obviously gone into its construction, and it was very modern in design. It was nearly hidden by the hanging branches of trees and mountain shrubbery.

The man made a sharp right turn and his tires crunched on the gravel as the car moved toward the garage.

And then suddenly his foot slammed hard on the brakes and the vehicle skidded to a halt. He made himself sit quietly for a moment in order to calm the pounding of his heart.

A car was parked in front of the steps leading to his front door and a man was sitting behind the wheel.

Regaining his composure, he snapped off the lights and ignition and lifted a revolver out of a rack under the instrument panel of the jeep. He shoved the weapon into his jacket pocket and lowered the window.

"What are you doing here?" he leaned out and shouted.

"I'm waiting," the man answered pleasantly. "There are some people inside."

The living room of the isolated Puebla Lake ranch house was cheerful and richly furnished. A professional decorator with an eye for detail had captured the look and feel of a cozy hacienda.

The owner entered and stood motionless in the center of the room as three men rose to their feet.

They studied him coldly until he had removed his right hand from the pocket of the hunting jacket.

Thomas Whiting recognized his visitors and shuddered. "I don't want any trouble," he mumbled nervously.

"Nobody wants any trouble," the tallest of the three commented smoothly, sitting down. "We want to complete our business and get home as quickly as possible."

"How did you find this place?" Whiting asked in a trembling voice.

The tall man in the chair smiled and stretched his long legs. "It wasn't easy," he drawled. "We persuaded your old partner to tell us what he knew and we picked up the rest from a builder in Santo Salinas and a real estate agent in Albuquerque." Clete Hardigan shook his head wearily. "It sure wasn't easy," he repeated.

"What do you want?" Whiting inquired nervously.

Hardigan made a gesture and one of the men left the room quickly. His shadow could be seen just outside the front door of the house.

"Now you know damn well what we want," Hardigan replied impatiently. "Let's save a lot of time and trouble and get this over with fast."

"I don't know what you're talking about."

The Texan sat up and his features hardened as he leaned forward in the chair.

"I suggest that you take a seat, Mr. Whiting."

After a brief, uneasy pause, the former lawyer sat stiffly on a divan and faced his uninvited guest.

The other member of the team, a dark man with strong Latin features, remained standing and moved back to a wall near the fireplace. He folded his arms and watched silently.

"Give me your papers on the Hawthorne case and then pour us all a stiff drink, Mr. Whiting," Hardigan said in a mock-friendly manner. "You certainly made us work for it this time. Only mountain goats should be allowed up here."

"I don't have any papers," Whiting replied sharply. "Rambeau took them years ago."

"*Bought* them, Mr. Whiting," the agent corrected.

"Whatever you say. But he has them and I have nothing more to add to the story. I'm sick and tired of the entire affair and I do not wish to be involved again. That's why I'm here in Puebla."

Hardigan shook his head. "You forgot to inform Mr. Rambeau that you made a copy of all that research material."

"That is not true."

"It *is* true," the agent contradicted. "That copy belongs to the buyer. Wouldn't you agree, counselor?"

Thomas Whiting's uneasiness was now more apparent as he saw Santo Morales remove a pad and pencil from his pocket and begin an inspection tour of the living room.

"I do not have a copy of my research material," Whiting insisted. Perspiration was beginning to appear on his forehead and he could no longer control the quiver in his voice. "You must believe me."

"How the heck can you live way up here without a telephone, Mr. Whiting?" the agent asked seriously.

"What?"

"Put that on your list, Santo," Hardigan called to his associate, who was in the process of examining windows, doors and various furnishings in the room. "He has no direct way to communicate from here."

"What the hell are you people doing?" The former attorney twisted on the divan and anxiously watched the proceedings.

"Mr. Morales is taking an inventory," Hardigan explained calmly. "We might want to buy this place someday."

Whiting turned back to the Texan and scratched at his beard with trembling fingers.

The agent's casual manner changed abruptly and his tone became cold and menacing. "Or the information might be useful if you want to take out an insurance policy," he said. "You need a lot of good coverage up here, Mr. Whiting. Don't you agree, Santo?"

"Absolutely," the other Rambeau agent commented.

"You have a copy, Whiting," the Texan drawled. "That funny boy from China is back and we don't like certain rumbles." His eyes narrowed. "Give me the papers." It was a direct order.

Thomas Whiting removed a handkerchief from his jacket pocket and wiped his forehead.

"Mr. Rambeau received the only copy at the time," he stuttered hoarsely. "That's the truth, Hardigan."

"Keep talking."

"I did not cheat Mr. Rambeau."

"You still haven't said anything important."

"I made fresh notes from memory when Hawthorne returned to America," Whiting admitted nervously. "This was not a copy of the research which I . . . submitted to Mr. Rambeau."

"Now why would you want to do a nasty thing like that?"

Whiting mopped his forehead with the handkerchief again and then took a deep breath.

"I don't know exactly, Mr. Hardigan," he muttered. "Perhaps I thought the American government would call me and demand accurate testimony or . . . I don't know."

"Or maybe you could sell the stuff all over again. Isn't that more like it, Mr. Whiting?"

He was too distraught to answer.

Santo Morales took a seat in a chair next to Hardigan. They both glared at Whiting.

"You were warned once before that all this information is

too damn sensitive to be put down on paper," said Hardigan. "Don't you remember that, counselor?"

Thomas Whiting bowed his head and nodded.

"We can't cut facts out of your brain unless we kill you," the Texan added smoothly. "And nobody wants to do that," he continued. "But we just can't afford to have this information floating around."

"Give us your notes," Morales demanded harshly.

Whiting began to shake violently and soon tears were streaming down his cheeks.

"I don't have the notes," he sobbed. "Please believe me."

"Just what the hell are you saying?" Hardigan asked, alarmed.

"I gave them away," Whiting blurted out. "I sold them to somebody."

He buried his face in his hands.

"I'm sorry," he gasped. "I needed the money and . . ."

Morales suddenly jumped to his feet and lunged forward as Whiting pulled a revolver from the side pocket of his hunting jacket.

"*I want to die*," Whiting screamed hysterically, pointing the weapon at his own throat. Morales knocked the gun from his hand and punched him, knocking him to the floor.

Morales tossed the gun to Hardigan, who had been watching the scene with mild interest from his armchair. He checked the weapon briefly and then placed it on a nearby coffee table. It was loaded and primed for firing.

"Who bought your papers?" Hardigan lifted himself out of the chair and walked toward Whiting. "Where are the papers right now?"

"I can't tell you that, Hardigan," Whiting stammered. "I took an oath to God . . . and a lot of money."

Without a change of expression, Hardigan grabbed Whiting savagely by the hair.

"Who bought your papers?" he asked again in a monotone.

"We don't like blood or bruises," Hardigan said, tightening his grip on Whiting's hair. "But you are really making things difficult for us, counselor."

"I . . . won't . . . tell." He was sobbing as he struggled to pull away.

Hardigan twisted Whiting's head into a workable position and Morales was then able to locate a nerve in the back of the victim's neck. His thumb dug deeply into the flesh and Whiting's eyes bulged. The blood drained completely from his contorted face and his body became rigid. He opened his mouth to scream but no sound came out.

"Listen real good, counselor," Hardigan whispered while his associate continued to apply the special treatment. "We have to know what you did with the Hawthorne files. Nobody leaves this house until we find out. Understand?"

Whiting seemed to be losing consciousness and Hardigan quickly gestured to Morales.

He released the pressure and Whiting fell back on the divan.

"Where did you stash the Hawthorne files, counselor?" Hardigan waited. "I might not ask you again."

Whiting cleared his throat and swallowed hard several times before speaking. His voice was hoarse.

"I . . . sold them . . . to . . . Charles Manning."

Hardigan stared up at Morales and there was complete silence in the room.

Thomas Whiting was sitting in a dazed condition with his head bowed. He appeared to be praying.

"I'll be a son-of-a-bitch," Morales mumbled incredulously. "Manning of Michigan."

Clete Hardigan shook his head in amazement and then glared at the pathetic figure on the divan. "You sure are a barrel of trouble."

He pulled himself up and tightened his belt. "This time you really did it, counselor."

Whiting looked up very slowly. His voice trembled. "What happens now?"

Morales removed the notepad from his pocket. "Should I finish the information for Rambeau?" he asked Hardigan. "All I have is part of the living room."

"It might be a waste of effort, Santo," the agent answered.

"I don't think Mr. Whiting is going to be around these parts for any length of time."

Thomas Whiting looked up at both men.

"What will happen to me, Mr. Hardigan?" he asked.

The Texan stared at him and then smiled sardonically.

"I don't know what's going to happen to you, counselor." He walked toward the coffee table. "But I have some very good advice."

The agent pointed to the loaded pistol.

"Why don't you use this and save us all a lot of time and trouble?"

JANUARY 28, 1962
RAVENHURST
WINCHESTER ESTATES
DETROIT, MICHIGAN

37

CHARLES MANNING CLOSED a thin folder and placed it with a stack of documents in the bottom drawer of his desk. He took a set of keys from the pocket of his lounging robe and securely locked up the important material. Then he switched off the reading lamp in his private study and reached over to tug at a slender cord which opened the velvet drapes. Moonlight streamed through the windows of the room and he sat, trying to assimilate the staggering information he had just read. It would have to be professionally investigated and legally confirmed but he felt it was genuine. He was astounded by Whiting's documentation and intimate knowledge of American political manipulations.

Manning already knew that certain minor accusations involving a particular Washington official were true; there seemed to be little reason to doubt the other incredible charges which touched some of the highest offices in the government.

He closed his eyes and thought of Roger D'Allesandro's statement about the condition of the world and the constant need for faith in and respect for the governing process. He recalled the Secretary's question at the conclusion of the meeting in Washington.

Would you risk destroying this nation for the sake of one insignificant character in a town called Waverly, Michigan?

And then Manning thought about Gerald Howard Hawthorne.

Estelle Manning was trying her best to relax in the library, but it was impossible for her to enjoy an evening of quiet leisure when she was concerned about her husband.

He had not slept properly for several nights and she was worried about his despondent mood and lack of appetite. He was now spending hours alone in his private study upstairs and his entire manner had changed since a close business associate had brought the special package from Albuquerque. He had become irritable and short-tempered, even with her.

She knew that he had completed his examination of the Whiting notes on the previous evening, but he had said very little about the contents or the possibility of taking action. He appeared to have been shaken by what he'd read, and seemed to be struggling with his conscience. At some point a big decision would have to be made, and she decided to try to talk it over with him.

"Every scrap of information has to be dissected and analyzed," he explained wearily.

"I'm worried about your health, Charles."

"That's a minor consideration," Manning replied. He tapped the files on his desk. "This incredible dossier is a lot more important at the moment."

"When will you discuss the material with me?" she asked.

"After I've made a decision."

"For God's sake, Charles," the woman snapped, "I'm not a child. I do have a modicum of intelligence and a great deal of common sense."

He looked at her, and then stacked the Whiting papers into an orderly pile on his desk.

"I will not allow you or anyone else to influence my judgment, Estelle," he asserted. "This verdict has to be mine. Can you understand?"

She nodded.

Manning pointed to the files. "Go ahead and read them," he said. "But *I* will decide whether we act or back off."

"Does he have facts?"

"Enough to force an investigation at the highest level." Manning paused and turned to his wife. "*If* a man wants to drop a hydrogen bomb on his own country."

She settled back on the divan and her eyes were alive with interest. "What about Gerald Hawthorne?"

"He's the bomb," Charles Manning replied. "This character is in a position to confirm most of Whiting's information."

He got up and walked across to a bar near the window. "Goldenson was on the right track." He poured himself a drink. "Want one?"

"No."

"Whiting mentions the McCarthy investigator and the pressure on the former Secretary of Defense, followed by Hawthorne's dishonorable discharge."

"Illegal?"

"There was a repatriation agreement and the man had a right to go to China."

"So it *was* illegal."

"Probably," Manning answered, "but this is nothing compared to the rest of it. The most incredible part of Whiting's information concerns a wealthy and respected American diplomat."

"Does Whiting give his name?"

Manning brought the drink over to the divan and sat next to his wife. "Ambassador Stevens."

Estelle Manning was stunned. There was silence in the study while Manning sipped his drink.

"The Secretary of Defense was coerced into using his office and political prestige to cover for Stevens."

"I can't believe it." She shook her head in amazement. "You were duped by Whiting."

"No, dear."

"The Ambassador fought Joe McCarthy every inch of the way," the woman continued. "He was America's most respected diplomat. When he died, so did a lot of our prestige abroad."

"He was also extremely wealthy." Manning stood and walked back to his desk. She watched as he put the glass down and tapped the Whiting papers.

"Everyone suspected that Edward Stevens had a few cute investments going outside of the States." He sat and faced his wife. "But what the hell. It's easy to kick up a little mud if you open a man's books."

She listened quietly.

"But this Whiting information is something else." He stared at the folders and seemed to be thinking aloud. "At first I nearly threw the whole damn project into the wastebasket but then certain facts started to fall into place."

"Facts about what, Charles?"

"Industrial espionage. It seems that our respected ambassador solved the problem of finding a safe, lucrative outlet for every qualified industrial spy in the United States." He opened the folder and scanned the contents. "Mr. Stevens *organized* the damn piracy by setting up a professional network for selling U.S. information—confidential patent office stuff—to selected foreign countries."

"Go on."

"Russia and Red China, for example."

"I still don't understand."

"A very exclusive group was formed here in the States with Ambassador Stevens at the top," he explained. "Every stolen blueprint of significance was purchased by this operation and all details were taken care of swiftly and expertly until the product was in the hands of an appropriate buyer."

Manning turned a page in the file and read a few lines before continuing.

"These clever boys even financed certain important thefts

when specific requests were received from reliable clients. These Whiting files are dynamite."

"Or complete fiction."

"Special telephones in Zagreb and electronic recording devices for Sverdlovsk eventually became part of a much broader scheme."

He looked grave as he replaced the folders on the desk.

"A few Washington employees discreetly offered their services. In time, a more sophisticated line of products started to move on the Ambassador's busy network."

"What kind of products?"

"It's a technical jumble in Whiting's files," he answered, "but I have a feeling that the word 'industrial' should be erased and the official records might read just plain espionage."

"That's a very serious charge."

"The group shared the profits and made a fortune," Manning went on. "They had a complicated, illegal and unorthodox Swiss arrangement."

"I see."

"Our shrewd McCarthy investigator was also on the payroll," he added. "This fellow had the best front in the world."

"Alive?"

"He died recently."

"Do you know the other Washington contacts?"

"No."

"They may be active in government right now."

"Anything is possible, Estelle."

Charles Manning leaned back in his chair. "Stevens and company had working contacts in all parts of the world," he continued. "The information shows that several dedicated Communists were operating for him in Russia and China."

"I'm going to have that drink now." She stood and walked to the bar. "This is shocking."

"The report indicates that Gerald Hawthorne was very friendly with two of these men." He watched her pour a small brandy. "One in Peiping and the other in a town called Tsinan."

"Does he give their names?"

"No," Manning replied. "But the government believes that Hawthorne was briefed in detail about the entire Stevens operation."

"Incredible." She moved back to the divan. "Communists dipping into a Swiss pot."

"That's probably the key to Hawthorne's silence." Manning closed his eyes for a few moments. "His pals would be slaughtered if the Red leaders ever found out about this unauthorized capitalistic arrangement."

"What did the investigator have on the former Secretary of Defense?" She took a sip of the drink.

"Enough to make him panic and act like a damn fool."

"How?"

"Files in several departments were tampered with and a minor employee from the Patent Office was bribed." Manning began to pace up and down the room. "The efforts were clumsy and one blunder led to another. He even made a foolish attempt to revoke Hawthorne's citizenship, at the beginning."

"It would have kept the boy in Red China for good."

"Correct." The industrialist's tone was grim. "A dishonorable discharge and public condemnation were probably the only alternatives."

"Smear his credibility."

"A little insurance in case the character ever decided to surface."

"Was the former Secretary acting on his own?" she asked.

"He took the advice of a powerful and understanding friend in government who checked into the situation and urged the head of Defense to back away."

"And?"

"Professionals were brought in by this influential friend."

"Gangsters?"

"Hell, no." The industrialist pulled his robe tighter around him. "Expertly trained fixers."

He turned to his wife. "Have you heard of a charmer by the name of Hector Rambeau?"

"The South American tycoon."

"Typhoon is more like it," Manning corrected. "His team moved in swiftly with brains, money, experience and a few muscles thrown in here and there. Everything was set in order and an American traitor by the name of Gerald Howard Hawthorne was safely out of the way in Red China."

The room was silent as Manning walked back to his desk and sat down.

"Time went by and the Party continued to gain strength and prestige." He tapped his fingers on the Whiting papers. "The sordid past was forgotten by all concerned."

"Surely other government officials were aware of the cover-up," his wife demanded.

"A few were involved in the original Rambeau operation and others received bits and pieces over the years," Manning explained. "No one was prepared to upset the apple cart for the sake of a few buried skeletons." He sighed deeply. "The Party was on the move."

"Are you insinuating that men like Roger D'Allesandro would ignore espionage for the sake of . . ."

"They may not have the actual facts," Manning interrupted. "Roger claims that the Stevens organization was commercial." He flipped through the files thoughtfully. "Today's diplomatic climate prohibits a closer examination."

"Who is Whiting?" she asked.

"He was hired along with another lawyer named Barlow years ago by a convicted Communist," Manning told her. "They fell over some Washington bones while trying to prove the man's innocence."

Estelle Manning finished her brandy. "So they're all guilty in some way." She placed the glass on a table.

"That's true, dear," replied her husband. "But Gerald Hawthorne is back and I'm worried about the country."

"This boy must be one of the most potentially dangerous human beings in America."

"In every way," Manning agreed. "He might have been programmed by the Chinese for a delayed explosion. It's been done before."

Estelle Manning left the divan and moved to her husband.

"You do have a frightening decision to make, Charles," the woman said gently.

"Things have become even more complicated," he told her. "The people involved are now in positions of leadership and they cannot afford scandals or wide-open investigations."

He glanced at the Whiting papers. "This time Hector Rambeau will go all the way to protect the government and the men at the top."

"Is the former Secretary's powerful friend still active in Washington politics?"

"Yes," he replied without looking up. "This man is the Vice President of the United States."

"Oh my God," she whispered.

The industrialist shoved the files toward his wife. "Go ahead," he insisted quietly. "Read them."

"I'm not in the mood at the moment, Charles," she stated as she headed for the door of the study. "My stomach is not as strong as I thought it would be."

She hesitated before leaving the room. "Please come to bed, darling," she begged. "I'm very worried about your health."

"I'll be there in a few minutes."

His wife mumbled a soft good night and closed the door.

Manning stood for a moment and gazed at the folders in his hands. He sighed deeply and then walked back to the desk, locking the Whiting report in the bottom drawer. He closed the drapes and was about to leave the room when he suddenly remembered something. His hand reached for a switch on the reading lamp.

Manning paused and glanced up at a framed photograph on the wall. It was a formal banquet scene—a huge banner was the background behind a group of distinguished-looking gentlemen who were seated at a long dining table.

"MANNING IS MICHIGAN," it read.

He stepped closer to the picture and inspected his own evening clothes and broad smile.

Then he concentrated on his two dinner companions who were posed stiffly with their arms outstretched in a gesture of warm congratulations.

Manning looked down to the lower right-hand corner of the frame.

The photograph had been signed by the President and the Vice President of the United States.

FEBRUARY 6, 1962
PRIVATE CHAMBERS
JUDGE EZRA STONEHAM ROPER
COURTHOUSE
WAVERLY, MICHIGAN

38

CHIEF OF POLICE CYRUS Crawford was furious. He sat on the edge of a chair and pounded on the judge's desk.

"I demand an explanation," Crawford fumed. "This action is unprecedented and I refuse to sit back and let these political hoodlums from Detroit interfere with proper law enforcement here in Waverly."

Judge Ezra Roper ignored the outburst and continued to light his cigar.

"You could have called me at the office and explained this thing before sending it around with one of your court messenger boys," said Crawford resentfully. "I don't like formal papers served on me without prior notice."

Crawford had been a member of the Waverly force since his graduation from high school and had a reputation as an efficient protector of the peace.

"I think the document is self-explanatory," Judge Roper commented in a professional manner. "The State of Michigan is interested in your prisoner."

Crawford tried his best to control another eruption. He poured himself a glass of water from a decanter on the judge's desk and swallowed before speaking.

"I've got this man on a drunk and disorderly, a peace disturbance and assault with a deadly weapon," he announced harshly. "Now he's in protective custody. And that assault charge can be stretched into something a lot more serious if I work at it hard enough."

Crawford drained the glass and slammed it down. "It's a local affair and it has nothing to do with the State of Michigan." He paused and started to button his jacket. "Lots of decent citizens are beginning to come forward now that I've got this bastard in custody on a good one."

"I'll bet."

"Robie at the tavern wants to file formal charges," Crawford went on. "So does Packard. The whole damn town has something on this character."

Roper lifted the paper out of the mail tray and glared at Crawford. "This document might help you, Cyrus," the judge commented seriously. "It all breaks down to a few basic facts," he explained. "The State wants this boy examined by psychiatrists in Detroit and you will have to cooperate."

"Doc Royston does that kind of work for us right here in Waverly."

The judge shoved the paper toward Crawford. "You'd better read this very carefully and do some rational thinking. They want Hawthorne in Detroit for a series of psychiatric examinations by specialists," he repeated calmly.

"Who the hell is *they?*" Crawford pounded the desk and Roper looked at him with irritation.

"Senator Samuel C. Brewster issued a special request for the transfer of custody and I signed the necessary papers," he stated sharply. "Gerald Hawthorne's background and his recent conduct indicate a possibility of mental illness and the State wants this man hospitalized and properly treated *if* specialists confirm these suspicions."

"And if they don't?"

"He goes back in court for assault with a deadly weapon," said Roper, "and to the penitentiary *if* you can prove your case."

The police chief's face relaxed a little.

"We get him back if the reports are negative. Is that right, Ezra?"

The judge took a long draw on his cigar. "I guess we do, Cyrus."

"How do you rate our chances?"

Roper swiveled toward the courthouse windows. "I figure that the report to the court will state that Gerald Hawthorne is mentally disturbed due to his unusual experiences in Korea and Communist China."

"Horseshit."

The judge ignored the remark. "The man will be confined to the Clifton State Mental Hospital for an indefinite period of time. And this decision will be handed down very quickly. That's how I figure the situation."

"What makes you so damn sure?"

Roper's expression was solemn as he turned and faced Crawford. "Quite a few very important people consider this boy to be unstable and a menace to society."

"You mean Senator Brewster?"

Roper thought for a moment and then grinned at his old friend.

"I mean the important police chief of Waverly, Michigan," he replied. "Cyrus Crawford. Am I correct, Cy?"

Hawthorne's room was small and dreary but at least it was private and more comfortable than the noisy and overcrowded wards on the upper floor of the institution.

There was a washbasin, a toilet, and a narrow window with two bars and a view of the garbage disposal unit behind the hospital kitchen.

Clifton State was an escape-proof asylum designed especially by two of Michigan's most experienced architects. The four levels were solidly constructed of stone and iron and most of the security features, including the guard towers and intricate alarm systems, had been publicized as structural innovations when the building was dedicated by the Governor of Michigan in 1912. It was located in a remote section of the Detroit suburbs and it was surrounded by high walls and open fields.

Hawthorne had completed one week of confinement at Clifton State, and he was determined to survive the ordeal without signing false confessions in exchange for special favors. Another interrogation session was scheduled for three o'clock. He sat on the edge of his uncomfortable cot and reminded himself to be patient, alert and unyielding. Events were moving too quickly. Only three weeks had gone by since he had thrown the knife in Ted's Tavern.

He scanned the bare cement partition of his hospital room and thought about the man's bleeding arm and his own subsequent beating. The memory was still fresh in his mind but the experience had not upset him emotionally.

He reclined on the bunk and gazed at the cracked toilet seat and antiquated plumbing fixture.

Once again he had fallen into an obvious trap. He had prepared himself earlier for a slick interrogation about Robie, Packard and the incident in Ted's Tavern. He had also thought up what he considered to be a brilliant line of deceptive responses to all possible questions involving his life at Camp Six and in Tsinan.

But the insidious medical team had caught him off-guard during the very first session by probing his childhood. He had tried in every possible way to control a growing sense of outrage as their questions relentlessly invaded his privacy, but it was useless.

A series of delicate questions pertaining to the love he felt for his mother had provoked him to attack the doctor, and the panel's diagnosis was completed much earlier than anticipated. He had almost strangled Dr. Quentin Jameson, who had been flown in from Washington, D.C., for the examination. A police attendant finally strapped the patient in a restraining device.

Hawthorne, thinking over the events, suddenly pounded his fist on the bed and sat up.

It had all been so expertly handled, he realized. The formal interrogation had surely been designed to set off an explosion in him and trigger the exact amount of bedlam required for official admittance to a state mental institution. He was beginning to feel some strain, but he had managed to protect the privacy of his thoughts and feelings in spite of continuous pressure and hostility.

A key twisted in the lock and he turned to face the door.

"Let's go, Hawthorne," a voice shouted from the corridor. *"Upstairs."*

He moved slowly and wondered whether he was destined to be a prisoner of war for the rest of his life.

The phone rang and the Rambeau agent reached for it from the sofa while he continued to study the sports pages of the *Detroit Herald.*

"Yeah," he muttered.

"A call from Washington, Mr. Morales." It was the hotel operator.

"Okay."

He was still absorbed in an editorial on boxing when he heard his boss's voice.

"Good morning, Santo."

"Good morning, Mr. Rambeau." He was tired but trying not to let it show in his tone. He put the paper down at once.

"You sound terrible," said Rambeau. "A bad night?"

"A very bad night," Morales answered. "What's it about, sir?" he asked.

There was a brief pause on the other end. "I was calling to tell you how pleased everyone is. Your work in Detroit was fabulous. Even better than the job you did in New Mexico."

"Thanks."

"There was a meeting last night in Atken's other office in Arlington and the compliments would have doubled the size of your head. The chairman's proposal could not have been timed any better."

"I know."

"The insane bit with the knife made everything fall neatly into place," said Rambeau. "We think your action there should hold up for a long time. Our good Dr. Quentin Jameson is sitting right here in the office, as a matter of fact. Whatever the strange gentleman says now becomes nothing more than a clinical notation in a serious medical case history." Rambeau went on. "Know what I mean?"

"I know what you mean," the agent answered soberly. "When can I get out of here?"

"I'll have to let you know later this evening," Rambeau replied. "But I'll want you to stay until the court papers are officially signed and certified. I'm not sure of the schedule."

"Thanks, sir."

"Talk to you tonight. So long."

February 7, 1962
Detroit, Michigan

It was late evening.

A long black limousine moved smoothly along the road toward Charles Manning's home in the fashionable section of Winchester Estates. Manning and his wife were tense and silent in the back seat.

The annual Civil Rights Association dinner had been as impressive as ever, but a brief conversation with Alan Purvis toward the end of the evening had upset the Mannings. They were now thoughtful as they considered the lawyer's startling disclosure about the accident.

Estelle Manning's expression was grave when she finally interrupted the lengthy silence.

"I'm frightened, Charles." She continued to gaze out of the car window, toying nervously with a thin gold bracelet. "We should act at once."

"I'll make a decision based on facts," he said firmly, "not conjecture."

"It's been weeks since you've had the files."

"I frankly don't give a damn if it takes years," Manning stated. "These notes are vital, but I need additional information from other sources before I tackle the government of the United States." He turned back to the window. "I'm not senile yet," he added quietly.

The limousine made a turn off the main highway and started up the winding road to the Manning estate.

"What about tonight, Charles?" she asked bitterly. "Can't you react openly to Alan's letter?"

"It's shocking and I'm very upset by the news," he answered without looking at her. "But then, many people are seriously injured in automobile accidents in Caracas, Venezuela. I'm upset to hear about it."

"Is that all? You said approximately the same thing when they shanghaied Gerald Hawthorne into Clifton State last week."

"The man put a Chinese dagger into someone's arm."

She glowered and he avoided her eyes.

"I'm not naïve, Charles," she said caustically. "Getting him in there was part of a master plan and you have the blueprints in your study."

"Listen to me." Manning was breathing heavily. "I'm not a fool. I know the whole damn thing is part of an involved conspiracy, but I'm afraid to move. I've been stalling," he admitted, "and I don't know whether it's due to patriotism or cowardice."

The driver accelerated unexpectedly into their driveway and the conversation stopped. Two state police cars with revolving lights were parked in front of the steps of Charles Manning's estate.

"We received the call about fifty minutes ago, sir," an officer explained. "It came from a member of your household staff." He checked a notepad. "Mrs. Maureen Kelly. A cook."

Manning and his wife, both extremely concerned, were standing in the center of the living room while uniformed police and plainclothesmen continued with a detailed inspection of the premises.

"These people were experts," the officer said. "We still haven't been able to locate the exact point of entry and everything was left neat and orderly."

The officer pointed to a plainclothes detective who was examining one of the living room doors. "Lieutenant Renaldo and his men will be finished with the downstairs in a few minutes and they'd like you to help with a complete inventory of each . . ."

Charles Manning suddenly bolted away from the group and headed for the spiral staircase. He bounded up the stairs to his private study.

His wife made an instinctive move to follow her husband but hesitated and stayed where she was.

"Something of value up there, Mrs. Manning?" the officer inquired.

"Important business papers," she answered.

Lieutenant Renaldo and a colleague started for the stairs. At the top, Manning dashed past an astonished detective and lunged for the handle of the study door.

He stood rigidly in front of the window and watched a uniformed policeman check the front driveway while Lieutenant Renaldo examined his desk.

"How many files are gone, Mr. Manning?" Renaldo was gently probing a lock on the bottom drawer with a thin metal instrument.

There was no reply.

"How many files are missing?" he asked again, looking up expectantly.

"Six," Manning replied grimly as he continued to stare at the grounds below.

"They must have been very important to somebody," said Renaldo. He tapped the delicate metal tool against his knuckles and studied the grave expression on Manning's face. "I don't think they removed anything else."

Charles Manning did not reply. He seemed to be deeply absorbed in his own thoughts.

"These were all business files?" Renaldo asked.

"Yes."

"Confidential plans and things like that?"

Manning hesitated and then replied impatiently. "They were very important business files."

"Any idea who might be interested in them?" Renaldo prodded.

Manning suddenly turned and scowled at the policeman.

"Every competitor," he replied sharply. "And I have thousands."

Renaldo placed the metal instrument in his jacket pocket. "Some very expensive outside talent was hired for this job." He walked back to the desk and shook his head. "This is the best work I've seen in Detroit and I go back a long way."

"Charles," Estelle Manning called softly from the doorway of the study, and he motioned for her to enter.

"I'd like to talk to my wife privately for a few minutes," he said to Renaldo.

The detective nodded. "Of course." He paused at the door. "We have some work to do up here, Mr. Manning. Please try not to disturb anything and let us know when the room is available."

He closed the door.

Estelle stood looking at her husband until he turned back to the window.

"I've gone through most of the house with the police," she told him in an unsteady voice. "Everything seems to be in order. They want to see us downstairs later for statements or something."

Manning's features were expressionless, but she could hear his unnatural, nervous breathing.

"Poor Kelly," she rambled on shakily. "I gave her a sedative and the police want to . . ."

Manning suddenly walked to the bar and dialed a number on the private telephone.

He drummed his fingers on a glass and waited for the connection. "This is Charles Manning," he announced authoritatively. "I'm sorry to disturb the household at such a late hour but I must speak to Dr. Myerson. It's urgent." He paused. "Thank you."

Estelle Manning studied her husband as he held the receiver.

"How are you, Barry?" she heard him ask. "I'd like to meet with you tomorrow morning at nine and I need about three hours. Can you make it?" He waited. "Here at my home. Strictly confidential and very sensitive." There was another brief pause. "Good. That's kind of you." Manning listened and then turned to face his wife before answering the voice on the phone.

"I want to release a patient from the Clifton State asylum," he announced. "I'll explain the details tomorrow. Give my best regards to Edith. Good night, Barry."

There was a soft tap on the study door and a man's voice called. "This is Lieutenant Renaldo, Mr. Manning."

"Yes, Lieutenant."

"I hate to disturb you but we'd like to finish up in the study."

"Come in."

The detective and two other plainclothesmen entered and went to the desk.

"Sorry, but I used the telephone and touched a glass," Charles Manning admitted. "I hope it doesn't spoil your investigation."

Renaldo laughed as he resumed his inspection of the lock on the bottom drawer.

"It won't mean a thing in this particular case," he stated. "These boys don't seem to have made any mistakes at all."

"You never know, Lieutenant," Charles Manning commented very seriously. "Nobody is perfect."

He led his wife to the door and they left the study.

MARCH 21, 1962
CLIFTON STATE HOSPITAL

39

GERALD HAWTHORNE'S TRANSFER to the maximum security wing of the institution had been approved by the administrator in his third week of confinement at Clifton State.

His mental condition and general conduct had deteriorated rapidly and the staff felt that the isolated section of the hospital would be better suited to handle his violent and uncontrollable outbursts of temper.

He had undergone lengthy therapeutic sessions with several psychiatrists in an attempt to locate the source of his mental disturbance.

It was evident to them that his experiences in Korea and Red China had aggravated a previous condition, so the psychiatric staff had concentrated on his parents and his early childhood in Waverly. One member of the Clifton team had intensified the patient's disquiet by hammering away at the intimate details of his marriage.

In a brief period of time Hawthorne's sullen attitude had developed into fury and he had physically assaulted three of the resident psychiatrists.

His new home reminded him of the underground pit during the days and nights of solitary confinement at Camp Six. There were four bare cement walls and a high ceiling. Toilet and washing facilities were situated outside the iron door of the cell and he was not allowed to leave unaccompanied.

An attendant had unofficially informed him that he was on a list for sodium pentothal. Hawthorne was fearful of the injections because the man had exaggerated the procedures of administering the drug and the effects of the truth serum.

He paced the cold floor of his cubicle and pondered the consequences of psychotherapy and prolonged questioning while under the influence of Clifton's potent "talk-out drug."

He shuddered when he thought of involuntarily releasing precious confidences about his mother, Ling Yu and information about certain experiences in Red China.

The patient gripped the bars of a tiny window and pledged to fight valiantly against all the destructive forces until he could find a safe way to freedom.

The furnishings in the spacious room were bright and cheerful, and members of the staff were always pleasant and cooperative.

Patients in robes and slippers could be seen shuffling around the area or sitting at tables with relatives and friends. A few inmates were allowed to stroll around the enclosed grounds at the rear of the main building, but even these privileged cases were monitored by a small army of guards in white uniforms.

Dr. Barry Myerson sat quietly in a comfortable leather armchair and surveyed the lobby of Clifton State. He glanced toward the hallway and saw Gerald Howard Hawthorne for the first time.

An imposing guard in a starched uniform was holding the patient by the arm and scanning the lobby in search of his authorized visitor.

Dr. Myerson stood and motioned to the attendant.

Hawthorne lowered his eyes as he was led across the lobby to meet the Chairman of Michigan's State Board of Mental Health.

The huge man in white was still gripping his arm when Myerson waved a finger at him. "You can leave Mr. Hawthorne with me," he instructed.

"But I was told that . . ." The attendant hesitated. "Yes, Dr. Myerson," the man finally replied. He moved away but glanced back over his shoulder several times before leaving the area.

Hawthorne sullenly refused to raise his head or acknowledge the doctor's presence.

"Let's go, Hawthorne," said Myerson. He headed for the closely guarded door leading to the hospital grounds.

The psychiatrist was certain that Hawthorne would not follow. He finally stopped and turned. As expected, the patient was standing by the leather chair but he had lifted his head and was now glaring suspiciously at the strange visitor.

Myerson took a few steps back and faced him. "Are you coming with me or not?"

Hawthorne continued to watch the doctor but refused to answer. Myerson suddenly wheeled about and started for the door again.

"*Where?*" The psychiatrist turned back slowly at Hawthorne's question.

"Outside," he replied, faking impatience. "This lobby gives me the creeps."

"I'm not allowed on the grounds."

"I say you are," Myerson stated firmly.

Hawthorne looked him up and down.

"Don't let my appearance throw you," the chairman grinned. "I'm a big shot."

"You don't even look like a doctor," Hawthorne said suspiciously.

Myerson then examined the patient very carefully from head to foot in the same manner. "You don't look so damn good yourself," he commented dryly.

He turned and walked briskly toward the doors leading to the hospital grounds. This time he did not pause or look back, since he was aware that Hawthorne was following him.

A guard issued a heavy robe at the entrance and the patient bundled himself into it reluctantly.

The air was fresh and crisp and there were trees and flowers and sunshine. Shrubbery lined the garden paths and wooden benches were spaced at intervals along the way.

Rolling green hills could be seen beyond the high walls and Hawthorne stared longingly at freedom as he walked in silence with the doctor.

A few elderly patients and several visitors were lounging around a fountain in the center of a shaded mall and Myerson guided his companion toward the spraying water.

"I don't really like fountains," he said. "But they have lovely roses on the other side." They continued to walk. "Do roses bloom in March?" he asked, fully aware that Hawthorne would not answer.

"I don't know a thing about nature," said Myerson to himself as they neared their destination. "But a man should appreciate nature. It should be a criminal offense to ignore such natural beauty."

They stood a short distance from the fountain and observed that the flowers were not in bloom. Myerson shook his head regretfully and they resumed their tour.

The patient kept his eyes on the paving and jammed his hands into the pockets of his robe. They moved casually along a trail which led to the high walls.

He was still wary and confused a little but more at ease. He kicked a pebble aside with his slipper.

"I thought you were supposed to interrogate me," he muttered without looking up.

"Do you want to be interrogated?"

"No."

"Then why don't you just enjoy the walk?"

They finally stopped a few steps from the surrounding wall and Myerson flopped down on a bench.

"I'm out of condition," he announced. "Besides, you're much younger than I am."

Hawthorne accepted a cigarette and a light. He squinted at the wall and then took a seat next to the doctor.

"How did you get me out of the building?" he asked the psychiatrist.

"I told you," Myerson replied in a friendly manner, "I'm a big shot."

"Are you a doctor?"

"Yes," he answered. "My name's Barry Myerson."

"A head shrinker?"

"A psychiatrist."

"Oh," Hawthorne said dejectedly.

"I run the Michigan State Board of Mental Health," said the psychiatrist.

"Then why don't you pull these bastards off my back?" Hawthorne asked, turning away.

"This staff is qualified," he answered. "They should be working on your head and not on your back."

Hawthorne tossed the cigarette to the ground and stomped on it with his slipper.

"They work on my mother and my wife," he burst out. "To hell with them. I'll never share my private thoughts with strangers."

Hawthorne peered up at one of the guard towers and thought of Camp Six as Myerson leaned his back against the cold cement bench.

"You'll never make it," said the psychiatrist, following his glance.

"I'm smarter than that," Hawthorne answered. Then he asked flatly, "Do *you* think I'm crazy?"

"I don't know what the word 'crazy' is supposed to mean," the doctor answered.

"Insane," Hawthorne snapped. "A lunatic."

"I don't know that much about you."

"What about anxiety neurosis?"

Myerson smiled. "Where did you hear that one?"

"In the Army," Hawthorne answered quickly. "A guy in my outfit had it and they gave him a medical discharge."

"So?"

"Should an anxiety neurotic be confined to the maximum security ward of this asylum?"

"Who diagnosed your case as anxiety neurosis?" Myerson asked.

"I did."

"You did," he repeated and then snapped his fingers. "Just like that. Anxiety neurosis."

"Sometimes I get the same symptoms as the guy in my outfit," said Hawthorne. "But I'm not insane."

"How would you like to get out of here?" the doctor asked suddenly.

"You mean the security ward?"

"I mean the hospital."

The inmate was interested but suspicious. "You might be a big shot but I don't think you're God."

"I'm not," said Myerson. "But a very important man wants to have you released and placed in his custody."

"What man?"

"Mr. Charles Manning."

The doctor spoke very seriously. "I will attempt to secure your immediate release from this institution."

"*If* I want to be released," Hawthorne reminded him.

Myerson ignored the statement and went on, "You'll live with the Mannings in Winchester Estates."

Hawthorne glowered at the psychiatrist. "I've been locked up in the strangest damn prisons." He forced a laugh.

"Ravenhurst is not a prison and the Mannings are sincere and understanding people," said Myerson. "They are my friends."

Hawthorne turned away, but he was listening.

"These people will do everything possible to make you feel at home," the official went on. "They have a swimming pool and a tennis court and a rare art collection and one of the best private libraries in the world."

A spark of interest registered on Hawthorne's face and the doctor decided he was on the right track.

"I've read that you attended special classes at a university in China," said Myerson. "Chuck Manning will probably hire a tutor and you could continue with your education at home."

Hawthorne spun around, his eyes ablaze with excitement.

"Charles and Estelle Manning are very intelligent and worldly people," the psychiatrist added. "The court and the State will consider their guardianship to be the best possible form of rehabilitation in a case of your kind."

Hawthorne's glowing expression slowly faded. He yanked a blade of grass and chewed on it.

"Mrs. Beatrice Powell told me about Mrs. Manning," he stated grimly.

"What about her?"

"This civil rights crap."

"It isn't crap," said the doctor. "Estelle Manning is active in many worthwhile civic projects."

"I don't want to be a hobby for a rich broad," he remarked coldly. "I'm just looking for peace and quiet and a normal life."

"Is this what you consider a normal life?" Myerson asked, glancing at the drab hospital building a distance away.

"I don't want to fight the government or hot-shot Army vets in barrooms," he protested.

"Explain your feelings to the Mannings," urged the doctor. "Discuss your problems with them."

"Interrogation again," Hawthorne reflected somberly. "The Army and Korea."

"Perhaps."

"Red China."

"Probably."

"*Never*," the patient raised his voice.

"They want to help," Myerson assured him. "You might have been the victim of unintentional but illegal governmental action and the Mannings will do everything possible to protect your rights as an American citizen."

Hawthorne laughed. "Mr. Manning will waste his time and money. I'll never tell them about Camp Six or Red China. It's *my* business."

"I see," the doctor commented grimly. "You'd rather sit here and have trained medical personnel concentrate on your precious childhood. Am I right?"

"It's safer," Hawthorne replied quietly. "For everybody."

"I don't understand what you mean, Hawthorne."

The patient pulled himself to his feet and Myerson followed.

"Mrs. Manning gets a big charge out of helping little people with their problems, right?" he sneered. "What's her husband's excuse?"

"Why don't you ask him?" They started back toward the main building. "I'll bring him over at four tomorrow afternoon."

"He'd come out here to Clifton?"

"If you agreed to see him."

Hawthorne concentrated on the trees and flowers as they strolled back through the hospital grounds. He breathed deeply and made the most of his last minutes in the garden.

"My wife and I are also going to be staying with the Mannings for a few months," said Myerson. "We do it every year. Edith adores the place." He watched Hawthorne struggle with his thoughts. "We'd have some interesting talks if you decided to join us."

They neared the door leading to the visitors' lobby.

Hawthorne stopped and looked down at his slippers. He demanded insistently, "Why does Manning want to know about my experiences in Red China?"

"Ask him," Myerson suggested. "Shall I bring him tomorrow?"

"Can I think about it?"

"No." He glanced at his watch. "Make up your mind, Hawthorne. I'm late for an appointment."

"I'll talk to him," the patient finally agreed. "But that doesn't mean that I want a transfer to Winchester Estates."

The official smiled. "You'll be taken to a room adjoining the administrator's office at three forty-five. I'll meet you there."

Hawthorne nodded his reluctant agreement and then gazed somberly at the doctor.

"Do you agree with my theory about anxiety neurosis?" he asked.

"I'd say very stubborn and a little crazy," the doctor replied. "Whatever that means."

He laughed and turned away, heading for the main gates of the mental institution instead of walking to the lobby door. "See you tomorrow," he called over his shoulder.

"Hey," shouted Hawthorne, "you're supposed to take me back inside."

"I trust you." The psychiatrist waved and continued walking without looking back. "You'll find your way home," he added.

11:30 PM
APRIL 2, 1962
OFFICE OF THE SECRETARY OF STATE
WASHINGTON, D.C.

40

ROGER D'ALLESANDRO WAS WORRIED—irritability and frequent outbursts of temper were beginning to interfere with his work. The job of running one of America's most sensitive departments was awesome and laborious, of course, but he knew that his condition was being aggravated by a personal conflict which had nothing to do with long hours, burdensome responsibility or the gravity of world affairs.

He sat at the oval desk and picked up an official document.

His eyes skimmed the opening lines and then he arranged the paper neatly on a large green blotter. He had finally taken formal action.

He looked up as Senator Edward Atken and General Roland Fawcett entered his office. Both men seemed weary and ill-humored.

The elderly chairman of the Foreign Relations Committee flopped on the sofa and removed his shoes. He settled back against the comfortable .cushions and pushed a thatch of tangled gray hair out of his eyes as he placed both feet on a low serving table.

Fawcett sat erect in a chair facing the Secretary of State's desk. The tall officer's crew-cut was now beginning to thin but his stern features and crisp mannerisms had not changed since his days at Camp Six. He suppressed a yawn and made an effort to smooth the wrinkles in his uniform.

The senior senator muttered something about a lengthy Pentagon conference and cursed under his breath. He glared at D'Allesandro. "I think we've had enough for one day."

"This meeting will be brief," the Secretary assured him.

"I hope so," said Atken. He nodded toward the General. "The test ban conference is going to be restricted. What the hell is Roland doing here?"

D'Allesandro looked at the old man and indicated the paper on his desk. "I'm not interested in the treaty or the Pentagon at the moment," he explained solemnly. "This is a personal matter and the General is involved."

Fawcett shifted in his seat and Atken looked perplexed as D'Allesandro continued. "A member of my staff gave me a detailed report on the Rambeau meeting held in Arlington last night," he stated grimly. "I want to know if the facts are accurate."

Senator Atken turned away instantly and lifted his feet off the table. Fawcett fingered his collar and glanced at Atken.

"Your interest in this affair has always baffled me, Roland," D'Allesandro snarled. "I understand the connection now."

"What do you mean?" the General asked, startled by D'Allesandro's tone.

"Were you present at the Rambeau meeting last night?"

"I was not," the General replied.

"Don't be a damn fool, Roger," Atken interrupted. "Nobody in this government knows anything about a meeting in Arlington, Virginia, last night. Your man is completely out of line and should be disciplined." He leaned back. "And you certainly owe Roland an explanation."

D'Allesandro continued to stare at Fawcett. "Did you know that Hector Rambeau held a meeting with his entire staff at a private residence in Arlington, Virginia, last night?"

"Roland doesn't know a damn thing about a Rambeau meeting," Atken broke in. "Deal with me," he instructed harshly.

"Well?" D'Allesandro asked.

"I heard some rumors," Atken replied. He turned to the General. "You go ahead, Roland. I'll talk to the Secretary."

D'Allesandro motioned Fawcett back into his chair. "Just sit there until I'm finished," he ordered.

The General looked furious and humiliated. Atken took a step closer to D'Allesandro. "Mr. Secretary, you are building mountains out of anthills and I personally resent your hostile attitude."

"I've just discovered a few things about your anthills, Edward." D'Allesandro wheeled about and returned to his seat behind the oval desk. He gazed sternly at both men.

"Did you also hear rumors about the Hector Rambeau plans, Mr. Chairman?" he asked angrily. "The closing stages of Operation Red Watch? The final solution to the Hawthorne problem?"

"Hector Rambeau is a private citizen," Senator Atken explained calmly. "And so are his associates. I can assure you that this government has neither advised nor instructed Mr. Rambeau in reference to Operation Red Watch or Gerald Howard Hawthorne."

D'Allesandro managed to control his disgust and outrage as he looked from one man to the other.

"You boys made a stupid blunder," he asserted coldly. "Charles Manning is a loyal American citizen but Rambeau has pushed him too far. He's decided to take action. Manning isn't a shifty television producer or a frightened Washington lawyer," he went on, trying to compose himself. "Manning is Michigan and he has the power and influence to set up a formal investigation and pulverize this whole damn Administration."

"Don't count on it, my friend," the Senator interjected.

"This man has enormous power," D'Allesandro said. "Senator Brewster and Governor Pike were forced to sign Myerson's release order for Hawthorne because Manning put the screws on them from several directions."

"Brewster and Pike are Michigan boys," Atken pointed out coolly. "Charles Manning's political screws won't fit in the same holes here in Washington, D.C."

Roger D'Allesandro stared at Atken and lowered his voice.

"Gerald Hawthorne is now living in Winchester Estates and he will soon rip this government to pieces. Manning will take him straight to the top." He paused, noticing Atken's troubled expression. "It was a good try, Ed," he added softly, "but don't you think we've all reached the end of the line?"

"What do you want to do, Mr. Secretary," the Senator asked.

"The President or the Vice President should face the nation right now and put it all on the table," said D'Allesandro. "It's better than waiting for this character to kick off an avalanche which will eventually bury the Party and cripple the government."

"Don't jump to conclusions, Roger," the old man advised. "Charles Manning can't begin a formal investigation unless Gerald Hawthorne agreed to shoot his mouth off all the way."

The Secretary of State narrowed his eyes. "I think that the Rambeau plan, as outlined to me, will eliminate that possibility forever," he stated grimly.

Senator Edward Atken stood and moved to the desk. He looked down at the Secretary of State.

"This meeting is over," he announced.

D'Allesandro suddenly rose to his feet and faced Atken.

"Edward," he said hoarsely, "it appears that our anthills were actually mountains from the very beginning." D'Allesandro glanced at the granite features of Roland Fawcett and then turned back to the Senator. "Are you aware that we have been covering up a great deal?"

There was a long pause before Atken spoke. "I think you've just about finished, Roger," he advised quietly.

"Not quite." D'Allesandro picked up the document from his desk. "I wanted you to see this before the President receives it in the morning."

He presented the paper to the elderly politician.

Atken read very slowly, glancing up several times with an expression of disbelief.

The Secretary gazed unemotionally at Roland Fawcett. Their eyes met for a moment and the General turned away.

Edward Atken finished reading the document and put it back on D'Allesandro's desk. He walked pensively to the bookcase and began to pace behind Fawcett's chair.

"Tear it up now, Roger," the Senator finally ordered, stopping near the ornate globe of the world. "You'll regret this move for the rest of your life."

"Not a chance," D'Allesandro replied firmly. "My decision is final."

The old politician marched to the oval desk and leaned on it heavily with both hands.

"You can't do this! The treaty negotiations will come to a grinding halt and you'll wreck every damn bit of diplomatic progress we've made so far," he pleaded. *"Tear it up!"*

"Let others have the pleasure."

"The others are imbeciles."

"Our President will find the right man." He smiled sardonically. "What about Hector Rambeau?"

D'Allesandro folded the paper very carefully and placed it in an official envelope. He then sealed it and locked it in the top drawer of his desk.

"My physicians have recommended this action," he explained. "The pressures of public life are much too great."

"A goddamn lie," Atken blurted out. "This resignation will create panic and speculation."

"Have you been to a doctor lately, Edward?" D'Allesandro

asked sarcastically. "What about the Vice President? I think that most of you fellows need the same kind of thorough examination."

"The President will refuse to accept the resignation."

"He will accept it with regret during tomorrow's press conference."

General Fawcett eased himself cautiously to his feet. "I don't think that you'll need me any further," he said hesitantly.

"Hell, no," D'Allesandro stated.

Atken turned abruptly. "Keep your mouth closed about all this, Roland," the Senator warned. "You were never in this office tonight. Is that clear?"

"Very clear."

"*Fawcett!*" D'Allesandro's shout halted him at the door and he turned.

"That corporal seems to know something detrimental to your proud military record," said the official. "I intend to recommend a complete investigation before you take one more step in the Army of the United States."

The General straightened up and stared contemptuously into D'Allesandro's eyes.

"As you wish," he stated in a clipped fashion.

Fawcett glanced at Senator Edward Atken and then marched briskly out of the office.

Gerald Hawthorne stood in front of an ornamental dressing mirror and inspected his latest prison uniform. It was two o'clock in the morning.

The expensive red silk pajamas and comfortable slippers were unlike anything he had ever been issued before, and the personal monogram on the top pocket made him blink in amazement. The mirror also showed him a head of neatly trimmed hair and a clean-shaven complexion.

He turned away from his reflection and examined the splendor of the Ravenhurst guest suite. It was still a fantasy after six nights of regal confinement.

A grandiose four-poster bed, the luxurious furnishings, the thick rugs were all somehow unreal. There were several interesting books on a side table but he was not in the mood for reading. He was confused and impatient to complete the preliminary stages of the unusual Winchester indoctrination program.

His new jailers were pleasant and generous. They had tried to make him feel welcome in every way but he knew that the time for serious interrogation was rapidly approaching. He was prepared.

Charles Manning had suggested that he spend the first week of his visit in a very relaxed atmosphere without establishing any formal routines or daily schedules.

Estelle Manning had given the boy a grand tour of the estate, and they had spent a long time in the Ravenhurst library. He was stunned by the fascinating collection of books and magazines and was amazed to find two shelves devoted to the works of famous Chinese authors. The Mannings had obviously purchased these books especially for him.

Mrs. Manning was away from the house a good deal, and the chauffeur had informed Hawthorne that she visited the offices of the Michigan Civil Rights Association every afternoon.

The informal atmosphere and casual attitude of the Mannings and the Myersons, who were also staying in the house, were evidently intended to soften him up for the tedious sessions ahead, Hawthorne decided as he climbed off the bed and walked barefoot over the warm carpeting. The moon was full and bright, and a corner window seat afforded a panoramic view of the forests and distant hills beyond the grounds of Ravenhurst. A slight movement in front of the massive iron gates caught his attention.

Two men were conversing quietly in the shadows and Hawthorne observed that they were both wearing leather holsters at their sides. The entrance to the estate had not been guarded in this fashion on previous nights.

Another shadowy figure could be seen patrolling near the tennis courts, and Hawthorne made out the barely visible shapes of a jeep and a motorcycle parked near the outdoor swimming pool.

He craned forward in the direction of the gymnasium in time to see another security man, who was gripping the lead of a ferocious-looking police dog.

Hawthorne counted in all seven armed men, four dogs, two jeeps and the motorcycle. Several of the guards were in uniform. The vehicles could have belonged to the state police but it was difficult to tell.

He sat on the window seat and tried to figure out the reason for so much professional security. He knew that no one had left the house after dark since his arrival, but no one had mentioned these protective arrangements.

Apparently, he was not the only prisoner at Ravenhurst and this realization confused him even more.

APRIL 10, 1962
DETROIT, MICHIGAN

41

THE WINCHESTER INTERROGATION panel was ready when Hawthorne entered the upstairs study at eleven o'clock on the following morning.

Charles Manning was seated behind his desk. Barry Myerson and Estelle Manning were sitting on the sofa and a comfortable armchair had been positioned near them for him.

Mrs. Manning proceeded to pour coffee from a serving tray as soon as Hawthorne took his place.

"Would you like some cake, Gerald?" she asked.

"No, thank you." He accepted his cup and stared at Charles Manning.

Hawthorne could feel the tension in the room and it was evident that a discussion on strategy had taken place before his arrival.

"I'll get straight to the point," said Manning. He took a sip of his coffee. "You have a right to hear the facts and I intend to be as brief as possible. First of all, let's take a look at the conditions of your release from Clifton," said Manning. He motioned to the psychiatrist.

"It's a special arrangement, Gerald," Myerson explained pleasantly. "The Mannings have practically adopted you. They have assumed total responsibility for your conduct and welfare. The Board will assess the extent of your rehabilitation on a monthly basis."

Hawthorne sat rigidly, a sullen expression on his face.

"Do I have to live here in Winchester Estates?" he asked.

"Yes," Manning answered before his wife could respond. "It's an important clause in the release conditions."

"I have property and belongings in Waverly," he protested.

"We'll talk about it later," Manning stated. "But I promise that you and your property will be protected." He finished his coffee and shoved the cup to one side. "Of course, the State has a right to send you back to Clifton immediately if you do not comply with the conditions of release or if we feel that the probationary arrangement is not working out satisfactorily."

"It's only a technical stipulation, Gerald," Mrs. Manning interjected. "Everything will go smoothly."

Hawthorne ignored her and watched Charles Manning settle back in his chair.

"There will be many personal advantages for you here at Ravenhurst. I'm offering you a brand-new life." Manning smiled.

"In exchange for what?" asked Hawthorne.

His host leaned forward across the desk.

"There are plenty of strings attached," he said. "But I want to outline the good things first. Do you mind?"

Hawthorne folded his arms and scowled as Manning proceeded to explain.

"I won't pretend to be modest." He indicated the rich furnishings in the study with a sweeping motion of his arm. "This is a taste of the good life, Hawthorne. You'll have expensive clothes, good food and every possible comfort and convenience. We want you to consider our home as your own. If you want, I'll hire private tutors and you will be able to go on with your education."

Hawthorne's expression remained cold as Manning continued. "Your work at the Chinese university should not be wasted," he added.

"We'll introduce you to interesting, intelligent people, Gerald," Estelle Manning promised.

"In time," said Charles Manning, "many interesting situations will be available to you. In time, Hawthorne. A career, for example."

Hawthorne accepted more coffee from Mrs. Manning. He could not conceal his growing interest.

"I'd have you start at the bottom in order to learn every phase of my diversified operations. If you prove that you've got the ability and are conscientious, this opportunity could serve as a launching pad to a position of importance in my organization."

"We do not have children of our own, Gerald," Mrs. Manning said. "My husband would try his best to move you along as quickly as possible."

"No preferential treatment, though," Manning cautioned. "You'll have to prove yourself to a lot of people. But if nothing else, I could guarantee you a damn good job somewhere in my company. I'm not trying to play God," he assured him. "But I am offering you a chance to start over."

Hawthorne glanced down at the floor and then at Barry Myerson as the psychiatrist cleared his throat.

"The State Board is in a position to issue a clean bill of health in one year if you stay out of trouble and on the right track," the doctor explained.

"Complete freedom in one year?" Hawthorne asked earnestly.

"The case will be reviewed and you'll have to submit to a series of examinations by my staff of competent quacks," said Myerson. "But a good conduct certificate and a few words from the Mannings should put you on your own without complications."

Hawthorne slowly finished his coffee and put the cup down.

"That's the good part," he said flatly. "Now tell me about the strings."

Manning glanced at Myerson and the doctor made a move to leave. He took Estelle Manning's hand and they both stood up. "I'd better find my wife," he announced. "She was last seen talking to your damn chauffeur and I never trust any man who looks as good as he does."

In a few moments, the door of the study was closed and locked and Gerald Howard Hawthorne prepared himself for another interrogation. The former prisoner of war was both experienced and confident but he had underestimated the importance of this encounter.

Myerson and Estelle Manning had just reached the foot of the stairs when a Michigan State Police car rolled to a smooth stop at the entrance to the mansion. A butler opened the door and stepped outside in order to greet the visitors.

The motor of the police car was still running, and two plainclothesmen examined various documents in the back seat. A uniformed officer sat at the wheel and the Mannings' butler waited patiently at attention as the men climbed out of the car. He led the visitors up the steps and into the foyer.

Mrs. Manning, Edith Myerson and the psychiatrist were just beginning a game of cards when the men were ushered into the living room.

"My husband is busy upstairs at the moment," said Estelle Manning apologetically. "Perhaps you could organize your things and freshen up while he completes his business."

"We'll wait in another room if you don't mind, Mrs. Manning," one of the men replied. "Another car should be here with our suitcases in about an hour. I'm Sergeant Andrew Castle." The officer was about thirty-five years old with a smooth complexion, a rugged build and blond hair. He was dressed in a dark business suit, white shirt and conservative tie.

"I'm Sergeant Paul De Marco." The other man was thin but muscular and in his late twenties. The policeman's dark skin was slightly pockmarked and his straight black hair had been heavily greased into place.

Mrs. Manning introduced the Myersons and instructed the

butler to make the officers comfortable in the recreation room.

"Seems like you've got the entire Michigan police force here in Winchester," Barry Myerson commented after they had left. "It's beginning to frighten the hell out of me."

"These two men are special," Mrs. Manning explained confidentially. "They were personally selected by Chief Saunders."

"For what?" asked the psychiatrist's wife.

"Charles asked for close protection at all times because of the recent burglary," Mrs. Manning replied.

"They'll live here in the house?" Myerson asked.

"Yes. And we will not make a move without them. Charles is mainly concerned about Hawthorne and wants him watched constantly for his own good."

"What about the other cops who roam all over the grounds at night?" Edith Myerson asked. "Your place is beginning to look like Clifton State."

"They work for a private security company," Mrs. Manning told her. "Charles might discharge most of them now that Chief Saunders has arranged for personal security from the state police."

Edith Myerson shook her head in bewilderment and picked up the cards. "I still don't understand exactly what's going on," she said. "But at least I know we're all safe." She dealt the cards.

Hawthorne had watched the industrialist pace and sit and stand up and pace again. He had been both eloquent and sincere, but his approach, Hawthorne felt, was standard. Charles Manning was proving to be a predictable opponent so far. Typical civil rights counsel—he had heard it all before from experts.

His dishonorable discharge had probably been issued illegally because the repatriation agreement had given him a right to settle in China. There was a strong possibility that the government owed him back pay because of his confinement as a prisoner of war in Camp Six. He had been accused and then pronounced guilty without a formal trial. Television and the press had treated him unfairly. The people of America had abused him without hearing his side of the story. He had a strong case against the United States.

Manning talked and paced and finally walked to the bar to pour himself a drink. He turned to Hawthorne.

"The conditions of your release clearly specify that the probationary period will terminate immediately if you consume one drop of alcohol."

Hawthorne stared coldly but did not respond.

Manning took a long gulp of whiskey. "It further states that if you are observed drinking in a public place while in my custody, the courts have the right to place the assault charge back on the books and this could mean the state penitentiary instead of Clifton."

He removed another glass from the cabinet and poured an ample amount of Scotch whiskey, then handed it to Hawthorne.

"This is the only exception," Manning decreed. "Don't ever take advantage of me."

He moved to the sofa without waiting for a reply and sat down. There was silence in the room as both men sipped their drinks.

"*I* have decided to declare war against the United States and the reasons are more complicated than your personal claims for money and justice," said Manning. "With your help I might be able to fight a respectable battle." He paused. "Without you I'll be screaming into the wind and eventually some very rough customers will destroy me and wreck my business operations. The questionable actions taken against you are part of a much larger conspiracy," he went on. "And that's putting it mildly."

"I'm not that important," Hawthorne said without much interest.

"You are," Manning corrected. "Your information and personal testimony is a key to a vault which is packed with corruption and misconduct."

"I don't know a damn thing," Hawthorne insisted. "You'd better find another key."

Charles Manning paused thoughtfully and then edged forward. "Ambassador Edward Stevens," he whispered. "A Mr. X who is still in a position of trust in the Defense Department." He hesitated. "General Roland Fawcett."

"What?" Hawthorne was finally interested. "He's a general?"

"Not only a general," Manning pointed out eagerly. "Fawcett will soon be appointed to the Joint Chiefs of Staff."

Hawthorne snickered and took another slug of whiskey. "*General,*" he muttered to himself.

"You know about these people, Gerald," said Manning. "Your disclosures will help to substantiate the initial misconduct and get things rolling." He watched Hawthorne finish his drink. "Trained investigators will then be able to do a thorough examination."

The veteran shoved his glass toward Manning.

"Absolutely not," his host responded.

Hawthorne glared at the man and then placed the glass on the floor.

"Will you help?" Manning asked.

"No." The reply was emphatic.

"It took me a long time to make this decision to act against my own country." Manning appeared to be thinking aloud. "The nation is involved in complicated foreign relations and a scandal now will ruin our progress in many areas."

He took a seat and rested his empty whiskey glass on a table next to the desk. "But I don't want this super-mafia to demolish the United States."

"What's a super-mafia?" Hawthorne asked.

"Slick and experienced gorillas who do the dirty work for our reputable public officials," Manning replied bitterly. "What the hell do you think those men were doing out on the grounds earlier this morning?"

"Making sure that I don't take off," the other man answered. "But now that I think ..."

"Don't flatter yourself, Hawthorne," Manning interrupted angrily. "They were protecting *all* of us. These thugs from

Washington pushed me into action. Frankly, your case was my wife's affair until those animals went to work."

"Who are they?"

"*What* are they doing is a better question," Manning stated. "Bribery, theft, assault—even murder whenever it becomes necessary. They broke in here and burglarized my files. I'm sure that we'll be hearing from them again very shortly."

"You knew about these guys when you had me released?"

"Yes."

Hawthorne scratched his chin and seemed to be contemplating something important. "Can I have another drink?"

"No," Manning replied bluntly. "We could all have our heads blown off before this thing is over," he said.

"Why should *I* help you?" asked Hawthorne. "I'm willing to go back to Clifton State and avoid all this trouble."

"I've offered you a new life with a career and an education."

"Fantasy."

"No, Hawthorne," Manning snapped. "The real thing if you have the nerve to help me."

Manning walked to a chair facing his houseguest. "Will you do it?"

"I can't." Hawthorne avoided his eyes.

"Why not?"

He hesitated and then looked down at the floor. "I have an obligation to my friends in China. They'll die if I say too many things over here."

Manning looked at Hawthorne for a moment and then lost his temper.

"Screw your friends in Red China!" he shouted.

Hawthorne leapt to his feet, wheeled about, and glared at him.

Manning finally brought himself under control. "I have very close friends in Washington and this investigation will destroy their lives completely," he responded. "The Secretary of State has already resigned and I am responsible for his decision. How the hell do you think *I* feel?"

There was a light tap and Manning walked to the door and opened it.

"The police are waiting for you downstairs," said Barry Myerson. "De Marco and Castle."

"I'll go down and talk to them," said Manning. He turned back to Hawthorne. "Think about everything very carefully and remember that a chance to start life over again is seldom available to any of us. I'll talk to you later."

April 11, 1962

Mr. Gerald Howard Hawthorne
c/o Mr. Charles Manning
Ravenhurst
Winchester Estates
Detroit, Michigan

Dear Sir,

42 I represent the Craddock Real Estate Corporation of Waverly, Michigan. We are the oldest and most experienced property firm in the district. Mr. Carl Farrow, one of our associates, has received numerous inquiries in reference to your property on Elm Drive. A particular customer here in Waverly is prepared to make a very substantial offer if you are interested in immediate negotiation.

Please contact Mr. Farrow at your earliest convenience and let him know whether you wish to explore the possibility of an outright sale. We could also discuss several rental propositions if you do not wish to dispose of the premises at the present time.

The house is located in a desirable residential area of the town and we feel that our company is in a position to conclude a profitable transaction if you are willing to grant us authority to act as your agents here in Waverly.

Mr. Farrow is prepared to meet with you in Detroit if necessary although we feel that a conference with our entire staff would guarantee a more effective course of action.

We anxiously await your reply and hope that our firm can be of service.

Yours sincerely,
Cass Holbrook
Vice President
Craddock Real
Estate Corporation

A personal invitation to spend an evening at the home of Charles Manning was quite an honor.

The giants of industry, politics and show business were thrilled to be received by the Mannings, and many illustrious guests were transported to Michigan from all parts of the world for these events.

The luxurious mansion in Winchester was bustling with activity during the month of April 1962, but the household staff was baffled by the secrecy of the arrangements and the lack of fanfare.

Important visitors were arriving and departing without prior notice and most of the conferences were being held behind locked doors in the upstairs study.

Maureen Kelly, the cook, was seldom requested to prepare a formal meal for the guests, and even Mr. Manning's annual June 3 birthday ball had been canceled.

The strange houseguest, Gerald Hawthorne, was still on the premises and Dr. Myerson appeared to be involved daily in Charles Manning's hectic schedule.

The doorman had greeted Senator Samuel Brewster at four o'clock on a wet Saturday afternoon, and Governor Pike's limousine had arrived at a very late hour in the evening with a police escort.

Representative Howard Dutton, of the House Judiciary Committee, had spent over three hours in the locked study on two separate occasions, and Senator Jacob Steiner had stayed at Ravenhurst overnight after a lengthy conference with Charles Manning and two men from Los Angeles. A Federal judge and numerous lawyers had turned up for secluded meetings, and a Washington journalist had arrived, accompanying several high-ranking military officials.

The staff of Ravenhurst also wondered about the bolted room on the third floor and Gerald Hawthorne's regular visits with Dr. Barry Myerson and two grim-looking gentlemen with thick briefcases and recording machines.

"Tell us the name of the Chinese official who persuaded you to inform on Martino as the killer of Chow."

"I told you exactly what happened about Martino," Hawthorne snapped. "Don't put me through that crap again."

"Just give me the name of the Chinese official who forced you into a confession."

"He didn't force me."

"I understand that, but give me his name."

"Kwen San."

"Who?"

"Kwen San."

"Was this man your usual interrogator at Camp Six?"

"He was the jailer."

"What about the interrogator?"

"When they questioned me about Chow Chow?"

"Yes."

"He was a new guy," said Hawthorne. "I never saw him before."

"Did you see him later in China?"

"No."

"What about Kwen San?"

"Never."

"What was the name of your usual interrogator at Camp Six?" the man tried again.

"I don't remember."

"Did you ever see him again in China?"

"Yes."

"But you don't remember his name."

"No."

Barry Myerson halted the frustrating session.

"Why don't you fellows take a break?" he suggested to the investigators. "Get back in about twenty minutes."

He switched off the machine and the two other men left the room.

Myerson put his feet up on a table and waited for Hawthorne to calm down.

"You know what they want," the psychiatrist commented bluntly. "They'll pound away until you tell them."

"I can't murder my friends so casually," he stated. "My stomach turns when I think about what might happen to them in China."

"What about Chuck Manning? This plan of action will certainly be responsible for bumping off some of his close *American* friends and shake hell out of the country."

"I'll help him because I made a deal," Hawthorne replied. "But don't let these bastards push me too fast."

"You know the names of two important contacts in Red China and this information is vital to Ambassador Stevens's phase of the case."

"I know."

"So far, you've talked candidly about personal experiences in Korea and Camp Six and this testimony will help to clarify your *own* position," Myerson explained. "Now they'll expect cooperation in other areas."

"I'll cooperate," he answered huskily. "But I don't want to be pushed around."

The door suddenly swung open and Charles Manning walked into the room.

"I'm leaving for Washington tonight," he announced. "Both investigators are returning with me."

"What happened?"

"Everyone is convinced and we're on our way," he replied excitedly. "A full meeting is scheduled with the committee chairman, chief counsel and several important panel members."

"Great," Myerson exclaimed. "Based on what you've got?"

The industrialist turned to look at Hawthorne. "Yes, and

also on what Gerald is going to tell a man by the name of Alan Maugham."

"I've read about him," the psychiatrist commented.

"He's the committee's sharpest legal brain—the one who can pull the trigger if everything falls into place," Manning explained. "Maugham intends to come and chat with Gerald here at Ravenhurst tomorrow afternoon and then he'll return and report to the chairman while I'm still in Washington."

Hawthorne got up and walked to the window, where he glared out at the roses which were now beginning to bloom.

"Ever been to Washington, Gerald?" Manning asked.

"No," he answered moodily.

"You'll be going for a visit very shortly," Manning told him. Hawthorne continued to scowl at the flowers.

Myerson walked over to Charles Manning. "He's had a rough time," he whispered. "Your two private investigators have the sensitivity of charging bulls."

"They did very well, Barry," Manning corrected. "We have powerful material from many sources and the information has been coordinated brilliantly for the government."

"He held on to his secrets," said Myerson, nodding toward Hawthorne's back. "Mentioned no names."

"The Korean background was the main purpose of the exercise," Manning assured him. He then raised his voice for Hawthorne's benefit. "You'll have a much easier time with Alan Maugham, Gerald. He won't be so rough about probing for facts. His main job is to determine the importance of your information and whether you are willing to testify under oath in front of a Congressional committee."

"It's going to hit like a bombshell," Myerson predicted. "The story of the investigation will be on every front page in less than a week. Will the President officially acknowledge the damn thing?"

"Dutton of the House and a few others will brief Atken and the Attorney General tomorrow," Manning replied. "They intend to urge somebody at the top to prepare a statement before the news begins to break in the world press. They smell a scandal already, of course. A couple of columnists might bust it wide open before anything official can be distributed."

Hawthorne suddenly turned away from the window and faced Manning.

"I want to go to Waverly and take an inventory of my house," he stated somberly.

"Your timing is a little off, Gerald," his host replied. "Alan Maugham will be here tomorrow, and we should wait until we have a definite schedule from Washington."

"I might want to sell or rent *my* property," he declared. "Besides, I feel like checking through my belongings and bringing a few things back here with me from Waverly."

"At least wait until I return from Washington," Manning advised.

"I'll go to Elm Drive after I talk to this guy Maugham," Hawthorne persisted.

Manning was about to answer when Myerson put a hand on his arm. "I don't want to interfere, Chuck, but we've all agreed that Gerald should dispose of his property and he must take a personal inventory before considering any transactions."

"Fine," Manning answered. "We can do that when I return from Washington with a confirmed schedule."

Hawthorne scowled and turned back to the window. Myerson moved closer to his old friend and spoke quietly but firmly.

"In a very short time this boy is going to be too hot to leave the grounds without an army of specialized cops and bodyguards. Reporters will be at him every step of the way. Why not let him talk to Maugham tomorrow and then leave for Waverly quietly before the storm breaks."

Manning paced up and down while he debated the wisdom of the move.

"Estelle could go with him," Myerson added. "She knows more about real estate than any of these damn Craddock people. She's in a position to protect Gerald's property and move swiftly. Everything could be arranged in one visit."

He glanced at Hawthorne who was still facing the window.

"The damn trip," Manning commented. "I don't like the idea of Estelle leaving Ravenhurst at a time like this."

"We can't be prisoners here forever, Chuck," said the psychiatrist. "And things will get worse. The time for Waverly is now. Why don't you send Andy Castle with Gerald and Estelle? He appears to be a very dependable officer. You have to take some risks if you intend to fight the U.S. government."

"I wouldn't call Craddock Real Estate or alert anyone in advance of this trip."

"Absolutely not," Myerson agreed.

"What about you and Edith?"

"We'll hold the fort here at Ravenhurst," the psychiatrist replied.

"All right. Let's talk to Castle tonight and see what he thinks," Manning decided. "Special security measures will have to be taken and scrupulously observed."

He stood and walked over to Hawthorne at the window.

"You understand the importance of obedience on a trip of this kind," said Manning. "If we decide to proceed with the visit, I must remind you that my wife and Sergeant Andrew Castle will be in complete charge at all times. Any mistake on your part in Waverly will wreck this whole project and make damn fools out of us all," Manning warned.

"Don't worry, Mr. Manning," Hawthorne said mockingly. "I'm an experienced prisoner."

APRIL 14, 1962
DETROIT, MICHIGAN

43 ALAN MAUGHAM WAS surprisingly pleasant and very informal. He was much younger than Hawthorne had imagined and the session in the upstairs room was handled like a conversation between friends instead of a formal investigation prior to possible Congressional action.

The man was tall and thin and his soft voice and relaxed manner had eased the strain and tensions built up by the previous inquisitions.

Maugham was able to explore sensitive areas without provoking the usual explosions of temper.

There was no recording or stenographic equipment in the room, and this had relieved Hawthorne. Maugham stood behind a large work table and often referred to the official documents and files in front of him.

He had explained his mission patiently, and Hawthorne had finally understood the importance of the afternoon conference in reference to Charles Manning's assault on the government.

The early phases of the discussion had centered on the military aspects of his experiences in Korea, and Hawthorne had cooperated without exaggeration or omission.

"Be prepared to give a detailed account of the blunder because the Reds probably distorted your version while you were a prisoner in Camp Six," Alan Maugham had advised.

"I don't understand."

"Your report about the slaughter of the American troops."

"I told the truth in that document."

"We have to assume that they adjusted it and faked the photographs."

"What the hell do you mean?"

The investigator held up his hand politely. "We'll talk about the possible distortion later but be ready to testify about the actual incident."

Hawthorne's mind raced back to K. M. Wing but his thoughts were interrupted by the counsel's next statement.

"Expect a lengthy cross-examination by the entire panel when General Fawcett is mentioned," said Maugham. "I suggest that this phase of your testimony be omitted entirely unless you have specific facts." He hesitated. "The General has an impeccable record."

"The *General* is a goddamn fraud!"

"Any emotional response to questioning will be a futile exercise in front of the committee," Maugham cautioned. "Are you prepared to introduce solid testimony against General Roland Fawcett?"

"Yes."

"Facts?"

"The truth."

Maugham nodded his head and scribbled a few words on a sheet of paper.

"I found out plenty about that traitor when I was at Camp Six and later on in Tsinan," Hawthorne added. "I'll face him and watch him squirm."

The interrogator moved to a seat behind the improvised conference table.

"You will certainly be questioned about the paper factory," Maugham said.

"That's easy," said Hawthorne. "When I first got to Tsinan, the Red Cross gave me enough to last for a few weeks and Dr. Liang Yu, my father-in-law, eventually, arranged a small loan through a friend of his. This same man helped me find a place to live when I arrived—a dirty little room inside the Old City, but it was fine for me. Then he found me a good job in the paper factory. The work was very hard and the hours were long. My pay was about forty dollars a month in American money but it was a very happy period of my life."

"Were you an active member of the Communist Party at any time?"

"No."

"Were you ordered to participate?"

"A funny little guy came to see me from Peiping," Hawthorne replied. "He pushed me hard but I refused."

"How did you manage to get away with this open disobedience?"

"A friend helped me in Tsinan," he answered with a touch of pride. "An important local official."

"You will have to give his name to the committee, Hawthorne."

"I know," he mumbled. "They'll get it in Washington."

Maugham placed a check mark on one of the documents and Hawthorne spoke very softly without being questioned.

"Life was beautiful for me when my wife was alive," he recalled. "I lived and worked in peace and we had many friends from the university."

"I understand that you speak and read Chinese," said Maugham, continuing to examine one of the papers.

"Yes," Hawthorne replied. "And I also think Chinese," he added.

The government counsel ignored the remark and stood up. He searched for and then located a particular document, and the conversation proceeded.

"Did you visit Peiping while you were employed in the Tsinan paper factory?"

"Yes."

"For what purpose?"

Hawthorne paused and lit a cigarette while he organized a concise response. "The new factory manager offered me a job supervising a department."

"Can I have his name?"

"Yen," Hawthorne answered without hesitation. "Ho Yen."

Maugham placed his pencil on the table and leaned forward.

"Tell me about this department."

"The government was putting up a lot of money for certain projects," Hawthorne answered. "There were many benefits for the workers."

"Did Mr. Yen explain the projects?"

"No," he answered. "Peiping selected five plants to manufacture different parts."

"And the completed products?"

"Yen didn't know himself," Hawthorne replied cautiously. "Each blueprint was going to be delivered in sections."

"Were you interested?"

"Yes," he answered. "But I didn't think I wanted to become a Chinese citizen just yet. That was the catch. So I talked to my friend in Peiping. A very important government official." Hawthorne noticed the excitement in the counsel's face and spoke before Maugham could ask the obvious question. "You'll have the name in Washington."

"Was this man your regular interrogator in Camp Six?"

"Yes."

"Was he the Peiping contact for the Stevens operation?"

"Yes," he answered softly.

"What did he tell you?"

Hawthorne stood up and walked to the window.

"He briefed me about the Turncoat crap in the States," Hawthorne commented bitterly as he stared out of the window. "He told me about my dishonorable discharge and showed American newspaper clippings about my *defection* to Red China."

Maugham sat on the edge of the table and listened attentively.

"He let me read official papers about the American prisoners in Korea and I saw Fawcett's true military record." Hawthorne sneered. "It was like a damn comic book."

"This friend eased your conscience?"

Hawthorne turned sharply. "I didn't have a guilty conscience about being in China and my feelings are the same right now."

Maugham picked up a document. "Did he talk to you about the Stevens operation?"

"Yes." Hawthorne turned back to the window. "Only the soft parts."

"I don't understand."

"There were soft areas and hard stuff," he explained tensely. "Soft was industrial."

"Commercial blueprints?"

"Yes."

"From American companies?"

"Also British and a few others," Hawthorne answered. "Stevens had this stuff moving for years."

"When did it change?"

"Some Washington people joined the group."

"Were the soft products eliminated?"

"No," he replied. "They became more complicated and the payoff was bigger for everybody."

"Was the special unit at your factory organized for soft operations?"

"Yes." Hawthorne was becoming uneasy. "In the beginning."

"Was there an American contact for these soft products?" Maugham inquired. "In the beginning?"

"A guy in the Commerce Department," he replied irritably.

"Can I have his name?"

Hawthorne watched Sergeant Andrew Castle walking toward the main gate.

"Davidson," he answered suddenly. "Warner Davidson."

The interrogator stared for a moment and then made a hasty note.

"What about the hard stuff?" Maugham asked as casually as possible. "Espionage?"

Hawthorne continued to gaze out of the window. He did not reply.

"Did your friend in Peiping talk about the hard areas?" the interrogator persisted.

"Not when I went for the interview."

Maugham paused briefly in order to study a page of notes.

"Did you continue at the factory after refusing to join the special work unit?"

"Yes."

"Was there any trouble?"

"Mr. Yen wanted to ease me out but my friends stopped him."

The Washington investigator moved behind the table and sat.

"Your friends in Peiping and Tsinan were unusually kind to you," he said. "And protective."

"That's right."

"Were you aware of their personal financial arrangements in the Stevens operation?"

Hawthorne turned away from the window and glared at the interrogator.

"That's none of your goddamn business," he thundered.

"It is," Maugham answered firmly. "Your testimony has to be logical in order to be convincing."

"Do you think I was blackmailing them or something?" Hawthorne asked in amazement. "They were my friends. I don't want to discuss their private affairs."

"Most of the facts are known anyway," the investigator announced with conviction. "They were all pulling funds out of a Swiss account."

The former prisoner of war tried to control his temper. He moved dejectedly to a chair and slumped down with his legs outstretched.

"We never discussed money," said Hawthorne. "It wasn't something I cared much about then."

Maugham opened another folder and examined the material before speaking.

"When did you find out about the hard stuff?" he asked bluntly.

"After my wife died," Hawthorne answered. "Ask me straight and let's get this damn thing over with. I know plenty, and I'll honor my pledge to Manning." His smile was forced. "Caviar and a brand-new life in exchange for a couple of gook necks."

"This is your personal decision, Hawthorne."

"You bet your ass, Mr. Maugham."

"After your wife died . . ."

"I did a lot of stupid things," Hawthorne interrupted coldly. "Like a lot of crying, and drinking, and fighting, and they finally threw me out of the factory in Tsinan."

"How did you live?"

"I stayed with Dr. Yu until he died."

"And then?"

"More drinking and fighting and a few Chinese jails."

Maugham leaned back in his chair and examined Hawthorne's anguished expression.

"My friends had to help me again," Hawthorne continued in a husky voice. "I lived with the official and his family in Tsinan and my good friend from Peiping visited us many times."

"Did you work with them on the Stevens project?"

"Only once." Hawthorne smiled. "It was just soft." His features tightened again. "But I knew the score."

"Were your friends able to . . ."

"Ask me about some patriotic Americans," he cut in. "My Chinese friends didn't play this game alone."

"Very well," Maugham agreed. He prepared a fresh sheet of

paper. "The information about Warner Davidson is very important. Do you know the names of any other involved officials?"

"One guy is dead," Hawthorne answered. "He used to work for that character Joseph McCarthy."

Maugham was now preparing an informal written record of the conversation. "Soft areas?" he asked without bothering to look up.

"The sleazy bastard was like a coordinator," Hawthorne replied. "He walked a thin line down the middle of everything."

The investigator nodded.

"Stevens had two more Washington contacts. A man named Turner—in the Defense Department."

Maugham stared at Hawthorne and waited for him to continue.

"He used to feed maps and charts and percentages," said Hawthorne. "Up-to-date information from the States and most of the strategic bases," he added matter-of-factly. "My friends used to call him the Reporter."

The investigator scribbled a few additional notes and then glanced up again. It was evident that he had not expected the blunt disclosures.

"Turner is still in the Department," Maugham remarked. "Anything else?"

"This guy handled a few assignments with the help of *General* Fawcett and somebody in the Pentagon," he snarled. "They supplied paper shipments for MV in Moscow."

"Explain."

"It's real technical." Hawthorne shook his head. "Richard Fulham was the MV key in the States, and they called his outfit WMO, or something like that."

"World Meteorological Organization?" Maugham inquired in a shocked tone of voice.

"It was a part of the United Nations."

The investigator put down his pencil and shoved the papers to one side. He covered the notes with a folder before speaking again.

"We have to prove your allegations in front of an experienced committee in Washington, D.C.," he commented soberly. "You must understand the seriousness of these charges and the consequences for the people involved."

"Fat politicians knew about Stevens and they'll all be shot in the head for treason after I tell my story." Hawthorne lit another cigarette and scowled. "They probably figured that the Ambassador was shipping toilet paper and oranges to the Communists."

"Was Richard Fulham dealing in hard stuff for the organization?" the investigator asked with more than a little uneasiness.

"He was a fucking spy!"

Hawthorne stood up and paced to the window. "I watched these dirty bastards sell the United States down the river." He scanned the rolling hills of the Manning estate. "And they were calling me a traitor because I stayed in China."

"You should have made an attempt to contact your government," Maugham chided.

"And die on the streets of Tsinan for the glory of Roland Fawcett?" Hawthorne turned and faced him. "Besides," he added bitterly, "my American contacts were a little unreliable at the time."

"Tell me something about MV in Moscow," Alan Maugham demanded, changing the subject. "Missiles?"

A sarcastic grin spread across Hawthorne's face. "Are you testing my information, Mr. Maugham?"

"No," the investigator answered truthfully, "your pledge to cooperate as a responsible witness."

"These people have been working on range and accuracy for years." Hawthorne's expression was serious once again as he walked to the desk. "Stevens handed it to them on a platter and the entire American government is guilty."

"Are you talking about intercontinental ballistic . . ."

"Land- and submarine-launched," he interrupted. "They'll beat hell out of America in about ten years because of the Ambassador."

"What do you mean, Hawthorne?"

"Range and accuracy. Their new subs are going to throw

stuff over six thousand miles in front and hit dead center every time."

"I don't know much about military technology," the interrogator said.

"You don't have to be *General* Roland Fawcett to understand," Hawthorne continued. "American sub missiles won't get past two thousand miles in ten years and they'll miss the target with every other shot."

Hawthorne moved back to the leather chair and sat down, allowing the statement to register. "The Reds are far ahead of the game," he announced, "playing with American marbles."

The investigator was transfixed by Hawthorne's unexpected candor. He decided to continue the line of questioning.

"Single warheads?"

"On the submarines," Hawthorne replied with authority. "But these guys are working on special multiples from land." He took a drag of his cigarette and inhaled deeply. "Mr. Fulham handed over a few new diagrams."

"Can you explain?"

"Multiple warheads," Hawthorne answered, "but each one can be aimed to hit a different bull's-eye from the same launch." His face looked somber. "In a few years one clean shot could knock out the world."

"Do you know about stockpiles?"

"I know that secret bases are being set up right now for the sub missiles," he replied. "Ask Turner and *General* Fawcett."

The investigator stared in awe as Gerald Hawthorne nervously stubbed out his cigarette in the ashtray.

"You said that MV was a project for Russia," Maugham proceeded. "How did this information end up in Peiping and Tsinan?"

"Fulham and the others were greedy. They leaked them to Red China."

"Is the Russian government aware of this leak?"

"How the hell should I know a thing like that?"

"Do you have specific details about Chinese progress in this area?"

"Nothing technical," Hawthorne stated frankly. "But I

know that both of these countries have been working fast while America keeps on pitching test bans and other political crap."

Alan Maugham reached for a briefcase. He opened it and removed several official documents.

"Why did you leave China, Hawthorne?" the investigator asked while inspecting one of the papers.

"There was nothing left for me in Tsinan after my wife died," he answered impatiently.

"You had good friends."

"Yes." Hawthorne sat up. "But nothing mattered once Ling Yu and the doctor were gone."

"Did you miss this country?"

"No."

"Was it your idea to come home?"

"No," Hawthorne answered. "My friend in Tsinan suggested the idea." There was a long, thoughtful pause. "Some of the local officials were starting to complain about me. So my friend in Peiping convinced the government."

"You were stranded in Hong Kong without funds..."

"Both friends gave me enough for the trip." He glared angrily at Maugham. "People don't earn much money working in Communist China."

The investigator nodded. "How could they allow you to leave the country with so much privileged information?"

"What?"

"The Stevens operation, for example."

"It's old news," Hawthorne answered. "They have a new system in China now, and I don't know a damn thing about it."

"You were still permitted to return with enough knowledge to wreck an entire government," Maugham insisted.

"*This* government," Hawthorne declared emphatically. "Peiping won't cry if I smash Washington."

"You might, Hawthorne," said Maugham grimly, "if we prove this case."

"I didn't come back here to cause trouble," Hawthorne muttered, "but these bastards were killing me. Why should I stay locked up in a nut house because of some filthy American traitors?"

"What about the officials in Tsinan and Peiping?" Maugham quizzed softly.

"Maybe they'll understand." Hawthorne bowed his head. "And forgive me."

The Washington counsel picked up his pencil and shuffled through a stack of papers. "Do you intend to deliver this testimony under oath before an official committee of the United States government?" he asked formally.

"Yes."

"Give me the names of the two Chinese officials," Maugham instructed with the pencil poised over a notepad.

"Let's wait until we get to Washington," Hawthorne said. "I have very few friends on this earth and I'd like to hold on to them for as long as possible."

Maugham stared at the man curiously for a moment, then the conference continued without further reference to K. M. Wing or Sung Tsen Tson.

Hawthorne sat beside Dr. Barry Myerson and breathed deeply, filling his lungs with the fresh evening air.

It was over.

Alan Maugham had returned to Washington with the fuse for Manning's hydrogen bomb, and arrangements for a morning visit to Waverly were scheduled to be discussed at a nine o'clock meeting with Sergeant Andrew Castle.

The psychiatrist closed his eyes and slid into a more comfortable position on the bench.

"The case will now move very quickly," he commented. "Maugham is impressed with your information and willingness to cooperate."

Hawthorne did not respond.

"You have courage, Gerald," the doctor added. "Maugham was secretive about the details of the conference but he did say that you mentioned names." Myerson opened his eyes and glanced up at the branches of a tree. "It must have been very difficult for you."

Hawthorne wondered how the sale of the property could be accomplished without disturbing the upstairs shrine or the spirit of his mother.

"I can certainly understand your feelings of guilt and confusion at the moment," the psychiatrist went on. "When a man is required to expose his friends in order to . . ."

"Skip the speeches," Hawthorne interrupted. "I haven't exposed them yet."

The doctor straightened up and rubbed his arms. "Alan Maugham is an experienced Washington counsel and your testimony will be handled with great discretion."

"I don't give a damn how he handles my testimony," Hawthorne stated bluntly. "He didn't force me into anything. Will Mrs. Manning let me go home tomorrow?"

"I think so," the psychiatrist answered. "She was very pleased and excited after Maugham spoke to her."

Hawthorne laughed. "She's an understanding lady and a lenient jailer." He turned to Barry Myerson. "Confession is good for the soul and lots of other things. Right, Doc?"

"It's good for the mind."

There was silence while both men lit cigarettes and scanned the beauty of Winchester Estates.

"Why don't *you* confess?" Hawthorne asked suddenly.

"What?"

"Confess," he persisted. "It's good for the soul and the mind."

"What are you talking about?"

"Something important. Your mother, maybe."

Barry Myerson stared at him. "Is it important to you?"

"Yes."

"Why?"

"Because I want to hear somebody else spill their guts for a change."

Myerson was about to walk away but changed his mind when he saw the expression on Hawthorne's face.

"My mother struggled in a small Polish village while I became a rich Jewish doctor here in America." He hesitated and forced a smile.

"The plan was to bring her over as quickly as possible but I became richer and busier each year and one delay led to another. I finally stopped counting my money long enough to make the move but it was a little too late. Adolf Hitler had already saved me the cost of a ticket."

Hawthorne stared at the doctor without displaying any emotion.

"I just spilled some of my guts," the psychiatrist announced. "Does it make you feel any better?"

"Maybe."

Barry Myerson stood. "Perhaps you can tell me the story of *your* mother someday, Gerald."

"She doesn't have a story," he replied, pulling himself to his feet.

They walked slowly toward the main house.

"I just loved her too much," Hawthorne whispered as he entered the mansion.

MAY 21, 1962
DETROIT, MICHIGAN

44   EVERY DETAIL OF THE trip to Waverly had been thoroughly discussed and meticulously organized. The final plans had been approved by Charles Manning during a lengthy telephone call to Washington, D.C. The conversation had lasted for more than an hour and Manning had stressed the need for tight security and prompt action.

He had reiterated to Hawthorne over the phone the terms and conditions of the probationary release from Clifton State, and had reminded him of Myerson's pledge to work toward obtaining his complete freedom in one year if a record of good conduct could be presented to the State Board of Mental Health.

He also warned Hawthorne that Sergeant Andrew Castle was officially in a position to place him under arrest in the event of any disobedience or trouble during the visit to Waverly.

Finally, Charles Manning had extended his best wishes for a safe and productive journey.

4:00 PM
May 26, 1962
Waverly, Michigan

The plan had worked perfectly right from their departure at ten-thirty in the morning.

Sergeant Castle was dressed in a drab blue suit but his specially designed jacket concealed an accessible shoulder holster.

Both he and Mrs. Manning wanted to attract as little attention as possible in the community. To this end, Castle drove an unfashionable black 1957 Chevrolet sedan which belonged to one of the Ravenhurst butlers.

Mrs. Manning had anonymously telephoned the Craddock Realty Corporation at nine o'clock in the morning and had arranged an appointment with Carl Farrow and Cass Holbrook in the name of Mr. Andrew G. Castle of Dearborn, Michigan.

Hawthorne sat alone in the back seat. His thoughts drifted back to his childhood and adolescence as the car approached the Waverly town limits.

The Craddock representatives were surprised but very pleased to welcome Estelle Manning and her two silent male companions.

Mrs. Manning had expertly investigated every facet of Gerald Hawthorne's intended property arrangement with the Craddock Real Estate Corporation, and easily manipulated the formal meeting, which continued until one o'clock.

Carl Farrow was a chunky man in his early fifties with a bulbous nose, deep-set eyes and a complexion which testified to heavy drinking.

Cass Holbrook—a tall, very thin character with pince-nez glasses and straight black hair—was the senior partner in the organization and led most of the serious conversations with Mrs. Manning.

Both men had tried to include Hawthorne in particular discussions about the value of the Elm Drive property, but it was obvious that their cordiality toward the man known as the Turncoat was strained.

Mainly they avoided his eyes and concentrated on Estelle Manning and Andrew Castle, who had been introduced as a close friend and business associate of the Mannings.

Sandwiches and coffee had been ordered earlier and served in the office.

Hawthorne ate while sitting alone by the window. He gazed out at the familiar shops and traffic on the Waverly streets and ignored the social chatter in the office.

A vivid image of the house on Elm Drive suddenly blocked out all other sights and sounds and all at once the situation became unthinkable. The sale of the family property signified the permanent loss of his only sanctuary. He was about to be exposed to a hostile world forever.

Hawthorne pictured the intimate and nostalgic items in each room and the boxes in the basement. His whole body trembled as he realized that the sealed upstairs chamber would have to be inspected before any formal transactions could be completed.

He was still dazed by the predicament when Estelle Manning announced that the group was ready to proceed with the next phase of "Operation Waverly."

At two o'clock in the afternoon the three visitors from Winchester Estates, accompanied by Carl Farrow and Cass Holbrook, left the Front Street office building in the black Chevrolet sedan and drove to Gerald Hawthorne's house on Elm Drive.

The silent owner of the property remained in the living room, ignoring Andrew Castle, sitting opposite, while Estelle Manning and the two estate agents professionally surveyed the grounds and general layout of the interior.

Hawthorne had explained earlier that the bolted upstairs bedroom contained very personal belongings and it would not be available for inspection until later in the evening, after his inventory. They had accepted this without question.

Mrs. Manning announced that the preliminary examination of the residence would be conducted in an informal manner and he would have sufficient time to check through his effects while she attended several meetings, including a four o'clock session in the Deeds and Records Office of City Hall with Farrow and Holbrook.

Sergeant Andrew Castle was to remain with Hawthorne until Mrs. Manning completed her conferences.

"She's a brilliant woman," the police officer commented, when the two men were left alone in the house. "This place will be signed, sealed and delivered by the time she gets back here tonight."

The state trooper watched Mrs. Manning drive away from the front of the house and head down Elm Drive. He turned slowly from the windows and walked to the middle of the living room.

"Do you mind if I relax?" he asked politely. "It's been quite a day."

Hawthorne did not answer. He sat with both legs outstretched, staring vacantly at a fixture on the ceiling.

Castle removed his jacket and draped it neatly over a chair. He shifted the position of the gun and holster as he made himself comfortable on the sofa.

"I'm sorry about this damn weapon, Hawthorne," he said. He adjusted the strap. "I have to follow orders just like everybody else. I'm responsible for you and Mrs. Manning."

There was silence in the room until Andrew Castle tried once again to force conversation.

"She'll probably negotiate a very good deal tonight," he predicted brightly. "I'll bet the lady has everything arranged before they finish dinner at the hotel. Do you know the prospective customer?"

Hawthorne shook his head without looking.

"The Craddock people told us that Phil Prager is buying up most of the town." He grinned broadly. "Estelle Manning will charm his tail off and you'll end up with a very good price for this house, Gerald."

The use of his first name prompted Hawthorne to twist around and glare at the trooper.

"You can call me Andy," the officer suggested with a warm smile. "She won't be back until at least nine o'clock so we might as well keep things friendly in here."

"When do we eat our dinner?" Hawthorne asked in an irritable tone.

"Mrs. Manning will bring food back for us."

"Why can't we go out?"

"We don't leave this house until our vehicle is pointed toward Winchester Estates."

"I know where to pick up a hot pizza and some beer," Hawthorne persisted.

"I understand your situation," said Castle sympathetically, "but I'm just a cop who works for a living," he explained. "We can't move until Estelle Manning gives the word and you know damn well that nothing will change these orders."

Hawthorne turned away. "It's my own goddamn fault," he mumbled under his breath. "I jumped for the bait and they hooked my ass real good."

The policeman narrowed his eyes and studied Hawthorne's bitter expression. "The Mannings are fine people," said Castle. "You did very well, you'll excuse the personal comment."

"You don't know what the hell this is all about," the prisoner stated grimly. He stood and walked to the far end of the room.

Castle watched every move as Hawthorne opened a cabinet and stooped to look inside.

"I know that Ravenhurst is a lot better than Clifton or the state penitentiary," the officer commented. "You might have the opportunity of a lifetime if you cooperate."

Hawthorne closed the door of the cabinet and straightened

up. "True," he replied. There was an unexpected touch of excitement in his voice and manner. "But I have to deliver plenty in exchange for all this. Do you know what I have to give them?" he asked with his back to the policeman.

"I have a general idea."

"Did they brief you about Washington?"

"No."

"Korea?"

"No."

"Red China?"

"No."

Hawthorne suddenly wheeled about and faced Sergeant Andrew Castle. "Then don't talk to me about arrangements with Charles Manning," he shouted. "Mind your own fucking business."

The officer nodded calmly. "Fair enough." He leaned forward and pointed. "What do you have stashed in that cabinet?"

Hawthorne turned away and stared pensively at the trees and shrubbery in his front yard.

"Whiskey?" Castle asked. He waited but the prisoner refused to respond. "Do you want to make a deal?"

This time Hawthorne reacted by folding his arms. "Sit down and listen to what I have to say," Castle suggested as pleasantly as he could.

Hawthorne finally moved away from the windows and sat in his favorite chair, where he scowled at the officer.

"I have a right to place you under immediate arrest if you consume a drop of the alcohol in that cabinet," Castle explained. "The stuff should be poured down your kitchen sink right now. It might avoid serious trouble later this evening."

"Get to the point," Hawthorne snapped. "I'm sick and tired of long speeches."

Castle looked intently at him.

"I intend to leave the whiskey in your cabinet," he stated. "It's a dangerous temptation but we had better begin to trust each other."

"Why?"

"I'll probably be with you all the way to Washington and back."

"How thrilling."

Sergeant Castle settled back on the sofa and tried to change the subject.

"Did you grow up in this house?" he asked.

The question surprised Hawthorne. "What?"

"Is Mrs. Manning selling your family home?"

"Yes," the prisoner replied, and then looked down at the floor.

"It must be an emotional experience, and I'm sorry that the situation has to be handled this way." He touched the shoulder strap. "I'll do everything possible to make things easier for you."

Hawthorne's features hardened as he glared at the officer. "I thought you had a deal to offer," he snarled.

Castle looked at his watch and seemed to be calculating a schedule. Then he walked over to the cabinet, looked inside and slammed the door shut.

"You have two full quarts of Scotch there," he stated.

"Three," Hawthorne corrected.

The officer stood with his back to the whiskey. "Are you going to check every room in this house?" he asked brusquely.

Hawthorne swallowed hard before answering. "Yes." He paused. "And also the basement."

"I'll gamble with you."

Hawthorne looked at the Sergeant curiously. "I don't understand."

"You go ahead and inspect the house and I'll forget the rules for once in my life."

"Meaning?"

"I'm tired and I might take a long nap in the study."

Hawthorne watched the man pick up his blue jacket from the chair and sling it over his shoulder. "I'll respect your privacy in exchange for a few pledges.

"You will not leave this house under any circumstances," the officer declared firmly, "and no one is permitted to enter."

"And?"

"No whiskey."

"Go ahead."

"You will alert me at once if you see or hear anything of a suspicious nature."

"What does that mean?"

"You know damn well what it means," Castle snapped. "*Anything.* Especially the appearance of strangers on the grounds."

"Is that your complete list?" Hawthorne asked sarcastically.

"No," the policeman barked. "Make certain that I'm awake and in the living room by seven-thirty."

"Anything else, sir?"

"Yes." Castle took a few steps toward him. "You'll never mention this special favor of mine to anyone. I want your solemn oath."

Hawthorne met the trooper's gaze for an instant and then his eyes moved to the revolver.

"Suppose I try to steal that while you sleep?" he asked derisively.

"Be my guest," Castle replied. "It's been tried several times before by experts." The officer moved casually to the door. "I wouldn't recommend it, friend." He turned and faced Hawthorne. "Do you want to make a deal or not?"

"Why are you being so damn accommodating?" Hawthorne asked caustically. "I could drink that booze and rip this town apart while you . . ."

"Not a chance."

"How the hell do you know?"

"Because this favor gives you an opportunity to examine your personal belongings in private, without the interference of an outsider. We're both finished if you break any of the rules. But you'll fall much harder. Do you understand?"

"Yes."

"This is the start of a new life with Mr. and Mrs. Manning," Castle continued. "Here's your first chance to prove something to them. And possibly to yourself."

"I'll do my best," Hawthorne commented. He stared at the officer suspiciously. "Why do you want me to wake you up at seven-thirty?"

Andrew Castle pushed aside the living room portieres.

"Everything changes after the sun goes down." He looked at Hawthorne. "Including me," he added.

Castle left the room and closed the door.

7:00 PM
MAY 26, 1962
ELM DRIVE
WAVERLY, MICHIGAN

45 HAWTHORNE HAD COMPLETED his inspection of the downstairs rooms in less than fifteen minutes. He was not particularly interested in kitchen equipment, carpeting, fixtures or furniture. Mrs. Manning's experience in complicated real estate matters would surely obviate the need for his own appraisal, anyway.

He had spent most of the time in the basement of the house. After carefully examining two of the large cardboard boxes, Hawthorne had decided that most of his father's things, including the box marked "MY SON," would have to be burned in the backyard rubbish heap before any inspection by prying strangers could be permitted.

However, he had removed a kindergarten drawing of a house, three handwritten birthday cards, and a cigarette box which he had once purchased for his father, and packed them in a small wooden crate which he had found earlier in the kitchen closet.

The experience had been disturbing but by six o'clock Hawthorne had finished his investigation of the cellar boxes, and with the exception of a few selected articles, the contents were ready for the cremation which he intended to demand as a condition of sale. He then prepared himself for a survey of the upstairs rooms.

The thought of the Scotch whiskey occurred to him for the first time when he was going past the bolted door of his mother's shrine. A familiar pounding sensation started in his chest by the time he entered his father's room at the end of the hall, and this forced him to sit on the edge of the bed in order to regulate his rapid and uneven breathing.

After a short rest, he checked the drawers and closets, but he placed only a few souvenirs in the storage box.

At six-thirty Hawthorne moved the wooden crate into his own room, and knew that the time had finally arrived for a showdown with the Elm Drive ghosts and memories of the past.

Impossible, Hawthorne mumbled over and over to himself as he felt the throbbing chest pain begin to spread to other parts of his body.

He had packed several personal items by seven-fifteen, but halted his inventory when he realized that the room contained too many intimate documents and important keepsakes. He could not bear to imagine precious gifts from his mother being handled by outsiders or destroyed by fire.

He sat at the desk and studied the framed photograph of his beautiful Chinese wife.

It was nearly seven-thirty.

Hawthorne decided to wake the trooper and ask for an additional hour of privacy in order to complete his work in the upstairs rooms.

He tapped lightly on the door of the study but there was no reply. He knocked harder and called Andrew Castle's name, but the police officer did not answer.

Hawthorne put his ear to the door and could hear the man snoring. He reached for the brass knob and turned it gently.

Castle had apparently locked himself in the study.

Hawthorne was about to pound the door when an intriguing thought occurred to him.

The police officer had said earlier that he had observed two quarts of Scotch whiskey in the living room cabinet and Hawthorne suddenly remembered that the man had been correct. He recalled hiding the third bottle under a pile of old underwear in the bottom drawer of the dressing table in his father's room.

Hawthorne had intended to honor his pledge to stay away from alcohol but the fact that a drink was available upstairs filled him with courage. He hammered insistently on the door until Castle responded.

"I hear you," a drowsy voice answered.

"It's seven-thirty," said Hawthorne. "Can we talk for a minute?"

There were sounds of movement inside and then the door of the study was opened. Castle yawned as he adjusted the strap on his shoulder holster. He finally looked up and inspected Hawthorne from head to foot before speaking.

"I'll be damned," he exclaimed. "Sober."

"Are you disappointed?"

"I'm relieved," the officer replied. "It was a tense situation. I just fell asleep about twenty minutes ago.'

He removed a comb from his back pocket. "Are you finished with your inventory?"

"Not yet."

"We have until about nine o'clock. Let's finish your part of the operation before Mrs. Manning returns."

Castle moved past Hawthorne and headed toward the living room with his blue jacket draped over the leather shoulder strap.

"Sergeant," the prisoner called.

Castle stopped and turned in front of the portieres.

"I'd like to finish the upstairs alone," said Hawthorne. "My mother's room is special. She's been dead a very long time," he added in a whisper.

The policeman stared at him curiously without responding.

"I'm taking a few more boxes out of the kitchen," Hawthorne continued. "I might pack some personal items and take them back to Ravenhurst tonight."

Andrew Castle nodded. "We have plenty of room in the car. Take what you want."

"Can I do this thing alone?" Hawthorne asked.

"You followed the rules," the trooper said casually. "I trust you now."

"I'll get through before nine o'clock."

Castle leaned against the wall in the corridor. "Look for me outside if you need anything." He smiled. "I'll be on the front porch or in back of the house."

Hawthorne was puzzled. "Outside?"

"I begin to move around when the sun goes down," he explained. "Remember to stay inside if you hear any commotion."

"Do you expect some kind of trouble?"

"I always expect trouble," Castle informed him solemnly. He fingered the butt of the revolver. "It's going to be late when we leave this house. Mrs. Manning is a rich lady and I understand that you have a few dedicated enemies in this town."

"A few drunken bums," he corrected. "Waverly patriots."

"We're all patriots, friend," the policeman answered with a touch of hostility. But then he grinned broadly. "You go ahead and finish the upstairs inventory. I'll worry about everything else."

Hawthorne watched him swagger into the living room.

The floor of his bedroom was cluttered with old newspaper. He wrapped selected items carefully and then packed them into a cardboard box.

He still had the wooden crate for smaller articles and there was always his Chinese traveling bag in which his mementos of Korea and Tsinan had remained safely locked away, along with a new and very important acquisition which he'd found in his father's basement files.

He stored childhood gifts and letters from his mother and covered the family picture albums with layers of paper before placing them into the box. He worked feverishly in an attempt to sort out and have ready for removal all his most treasured possessions before the start of Mrs. Manning's formal inventory.

Perspiration soon moistened his hair and forehead and he was unable to blink away the haze which settled over his vision, or ignore the sharp pains shooting through his skull.

From time to time he paused and glanced toward the desk. The photograph of his wife seemed to urge him on and he tried to disregard the frightening symptoms which had paralyzed him on so many other occasions.

Suddenly, a shuffling sound in the backyard jolted him upright. Ordinarily, he would have snapped off the lights and prepared himself for trouble. This time he walked to the window and pulled the shade, realizing that the sound must have been made by Castle who was patrolling the yard. He wiped the dampness away from his eyes with a handkerchief.

It was eight-fifteen and he had nearly completed the work in his bedroom.

Another noise drifted up from the yard and he was temporarily immobilized by the sound of a hacking cough.

Hawthorne leaned closer to the window and listened anxiously. There was silence. He walked unsteadily to the desk and removed several items from each of the drawers, and at eight-thirty, as estimated, his personal belongings were organized. Soon he could allow the family ghosts to be dispossessed by strangers.

The box and the wooden crate had been sealed with heavy black tape and they were both neatly positioned in a corner of the bedroom. However, the Chinese traveling case was still at the bottom of his locked closet, and one cherished belonging remained untouched. He would not put Ling Yu's photograph away until the last minute. He needed the influence of her memory in order to take the final terrifying step. He stared longingly at the photograph of his wife and then removed a set of rusty keys from the desk drawer.

He faced the barricaded door of his mother's room. Estelle Manning would soon return for her inspection and he had to visit his mother's shrine before any outsider violated the spirit of her memory.

Dizziness and nausea caused him to reel and back away but he gripped the hall railing firmly and pushed himself forward. His hands touched the smooth wood and the shock forced him to gasp for breath and sink to the floor.

He reached up and grasped a chain.

The feel of the heavy metal rings made him shudder but he managed to pull himself slowly to his feet.

His face was covered with perspiration as he leaned against the wall for support and tried to bring himself to examine the three separate locks on the door.

He steadied the jangling keys and his fingers somehow responded. The tumbler of a lock clicked loudly.

The entire house seemed to tilt without warning and Hawthorne swayed crazily and nearly fell to the floor. A strong feeling of nausea hit him and he swallowed an urge to retch.

After several agonizing moments, his eyes focused on the door handle. An unexpected stream of tears rolled down his cheeks and mixed with the sweat of anxiety.

The final step had to be taken.

Hawthorne glanced down at the key in his hand. The opportunity for complete freedom might be lost forever if he did not act immediately.

Only a few simple moves were required. The twist of a corroded padlock would unfasten the chain and expose a heavy iron bolt. These locks had sealed the spirit of his mother since the night of her death.

He closed his eyes for a moment and attempted to block out all thoughts and feelings. Then, ignoring the pain and tears and anguish, he worked frantically to earn the right to a new life. He completed the task and then slumped to the floor.

Blackness was beginning to roll over him. He stretched full-length on the carpet and stared up at the door. The dangling chain caught his attention. The sacred tomb was open at last, and he was now obliged to enter.

He heard noises again. The unmistakable sounds of quiet conversation and subdued laughter were coming from the yard in front of the house. Sergeant Castle was talking with someone outside.

Hawthorne took hold of the railing and hauled himself upright.

He moved unsteadily to the entrance of the room and stood mesmerized by the unfastened chain.

He clutched the handle with both hands, and the door opened slightly. Not more than three inches. But it was enough for him to catch a fleeting glimpse of color and beauty. He recognized familiar articles of silk and lace, and the faint scent of her perfume shocked him out of his stupefied condition.

He managed to slam the door shut and drop back to his knees.

Hawthorne gulped his second tall glass of whiskey and cursed because it was not taking effect quickly enough.

At first he had intended to take the bottle into his own room but the thought of Ling Yu's photograph had prompted him to stay in his father's room.

Suddenly he heard the distinct sound of glass shattering against the side of the house, and he instantly switched the room into darkness.

A piercing shriek of drunken laughter cut through the stillness of the night.

Hawthorne dashed to the window and listened as an authoritative whisper stifled the disturbance. He pulled the shade aside cautiously and debated whether to call for Castle.

A generous swallow of whiskey helped him with his decision and he remained silent in order to comply with the trooper's instructions. It was obvious that trespassers were gathering in the shadows and he began to wonder about the tactics of the Michigan State Police.

A rock crashed through one of the skylights on the roof, and again Hawthorne heard raucous laughter, whispers and a hacking cough.

Another bottle hit close to the drawn shades and splintered into the bedroom. There were sounds of scuffling, a loud groan and then complete silence.

Hawthorne took another drink and crouched by the window.

"Castle!" he yelled. *"What the hell is going on?"*

The grounds were quiet.

"*Castle!*" Hawthorne screamed again.

He waited anxiously for an answer but only the crickets and the rustling of leaves could be heard outside.

Suddenly he was startled by a loud pounding on the wooden planks of the house, just below the bedroom window.

"Stay inside." It was Castle's voice.

Hawthorne opened the shade but was careful not to expose himself to the possibility of an attack by the concealed enemy.

"*What the hell is going on out there?*" he yelled from his squatting position on the floor.

"A couple of local drunks," the officer replied sternly. "I told you not to interfere with my work," he added.

Hawthorne jumped to his feet and leaned out of the window. "*I know these bastards!*" he shouted angrily. "*They mean business!*"

The policeman was massaging his fists. "So do I, friend." He glared up at Hawthorne suspiciously. "Are you finished with the inventory?"

"Almost."

"It's nine-thirty," Castle announced. "Mrs. Manning is late."

Hawthorne glanced at the shattered pieces of glass and then surveyed the grounds.

"Are they still around?" he inquired bitterly.

"Get back inside and take care of your own business," the trooper answered in an icy tone.

The bright headlights of an approaching vehicle attracted Hawthorne's attention and he did not have time to respond.

"Here comes Mrs. Manning," Castle said. "Don't bother her with talk about drunken bums." He disappeared into the shadows.

Hawthorne corked the bottle of Scotch and tossed it under the bed.

There were still a few strong-flavored mints in a porcelain jar on the night table. He chewed and swallowed several as he staggered toward the unlocked bedroom door in the center of the hallway. The alcohol had eased some of his anxiety and he was able to face the ordeal with less trepidation.

It was his last chance. He closed his eyes tightly and took a firm grip on the handle.

"*Gerald!*" a woman's voice called excitedly from the living room.

Estelle Manning had entered the house. He heard her footsteps as she moved down the hall at a brisk pace.

"Gerald?"

"Yes."

"It's very late." Mrs. Manning had stopped at the bottom of the stairs. "Please come down to the study right away."

Hawthorne gazed sadly at the unlocked door.

"We have to work quickly," the woman urged. "I'm waiting, Gerald."

He released his grip and backed away from his mother's shrine.

46

"ARE YOU ILL?" Mrs. Manning asked casually.

"No," Hawthorne replied. "Just tired."

She was sitting at the antique desk in the study and her eyes sparkled with excitement as she scribbled in a notepad.

"The Craddock people will conclude a very good sale with Prager in a few weeks," she explained without bothering to look up. "Prager knows the house very well. Did you realize that the buyer was acquainted with your family?"

"No."

"Your father did some plumbing jobs for him many years ago," she added.

Hawthorne sat hunched in a dim corner of the sofa and tried to conceal the fact that he was drunk.

"We'll discuss the details later," she was saying. "I'm leaving a set of keys with Mr. Holbrook. His organization is experienced and reliable."

"The keys?"

Hawthorne's question and peculiar tone of voice caused Mrs. Manning to look up at him.

"He has to show the property, Gerald," she explained. "We're taking a complete inventory tonight before we leave for Ravenhurst."

"I understand." He shrank back deeper into the shadows as the woman continued to stare.

"This is an unusual situation," Mrs. Manning commented quietly. "I doubt very much if any of us will be in a position to return to Waverly once our Washington commitments begin. Do you understand?"

"Yes."

"Have you packed your personal belongings?"

"A few things," he answered hesitantly.

"We'll store the rest or include particular items in the sale if Mr. Prager is interested," she said.

Hawthorne could not control a trembling in his right hand. He shifted his position on the sofa.

The snap of a twig outside the window attracted Hawthorne's attention. Mrs. Manning continued to work without reacting to the noise.

"Did you see Castle?" he asked as nonchalantly as possible.

"No," the woman answered. "He told me earlier that he was going to patrol the grounds."

"Did you hear anything when you drove up to the house?" Hawthorne questioned cautiously.

Mrs. Manning looked up from the paper. "Everything appeared to be quiet and normal." She tried to get a better look at him as he leaned into the darkness. "Why?"

He remembered the trooper's warning about mentioning the disturbances. "Nothing," the prisoner shrugged. "I just wondered."

"Andy Castle is extremely qualified," she assured him. "He was personally selected by Chief Saunders of Detroit."

Hawthorne ignored a rustling sound but knew that someone was moving in the bushes at the side of the house. He hoped that it was the Michigan State Police.

"I spoke to my husband this evening," said Mrs. Manning.

She closed the notepad and turned to face him. "All hell is breaking loose in Washington because of you."

He sighed deeply in an attempt to regulate his breathing.

"A man by the name of Turner quit the Defense Department, and other ranking officials are expected to resign during the next few days. You will personally cleanse this government and go into the history books, Gerald."

Hawthorne could not suppress a laugh.

"I'm serious," the woman insisted. "Even the White House is concerned about your testimony. Did you know that?"

"Don't overestimate my information," he replied quietly.

"You've started a chain reaction. Charles will explain in detail when we see him. My husband has proven himself to be a man of rare courage. He has accepted every risk in order to rid this nation of corruption. Many of his dear friends may be destroyed in the process but Charles will follow it through to the end. I'm very proud. Friendship is the most precious thing on earth," she said. "Charles will suffer for the rest of his life because of this affair in Washington."

There was silence in the study as Estelle Manning walked toward the door.

Hawthorne muttered something in Chinese and she turned. "What did you say?"

"Nothing important."

"I'm curious, Gerald." She walked closer to the sofa. "We've never heard you speak the language."

Hawthorne leaned forward and the lamplight accentuated the deeply etched lines around his mouth and eyes. "Friendship is also valued in China," he explained coldly. "You don't need luxury if you have friends. They say that with true friends, even water is sweet enough."

Estelle Manning stared at him until he moved back into the darkness. "That's a lovely thought." She walked to the edge of the sofa. "I see that you do understand my husband's ordeal."

"And my own," he snapped irritably.

"Of course, dear," she told him, "but thank the Lord that

your testimony will only involve strangers in the government. Charles must deal with his friends."

"They also want the names of *my* close friends," he insisted.

"In Red China, Gerald," the woman retorted sharply. "Not in the United States of America."

Hawthorne turned away.

"I'm going to begin the inventory in the basement," she announced. Her tone and attitude had softened. "Are you ready?"

His heart began to thump loudly as he was reminded of the unfinished business at the top of the stairs.

"Do I have to go with you?" he asked.

"Not necessarily," Mrs. Manning answered. "Have you finished down there?"

"Yes," he replied. "I left two cardboard boxes. They have to be burned in the yard before we leave tonight."

"I understand," the woman assured him. "Andy will help you later."

Hawthorne frowned. "What's your schedule after the basement?" he asked.

Mrs. Manning checked the pad in her hand. "The kitchen, this study and the living room."

"And then?"

"Upstairs." She moved toward the door again. "Have you finished upstairs?"

There was a very long pause before Mrs. Manning received an answer. "I have one thing to do," he replied in a husky voice.

"You have plenty of time," she told him. "I intend to inspect closets and shelves and all hidden places. Treasures have been discovered under carpets and even in chandeliers after the sale of an old house.

"I suggest that you sleep for a while," Mrs. Manning advised gently. "You look very tired."

"Maybe I'll rest on the couch in the living room," he replied. "It's been a rough night for me and I still have something very important to do upstairs."

"Good," the woman said brightly. She hesitated in the

doorway. "Finish it up. Sweep away every detail of the past and look forward to a bright and rewarding future at Raven-hurst."

She turned and looked at him.

"Manning of Michigan has promised you a new life." She smiled warmly. "You are a very fortunate man, Gerald Haw-thorne."

Sergeant Castle checked the luminous dial of his wristwatch and then strolled to the front yard gate.

It was 10:45 PM and conditions were excellent.

The moon was hidden in an overcast sky and the Elm Drive street lights had been extinguished earlier by a sudden local power failure.

Castle propped his foot on the rusty metal and smiled as a black automobile coasted silently past the entrance and came to a halt a short distance away. The vehicle was concealed by the low-hanging branches of a large tree but Castle knew that the Waverly police department had arrived. He imagined the excitement in the car and tried to visualize Chief Cyrus Crawford's face.

The officer smoothed his suit jacket over the leather holster and chuckled as he estimated the number of deadly weapons now poised and ready to be used against a skinny, mixed-up, confused former Army corporal.

He heard whispers and suppressed laughter coming from a clump of bushes at the far side of the house. The crew from Ted's Tavern was still much too noisy but the trap could now be sprung at any time.

Castle thought about Packard and his drunken associates. A few swift punches had sent the hooligans crashing into the bushes but, as he'd expected, they were all back for more. This time, however, the local patriots would wait for their victim with better manners.

The suburban cops were unaware of Hawthorne's impor-tance in Washington, D.C. It would be Chief Crawford, he was sure, who would pull a trigger in the darkness and complete Hector Rambeau's mission. He felt the revolver on his shoulder and hoped that the responsibility for the actual finish could be shifted to the local police. He was not especially anxious for another notch on his belt.

He noted that the hidden intruders were quiet as he turned and slowly walked back toward the house. He sat on the steps and thought about the United States government and Rambeau and Manning and his own participation in the final stages of Operation Red Watch.

The clinking sound of glass attracted his attention.

He glanced around at the living room window and observed that the lights were out and the shades had been drawn. Andrew Castle knew that the victim was in the process of simplifying the basic plan for his own extermination.

The policeman lit a cigarette and leaned his head back against the wooden pillar of Hawthorne's front porch. He calmly blew smoke toward the cloudy sky while inside, his prisoner gulped whiskey, transgressing the terms of his parole and forfeiting his chance for salvation.

The dark corner of the living room provided tranquil and welcome seclusion. This was Hawthorne's only concern at the moment.

He had already consumed one full bottle of Scotch and was now draining the second. Estelle Manning's footsteps no longer bothered him as she moved about in his father's room overhead. The past would soon be buried. Hawthorne decided to drink a toast to its funeral, and then drank again in honor of his new start in life with the Mannings of Michigan. After the brief ceremony, he placed his bottle on the floor and walked unsteadily to the front window.

"Castle," Hawthorne called quietly. There was no reply from the porch. He pulled the shade aside cautiously and tried again. "Castle."

"What do you want?" the officer finally whispered back.

"Is everything quiet?" He was certain that the alcohol had not slurred his speech.

"Get back inside the house and keep your mouth shut," Castle ordered harshly. "Everything is quiet."

"I have to burn some papers."

"What?"

"In the rubbish heap out back."

The trooper did not answer immediately but in a few seconds his head appeared at the window. "What papers?"

"Personal things," Hawthorne replied. "I have to burn some boxes in the rubbish heap." He lost his balance for an instant but managed to grip the edge of a radiator and prevent himself from falling.

Castle pretended not to notice. "Did you talk to Mrs. Manning about this?" he asked.

"She wants you to help me."

"We'll burn your damn boxes when I give the word." His voice was low and grating. "Stay inside and don't interfere. I want to be notified exactly fifteen minutes before you and Mrs. Manning are finished in the house," Andrew Castle ordered. "Understand?"

"Yes."

"I'll be here on the porch."

Hawthorne swayed in the darkness and took a firmer grip on the radiator.

"On the porch," he repeated, slurring his words noticeably. "Fifteen minutes before."

"You come and get me."

"I understand," Hawthorne mumbled.

"We'll both haul the boxes out to the yard," the officer went on. "I'll have the fire going."

"Right."

"Are you getting this?"

"Yes, Sergeant."

"Tell Mrs. Manning that I want her to remain in the house until we complete the job out back," Castle instructed. "Security reasons," he added.

"I'll tell her."

The trooper flipped the shade back into place and moved away from the window. Hawthorne heard him leave the porch and then head toward the rear of the house.

A closet door slammed upstairs.

He released his grip on the radiator and navigated a shaky turn. The living room tilted to one side but he managed to remain on his feet.

The emergency treatment with the alcohol had worked very well. A comforting haze was beginning to settle over him and his nerves were steady and under control. He decided he was now strong enough to complete his self-imposed assignment.

The loud snapping of twigs and branches alarmed him momentarily but then he realized that it was only Castle preparing a funeral pyre in the backyard.

He staggered toward the portieres.

As Hawthorne made his way down the hall to the bottom of the stairs, he used the walls and various articles of furniture frequently for support. The actual climb was strenuous, and he had to drag himself up by the banister as he made his way to the top.

The muscles of both arms were beginning to cramp. His uneven breathing forced him to hesitate just before reaching the top. He gripped the railing again.

"Gerald?" It was a woman's voice. "Is that you?"

Hawthorne looked up, startled, and his hands suddenly froze to the wood. His vision blurred and he was unable to swallow. A sharp pain cut into his chest as he gasped for air and struggled to remain conscious.

"I'm in here, Gerald," the voice announced. "What a magnificent room."

His tongue was swollen. It had somehow lodged in his throat and he felt he was choking. He ordered his body to move forward but it refused to respond.

"I need some help, dear."

It was inconceivable. An unmistakable case of fantasy or wild imagination. A voice was coming from his mother's tomb. There was the sound of movement. It was his obligation to investigate and scatter the disturbances.

"It's difficult to work in here," said the voice in his mother's room. "Are there any other lights?"

It was almost impossible for him to hear properly because of a weird reverberating in his ears. The haze before his eyes was beginning to thicken and swirl and block his vision entirely.

Hawthorne dragged himself to the doorway. Bureau drawers and closets were being opened and inspected. He listened to a jumble of comments but they seemed muffled, as though coming from a great distance.

"Please hurry, Gerald," the words resounded. "It's very late."

He could now make out the vague shapes of the dressing table and a small, familiar chair. He saw a hairbrush and a gold hand mirror and her favorite comb. He recognized other personal things, including a lace nightgown which had been casually draped over a chair.

"Some of these clothes should be given to Welfare in Detroit," the voice suggested. "I know the organizations."

Hawthorne stood as though in a dream. He had expected convulsions followed by unconsciousness. Instead, his mind was strangely at ease for the first time in years and every symptom of anxiety had miraculously vanished.

47

ESTELLE MANNING WAS inspecting an outmoded wardrobe in the closet when she heard Hawthorne enter quietly.

A small table lamp was the only source of light and the room smelled musty. Both windows had been nailed shut.

"Do you agree?" She took out a dress with a gaudy floral design and brought it closer to the light. "We'll have Detroit Welfare make a collection before we leave for Washington."

Hawthorne was silent.

"It's up to you," she added. "Perhaps you know someone here in Waverly." She tossed the garment on the bed with several others. "Everything will be appreciated. Especially in black neighborhoods."

He stood in the darkness and watched as the woman picked up the lace nightgown and moved to the lamp. She ran her fingers gently over the material and then faced the dressing mirror, holding the intimate article of clothing next to her body.

"My size," she commented. "I noticed it before."

There was no response from the shadows.

Estelle Manning lowered the gown self-consciously. She suddenly realized that Hawthorne had neither moved nor spoken since entering the room.

She turned and peered into the darkness. "Are you all right? I can't see a damn thing in here."

Unexpectedly the silence was broken by a hoarse whisper. The voice was unfamiliar and chilling.

"Mommy."

"What did you say, Gerald?"

"Mommy."

Hawthorne was invisible but she could hear the sounds of his heavy breathing.

He was obviously emotionally upset, she thought. Nevertheless, Estelle Manning was determined to maintain her composure.

She moved to the closet and took her time arranging the nightgown on a wire hanger.

"Mommy."

The plea was infantile and terrifying but she managed to place the garment on one of the wardrobe racks.

"We'll go downstairs now, Gerald," she announced, trying to sound as casual as possible. "Andrew is probably worried and impatient."

The bedroom door closed very quietly.

Instinctively, Estelle Manning knew that Hawthorne was still in the room. "Gerald?" She could no longer control a growing sense of apprehension. "What's the matter with you?" Her voice was beginning to tremble.

The silent figure was emerging from the shadows.

"That's enough." Mrs. Manning backed away. "*What are you doing?*"

Her slow retreat ended abruptly at the dressing table. She stood transfixed as the dim light revealed Hawthorne's face. His features had the lifeless hue of wax, the white skin drawn tightly over sharp cheekbones. His saucer-wide eyes reflected years of pain and sorrow but they stared innocently, childishly, longingly at her. His mouth was set in the expression of a pouting infant. The thin lower lip protruded, trembling.

She turned away in horror. Tears were flowing down his face and yet she could not hear a sound. He moved toward her.

"Gerald. Don't!" she begged.

She twisted away from the dressing table but Hawthorne placed his arms around her and pinned her against the wall.

"Mommy. Mommy."

The child was smearing kisses on her face and neck as she struggled desperately to loosen his grip. A strong hand was clamped over her mouth. She could not breathe properly, let alone call for help.

"Let me stay, Mommy," he slobbered. "Please let me stay."

He attempted to stroke her hair. She pulled away and the back of her head smashed against the wall. She was dazed as Hawthorne wrestled her across the room.

The sight of the bed, however, jolted her into action once again. She squirmed and fought as her body was pressed back into a reclining position on the silk covering.

"I love you, Mommy." His voice was shrill and boyish. "Please let me stay." He laid his head against her breasts. "Don't push me away, Mommy."

She stopped struggling and allowed him to feel the heaving of her chest. The excitement caused him to relax his guard for an instant and she managed to pull one hand free.

Her long nails dug deeply into his face and the blood stained his cheeks and mixed with the tears. He threw back his head and she saw the grotesque transformation of his features.

"*You goddamn whore!*" His fist slammed into her face. "*You whore bastard!*"

She stared blankly as he swung again. "*I've got a Silver*

Star!" Another powerful blow shattered her teeth. "YOU GODDAMN WHORE BASTARD!" His knuckles crashed against the side of her jaw and split the flesh. "I'VE GOT A SILVER STAR!" Hawthorne continued to pound with barbaric fury. "DIRTY FILTHY BASTARD!" Again and again his fists connected until he had completely smashed her face. He stopped the assault and gazed at the woman on the bed.

Blood was flowing from her nose and mouth. Several facial bones were badly damaged and most of her front teeth were gone. But she was conscious and alive.

Hawthorne fell across Estelle Manning's body and began to smother her mutilated face with kisses.

"Mommy. Mommy," he sobbed. "I love you, Mommy."

She stared unblinkingly at a spot on the ceiling while the gurgling infant spread blood and tears and saliva over her swollen lips.

"Let me stay, Mommy," he whispered. "Please, Mommy."

He rubbed and squeezed her breasts with trembling fingers. She moaned as his hand slid under her skirt and searched roughly between her legs.

"I need you, Mommy." Her undergarments were ripped away. "Don't ever leave me." He caressed the smoothness of her skin. "I love you, Mommy."

She remained in a state of shock, completely inert.

Fragments of teeth and bone clogged her throat, and she could not swallow. The deranged child was stroking and probing and she was unable to scream or fall into unconsciousness.

His wet mouth was pressed against her ear. "I'll never tell," he promised hoarsely. "Never."

He lifted his body and sat upright on the bed. His breathing was rapid and irregular.

He knelt before her and prepared himself.

Then the rumpled skirt was eased up to her waist and she could feel him push closer. The boy was crying softly.

A merciful curtain of insensibility was beginning to descend which allowed her to ignore the pressure of his knees. She did not resist as her legs were forced apart. He thrust himself inside her and rocked violently.

"Mommy! Mommy! Mommy! Mommy!" His young and guiltless eyes were filled with tears. *"I love you, Mommy!"*

Estelle Manning watched the pathetic figure as it bounced and quivered.

"MOMMY! MOMMY! MOMMY!" he wailed.

She continued to stare, dully, as the hideous infant shuddered and then slumped forward to her naked breasts.

From far away came the sound of someone chopping wood.

Her eyes closed.

Sergeant Andrew Castle tossed several large branches into the bonfire and watched the flames leap to the sky.

The blaze was ready for Hawthorne's personal rubbish.

He added a few twigs to the roaring pile and glanced toward the house. Estelle Manning's thorough business approach had helped to strengthen the trap by providing additional time.

Sobriety had silenced the rowdy patrons of Ted's Tavern, made them more dangerous. And the local police had primed a deadly arsenal for the victim. He had observed Crawford pacing anxiously in the shadows of Elm Drive.

He kicked a few dry leaves into the heap and visualized the celebration which would follow this Rambeau victory. Certainly the official reward for the completion of the Waverly mission would be very substantial.

Slick broads and sunny vacations were usually the rewards for routine accomplishments. And Gerald Hawthorne had been listed in a special category. Some distinguished individuals had recently made their wishes very clearly known. They did not want Hawthorne shouting his mouth off. Especially in Washington, D.C.

He listened to the crackling of a heavy log and thought about his requesting a transfer to an administrative position in Washington.

Five minutes later, at 12:45 AM, Castle turned away from the fire and headed leisurely toward the front porch.

He passed the thick clump of bushes at the side of the house and ignored a muffled whisper from one of the trespassers.

Cyrus Crawford and his associate were hovering in the vicinity of the gate as he approached the wooden steps. His shoe touched the lower plank.

At that precise instant, the quiet was shattered and Andrew Castle was stunned by the deafening report of a pistol. He made an instinctive grab for his shoulder holster and the weapon was ready before he reached the front door of the house.

"Have you been shot?" Castle screamed.

Estelle Manning was conscious but unable to answer. Her face was an unrecognizable mass of torn flesh and splintered bone. Blood was still flowing from her wounds and soaking the bed.

"Go out to your car and call an ambulance!" the state officer blasted at Chief Crawford's assistant, who had come running to the house as soon as the shot was fired. *"Then notify Mr. Charles Manning in Washington."* He shoved a piece of paper at the local cop. *"Here's the number of the hotel."*

Crawford's assistant continued to gape at the woman's battered features. "TAKE OFF!" Castle bellowed, pointing the revolver at the young man's head. He lunged for the door of the bedroom and then headed for the stairs.

"You stay here!" Castle shouted excitedly to Chief Crawford. "Try to clean her up but don't fool around too much. Wait for the medics. She's in bad shape!"

Cyrus Crawford was also clutching a pistol. He scowled at Castle. "Who the hell do you think . . ."

"Shut up!" Castle yelled. "Your job is to protect this woman. Hawthorne is still in the house and the crazy bastard is armed!"

He rushed toward the hall but paused and turned to face Crawford before leaving.

"I ordered you to stay with Mrs. Manning," he stated in a low and menacing tone of voice. "Don't leave her side for *any reason*. Or God help you, friend."

Crawford watched Castle make a hasty exit and close the

door behind him. He obediently locked the room from the inside.

Castle switched the upstairs hallway into darkness. He took a firm grip on his revolver and then moved silently to the railing.

The police car radio could be heard crackling outside the front yard but the voices were faint and distorted.

A dim light from the living room enabled him to see hazy shapes on the lower floor. He surveyed the area and realized that conditions would make accurate marksmanship impossible.

"*Hawthorne!*" Castle shouted. "*You don't have a chance.*" He stooped low and aimed his gun for a killing. "*Step into the light and drop that damn weapon!*"

The house was still.

"*Mrs. Manning is alive,*" the officer yelled. "*Give up and I'll get you off the hook!*"

Something moved downstairs. The policeman lowered himself into a prone firing position. His gaze was fixed on the lighted section of the hallway. "*Hawthorne,*" he called again. "*They need you in Washington. Manning and Myerson will help. Come out so I can see you!*"

Castle heard another noise in the vicinity of the portieres. His finger remained steady on the trigger as he prepared himself for the completion of Operation Red Watch.

"Hey, Castle!" It was the voice of Crawford's assistant coming from the living room. "Hold your fire." Castle cursed under his breath before answering. "Did you get the ambulance?"

"It's on the way."

"I can't hear you."

"It's on the way."

"Mr. Manning?"

"The local operator has the information." He paused. "I know her. She'll get him."

Castle lifted himself to a crouch and then edged closer to the dark stairs.

"Get outside and help cover the house," Castle ordered. "Shoot to kill."

There was a hesitant sound from the front room. *"The house is covered from every possible angle, Sergeant,"* the local cop yelled a moment later. *"I armed a few of my best deputies!"*

Castle smiled as he thought of Packard and his hoodlums officially licensed to commit murder in the name of law enforcement.

"Hawthorne!" Castle called again. *"Did you hear that? Come into the light and drop your gun."* He waited. *"I'm your friend."*

He inched quietly along the railing until he reached the room at the end of the corridor. He stood with his back flat against the wall and listened.

The revolver was poised for immediate action and his senses were tuned to the slightest indication of movement. He waited and finally heard a rustling noise, or the flapping of heavy material. Just for an instant.

He came to the conclusion that the door in question led to Hawthorne's own bedroom.

"Hawthorne," he whispered with the gun leveled and his body stretched away from the entrance. "Come out of there."

The room was quiet.

"Hawthorne," the policeman tried again. "Don't be a fool. Toss the weapon out or I'll have to take you by force."

A dull bumping sound from inside the room confirmed his suspicion that the victim was cornered. But he intended to complete his assignment without exposing himself to unnecessary risks.

"Hawthorne," Castle whispered harshly. "The game is over. Are you listening to me?" He waited. There was silence. "You happen to be a worthless traitor, but Charles Manning needs your help in Washington. Give me the weapon and come out. This is your last chance."

Castle paused again but there was no answer.

"A psychotic queer without a conscience. That's you, Hawthorne," Castle taunted. "You even play in reverse for the right price. The names of your Chink lovers for Manning gold. What a filthy whore you are, Hawthorne. Your ass is for sale to anyone with a proposition."

He hesitated again. The room was quiet.

"Come out and make a deal with me. I might say that Estelle Manning fell down the steps. If you . . ."

His voice trailed off as something caught his eye at floor-level. Blood was seeping out from under the bedroom door and he watched it soak the carpet in the hallway. He leaned closer but did not lower the revolver. "Hawthorne?" he called softly. There was no reply. He reached out cautiously for the handle.

Another dull thump from inside caused him to freeze and hold his breath. But it was only for an instant. This time he was able to identify the sound of a fluttering window shade.

Castle held his position, back against the wall, clear of the entrance, while he slowly turned the handle. The revolver was aimed from hip level and his finger was beginning to apply pressure on the trigger as he completed the turn and then pushed gently. The door opened far enough for him to see the rug in the middle of the room.

He relaxed immediately and placed his weapon back in the shoulder holster. He walked inside and calmly inspected the results of Hector Rambeau's political operation.

Gerald Howard Hawthorne lay sprawled face-down on the floor with a pistol in his right hand. It was pointed directly at his head. Blood was gushing from a jagged wound above his ear. Castle moved closer and stooped in order to check for life.

Hawthorne was clutching a framed photograph in his left hand. The glass had shattered under his chest and Castle observed that blood stains were partially concealing the face of a young Chinese woman.

An Oriental traveling bag was overturned near the body and some of the contents had spilled out close to Hawthorne's face.

Castle looked down at an expert marksman's medal and a

Silver Star, awarded for gallantry in action. "Crazy bastard," he mumbled.

The portrait of another woman and several other articles were still packed in the traveling bag.

The officer stood and walked over to examine a strange work of art, an old Chinese painting which had been crudely taped to the wall above Hawthorne's desk.

It appeared to be a jumble of objects and characters but he was able to make out a graveyard and a young man lying on the ground next to a tomb.

The Chinese inscription had been translated. It read:

"Fear is my private weakness, but death is my public duty."

He heard the piercing sound of the ambulance siren as it approached the house.

Castle turned and stared thoughtfully at the bleeding figure on the floor. He watched Hawthorne's blood cover the photograph completely; then went to the door.

"*Crawford!*" Castle screamed down the hall.

A door was unlocked. "Yes?"

"How is she?"

"Still conscious," the Chief answered. "Busted up around the face and probably raped. But she wasn't shot."

"I know," Castle answered.

The Waverly hospital attendants were rushing into the house.

"Up here, fast! *I've also got a corpse up here.*"

May 27, 1962
New York City

Robert Calhoun Spangler folded a small piece of yellow teletype paper and arranged it neatly on his office desk. He leaned back and tried to concentrate on the excited voices of his television program staff.

Arnold Dorfman was animatedly briefing the group on

Amalgamated's elaborate plans for special coverage in Washington, D.C.

"We'll break 'Capital Commentary' at eleven-fifteen and pick up Atken's resignation speech live," the executive producer explained. "It's a network pool feed."

"Fifteen minutes?" Tim Henderson queried. His pencil was scribbling rapidly as usual.

"Probably more," Dorfman answered. "The Senator might decide to break things wide open before the investigation starts. First Turner in Defense, then Davidson, now Atken. Incredible."

"He can't plead age and health this time," said Henderson. "Did you see the evening papers?"

"Same on the wires," the producer added. "It's Pearl Harbor all over again."

"What about the late movie tonight?" asked Henderson. "First-run and heavy promotion."

"Screw the late movie." Dorfman glanced at his boss. Puzzled by his silence. "Washington is falling apart."

"These are resignations, Arnie," Henderson reminded, "not confessions of guilt at the moment."

The tense Amalgamated staff waited for instructions.

"We'll stay with the news panel and broadcast every development," Spangler announced roughly.

"And tomorrow?" asked Dorfman. "What about sponsored hours and the morning soap?"

"Keep the entire schedule flexible," the program chief replied. "I expect a few sudden explosions."

"What do you make of it, Bob?" Henderson asked seriously. "Forget the rumors."

Spangler rested his head on the back of the chair and stared thoughtfully at the folded piece of paper on his desk. "Somebody dropped a bomb on the White House and the fallout is just beginning to spread."

"Fawcett is the real shocker," Dorfman remarked, shaking his head in amazement. "The General was set for the Joint Chiefs."

"And what about Frank Turner?" Henderson stuffed his

pencil into a jacket pocket. "They were dusting off D'Allesandro's chair."

"Atken had better clarify this damn mess tonight," Dorfman stated emphatically. "Nobody is available for comment."

"We might be twisting everything out of proportion," Henderson decided. "I'll wait for an official statement."

Fran Patterson walked briskly into the office and handed Spangler a message.

He skimmed the information and then looked up at his executive producer.

"I have a program change for you, Arnie," he announced. "Kill Senator Edward Atken's eleven-fifteen network feed." Spangler paused somberly. "Insert a live address by the President of the United States."

There was complete silence in the room until Arnold Dorfman mumbled, "Jesus Christ."

The message was handed back to Fran Patterson. "Take it to the newsroom," Spangler instructed. "Arnie will be there in a few minutes."

"Do you want some food sent up?" the woman asked.

"No," Spangler answered quietly. "I'm going out for a couple of drinks."

She hesitated for an instant before turning and walking out of the office.

Dorfman and Henderson watched curiously as Spangler picked up the teletype paper. He unfolded it and read the contents again.

"Want to do a special Hawthorne obit?" Dorfman asked without much enthusiasm. "I can pull some clips from the interview."

"No," Spangler answered.

He crumpled the dispatch and tossed it into a wastebasket under the desk. "It's a regional news item, off the wire," he told them softly. "Keep it that way for as long as possible."

He rose to his feet and moved slowly across the thick carpeting.

"The Hawthorne obit would be a great feature on a night

like this," Tim Henderson called out. "The death of an American traitor."

Robert Calhoun Spangler paused at the entrance as he turned the handle.

"Forget it," he said without looking back. "Let the poor bastard rest in peace."

He slammed the door of the office behind him.